STAR TREK™

STRANGE NEW WORLDS

THE HIGH COUNTRY

STAR TREK™
STRANGE NEW WORLDS
THE HIGH COUNTRY

John Jackson Miller

Based upon *Star Trek*
created by Gene Roddenberry
and
Star Trek: Strange New Worlds
created by
Akiva Goldsman & Alex Kurtzman & Jenny Lumet

GALLERY BOOKS
New York   London   Toronto   Sydney   New Delhi   Havenbrook

G

Gallery Books
An Imprint of Simon & Schuster, Inc.
1230 Avenue of the Americas
New York, NY 10020

First Gallery Books hardcover edition February 2023

GALLERY BOOKS and colophon are registered trademarks
of Simon & Schuster, Inc.

For information about special discounts for bulk purchases,
please contact Simon & Schuster Special Sales at 1-866-506-1949
or business@simonandschuster.com

The Simon & Schuster Speakers Bureau can bring authors
to your live event. For more information or to book an event,
contact the Simon & Schuster Speakers Bureau at 1-866-248-3049
or visit our website at www.simonspeakers.com.

Interior design by Kathryn A. Kenney-Peterson
Interior art by John Jackson Miller

Manufactured in the United States of America

10   9   8   7   6   5   4   3   2   1

Library of Congress Cataloging-in-Publication Data is available.

ISBN 978-1-6680-0238-4
ISBN 978-1-6680-0240-7 (ebook)

This book is dedicated to three talented teachers:

Thomas Ford,
who took serious literature
and showed us where the laughs were

Gwen Rosenbluth,
who helped me become a wordsmith

And in memory of
Ellen Burns,
who adored comics, science fiction, and fantasy,
and who would have found no memorial cooler
than getting mentioned in a Star Trek *novel*

I can't say as ever I was lost—
but I was bewildered once for three days.
                                    —Daniel Boone

HISTORIAN'S NOTE

The events of this story take place in 2259, following the capture of the *U.S.S. Enterprise* by the pirates of the *Serene Squall* and the successful efforts to retake the ship (*Star Trek: Strange New Worlds*, "The Serene Squall") and before the routine survey of the Jonisian Nebula and the events that befall Doctor M'Benga and his daughter, Rukiya (*Star Trek: Strange New Worlds*, "The Elysian Kingdom").

Part One
OLD WORLDS

To Havenbrook

Tar Pits →

To Greenfield →

Magee Farm

To Valley Ranch →

CHAPTER 1

THE CAPTAIN

"Hey, *I* called shotgun!"

Spock turned in the shuttle's copilot seat and raised an eyebrow. "Captain, I do not—"

"Relax, Lieutenant." Coffee cup in hand, Christopher Pike grinned. "You're going to say you don't know what an ancient Earth weapon has to do with seating arrangements, and Uhura is going to explain how the expression originated with nineteenth-century stagecoaches. And Number One will give me the look she's giving me now."

"Which should need no translation," Lieutenant Commander Una Chin-Riley said from the pilot chair. "Does it, Cadet?"

Nyota Uhura smirked. "I was going to say there's no record 'riding shotgun' was used before 1900. No written record, anyway."

"Coach drivers: not big writers." Pike took a seat beside Uhura in the second row and looked forward to his first officer. "How's our new baby handling?"

"So far, as advertised." Chin-Riley patted the shuttle's control station.

Uhura touched her earpiece. "*Starship Enterprise* reports only intermittent visual contact with us. Only three sensors still detect us."

"Good," Pike said. "Maybe we'll get lucky and lose them entirely."

Eratosthenes was a shuttle built for the new Prime Directive era of exploration. Shielding protected it from infrared and radar detection, and its thermal and electromagnetic emissions were minimal. Voltage applied to a thin film on the shuttle's skin further controlled what colors it reflected. It wasn't a cloaking device such as the Klingons had used in their recent war with the Federation, but Starfleet didn't want to be in that business. This shuttle was about investigating new civilizations without causing a panic.

Its designer, a former *Enterprise* chief engineer, had sent the prototype to Pike to test. The captain had found an immediate use for it: entering the Bullseye Nebula to approach a planet so obscure neither it nor its parent star had names beyond the surveyors' catalog entries.

"Five hundred thousand kilometers from FGC-7781 b," Spock said. "We are now at the last reported position of the *Braidwood*."

"Full stop," Chin-Riley said, reading Pike's mind as always.

According to Starfleet, *Braidwood* was a civilian anthropological expedition that had been out of contact for nearly a year. Its last message, transmitted to the expedition's backers, spoke of the detection by long-range sensors of a society, apparently pre-warp, on FGC-7781's largest planet.

"Their supposition was correct," Spock said, consulting his readings. "Multiple life-forms and artificial structures in concentrated population centers, with smaller ones spread out across rural areas."

"City *and* country," Pike said. "Radio transmissions?"

"None detected." Uhura leaned back with a sigh. "I guess I'll just enjoy the ride, then."

Pike gave her a reassuring nod. Not every mission could be an adventure for everyone.

"Pollution levels minimal," Spock said, reeling off sensor reports as he received them. "A prime candidate for study."

The "prime" part is the problem, Pike thought. It was easy to guess what had transpired. Whether their expedition was Federation-approved or not, the *Braidwood* crew would have been obliged to report their discovery and hold position until a Starfleet survey team arrived to evaluate the planet. Of course, prospectors and colonists could never be convinced to do that, and Pike expected the scientists were no different. "They went down to look around and never came back. And their sponsors only *now* got rattled enough to ask for help." He glanced at Chin-Riley. "Sound about right?"

"Textbook." She shook her head. "Nobody ever learns."

Well, we *have*, Pike thought.

A pre-warp society would not be able to launch a starship like *Enterprise*, but it might see one overhead. Telescopes on Earth dated back to the seventeenth century. *Eratosthenes*, by contrast, was ideal for a recon, safely yielding more information than a probe could. "Uhura, signal *Enterprise* that we're going to establish planetary orbit. We'll scan for the *Braidwood* from above."

Pike stretched in his chair as the impulse engine restarted. He didn't need to join this voyage; test flights were Number One's specialty, and Spock's skills were equal to any reconnaissance task. But even accidental first contacts were a captain's concern, and he'd wanted a ringside seat. Security Chief La'an Noonien-Singh, now occupying the captain's chair back on *Enterprise*, had objected as her job required—but he had no intention of setting foot on the planet, which grew ever larger ahead of them.

The world was small enough to have an iron outer core and a protective magnetic field, while offering a wide range of terrains and ample seas. Retrograde rotation meant the sun rose in the west—while short days created additional bands of atmospheric and ocean circulation. The Bullseye Nebula's proximity to disputed space had kept it unexplored, but the Klingon War was over. If *Braidwood* hadn't dropped in, somebody else soon would have.

"Short years, twenty-hour days, and a significant axial tilt," his first officer said. "But there's a lot of green there. Nature gets busy fast because it has to."

"Nice planet," Uhura said. "Deserves a better name, though."

"You're the wordsmith," Chin-Riley replied, adjusting the controls. "Improve on *Eratosthenes* while you're at it."

Spock spoke without looking up. "Eratosthenes was the first human to calculate Earth's circumference and axial tilt. He required no technology: simply pillars and their shadows."

"I know, Mister Spock. I mean the name's a tongue twister. At least it still fits on the side of the—"

The cabin lights went out.

Pike looked up. "Mood lighting?"

"Very much not," Chin-Riley said. "The flight console's down. Engines offline."

"My station is also inoperable," Spock said.

"Same here," Uhura added.

Intending to check on the power systems aft, Pike stood—and immediately had to use his hands to keep from striking the overhead. "So much for gravity plating." He listened as he floated. The life-support systems were offline too.

He had started to make his way toward the darkened rear of the compartment when the ship lurched, causing him to fall to the deck. The impulse engine rumbled to life while lights and circulating air returned.

Pike picked himself up. "Well, I've said it before. Sometimes the best horse bucks."

"We only have half a horse," Chin-Riley noted, concern creeping into her voice. "Faults in multiple systems. Comms are out."

Pike rolled his eyes. He took out his personal communicator—and was startled to find that it didn't work either.

Spock found the same thing with his. "Curious."

Uhura brightened. "Mine works."

"That's why you're in communications," Pike said, accepting the device from her. He flashed a smile to calm the cadet. "Pike to *Enterprise*."

"Enterprise," responded an authoritative female voice. "*We weren't expecting you on this channel, Captain. I thought you said you weren't going down to the planet.*"

"Don't worry, La'an. I haven't jumped the fence. But we've got a problem." Pike glanced at his first officer. *How big?* he wondered.

As if in response, the cabin went dark again. Pike grabbed hold of the chair beside him this time. "Déjà vu." He faced Spock. "Electromagnetic pulses?"

"We detected no change in solar activity." Determining there was nothing he could do at his station, Spock rose and made his way aft. A minute later, he reported that there wasn't a single electrical tool functioning. "On reevaluation, Captain, your theory may hold some—"

Another jolt. Spock dropped to the deck.

"Around and around she goes," Pike said.

His first officer raised her voice, enough that Pike took notice. "More faults in multiple systems. They're either rebooting or down."

"We're still moving."

"That's the acceleration from before. We hadn't inserted into orbit yet." She stared ahead at the planet, growing bright ahead of them. "The guidance systems aren't getting enough time to reset."

Flying manually was nothing new to her, Pike knew. But it depended on having some control over the propulsion systems. "Reverse course when it lets you." Finding that his comm unit was still working, he decided to take no chances. "La'an, we're having mechanical issues here. Come get us."

"*Understood. Stand by.*"

"Buck up, folks. Help's coming." Pike said it more for Uhura's benefit than anyone else's. It wasn't so many years ago he was playing big brother to incoming cadets; now he was dad. It was important to show her that it was just another day at the office.

When power returned, Uhura's handheld comm came back online. He spoke into it. "Not to rush you, La'an, but it's getting a little stuffy over here."

"*This is Lieutenant Hemmer,*" declared the stern male voice of *Enterprise*'s chief of engineering.

"Hello, Hemmer. I'm afraid we're going to have to tell Professor Galadjian we broke his toy."

"*I would trade places with him in an instant. As near as I can tell, someone has broken science!*"

Pike and his companions looked at one another, baffled. "Mind repeating that, Hemmer?"

"*As* Enterprise *approached you, many of its systems shut down and then began restarting, the same as yours. And not just the ship. Everything with a transtator went down. Electrical flow appears impacted.*"

"An EM attack?" Number One asked.

Hemmer heard her. "*I have considered that. What I—*"

The communicator went silent. Pike spoke into it. "Hemmer, you there?"

He toggled the device a few times to make sure it was still working. It was—at least until the shuttle's few remaining stations went dark again. Hemmer, Pike hoped, might have better luck in such a situation: a blind member of the Aenar, an Andorian subspecies, he visualized items through a telepathic talent that few outsiders understood.

When the next restoration occurred, Pike heard Hemmer again, his volume lower but agitation higher.

"*—these flashes coincide with what seems to be a phenomenal increase in resistance, retarding electrical activity. The lengths of our operational windows are declining logarithmically as we approach the planet.*"

"But we're even closer," Pike said. "And closing."

"*We expect you will have no working electrical equipment in four minutes.*"

Uhura's eyes widened—and she touched her forehead. "*People* are electrical! Could it harm us?"

"I cannot speak to what Chief Hemmer is describing," Spock said. "But in the case of magnetic pulses, the brain is significantly less susceptible to electrostatic damage than electronic components."

"How do brains fare in uncontrolled descents?" Number One asked. *Eratosthenes* was not permitting a course change.

"*There are risks here as well,*" Hemmer said. "*Doctor M'Benga agrees with Spock on the biological question, but he fears these repeated outages will harm his patients if we remain in whatever is happening here.*"

Unaware of anyone in critical condition in sickbay, Pike looked to his first officer. She gave a quick nod. It wasn't unusual for her to know more than he did. "Understood," he finally said. "If I know you, Hemmer, you have a plan."

"*Unless the laws of motion also decide to rebel, we will coast past your position on the way out of the vicinity—and hopefully, this phenomenon. We are both going too fast, and on different headings, for any kind of rendezvous. But we should be able to attempt the transporter.*"

"The transporter!" Uhura said aloud, before whispering to Pike, "Is that wise?"

The shuttle felt the first grasp of the atmosphere, shaking the vessel. Pike spoke into Uhura's communicator. "Hemmer, we're in a place where basic physical laws can't be trusted, and random things are failing on *Enterprise*. You're sure the transporter is the right choice?"

"*It's the only one,*" the chief engineer said. "*If there's a problem, I can trick the system into reintegrating you on the planet's surface, rather than where you are now. An appropriate analogy would be—*"

"Sending a letter with a false return address?"

"*—I was going to say, 'something I don't have time to come up with.'*"

Spock sounded grave. "The lieutenant's plan would deposit us on a world we know nothing about."

"We're going in hard and hot," Chin-Riley said, struggling with the controls. "That might be as good as it gets."

Skipping rocks isn't much fun for the rocks, Pike thought. "Do it, Hemmer. And no matter what happens, get *Enterprise* out of here until you know what's going on." He stared at the world rushing toward them. "You have my full confidence."

"*Of course I do,*" Hemmer said. He paused. "*All the same, if you got into your environmental suits, I would not take offense.*"

CHAPTER 2

THE SHEPHERD

"Come on, where'd you go? Come on, where'd you go?"

It was more of a chant than a question, and Lila Talley knew her quarry wouldn't understand a word. But it was part of the patter her grandfather used when tracking lost sheep, and every so often, it worked.

That wasn't happening today. The runaway in question had been one of several ewes spooked by a sudden cloudburst the day before. Lila had grown up in a place where lightning storms could rage for hours. Out here, the sky got it out of its system all at once with a million tiny flashes. That meant more time for picnics but left a mark on the ovine nervous system.

The auburn-haired woman guided her stallion through a clump of brush. It barely required anything of her at all. A black leopard-spotted Appaloosa, Buckshot looked like his name—and while he'd only been hers since the previous winter, they functioned as one.

Not so for her other partner. Rufus emerged from a bush and plopped on the ground before the horse. She stopped and stared at the dog. "That all you have to say?"

Rufus whimpered and rolled in the dust.

"You're no help." Lila adjusted her hat and got Buckshot moving again, forcing the mutt to scramble to its feet to avoid the horse's hooves. Back home, she'd have had her choice of dogs for herding and tracking; here, the breeders had done their best with what little they had to work with.

Still, it was a small sacrifice. Entering a broad valley, Lila felt happier than she ever had. The tableau, all greens and golds, looked like a painting. A farmhouse, barn, and several outbuildings sat in a clearing, while the wooden wheel of a mill turned in a brook. The Magee place wasn't one of the nicer ones around; much about it was in disrepair. Yet scenes like these never failed to take her breath away.

I can't believe this place exists.

A sandy-haired girl saw her and waved. Jennie Magee was a couple years shy of adulthood, and while Lila hadn't interacted much with kids since coming to the area, she knew Joe, the girl's father: a widower and a bit of a troublemaker. Lila imagined he had to be challenging to live with.

"Just a second, Miz Talley." As Lila and Rufus approached, Jennie opened the door to the barn and disappeared inside. Seconds later, she nudged out a sheep. "Is this yours?"

Lila grinned. "Where was she?"

"In Ma's herb garden."

"Fine dining. I'm impressed." Lila dismounted and examined the animal. "She eat much?"

"No. I mean, I don't know." Jennie gestured to the plot and grimaced. "We don't really tend it anymore." Rufus loped up to her, looking for attention.

"You and your pals cost me two hours," Lila said to the ewe. She got a bleat in response.

Scratching the dog's belly, Jennie looked up. "The size your flock is, I don't know why you bother looking for strays. Sooner or later something out here would have eaten her up."

"That's what I'm afraid of," Lila said, walking back to Buckshot. "The predators we got around here, once they get a taste for mutton, will sniff out where it came from. And then we're forced to use these." She patted the saddle scabbard that held her rifle, safely tucked behind a stirrup fender.

Jennie rose. "Can I see?"

Lila removed the rifle and let her examine it. "I'm sure you've got one."

"Ours is old."

"Nothing wrong with old things, if you take care of them."

Jennie's study of the weapon ended in disappointment. "It's the same as ours."

"It works. No need to reinvent it." Lila gestured to the forest at the edge of the farm. "Anyway, last thing we need is a lot of wild things dropping in for dinner. Ammo's precious."

"I guess." Jennie started to put the rifle back in its scabbard.

Lila stopped her. "Right side up, so the motion doesn't rub on the sights." She stepped next to Jennie and showed the girl how to properly cinch the scabbard. "You don't want to lose the rifle every time you jump something."

"Pa carries ours—and we don't go anywhere but town."

"Well, you never know. Maybe you'll take up the sheep trade."

Jennie closed the barn door without enthusiasm. "Don't you get bored?"

Lila smiled. "Never. There's plenty to learn—even from sheep." She nodded to the errant ewe. "Be calm. Respect their space. Move 'em slow—don't let groups splinter off. Every day's a lesson."

"If you say so."

Lila climbed back aboard her horse. Kids never valued anything they had, but that passed. Jennie would see one day—though her father might be another matter. As she prodded the ewe forward, Lila craned her neck and looked about. "Where *is* your pa?"

"At the tar pit." Jennie gestured to the north. "Getting asphalt to line the cistern."

"Huh." Lila glanced over at the mill. "Your water wheel's running fast."

"It's fast water."

"I mean it's idling. Gears must not be engaged. Kind of odd for harvest time."

"It's always harvest time round here," Jennie said. She sighed. "Like I told you, he's out. He'll back later."

Lila got the impression Joe Magee had put them behind more than once. "Well, just don't let the work go too late today. You know the saying."

Jennie said it by rote: *"More than a candle, too much to handle."*

"That's right. People weren't meant to work at night. You don't want the Sorry coming down on you."

Before she could elaborate, a faraway gunshot rang out. Lila's hand felt for her scabbard. When another sounded, the rifle was out and in her hands.

Jennie looked to the north. "That's just Pa. Probably wants more buckets." She walked over to where several wooden pails sat piled within one another. "Feel like haulin' some tar?"

Lila shook her head. "He shouldn't waste ammo like that. I've got a flock to get back to. Enjoy, kiddo." She whistled to Rufus and got her animal entourage moving.

She occasionally worked as a circuit rider spreading the good word, but it wasn't bad to interact with people at other times. There was something natural about it. People in farming communities everywhere valued their freedom and solitude, yet they were always in one another's business. Lila found that a comfort. Neighbors looked out for each other.

Fences wouldn't be part of life here at all if it weren't for the animals. Folks didn't mark property lines: they just knew. Theft was for those without, in places where people went to bed hungry. Here, no one ever had. And if it weren't for the *wild* animals, she wouldn't need her rifle either. There was never a dispute so hot that it wasn't settled with a handshake and a birch beer.

Lila thought it was all about attitude. If you recognized the best things in life were right in front of you, you weren't likely to kick up a—

Boom!

It was a colossal sound, one Lila had never heard in any storm here. The panicked ewe darted off, with Rufus giving chase. Lila pulled the reins tight to steady Buckshot. *What was that?*

Her eyes turned first to the north, but it was much louder than Joe Magee's rifle shots. She looked next to the sky. It was clear of any weather. Nothing but the stray silver fronds of the afternoon aurora—and the *thing*.

There were objects of one kind or another in the air here all the time, but this was high and fast, lancing across cirrus clouds. Shiny too. Lila had barely set eyes on it when a second boom echoed across the farmland. The sound came from well behind the traveling object, and in the time it took for her eyes to go to that position, the fast-mover disappeared over the northeastern horizon.

She sat for several moments, waiting to see a return or hear another sound. She saw nothing but the aurora and heard nothing but the autumn wind rustling through a nearby stand of trees. That, and Rufus's barking, somewhere within the thicket.

Lila shrugged. She had a sheep to find—again. *"Come on, where'd you go?"*

CHAPTER 3

THE GARDENER

"Harjon, do we live in a perfect society?"

Drayko heard silence in response to his question. He looked up from the potting table and lifted his glasses. His new page, barely an adolescent, stood in the doorway to the arboretum and shuffled from one foot to the other, nearly dropping the bottles on the tray he was holding.

"I'm sorry," croaked a changing voice. "What was the question?"

"I asked if we lived in a perfect society." His own voice gravelly with age, Drayko gestured around the greenhouse with his spade. "You. Me. All the people of this world."

Harjon appeared to give it some thought. "If we measure perfection by prosperity, health, and mutual goodwill, then, *yes*: we live in a perfect society."

"Hmm. How long have you been memorizing that?"

"I did not—"

"Come. How long?"

Caught, Harjon spoke lower, his facial freckles doing nothing to hide his blushing skin. "Since they told me I was being assigned to your service, sir."

"Ah, you have hit upon the answer to the question." Drayko put down the plant he was potting and walked toward Harjon. "The fact is that we *were* living in a perfect society—up until you were assigned to me. Since then, teas have arrived late, fertilizers have been spilled on floors, and plants that have never seen an aphid are now plagued with them." He plucked one of the bottles from Harjon's tray. "All this you have done in nine days."

"Eight, sir."

"Quiet." Drayko affixed a spray nozzle to the container and walked back to the perennials. Harjon shadowed him, step by step.

Another growing season was coming to an end, and Drayko had much work to do. He had a means of heating the greenhouse, of course; its contents were too valuable not to protect. But he wanted everything just right before he brought more plants in from outside. So many factors went into his work. No assistant had ever fully understood that, and Harjon had given him no reason to be confident.

Still, it was his lot in life to continue to try.

"Every one of these species is from somewhere else," Drayko said as he sprayed. "And yet they are all here, coexisting. Overwater, overcrowd—and you could lose one or all."

"Yes, sir. There are rules."

"I didn't make them. I just keep them."

A human had once told him that "Drayko" sounded like the name of a great serpent in her people's ancient culture—and also an infamous harsh lawgiver. It was just like humans to draw the most peculiar connections. Drayko told her he was by no means harsh, except where weeds were concerned. But he liked the serpent thought, especially when she told him about another culture's legend involving a great snake encircling the world. Drayko felt that way about Epheska. He embraced his planet, protecting most of its lands and some of its seas. If he were to let go, everything would fall apart. And that was no myth.

He had the shears out and was trimming thorns when a woman in a lavender cloak entered the arboretum. Older even than Drayko, she was his link to the world outside the valley—and she had never shown the least respect for the privacy of his garden time. "I am done for the day, Zoryana. What is it now?"

"Your son has still not reported in."

"I thought your job was to bring news." He glanced over at her and saw several slips of parchment in her hands. "I see. You *did*."

"It's been a busy day. Wild horses have been seen near Jevarsk."

"Again, a thing I already knew."

"You see how he speaks to me?" Zoryana rolled her eyes, apparently for Harjon's benefit, before she soldiered on. "The warden of Jevarsk seeks guidance. She is concerned her people will find the horses an inconvenience."

"They'll probably find them absolutely terrifying." Drayko chortled. "Her people are barely a meter tall."

Having heard a topic he understood, Harjon piped up. "My sister says that horses are everywhere."

"So that is where the wisdom went in your family," Drayko grumbled. "It's a good thing people don't multiply as fast. Still, it's hard to call the equines an invasive species, considering . . ."

He trailed off, as he often did when an idea overtook his observation. He had the solution in seconds. "Tell the warden to prepare for a burn on the Veros Slope. There won't be anything for the horses to eat—and winter is coming, so they won't approach any closer. That buys time for a more comprehensive solution."

Zoryana made a note. "And what do I tell the Jevarskans to do about the horses that are already there?"

"Tell them not to walk too closely behind them. And whatever they do, don't look up."

It went like that, eating into his precious private time. More routine messages, all requesting his guidance on everything from commodities to infrastructure to forestry. In nearly every case, his querants already knew what the proper thing to do was; they just wanted Drayko to validate their choices. He did so quickly, without looking away from his plants. Only a report of a rare disagreement between two settlements gave him a few seconds' pause. That was all the time it took for him to hit upon an answer that would make both parties happy, while remaining consistent with the beliefs that all shared.

Harjon listened intently—so much so that he was not properly positioned when Drayko turned to set his spray bottle on the tray. It smashed on the floor.

"Wonderful," the older man said as his aide hurried to recover the shards. Drayko glared at Zoryana. "Now, unless you want poor Harjon to decide that our perfect society is in fact a deeply boring one, I ask that you leave any further matters until tomorrow. Enough is enough."

Zoryana looked down on the fretful youth with a practiced patience. "Child, it must have come as a disappointment to you to learn the great Drayko is in fact an old—"

A bell sounded outside. Drayko and Zoryana looked at each other. "Expecting something?" he asked.

"No." She shuffled her papers. The bell rang again.

Two rings was definitely unusual. Drayko stepped past Harjon and made for the exit, Zoryana in tow.

Drayko found his terrace bathed in autumn light. He walked to the edge and looked over. The bell was down there, outside a marbled temple. A runner exited the structure and ascended the long flights of stairs to his position. A second courier followed moments later.

The breathless messengers reached the landing ten seconds apart, each bearing scraps of parchment for Zoryana. She examined them before showing them to Drayko. "Flashes. From Hohlagad, and then Cherra Bay."

They were the most basic alert—messages sent when a party had no time to communicate more. A flash from Hohlagad could mean a tornado. A flash from Cherra Bay, a tsunami. But there was no reason he should get alerts from both places, one after the other in swift succession. *What could they have in common?*

The answer dawned on him.

"They're in a straight line. *To here*."

Drayko clutched the slips of paper and hurried around the side of the terrace to the patio facing southwest. He looked up—and gaped as a blazing object streaked just below the clouds several kilometers to the south. Its black contrail scarred the afternoon sky—and thunder resonated through the valley. It contin-ued to echo after the fireball disappeared over the mountains to the east.

Zoryana said nothing. Harjon, eyes wide, covered his mouth. "What was *that?*"

"Something we have to find," Drayko declared. He removed his apron and tossed it to the youth. His workday had just begun.

CHAPTER 4

THE FALLEN

Spock awoke, drowning.

Were he to be precise—as was his wont—he would have said he was suffocating, because no outside fluid had penetrated his environmental suit. But he did awake beneath a liquid surface, breathing only the air that was in his helmet when he donned it. The circulation system hadn't been functioning when he put it on, and it still wasn't.

That the transporter beam had not brought him to *Enterprise* was obvious. He surmised he had been deposited on the planet they had been hurtling toward, although the official catalog name for the world eluded his grasp at this difficult moment. The pain he felt suggested that he'd first materialized high above the surface and that he had blacked out on impact. And though he had no memory of that moment, he speculated it had not happened long before, as he had air to breathe and was still sinking into the depths. His descent further suggested something about the density of the medium, ruling out several substances he doubted were on the planet anyway.

It was as far as theorizing could take him, but given the circumstance, he expected that would be forgiven.

He had to do something, yet every option held risks. While Starfleet's new environmental suits were lightweight, they weren't something to swim in. At the same time, Spock couldn't see removing it. It had protected him thus far from whatever pressures were present, and his body might not fare as well without it. A further issue was the liquid itself. While he had detected bodies of water on FGC-7781 b—he remembered the name now—he might be surrounded by something more inhospitable.

When the last light around him vanished, he determined he had no alternative to playing the odds. The emergency release for the breastplate was manual, and he still had time to work it. He was feeling for the control when the fish appeared.

In fact, he knew it was *not* a fish, but some other suboceanic life-form. The luminescent pods on either side of the being's meter-wide mouth showed that much. Danger heaped upon danger as it lunged in his direction. He twisted his body and felt the thump as the massive creature knocked him aside. Spock, it turned out, was not the target, but rather a dangling object below and behind him. The beast seized upon it and was captured when a latticework trap sprang shut around it. The snare began ascending, prey and all.

Spock saw his chance—likely, his only one. He took a deep breath and removed his helmet. He then worked the latch attaching his breastplate and the backpack with its defunct circulation system and shed them both. As they descended into the deep, he kicked violently, fighting to catch the rising trap on its way up. He lodged his fingers between the slats at the bottom of it. His added mass paused its ascent.

He was preparing to follow the connecting line to the surface when the contraption began to rise again. The ride up was shorter than he had feared, and he broke the surface seconds after the trap did. Inhaling deeply, Spock felt he had done reasonably well, accounting for the probabilities of every danger he faced, from possible acid in the medium to nitrogen narcosis from quick decompression. They were all the things a good science officer would think of.

But he also remembered that unexpected variables always remained—a fact that was confirmed a moment later when a blunt object struck the back of his head, rendering him unconscious.

Una Chin-Riley awoke, hanging from a tree.

Specifically, she was *in* a tree—and the preposition was more appropriate than usual. Her environmental suit's backpack apparatus had materialized inside what appeared to be a colossal redwood. Her body, fortunately, was outside it— but the fusion of tree and pack had somehow functioned to keep her dangling, dozens of meters from the ground.

If there *was* a ground. She could barely move her head, and before her she saw nothing but dense forest.

It was not supposed to be possible. Phase discriminators had come a long way from the early days of transporter use. If solid matter occupied the space at a target location, the ship's systems either redirected the annular confinement beam to an area safe for materialization or aborted the transport entirely. But Hemmer had been trying something special. He'd jerry-rigged an impromptu site-to-site transport, a kind of operation Starfleet rarely undertook even in perfect conditions and with fully functional equipment. That wasn't the case here, and neither of the fallback alternatives was available. *Enterprise*'s systems were in no shape to rematerialize personnel in the transporter room, and leaving them on a plunging shuttle was not an option.

Things had not worked properly, but there was no catastrophe—at least not yet. As near as the commander could tell, the sudden synthesis of materials caused no explosion; Chin-Riley suspected it might have something to do with quantum phases, or maybe the peculiar physical conditions here. She'd have been interested to know what the combination looked like, were she able to turn her head. There was almost certainly a scientific paper to be written about the experience.

Too bad I'm in no position to write it. This must be what it feels like to be a coat on a rack.

Thankfully, Spock had determined the planet's atmospheric content before things went haywire. She removed her helmet and breathed tentatively. Her caution wasn't necessary. The breeze was nice after being aboard a shuttle with no air circulating, and the smell of the forest was enticing.

It was clear to her what she'd have to do to get free, though that wasn't much comfort. The backpack was joined to her spacesuit's breastplate, the release for which she could easily access. Once it disengaged, she'd fall unless she somehow pivoted and grabbed onto the tree. Dropping was an option: she could see a large limb below and slightly to her right, but she wasn't sure she could grab hold of it on the way down. It wasn't something she'd get a second try at.

Chin-Riley needed to decide. Daylight was waning and she was attracting attention of the flying kind. The yellow-feathered avian that swooped in to hover before her reminded her of a hummingbird, if that species came in a parrot-sized variety. She didn't know what the thing's food looked like and had no desire to find out. "Shoo! Shoo!"

The bird darted in closer. She threw the helmet at it. She missed, producing a procession of clunks as the headgear ping-ponged down through the branches. Ten seconds passed before it hit bottom. Chin-Riley smiled meekly at the avian. "We're pretty high, huh?"

The bird moved again, causing her to cover her face with her armored hands. It was no attack, she quickly realized; rather, the critter landed on her shoulder and began idly pulling at her hair. *Enterprise*'s first officer pawed at it repeatedly, trying to dislodge it.

Finally convinced of the futility, she let her arms go slack. The bird squawked at her.

"Squawk, yourself," she replied.

This is embarrassing.

Nyota Uhura woke up, melting. And screaming.

When it came to protective wear, Starfleet's new environmental suits were the top of the line. Officers needed protection from the usual extreme conditions found in space, but also from many exotic particles and biohazards. The spacesuit designer's work was never done but was usually done well. In Uhura's case, it had kept her alive for however long she'd been lying on her back adjacent to an active lava flow.

She screamed because she couldn't move. Her body rested several centimeters deep in blackened basalt, and while she assumed the suit's material could not catch fire, melting was another matter. She had no idea how she'd gotten there; she remembered nothing after snapping on her helmet aboard *Eratosthenes*. She'd woken up immobilized in heat that she was starting to feel, even through the suit. Its coolant systems down, only passive protection remained. And that was starting to go.

Still, she fought. The superheated rock was less viscous than quicksand, but she lacked anything to grab onto. By impulse, she remembered her childhood fire safety lessons. She'd already stopped and dropped; now she rolled, heaving herself over once in the blazing muck. Being facedown in the stuff wasn't fun, but at least that side of the armor hadn't been as exposed yet. She pushed and rolled over again and again, hoping there was a way out and that she wasn't headed somewhere worse.

Covered on all sides by the goop, she stiffened—but now she had direction: down. The flow was a *flow*, after all, heading slowly down a slope. She just had to get ahead of it. All the time, the temperature rose and her breaths and heartbeats came faster. There was no time to waste with screaming. She could only urge herself on.

Go, Nyota, go!

Uhura gave one final heave and threw herself over. This time, nothing caught her. She slammed against solid rock and rolled without assistance. It wasn't a painless experience, but she felt wonderful and stayed in the roll, getting some distance.

She rested on her hands and knees, panting, near the edge of a smoking fumarole. The possible dangers of breathing the air, however, paled before her need to remove the helmet and suit before she either cooked within the hot basalt batter or froze in place when it hardened. She'd been wearing her *Enterprise* uniform underneath—there'd been no time to change on the shuttle. She acted quickly but carefully, maneuvering so as not to touch any of the molten rock with her hands. At last, the suit lay in a steaming pile at her feet.

She had a moment to look around. Uhura's homeland had several volcanic features: colossal Mount Kenya had long been extinct, while Emuruangogolak on the Gregory Rift had been active in recent times. But nothing she'd seen before resembled this place. The hellscape that surrounded her went on forever, and the sweltering air had a sulfurous stench.

She needed to get away—but first, she knelt to examine the mess of the suit, wondering if anything from it could be salvaged. It didn't look promising, but she figured it was worth a try. What she didn't figure on, however, was the sudden emergence of flames from the nearby hot seam.

Uhura stumbled away from the wrecked suit, landing on her backside. She was about to rise and run when the flames curled and drifted downward, crossing the blasted ground almost purposefully—serpents on a search. They found something: the gear she'd removed. Uhura scooted back several meters as more fiery tendrils emerged from the fumarole to assault the ruined spacesuit. It glowed white before melting away to nothing.

That could have been me, she thought. Knowing that it still could be, she scrambled to her feet. The flames before her rose as well, evoking a squeal of fright. But then they simply wafted into the sky, eventually becoming indistinguishable from the daytime aurora.

Uhura had no idea what she had just seen and decided just as quickly that she didn't want to know. She picked a direction at random and ran.

Captain Pike had not yet awakened.

And when he did, he regretted it. Immediately.

CHAPTER 5

THE MILL

"*Fire!*"

Christopher Pike opened his eyes at the sound of the word—and tried to get up. Instead, he tumbled downward in a tangle of sheets and struck the floor with a thud.

He winced. Even with his eyes tightly shut, he saw lights. The side of his face pressed against what felt like a wooden floor. His eyes opened. That didn't help much: the room was unlit, with deep shadows dancing before him. As he tried to sit up, he realized he was in a bedroom. It just wasn't his. He was not on the *Enterprise*.

Every bone ached. He didn't remember drinking or anything else that could have put him in this state. As a teenager, he'd nearly been crushed in a cavern collapse; this felt like that.

Removing the quilt that had ensnared him, he realized he was wearing someone else's clothes. Comfortable, but not his. He hoisted himself up and saw the shadows were caused by orange light flickering outside a window. And while throbs had been assaulting his eardrums since he awoke, he now heard something else. A girl's shout—and animal sounds, as well. A horse whinnied. *Is there a barn on fire?*

"This is a hell of a dream," he muttered as he tried to stand. A curtain provided a lifeline when he nearly fell, and he rested his head against the glass windowpane while he got his bearings. Eyes focusing, he saw a large millhouse outside, its roof ablaze in the night. Dream or not, he decided he had to take a look.

He stumbled across the small square room and found a door. The knob wouldn't turn—and his attempt to put force against it nearly drove him to the floor again. He crossed back to the window. With effort, he heaved up the sash. Confirming that he was on the ground floor above a short slope, he climbed outside, one leg at a time.

This time, Pike did fall. He avoided further pain only by going into a roll. He looked back to see he'd indeed exited a farmhouse, but the window was higher off the ground than he'd thought. No matter: the mill was the important thing—and the teenage girl, pounding at its door.

Pike stood and staggered toward her. She was surprised when he arrived at her side. "What are *you* doing here?" she asked.

"I don't know," he honestly answered. He had no idea who she was—just that she spoke his language, in an accent that was vaguely familiar.

She shook her head. "My father's in there!"

Pike looked up. The roof was ablaze, and smoke was emerging from a high window. He tried the large door to no avail—and wondered if whatever had made him hurt and confused had also made him weak.

The girl provided an answer. "Pa's barred it from inside!"

In his haze, Pike wondered why anyone would do that—but it wasn't the time to ask. He looked left and right. "Is there another way in?"

"I tried the other way already."

Pike turned—and listened. He spied the source of the whinnying he'd heard earlier. Two mustangs stood ahead of a wagon. They hadn't fled but wanted nothing to do with the fire. He looked to the girl. "Are they still hitched?"

"Yeah, I'd just come home when I saw this."

"Come on!" Life reentering his legs, he led her to the wagon. They detached the wagon within moments and led the horses back to the door. They didn't want to go—much less obey a stranger—but they knew the girl, and she understood what Pike was trying to do. He slung a chain around the metal door handle and secured it to the horses' rig. He looked to the girl, ahead with the animals. "Go!"

The horses didn't need to be convinced to put some distance between themselves and the mill—and if the door put up a fight, the frame that held it did not. The wood shattered and the door snapped away, unleashing a torrent of smoke. Pike covered his face with his arm and coughed.

The girl arrived before him, breathless but not overwrought. Pike moved to detach the horses from the door they were dragging, and she joined him. "What's your name?" he asked.

"Jennie."

"Go for help, Jennie!" Pike grabbed a blanket he'd seen in the back of the wagon. "I'll get your dad!"

Pike ran, pausing only to look to the east, where a black shape hovered high in the night sky. It was moving, but there was no time to consider it. He had to move, as well. He found a rain barrel by the side of the mill and thrust the blanket into it.

The soaked cloth covering him, he turned back to the entrance of the burning mill—only to see Jennie running inside, ahead of him.

If this is a nightmare, it's the one where nobody follows my orders!

Water streaming from the blanket over his head, Pike entered, expecting an inferno. Instead, embers on the dirt floor were providing all of the smoke—and some of the light—on the bottom level. He found the millworks intact. Upstairs was another matter. A ladder rose through the ceiling to the levels above, as did a large opening where bags of grain were sent up on a pulley for insertion into the grinder. The apertures shone bright with light from the fire above, and Pike could see that the debris below had all come from up there.

Realizing Jennie could only have gone up the ladder, Pike shouted for her. No response, but he did hear arguing from above. Finding no good way to scale the ladder while staying wrapped, he slung the blanket over his shoulder and climbed. If anything fell on him, he didn't feel it. But, then, every muscle was screaming.

He found Jennie precariously positioned on a second floor that was partly on fire. Pike followed her gaze upward. The floor of the topmost level was a platform only a third the width of the millhouse, and Pike saw a figure up there shielding some dark object with his body, even as flames surrounded him.

Jennie covered her mouth with her hat and shouted, "Pa, get down here!"

Above, her father yelled back. "Get out of here, Jennie!"

Pike surprised Jennie by grabbing her arm. "You've got to go. He's right."

"Pa's drunk," she replied, making no move to exit.

He pulled harder. "Come on. We'll all burn up!"

"No, we won't." Jennie shook her head. "But we might all fall through the floor if he doesn't get down here!"

Pike squinted upward. "What's his name?"

"Joe Magee."

The captain cupped his hands together. "Joe!"

A hairy face peered over the side at him. "*You!*"

"Mister Magee, you've got to come down!"

"I ain't goin'. Get out—and get *her* out!"

Pike could only agree with part of that answer. "Go down," he told Jennie. "I'll do what I can."

"You?" She gawked at him, incredulous. "You were half dead this afternoon!"

Pike felt it. But he couldn't lose this argument. Fortunately—or not—a collapsing timber supporting the upper deck made his case for him. "Here," he said, draping the blanket over her shoulders, whether she wanted it or not. "Get help. And a doctor, just in case."

Calmly accepting the blanket, she appealed to him one last time. "You don't understand. He won't burn. Neither will you. You just have to get him to come down."

There was no making sense of that. "Go!"

Pike saw her to the ladder and waited until she had descended out of sight.

Then he scaled it to the loft, where he found the expected inferno. The roof, partially gone, vented smoke to the sky. Through the flames, he saw that her father's roost appeared to be a workshop of some kind, with implements hanging from the burning walls. Joe Magee was short—and standing, Pike now saw, on a wooden right leg. He was shielding a makeshift engine with his body. Pike wondered if that had caused the fire.

"Joe!"

Magee looked back over his shoulder and swore. "I told you to get!"

The floor was afire to either side of the space between them, but a path existed. Pike took several steps toward Joe—and halted when flames to his right billowed up, curling in the air before him. Pike backed up with a start, feeling their heat.

He darted to the left. Coruscating flames blocked him there too. They seemed almost independent of the burning wood below, connected only by an umbilical of plasma. *"What the hell?"*

There was nothing to be done. Pike knelt low and surged forward, like an old American footballer avoiding blockers. The flames licked at him, but he was able to barrel through. He seized Joe around his midsection and tried to move him from the engine.

"Don't!" the man yelled as he fought to remain in place. "You damned fool—they don't hurt what's next to you!"

Pike smelled the whiskey on the man's breath as they struggled. They were the same age—but even as banged up as the captain was, Pike was in better physical shape. At last, he ripped Joe from the blocky engine. In the next second, the flames in the loft, like a thing alive, descended upon the machine.

"No! No, don't!" Joe wailed drunkenly. "Please!"

Pike held on to him while the flames grew brighter—and hotter. He dragged Joe back as the metal block turned white. Before Pike knew it, the machine, whatever it was, had melted into slag.

Joe wept. "It took weeks to build that!"

He wrested free from Pike and dove forward, only to topple over. Pike looked down and saw why. Sometime during their struggle, the flames had burned Joe's prosthetic limb away, stopping just a few centimeters shy from his body.

The engine consumed, the flames darted about, will-o'-the-wisps looking for something to attack. Another section of the roof collapsed, landing atop the ladder well. Slumped to the floor in mourning, Joe seemed not to notice. "It's gone—all gone."

"We're not!" Pike looked about for a lifeline and found one. The gear system remained intact at the crown of the remaining ceiling. A chain led from it to a rope, already tied in a loop around a huge bag of grain. Pike removed the bag and tested the rope. It would hold.

"Come on!" He reached underneath Joe's shoulders to try to get him up. The man did not fight as the captain dragged him back to the opening. Pike lifted Joe's arms and cinched the rope around his chest. "When you get to the bottom, I'll try to follow," he shouted amid falling debris. "No matter what, get loose and make for the door as best you can."

Joe simply moaned.

Pike grabbed the loose end of the rope and helped Joe over the side. The line went taut immediately, and he gritted his teeth against the friction as the rope tried to slip from his hands. Finally, Joe touched bottom—and seconds later, Pike felt the line go slack. He looked over the edge, hoping to see the man untying himself. Instead, he heard a horrific creak from above. Joe's weight on the gear system combined with the fire to bring another timber down. Pike rolled—

—into flames.

Eyes wide, he stood and frantically patted down his limbs. Only there was no burning sensation. No pain at all. Even as it surrounded him, the plasma seemed to dab tentatively at his body, transferring no heat. In fact, it was the coolest he had been since entering the mill. *Was this what Jennie and Joe had meant?*

Pike stepped forward, almost hypnotized, and emerged from the miasma. When his eyes adjusted, they saw that whatever the flames had done to him, their effect on the mill had been something else. A deafening groan heralded the impending fall of the central framing timber above. Both routes down were out. He wondered what, if anything, that left.

"It's a mill!" Pike knew from the grain chute what side of the mill the water wheel was on—and he'd seen the millpond beside it. The wall that had once stood between him and the outside was now a barrier of flames instead. Knowing what he had just experienced, he figured he had to chance it. Pike ran through the fire and leapt, hoping he had remembered correctly.

Seconds later, he struck water. His feet touched bottom briefly before he came back up. He'd just surfaced when the last of the roof gave way—and, from the sound of it, the second level too. He paddled, trying to get upstream.

He turned in the water, expecting to see the millhouse collapse, taking the wheel and perhaps part of the dam with it. Instead, he stared as the flames rose from the upper level—and *flew away*, joining the brilliant aurora to the northeast.

Pike wiped water from his eyes. *What had he just seen?*

He'd left the house delirious; nothing had changed. Reaching the shore, he lay on his back, exhausted. There was no sign of the flames, no sign of the flying black shape he'd seen earlier.

Jennie appeared, helping Joe to walk. "He's okay!" she declared. Pike didn't know whether she was referring to him or her father, but he was glad to see her. She helped him get to his knees.

Pike glanced across the pond to see riders approaching from the west.

"It's the lookouts," Joe said to his daughter. "Whatever you do, don't say nothin' to nobody." He pointed to Pike. "That goes triple for you!"

Pike wouldn't know what to say if asked. He looked wearily at Jennie. "I don't understand any of this. Is this a dream—or a nightmare?"

She shrugged. "Kind of depends on your point of view."

CHAPTER 6

THE OUTSIDERS

La'an Noonien-Singh stared across the briefing room table at *Enterprise*'s chief engineer. "Give it to me straight, Hemmer. Are they dead?"

"That depends," he said, "on how you define dead."

La'an didn't know whether Hemmer could see her pained expression or not, but it was no time to plumb the secrets of Aenar telesthesia. Not when three of the ship's command crew and a cadet were missing, and she was on the hook to find them. She plodded on. "How do *you* define dead?"

"The cessation of life functions, of course." Hemmer clasped hands the color of snow together. "Under normal circumstances, the transporter evaluates the status of the transported individual during the moments at the beginning, middle, and end of a journey. We did not receive telemetry in this case."

"So they didn't rematerialize."

"Which I might conclude, if the transporter logs could be relied upon. As there is a chance that our own receiver failed before it could receive confirmation, from a mathematical perspective I would describe them as potential people."

That set off a buzz in the room. "Schrödinger's crew," Erica Ortegas muttered.

"I'm sure our crewmates would appreciate it if we didn't consider them as theoretical constructs," La'an said. She stared at Hemmer. "Is that all you have? The system failed, and you can't explain why, so it's out of your hands?"

"Yes."

"That sounds like passing the buck."

"If that expression means that I'm running away screaming from responsibility for this mess, then I plead guilty." Hemmer shuddered. "When physics goes on strike, you might as well send me to my quarters with the day off."

Enterprise had coasted from the area near FGC-7781 b to a location where its systems functioned once again. All attempts to return to the planet had met with the same result, as everything with a transtator threw faults. Observations since had suggested a constant zone of suppressed electromagnetic activity at the planet's surface, with split-second expansions that also impacted an area with a wider radius, enveloping an additional hundred thousand kilometers beyond its moons.

Enterprise could not safely approach, and its first couple of probes launched into the region had failed. But it could *observe*, even from a great distance—and between its main deflector dish, an array of sensors, and probes safely positioned around the zone's outer limit, the crew had seen a lot.

Including a very dispiriting moment from some hours earlier. Jenna Mitchell handed La'an a padd. "Here's the final report on the shuttle impact."

She scanned the navigator's information and blanched. "No one could have survived this."

"Commander Chin-Riley hadn't completed orbital injection yet. *Eratosthenes* just kept to the last course it had, with no correction possible." She pointed out the arc the doomed vessel had taken over the planet's dayside. "The markings indicate the moments when our transporter went into operation."

"Four transports," La'an observed. "They weren't evenly spaced."

Transporter Chief Kyle responded. "It's like Mister Hemmer said—we were only able to get out one person at a time. *Enterprise* rejected their pattern streams and sent them back, as we'd planned, to locations near the surface."

"*Near* the surface!"

"The way things were working—or rather, *weren't* working—we weren't getting reliable sensor readings from the surroundings. And the farther downrange they got, the farther they were likely deposited from the shuttle's track."

La'an let the padd clatter to the table. "So even if they lived up to their potential, as Hemmer put it—our people might not be safe." She looked to Samuel Kirk, seated in Spock's usual chair. "What about life signs?"

"Um . . . there are some?" The mustached science officer straightened uncomfortably. "We've been detecting signs all along, but we can't distinguish one sapient life-form from another. Certainly not at this distance, and without some knowledge of what else is down there."

"What *can* we see?"

"Population centers, both in visible light and in the infrared—though there's less light and heat coming from them than we expected. Tremendous biomass—large forested and jungle areas, vast grasslands, oceans with bioluminescence. We're working on refining what we can see, but the atmosphere is peculiar."

Ortegas piped in. "The better option is lidar."

"Laser mapping," La'an said. "Nothing in these conditions is interfering with that?"

"Not yet," Hemmer said. "We can build a relief map of higher quality than anything we can create visually, at this range." He tapped one of the antennae atop his head. "You might even say that sight is overrated."

La'an knew that Aenar vision was based on something more than that—you couldn't read a computer screen with echolocation—but she wasn't going to debate that now. "Could the crew receive a message from us?"

"Not unless they've got something capable of receiving what we're sending," Hemmer said.

Ensign Shankar, at communications in Uhura's stead, confirmed he had not received any transmissions whatsoever from the planet—nor any response to his subspace hails. "I'm reluctant to try anything detectable by more primitive means."

La'an nodded. The new Prime Directive was already a prime headache.

Having worked around the table questioning the various departments, she now came to her own. "This phenomenon. Is there hostile intent?"

"What do you mean?" Ortegas asked.

"Our command crew is severed from us in an area where another craft disappeared. Is there hostile intent?"

"That's security thinking," Hemmer said. "Every problem's a nail."

"Are you saying there's no hostile intent?"

"I'm saying sometimes an inexplicable electromagnetic disturbance is just an inexplicable electromagnetic disturbance. It doesn't have any motive, unless it's to drive engineers to distraction. Which it seems to be a smashing success at."

None of it was good enough for La'an. She placed her hands flat on the table and splayed her fingers, determined. "I won't accept that the captain and the others are gone—and I won't accept we're on the outside, and that they're on their own. We must do something."

"You have not asked my thoughts," came a voice from the far end of the table.

La'an looked up. M'Benga had sat so silently, she'd completely skipped him in her go-around. "Sorry, Doctor."

The starship's chief medical officer spoke slowly, his words bearing weight. "I reiterate what I said to the captain earlier," M'Benga said. "You do not want to have *Enterprise* in the situation it was in before. Even to sally into the zone expecting to cruise out means sudden shutdowns of many systems, including life-support and medical services."

"Some systems remained operational before."

"Because we were not so close. But the shuttle's final moments should tell us that worse awaits." M'Benga shook his head. "No one is saying we will crash. But we could freeze or asphyxiate." He paused. "And there are vulnerable people aboard who would suffer before the others."

Ortegas nodded. "He's telling us setting fires for warmth is not a plan."

La'an had always known the helm officer to try to lighten the mood, and it worked, to the extent possible in this situation.

"We'll make no sudden moves," La'an said, "but there must be other things we can do. Even with the laws of science taking a holiday."

Hemmer cleared his throat. "As I've said, my preference is for equipment based on electrons that go where they're told. But there's a lot of know-how on this ship associated with the various autonomous systems we've tested. I have Jallow and Ghalka tinkering with probes that might employ more primitive mechanics."

Ortegas chuckled. "Clockwork timers and photographic plates."

"Laugh if you want. Your planet's first lunar impactor reached the surface without any internal propulsion system at all—and its means of communicating back was to release a vapor cloud for telescopes to see. And that was three hundred years ago."

"We've come some distance since." La'an stood. "See what you can come up with—and the rest of us will work with the tools we have. We have a deflector dish, and I'm not afraid to use it."

CHAPTER 7

THE LOOKOUTS

"Same old story," said the white-haired man looking down from his horse. "Joe Magee, still tryin' to burn himself up!"

Christopher Pike might've expected more compassion from the fire brigade. But the group of seven men and women who'd ridden up to the ruined mill hadn't brought any buckets or offered any first aid. Instead, two of them stood guard over Joe as he sat on a crate, while Jennie wiped soot from her father's face. Some of the other riders had entered the smoldering structure. The youngest of the arrivals, a wild-eyed teen, stood near Pike as the starship captain sat on the back of the wagon, toweling off.

Like Joe and Jennie, all the riders wore clothing similar to what Pike expected to find in a part of the ancient American West where autumn meant something. Dusters over shirts and trousers, with stovepipe boots and felt cowboy hats. Pike would have thought them from a costume party or theatrical production if it weren't for the glowing lanterns several of them held. The peculiar green glows came not from fire inside the devices, but a chemical reaction.

Pike knew it for sure when the imperious rider shook his waning lantern vigorously, coaxing a more vibrant glow from it. "Damned thing."

Joe sneered at him. "Afraid of a little fire, Garr?"

"The righteous need not fear." The older man dismounted. "Even so, I don't tempt fate—which is more than I can say for you, Joe. Was that you I saw jumping into the pond?"

"Do I look wet to you?"

The boy standing near Pike spoke up. "This is the one." Seventeen at most, the kid held a rifle, the only weapon in sight. He prodded Pike with it.

"Watch what you do with that," Pike said.

"Put that away, Reedy!" Garr advanced toward the wagon and held his lantern before Pike. "Who we got here?"

Pike gave his name. Before he could add anything, Joe quickly called out, "Chris is Erin's brother."

Garr paused. "Your wife?"

"Yeah," Joe said. "He's just in from out west."

"*Pike*." Garr peered at the captain in the emerald light. "I knew some Pikes, over in Pleasant Ridge."

"That's where he's from," Jennie piped in.

"Good name. Goes right back to the First Days." He gave the lantern to Reedy and offered Pike his hand. "I'm Sebastian Garr. A fellow fish, you might say. Didn't know your sister well, but she was a fine person. We admired her . . . *patience*." He shot a disparaging glance at Joe before using the handshake to help Pike down. "Say, you look pretty roughed up."

Jennie stepped closer. "He pulled Pa out of the fire. Then he jumped into the pond."

Garr's bushy white eyebrow shot up. "That so?"

"It's so." Pike, whose head already hurt, squinted at the mill. "By chance, you didn't also happen to notice that the fire just *flew off*?"

That prompted a blank look from Garr—and a quick intervention from Joe. "Chris don't know what he's sayin'. He was already banged up when he got here, in fact. A critter spooked his horse. He got throwed. Walked the rest of the way."

"Things are pretty hazy," Pike muttered. That, at least, was the truth.

Pike didn't know if Garr was impressed or suspicious until the man chuckled. "That could happen to anyone. I know that ride too. Don't know why you'd bother to leave—Pleasant Ridge is a fine place." He looked at the mill, now missing its top level. "Climbing up there in your shape was pretty brave."

"Or foolish," Joe interjected.

"Lots of brave things start like that." Garr paced the area before the captain. "You might've guessed I'm deputy warden around here, Mister Pike." He gestured to his companions. "These here are the lookouts."

Pike rubbed the back of his neck. "Lookouts?"

"That's right."

"Oh." It was one more thing for Pike to ask about, but Jennie and Joe seemed to want him to keep his curiosity to himself. He didn't know why, but he felt he owed them—especially as Joe seemed to be in trouble for something.

He knew that for sure when a woman emerged from the mill carrying a gunnysack and a wooden pail. Garr stepped away from Pike when he saw her. "What you got there, Sal?"

"He had buckets with tar in 'em," the woman said. "And others that held something else."

Sal showed the pail to Garr, who dipped his finger in and drew it to his nose. "Kerosene. He's getting fuel from the tar." He glared at Joe. "You ain't gonna tell me it's for makin' hooch."

"I ain't telling you squat," Joe said.

She emptied the sack. Various tools tumbled out—as well as metal fittings, some of them melted. "Same as always. Stuff for motor making."

Garr looked keenly at Pike. "Did *you* know what he was up to?"

Pike shook his head. That, too, was the truth.

Garr kicked at the pieces. "Joe, your whole life I've been telling you this tinkering business was gonna be the end of you. It took your leg, drove your poor wife to distraction—and now it's done this." He gestured to the ruined mill.

"The machine didn't do nothin'," Joe retorted. "It was working fine."

"But what good is it?"

"Winter's comin'. That brook there'll freeze and there won't be any more flour. But if I don't use water to run the mill—"

"People weren't meant to mill in the winter. That's *why* the brook freezes." Garr looked to the ruins and spat in disgust. "There's a hundred eighty days in a year, and you can't expect them all to be the same. I wouldn't want to live in a world where you had to do *everything* all the time." With his boot heel, he stamped one of the melted valves into the dirt. "Bringing the Sorry down on yourself is bad enough. This time you nearly killed your whole family. You really ought to think about your daughter."

Joe erupted. "I am thinkin' of her! Jennie ain't like Erin, Seb. She's restless. She's cut out for more than what we got."

"There's nothing wrong with what we've got. It's been good enough for centuries."

Pike had heard talk like this before. As a kid in California, he'd lived near the Bar T Ranch. He'd enjoyed his visits there; the daughter of the owners had taught him how to ride a horse. Her parents, however, were Luddites, always propounding about the evils of civilization. Garr was soft-pedaling it by comparison.

The older man looked down and tut-tutted. "Some lessons gotta be taught over and over." He nodded to his companions on either side of Joe. "Hitch that wagon and take him to Havenbrook."

"Here we go again," Joe protested as Garr's people made him stand.

Pike took a step forward. "Are you taking him to jail?"

Garr did a double take. "To church." He grinned. "You *did* get a rap on the head."

Jennie began to object as well—but Joe pointed her toward Pike. "Get him inside. And block that window so he don't get out until I come back. Wandering around, he could hurt himself."

"I'll second that," Garr said as he mounted his horse. He looked down and tipped his hat. "Hope you'll feel better soon, Mister Pike. And come to our Jubilee. We're no Pleasant Ridge, but I think you'll like it."

Jennie hustled Pike away as the others hoisted her father onto the wagon.

"Did they say they were taking him to *church*?" Pike asked.

"Just overnight."

"What'll happen to him?"

"They're gonna bore him silly—and he'll be impossible to live with when he gets back. Make that *more* impossible." She opened the door to the darkened farmhouse. "Your room's at the end of the hall. Try to stay put this time."

"He's not concerned leaving you with a stranger?"

"He's concerned leaving you around anyone else," she said, peeking out the door. "You keep talking, they'll find out you're from *outer space*!"

CHAPTER 8

THE WOODSMAN

Nope, not here. Gotta go!

Elsewhere, Una Chin-Riley might have considered a cross-country run a fine start to a day. Not so for this mad dash at sunrise. Racing from one inadequate hiding place to another was just the continuation of an exercise that had lasted all night.

She'd extricated herself from the tree just before sunset the day before, unharnessing from the permanently lodged backpack and falling free. Chin-Riley had missed two thick branches on the way down before caroming off a third with her feet. That had sent her into a swan dive through the foliage, grasping frantically at one would-be lifeline after another.

Meters from the surface, she'd finally snagged a hanging vine. But the ground held so many dangers she soon began to miss the tree, pesky birds and all. The canopy overhead was so thick the time of day barely mattered, and the ground so mushy that every step threatened a twisted ankle.

All of which she could have coped with, were it not for the wild animals. Creatures on legs numbering from two to a dozen had seemed to find her irresistible. The first officer didn't know if she'd encroached on their hunting territory or if she was the prey, but that didn't much matter. Night added swooping nocturnal fliers, most less pleasant than the bird she'd met in the canopy.

Sam Kirk, *Enterprise*'s xenobiologist, might have suggested some tactic for dealing with the aggressive menagerie. Unfortunately, Chin-Riley's communicator hadn't worked any better than her phaser had. She'd finally been forced to hurl the devices in order to escape from a band of things that looked like primates. She would worry about the Prime Directive consequences of that later, when she wasn't running for her life.

Chin-Riley had just caught a fitful hour of sleep crouching within a large flowering shrub when what looked like a fur-covered triceratops arrived to chew on it, only to decide it liked the smell of her better. Now it thundered after her, smashing its way through the woods.

The commander exhausted herself trying to build up enough of a lead that would permit her to find another hiding place. The giant tree before her had looked promising from a distance, but up close she saw the recess in it was just a trick of the morning light. *Nope, not here*, she again thought. But she couldn't bring herself to press on, not yet. Even for one in her excellent physical shape, the ordeal had been too taxing.

She looked up when she heard leaves rustling somewhere ahead of her. With the behemoth catching up behind, this was the worst possible news. But before she could respond, a hairy-faced person emerged from the brush and yelled something she didn't understand.

The furry dino charged them, and her impulse was to yank the new arrival out of the way. But before she could, the man placed a narrow brown tube to his mouth. When the juggernaut was just meters away, he huffed, blasting the monster in the face with powder.

Chin-Riley saw particles sparkle in the air—but only for a second, as the man pulled *her* away. It was the right move. Her feral tormentor pitched over and slammed into the forest floor, sending the morning dew flying. Whatever was in the blowgun had put the thing to sleep immediately.

Catching her breath, she regarded her savior. He was a mountain of a man, and while he seemed human to her, he also looked as native to the forest as any of the creatures she'd seen. His bushy brown hair fell over his eyes, and his long beard had burrs caught in it here and there. His clothing, while primitive and soiled, seemed designed for a rugged terrain. The man could have been twenty or sixty. He clearly hadn't seen a shower—or a mirror—in a month.

At the same time, she noticed how quiet the raucous forest had become. She felt safe, somehow, for the first time since the day before. She let out a large breath. "Thank you."

"Just doing my job."

Chin-Riley did a double take. As surprising as it was to find a deep-voiced park ranger here, discovering one that spoke her language was even more so.

He gestured to the fallen beast. "Don't approach the *ollodon* until the crystals dissipate, or you'll sleep too. Bhavan root is powerful."

The *Enterprise* officer noticed he hadn't worried about using his breath to deliver the substance, but the warning was needless. She had no intention of approaching the sleeping beast—and her savior's appearance had newly enlivened her. He had spoken her language, and that could likely only mean one thing. "Are you from the *Braidwood*?"

"What did you say?"

"The *Braidwood*."

"I've never heard this forest called that," he said, brown eyes bright as he looked up and around. "It is the Grandwood, and no one is from here."

"But *you're* here."

He didn't answer. He turned and tromped back the way he'd come.

Uninvited, she followed him. Chin-Riley found the woodsman in the smallest of clearings, beside yet another tall creature. This one had antlers like an elk, even if the rest of it resembled no four-legged creature she'd ever seen. It was tied to a tree, and he was removing a large saddlebag from it.

"I'm Una," she said, deciding it was best to keep things simple.

"I am Celarius," he responded without looking at her. He put the bag over his shoulder and walked straight past her, back in the direction of the sleeping *ollodon*.

Flustered, she followed him again. "I've been lost for a day, Celarius."

"Not likely."

His tone startled her. "You don't believe me?"

"I do not," he said, kneeling beside the monster. "This location is a week's ride to anywhere, and you have no mount."

She considered the Prime Directive—and thought fast. She pointed. "One of *those* things got it."

"The *ollodon*."

"Yes."

"Along with all your supplies."

"I was running. I didn't take inventory."

"Life is full of difficulties," Celarius observed. "Isn't it, my friend?" He patted the *ollodon* on the snout before turning to rummage through his bag.

At last, he withdrew a silvery stick and swept the end of it against the gritty skin of his palm. The tip of the stick ignited—and kept sizzling as he planted the other end in the wet soil.

"I could have used a fire last night," she said.

"No, you couldn't have."

"What do you mean? It got cold."

"As anyone would know, at this time of year. What settlement are you from?"

She picked a random direction and gestured. "It's that way."

He gave her a moment's glance. "There is no settlement that way."

"That would be why I can't find it."

"Hmm." He withdrew two rods from his bag and strung a metal coil between them. Turning his back to her, he thrust the coil into the fire to warm. "Does this mystery settlement have a name?"

"What's the closest one?" she asked.

"Gorm Tigah."

"That's it."

"Nonsense. There's nobody like *you* in Gorm Tigah."

"My family used to say that."

"I mean the Tigans are particular about their guests. They have a xenophobia nobody has shaken in centuries. They would not welcome you."

So far, Celarius wasn't looking much more hospitable. If this was a rescue, it sure didn't feel like one. "I'm sorry to bother you," she said.

"You aren't bothering me. I am doing nothing now that I wasn't here to do already." Satisfied the coil was hot enough, Celarius found his way to the underside of the great beast. She couldn't see what he was doing, but the dazed creature noticed, letting out a sudden and sharp yelp.

"Easy," Celarius said. He started whistling.

"What are you doing?" she asked.

"Gelding it."

"*Here? Now?*"

"Here and now."

She looked about. "Something you just wander around the forest doing?"

"Yes."

The beast emitted a low moan, after which Celarius spoke again. "In the natural order, *ollodons* are omnivorous. But some have traits that allow them to more easily digest meat. When a supply is available, they seek it and become aggressive. If their kind flourishes, more will have the trait—and they will no longer be suitable to ride."

"Somebody *rides* these things?"

"You and I aren't built for it. But others are."

She wanted to know *what* others, but she decided to hold off on asking.

Celarius was matter-of-fact about the process, and the care he took with the mammoth beast impressed her. Even so, Una noted the animal's restless twitching. "He doesn't seem excited about this."

"I know *I* wouldn't be," Celarius replied. "And I don't enjoy having to do it. This is his realm. You and I—more *you* than *I*—are the invaders. But the reputation of his species will improve, and that is for his own good. It is the tragedy of nature that it is better to be seen as useful than as a threat."

Una stood, speechless. She'd traveled many light-years in her life, but Philosophic Mountain Man was a new one on her.

His work finished, Celarius wiped his hands on his pants and stood. "Our friend will rest now. But when the powder wears off, he will be unhappy—and he will still find people tasty. I recommend you be somewhere else."

"Good idea. Which way are *you* going?"

"I don't see how that could matter," he said, leaning over to douse the flame on the stick with his fingertips. "I'm indexing forest species. I travel quickly—and quietly. I don't want company."

"I wouldn't be any trouble."

"You haven't been traveling cautiously. I caught your trail twenty minutes ago."

"I told you, that's because I was being chased." She'd had enough. "I don't know where I am—and I don't know where I'm heading."

"Another tragedy." Celarius shoved his items in his bag and faced her. "I'm here to find out more about *these* creatures, not you. People, I don't need to know any more about. I see enough of them in my normal life."

"Would any of *them* be more helpful?"

He disregarded her remark. "Odds are the reason you're in this forest is something I wouldn't approve of. Poaching—"

"I'm unarmed."

"—or suicide, which is the same as entering this forest unarmed."

She stewed. He had her there.

Celarius walked back toward the animal he'd been riding. "At best, you are fleeing from someone," he said. "If they are in authority, then surrender yourself to their care. If it was over a personal matter, then it's none of my business and I will not intercede."

"Something tells me those *other people* aren't sad to see you gone for weeks at a time."

The remark brought her a surprised stare from Celarius—and then the hint of a smile as he looked back at her. "I suppose that's so. But they would never tell me that to my face. It's another reason I—"

Chin-Riley's eyes widened. "*Look out!*"

This time, she did grab Celarius, shoving him out of the way as his riding beast violently flipped over. Something large and robust had pounced upon it, and the two animals rolled together, screeching. The attacker was another *ollodon*, she saw. Brightly colored—and the possessor of sharp teeth that it used to tear into its prey. Celarius scrambled along with her to a position behind a nearby tree.

He scowled. It was clear he'd been taken by surprise. "That would be our sleeper's mate," he said.

"You don't have any procedure for her in that bag?"

"No procedure—and no bag." He gestured to where the bloody violence continued. His gear was somewhere underneath his fallen and writhing mount.

She looked to his side. "You still have the blowgun."

"But not the powder. Still, the *kuuko* will keep her occupied for a time—perhaps, time enough." Celarius let out a deep breath.

It was the first time Chin-Riley had seen him even a little off-balance, and she decided to make the most of it. "This is a good place to have another pair of eyes, I'd think."

"Perhaps you're right." He looked her over, as if seeing her for the first time. "What did you say your name was again?"

CHAPTER 9

THE CHORES

Christopher Pike had any number of questions for Jennie, but he'd wound up not asking any during the night of the fire. Sleep was too appealing, and it wasn't like the house was lit anyway.

He rose to sunlight through the window. He had no idea how long he'd slept—just that he was thankful for the washbasin and the change of clothes sitting on the dresser. Finding the door unlocked, he went to the kitchen, where he discovered a pot of something that tasted vaguely like coffee on the stove. The locals' concerns about fire apparently didn't prevent cooking.

A plate of biscuits sat on the table, dripping in something he guessed was lard. He imagined Spock would have wanted to run a tricorder over them; M'Benga probably would have advised against them entirely. Pike ate everything in sight, without question.

Soon after, he walked outside, examining in daylight what had confused him at night. Apart from the charred mill, the place was gorgeous. The greens, yellows, and browns of the farm rose to a cloudless sky—and the golden tendrils of the daytime aurora to the northeast grew and subdivided like a hydra in the heavens.

This isn't Earth. Why does it feel like it is?

A. E. Hodgkin had been studying termites more than a century earlier when he came up with his Law of Parallel Planetary Development, but it had become faddish for explorers to use it to explain every similarity that didn't come from direct cultural contamination. Everything from the existence of multiple worlds of handles on doors to choruses in songs had been ascribed, not always convincingly, to nature preferring things a certain way.

Pike remained dubious of the overapplied law, even despite the strange places he'd seen. Cultural contamination was easier to buy than assuming he was on a planet where people independently decided to speak his language and eat with flatware. At the same time, he couldn't imagine *Braidwood* causing this level of transformation in a year. It was easier to believe that he wasn't on FGC-7781 b at all, but rather had gone back in time somehow to Earth. Only the pesky aurorae suggested otherwise—not to mention flames that seemed to act with a mind of their own.

Indeed, he'd been around enough that he couldn't rule out that the whole thing was happening in his mind, and that he was still sitting on *Eratosthenes*, under the control of some mischievous alien intelligence. The possibilities were endless, and he could barely process them all.

"Where are you when I need you, Mister Spock?"

He got no response to his spoken-aloud query, unless he counted the sound of horses. Still aching, Pike walked gingerly around the corner of the house. The wagon and its team were still gone, having been used to take Joe Magee away, but he could see another pair of horses in a paddock next to a barn.

Pike was next to the barn door when the manure flew at him. He stepped aside quickly. "Hey, watch it!"

"Whoops!" Inside, he saw in one of the horse stalls a figure wearing his space suit and helmet and holding a shovel. The environmental suit, too large for its wearer, sagged in places, with sleeves scrunched up—and the whole thing was smeared black. The wearer turned toward him. Jennie smiled through the helmet. "This is great!" she said, her voice muffled. "I can't smell anything in here!"

None of the gear's indicator lights were on. "You'd better take off the helmet," Pike said.

"What'd you say?" Jennie shouted, unable to hear.

Pike stepped to her, worked the control, and removed the helmet. "You're not going to be able to breathe if you keep that on."

Jennie took a breath and winced. "Can't be much worse than it is without it."

Having mucked out a stable a few hundred times himself, Pike grinned. "I'd think you'd be used to it by now."

"Never." She pitched the shovel and walked out into the sun.

Following her, Pike saw what a mess the suit was. "That isn't all from the stable, I hope."

She looked down. "Oh, no. *You* did this."

"I did?"

"When you landed. Pa says you appeared in the air over the tar pit and fell right in." Jennie began removing the protective gear, revealing a flannel shirt and jeans underneath. "You went in hard. It knocked you out. You'd still be in it if he hadn't called me out to the pit to help free you. Took both of us to get you into the cart and back here."

Pike chewed on what she'd said. This was FGC-7781 b, all right. But now he had the Prime Directive to worry about. "You know, I'm not from outer space," he said, helping to gather the dingy equipment. "I'm . . . an inventor. I made this suit."

She laughed. "I've already had my load of manure for the day."

Pike blanched. "No good, huh?"

"No inventor on Epheska would ever admit to being one—you saw what happened to my dad. But that's not why we knew you were a spaceman." Jennie picked up the breastplate and gestured to the circular shield mounted on it. She'd meticulously cleaned that part, revealing the chevron symbol ringed by the words "Starfleet Command" and "United Federation of Planets."

Pike sighed. All the work to make *Eratosthenes* undetectable, and here their space suits were all labeled, right on the front. *It might as well say "If found, please return to . . ."*

He gave it one more try. "Jennie, no matter what this says, I don't—"

"Are you going to keep pretending? That would be fun." She smiled. "I can try to prove you wrong."

"Something tells me nobody ever proves you wrong," Pike said. He took a deep breath. "Okay. I am from space, but I didn't mean to come here. I have some friends who may be here too. I need to leave, but I also need to find them." He fished around in the utility belt's compartments.

"What's that thing?" Jennie asked when he found what he was looking for.

"A communicator." Pike wasn't surprised when it wouldn't activate. "Does anything electrical work here?"

"I don't know what you mean."

"Never mind." Pike pocketed it and searched for the phaser next. He could tell it was dead as well, but he had no desire for it to fall into the wrong hands. "Is there a place I can get rid of this? I mean, forever?"

Jennie chewed her lip. "If it's something the Sorry doesn't like, it might get rid of it for you."

"The Sorry. That's the . . . magic fire?" It was the only way he could think of to describe it.

She responded with a nod. "If you want to keep anyone from finding something, there's always that building over there. You know what it is?"

Pike looked. "I do."

"That's why I didn't lock you in last night. I figure even spacemen need the outhouse."

"Much obliged." Pike chuckled and pocketed the phaser. "I'll take care of this later."

She always kept her eyes on him, he noticed: her strange specimen from beyond. "What happened to you?" she asked. "Why are you here?"

"I was aboard a shuttle. It's kind of a carriage that goes between places in the sky."

"You're kidding!"

"Well, that's when they work. Ours was in trouble. We had to get out." His eyes widened. "My friends! Did your father see anyone else?"

"Falling from the sky? Or in the tar pit?"

"Anywhere."

"Not unless they'd already sunk." The news excited Jennie. "You mean there's more spacemen around?"

"I hope so." He peered at her. "Did you say this place was called Epheska?"

"The planet," she said, picking up the environmental suit. "We'd better get the rest of this stuff back into the cellar before someone else drops by."

Pike frowned. "Garr would have a problem?"

"More like a conniption."

She stowed his gear, locking the cellar door afterward. Then it was off to the well, where they both drank from a tin scoop. Pike couldn't recall anything more refreshing.

He followed as Jennie continued with her chores. The first stop was the corral. "Mustangs," he said. "Surprising for a farm."

"They're strong and we ride them."

"Mules would cost less."

"Not sure what you mean." She gestured to a tobiano paint mare in the corral. "Cricket there I found and broke myself."

"Nice." A black gelding that Jennie called Shadow reminded him of Tango, back home.

He helped her unload feed. "You work pretty hard."

"Folks say it's the perfect society—but some are just perfectly tired."

"Don't you go to school?"

"What do you mean?"

"Don't you know what a school is?"

"Yeah, but I graduated when I could read and cipher, just like everyone else. Deputy Garr would say any more's a waste."

"What do *you* say?"

Jennie straightened. "There wasn't much left to learn. I had my choice of trades, then, like everyone else—but Ma died, and suddenly I had a lot of work around here."

Pike looked down. "What happened to her?"

"She just died." The girl didn't want to go any further.

They walked in silence the rest of the way around the house. There, he got a better look at the fields. "Is that wheat?"

"Wheat. Jajako. Barley. Some *gormil* too." She stared at him. "How do *you* know wheat?"

"The same way I know horses. I'm from Earth."

She clapped her thigh. "I knew it! I told Pa, but he was betting you just looked human."

Interesting, Pike thought. "No, this is me. How do you know Earth?"

Jennie smirked. "Okay, this will be fun." She headed back toward the corral. "Aren't you going to tell me?"

"If you can ride a horse, I'll show you."

CHAPTER 10

THE ENCOUNTER

Nobody had asked Nyota Uhura if she'd wanted to go on the shuttle.

Everyone had her file. Starfleet was nothing *but* files on people, places, and things. They knew Uhura's parents had taught at the University of Nairobi. They knew she was a prodigy speaking dozens of languages. They knew she was following in the footsteps of her grandmother when she'd joined Starfleet. And they knew the extent to which she'd excelled, earning a posting on the flagship right out of the Academy.

It was also not a mystery that her parents had died in a shuttle accident, along with her brother.

She did not fear traveling in shuttles. You couldn't avoid them as a cadet, and it would have precluded opportunities if she had tried. You couldn't play interstellar translator very well while sitting at a subspace terminal at home.

She wasn't surprised that nobody had asked her if she wanted to go on *Eratosthenes*, an experimental vessel, into a zone where another ship had disappeared. She wouldn't have expected otherwise. Chin-Riley wanted her cadets to perform professionally in all circumstances. Pike seemed to think it was another opportunity for Uhura—an adventure, he'd said. They were not callous people: they had to know what she'd gone through, and she knew that if she'd voiced any reservations, they would have listened.

The last day and night had her wishing that someone had asked—and that she'd begged off.

She'd been the last person aboard *Eratosthenes*. She knew it wasn't intentional: Hemmer and *Enterprise* were lucky to transport people off even one at a time, and Pike had deliberately asked to be beamed off last. *The captain, going down with the ship*, she thought. Instead, due to whatever luck of the molecular draw was in play, he was the first to be whisked away. He was followed by Spock and Chin-Riley, leaving her alone on a ship that was in its death throes. She'd seen the flames all around outside the shuttle as it streaked through the atmosphere, wondering if it had been like this for her family.

And then she'd awakened in hell.

It was not, she now knew—but she couldn't imagine hell being much worse. She'd meandered from one volcanically active area to the next, finding her way between boiling mud pits while she coughed her lungs out. This might be a fine home for a microscopic extremophile, but less so for someone whose Starfleet survivalist training had often come with the instructor's caveat: "Now, of course, in *your* role, you'll never need to know this . . ."

She was thankful that she'd remembered any of it at all—and frustrated that so much of what she'd been told involved drawing on supplies in a suit she no longer had.

Uhura had slept the night before in the open, watching black clouds rising to obscure some really fantastic aurorae. She'd started moving again with no direction in mind: the terrain didn't permit one anyway. Spock's words about there being sentient life on the planet rang in her ears, but she couldn't imagine where it would be.

And while she'd happily take the sudden appearance of a city—preferably populated by hospitable denizens with ample water and food—she really only cared about finding three people. Pike, Chin-Riley, and Spock. Three more people from a dying shuttlecraft.

Her voice was parched and dry, but she strained nonetheless to call out for them. What if they, too, had transported into the lava fields?

I was last to leave. What if I'm too late?

The sun reached its apex. She knew she couldn't afford the moisture, but she sat down to cry anyway. It wasn't something her professor would have advised, and it certainly wasn't Starfleet. But the moment called for it.

In the nearby caldera, another volcanic vent opened up, outgassing. It was enough to make her look, but not move. She knew now which events were dangerous and which were simply there to terrorize her. *What a terrible thing to become proficient at.* She put her head back down.

But this time, something was different. Out of the corner of her eye, she saw a tongue of fire licking up from the vent. It curled, almost somersaulting. Improbably for this breezeless zone, it began to move across the cauldron, bumping along like an orange tumbleweed, until it dipped beneath the lip of the shelf and out of sight.

Until, that is, the fireball leapt onto the surface beside her.

"*Gah!*" Uhura shouted, jumping to her feet. The ball of flames went momentarily ovoid in that instant, darting back to the edge of the shelf and resuming its previous chaotic shape.

She stared. It was the size of a basketball, and that was almost what its bouncing reminded her of. It was on fire, yet she couldn't tell what, exactly, it was burning.

She took a step to the left and watched as it rolled in the same direction, mirroring her movement but going no farther. She went back the other way and watched as it did the same thing.

A bizarre thought possessing her, she faked another move to the left and bolted right a few steps. The fireball simply bobbed in place, almost as if conveying impatience.

Uhura looked back at it. "You guessed on that one, right?"

It was then she determined dehydration might be making her delirious. She also realized there wasn't a thing she could do about it.

"So I'm talking to a fireball. Why not?" She frowned. "I'm alone here. I'm lost, I'm hurt, I'm hot, and I'm scared. But most of all, I'm thirsty. Do you have any idea what that means?"

Of course not. She shook her head and closed her eyes. Visualization exercises had helped her before, and she tried to picture herself in a cooling stream.

She opened her eyes. The blob was gone. "*Huh?*"

Uhura looked around. She spotted the flame-thing again, bounding across a steaming outflow. Upon reaching the other side, it paused—and after several moments, it bobbed up and down, almost impatiently, she thought.

And as wrong as she knew it was to personalize the thing, Uhura was tired enough to play along. "I can't go that way," she shouted across. She turned to the right and zigzagged through the higher terrain bridging the area. No sooner had she arrived near the fireball than it hared off again, tumbling across the blasted ground.

Uhura followed. *What else did I have planned?*

She was beginning to think of other things to do a couple of kilometers later when the object topped a crest. She followed—and saw the volcanic field giving way to a brown valley. Beyond a slope farther away, she saw something reflecting the light.

Water!

Uhura hurried ahead as best she could. The fireball bounded along next to her, clearly headed in the same direction. When she arrived at the rivulet, she paused. She had no instruments, but her water safety training told her this place was too close to the volcanic region. Following its gradual descent, she watched the water grow clearer as the creek widened. Life appeared, as well: hardy mosses on rocks at first, followed by more diverse plant life.

Satisfied that it was worth a chance, she fell to her hands and knees and cupped her hands into it. She took a sip. The water had a nasty tang, but she didn't immediately retch. She figured it might be even better downstream.

She noticed that the phenomenon had followed her the whole way. It sat near the edge of the creek, consuming nothing but still somehow aflame.

"You're a fireball who knows what water is," Uhura said, leaning over to address the thing. "I wouldn't think you'd like it. But still—*thank you.*"

The plasma grew a warm blue.

Uhura had been instructed in methods of communicating with other species, but she wasn't a xenobiologist. She'd already decided her unusual companion was alive and with some intelligence; she also wondered if it was fire at all, or just something that expressed itself as something that had some of the properties of flame. There were stranger things in the cosmos. She'd been told she might meet a few on *Enterprise*, but she'd never expected to find one herself.

But if she couldn't analyze the being, she could at least name it. Words were her department. It had responded to her shock and fear earlier and seemed to recognize her thirst; it seemed to respond to her emotions now. Calling it a fire elemental wasn't good enough. It needed an extra dimension.

"You're . . . an *empatherm*," she said. "What do you think of that?"

The being shimmered.

She looked downstream. Where there was life, there might be more. "Follow me if you want. I'm going for a walk!"

CHAPTER 11

THE TOWN

Like most fans of old Westerns, Christopher Pike understood the dramatic saloon entrance. There was something satisfyingly abrupt about the wooden panels banging inward, heralding a new arrival. There was a time and a place for that sort of thing, however, and his visit to the town of Havenbrook wasn't one of them. He wasn't looking for attention.

Unfortunately, he also wasn't looking for the hinges of the tavern door at Lem's Dirty Duck to have so much give to them. The doors sprang open at his push, shattering the mug of a patron who was standing too close. When the captain saw the bruiser in the black hat, he realized he couldn't have picked a worse occupant to inconvenience. Pike could have hidden in the man's shadow and had room to invite a few friends.

The offended drinker wore a dark jacket and a clean white shirt with a string tie; in another context, Pike would have said he was wearing his Sunday best. He looked down on Pike, who looked up, trying to decide between what would have been an appropriate gesture of apology on *Enterprise* and something more appropriate for the setting. He decided displaying weakness was all wrong here. "Sorry," he said, leaving it at that.

Pike steeled himself for swear words or fighting words—but what came from the giant's lips was something else. "Think nothing of it, friend. Better spilt on the floor than on the finery!" He threw a beefy arm around Pike. "Grand day for a Jubilee, no?"

Pike shook under the man's embrace. "Let me get you another drink," the captain offered.

It was said on impulse, and he remembered only too late that he had no currency. He was searching the pocket of Joe Magee's loaner clothes when he noticed the floor, and the liquid pooling around the broken glass. It was white. "What was that, milk?"

"Of magnesia." The big man put his fist to his own midsection. "I have to speak at the service. Always gets me right there."

Pike looked over to see that the balding man at the bar had already poured a new drink. Pike shrank. "Afraid I don't have a way to pay for that—"

"You out-of-towners are a hoot," the giant said, grinning as he went for his concoction.

Meanwhile, the barman approached Pike with a cloth and a tray for the fragments. Pike prepared to accept them. *I guess this is how I'm paying for the drink.* But the worker cleaned the area himself.

Pike had expected to know more about this planet by now, but his ride into town with Jennie hadn't gone as he'd planned. They'd barely hit the trail riding Shadow and Cricket when they met another family, heading into town for an event. That had put a damper on their discussions. No sooner had they arrived in Havenbrook than a messenger approached Jennie with news about her father. Jennie had told Pike to stay where their horses were tied, but his curiosity had gotten the better of him. *Who could resist a saloon called Lem's Dirty Duck?*

But after a minute looking around the hall from the bar, he decided that Lem's duck must have been one clean waterfowl, indeed. He'd expected tables with poker and faro, and piles of dollars and coins. He saw trick-taking, and pads and pencils. He'd expected checkers; he saw chess. He did get the piano player he was expecting, but the woman was playing chamber music.

And the people were just like he'd seen outside. No shabby miners, bedraggled ranchers, or grizzled cavalrymen. Instead, the others were well dressed—and he saw several families. It was as wholesome as could be. Some people were actually reading.

Pike didn't need Uhura around to know that *saloon* had come from *salon*. This place seemed to have jumped back a bit to its drawing-room origins.

The bartender approached, having finished his cleanup. "Birch beer, stranger?"

Pike shook his head and looked behind the barman. "Isn't that liquor back there?"

"Sure—but you wouldn't want that *today*!"

Pike acted as if he understood. "No, I guess I don't." He glanced about. "Have you seen any other strangers around here? I'm looking for some friends of mine."

"What settlement are they from?"

"They kind of move around."

"They sound like clouds to me!" The bartender smiled. "You're the fella staying with the Magees."

"I guess. Are you Lem?"

"Oh, no. Lemuel Bottoms was the founder. The Duck's been a fixture in Havenbrook since the First Days. I'm the nineteenth or twentieth proprietor, depending on how you count."

"Twenty sounds better." Pike glanced at the window. "Have you thought about putting your own name out there?"

The bartender shrugged. "No need—everybody knows who I am. And I'll just be passing it along to number twenty—or twenty-one." He smiled. "Why make work for someone else?"

"Right." Pike also wanted to ask if the bartender knew what a duck was, but he decided to save it when he saw Jennie enter.

"There you are," she said, walking up to him.

"Should you be in a place like this?"

"Why wouldn't I be?"

He looked around. "Yeah, I guess you're right." It was hardly a den of in-iquity, ready to lead to the downfall of local kids. *It might put them to sleep*, he thought. "What's the story with your father?"

"What I expected. Come on." She led him out into the street.

The previous night, Pike had thought the lookouts appeared fit for some kind of theatrical production. He'd expected that the town, like the tavern, would evoke some version of the Old West: a re-creation for the recreation of tourists, maybe even including a mock gunfight at the top of every hour. The buildings did have that historic flavor, and certainly there were many artisans at work. But this simulation, if that was what it was, leaned into the mundane, seeming happy and peaceful.

And again, a lot of people were dressed up. *Did they have Sunday on this planet?*

Jennie had the answer. "Today's the Jubilee they're talking about. Every-one's decked out, and others come in from outside."

"I guess I'm one of them. But I doubt you get many—"

Pike stopped talking when he noticed a smithy—or more specifically, the blacksmith. He was orange, with stubby horns, webbed fingers, and a mashed proboscis. He pounded a white-hot horseshoe on an anvil. When Jennie said nothing about him, Pike spoke up. "There are other kinds of people here, I take it."

"How do you mean?"

"Not human."

"Oh. I never notice that. Some are visiting, in from their own settlements. Some stay. Weedaw there is a Strooh. He moved here years ago from Iklik."

Pike looked at the blacksmith's workspace, which he apparently shared with the gunsmith next door. "He doesn't seem to be afraid of fire."

"He's afraid of most everything else." She waved to Weedaw, who looked suddenly away.

The interaction—or lack of one—concerned Pike. "Do all . . . *outsiders* act that way?"

"Oh, no. Here's proof of that." Jennie nodded to the porch of a shop on the other side of Weedaw's place. "*Hey, Mochi!*"

A purple-skinned woman wearing white waved back. "Good to see you, Jennie!" She looked Pike over. "This must be the uncle!"

"I must be," Pike replied. *Garr and his lookouts must have told everyone under the sun.* "And you must be the barber."

"Good guess!" Mochi glimpsed at the colorful pole beside her and smiled. "Oh, you need a shave." She gestured to her open chair. "How about it, friend?"

Pike touched his chin. Jennie had provided him with shaving gear at the farm, but he'd taken one look at the perilously sharp straight-edge razor and decided he could go without experimenting. He apologized. "I'm not sure we have time—"

"Nonsense," Mochi declared. "I know where you're headed, and I'm happy to make time. Everyone wants to look good for the Jubilee."

Before he knew it, Pike was in the chair with foam on his face. Jennie stood by the wall, yawning. She'd had a late night too. "I saw Deputy Garr," the girl said. "We're to meet Dad at the Jubilee service. That's his sentence—he's got to attend."

"It will do him no harm," Mochi said, bringing out her razor. "I never see you there either."

"Pa took me to Jubilees when Ma was alive," Jennie said. "But it's the same every time."

"Oh, I don't think so. I'll be going myself when I'm done here. I can't wait!"

Pike wasn't thrilled to hear the person with a knife to his face was in a hurry, but when she expertly drew the blade across his cheek, he rested more easily. A few minutes later, he was toweled off and admiring the closest shave he'd had in years.

It begat another awkward moment. "What do I owe you?" he asked.

"Just save me a seat at the service," Mochi said, withdrawing the sheet covering him. "I'll be there in time, I swear!"

Returning to the street with Jennie, Pike admitted he was even more confused about things after visiting Havenbrook. And while he had taken a stab at a theory several times, many things simply didn't fit.

"There was a case a long time ago where humans were found on another planet," he said. "Their ancestors had been abducted from Earth in the 1800s. But this isn't that world. Technology doesn't work at all here. You've got flying fire. And other species, like the Strooh."

"And Mochi," Jennie said. "I think her people call themselves the Avgana."

"And I think I'm confused. What's this all about?"

She sighed. "It's simpler if I just let *him* tell you. That's what this whole silly day is about anyway."

"Who's *him*? Your pa?"

Jennie laughed. "That's funny. No, you'll see. Come on."

CHAPTER 12

THE PICNIC

Una Chin-Riley found Celarius had remained indifferent to her as they crossed the forest. So she wasn't expecting him to give her flowers. "They're . . . nice?"

"They're lunch," Celarius responded. He turned to pluck another handful from beside the log they were sitting on. Tulip-like, they had large orange bulbs—and he bit into one like a drumstick. He spoke with his mouth full. "Try some."

She sniffed at the bunch in her hand—and recoiled. "They smell awful."

"They're not for a vase. The *llaoths* are the most nutritious of the forest wildflowers."

Hungry enough to try anything, she pulled a petal from a flower with her teeth. Her nose crinkled. "They don't taste good."

"If they did, there wouldn't be as many around for us."

"If we eat these, the critters might not want us at all."

Every conversation with Celarius had gone that way. If she had been looking for an expert on the great forest, she couldn't have done better: he knew every plant and beast, and their place in the balance of nature. Chin-Riley had initially imagined that his food supplies had been crushed beneath the unfortunate *kuuko*. She'd since determined that he had brought no food into the forest at all.

"I'm sorry about your *kuuko*," she said between bites.

"Why?"

The question surprised her. "It got killed. Did you have it for long?"

"Not at all," Celarius said. "I captured her as I entered the woods—this is her species' habitat. They are remarkably tame and easy to train, but also poor at self-preservation. I probably bought her an extra week of life. And as I've said, the steps I've taken will benefit her kind in years to come."

"Just not her."

"If we only thought of the now, there would be no forest at all."

More pearls of wisdom from Nature Man, she thought. She quickly finished the impromptu meal without complaint. "Done."

"So fast?" Celarius was still chewing.

"I ate it, didn't I?" She stood up, ready to move again.

"Adaptable, but impatient. Is there somewhere you have to be?"

"I told you earlier: I'm looking for my friends. We got separated."

"And I told you if they overnighted on the forest floor, they are likely dead."

"I was on the ground last night."

"As was I. But I would not count on a third person being so fortunate."

Or a fourth or a fifth, she thought. She was concerned about all of them, but perhaps not as much Pike or Spock, who had shown time and again they could take care of themselves. But while she liked what she had seen of Uhura in action, this was no place for a cadet.

And the truth was, she had no idea if any of them were on the planet at all. Maybe she was the only one beamed to the surface. Maybe she was the only one who survived.

She shook her head, dispelling the thought. "Let's go on."

"Very well." He cast the uneaten stems to the ground. "Possibly my last taste of nature for a while."

That startled her. "What do you mean?"

"My journey is over. This was the last day."

"No more spaying and neutering?"

"Not this trip."

"An end." She looked about. "We're in the middle of nowhere."

"Every nowhere is somewhere." He picked a direction and began walking.

She followed him through the woods for twenty minutes, trying as before to get some indication of what might lie ahead. She was unsuccessful, as ever. The next half hour passed in silence, with Chin-Riley wondering whether she'd be better off on her own.

At last, she declared, "For a trip that's over, we seem to be—"

"Here we are," Celarius said. Strong arms pushed apart brush to reveal a green clearing ahead, a kilometer across. At the center was a solitary tree, huge and barren. After so much life crowded upon itself, it was unusual to see something so dead and exposed.

Emerging from the woods, Celarius ambled in the direction of the hulk. "That's a deciduous *alkeen*. Their root systems are so enormous no rival trees may grow. There are many glades like these on the periphery of the forest."

The commander walked beside him. "What happened to the tree?"

"An invasive insect species that no longer exists. I put a stop to it a few years ago."

"How?"

"Actually, by leading them here. I knew they would find the *alkeen* irresistible—and I knew the trees would poison them."

"You sacrificed the trees?"

"Only some."

Chin-Riley couldn't figure Celarius out. He was a self-professed environmentalist—but also a bit of an engineer, tweaking nature to specific ends. Good ends, as far as she could tell. But whether it was for himself or someone else, she had no idea.

Then something else dawned on her. "Wait. How did you lead insects anywhere?"

She realized he had already stopped walking. He stood beside her, staring at a point in the sky. He pointed. "Look there. The moons."

Taking her first good look at the daytime sky since arriving, she saw aurorae—and the two moons she'd seen in orbit, both in their first quarters and visible by day. "They seem to be taking a meeting."

He rolled his eyes. "Now there's an educated view."

Annoyed, she watched the satellites' movement, barely perceptible. "There's a couple of arc minutes separating them," she said. "They'll be at appulse probably in the next ten minutes."

"Appulse? You mean a conjunction?"

"An appulse isn't a conjunction," Chin-Riley said. "The appulse is just the time of minimum separation. The conjunction is when they have the same right ascension or ecliptic longitude."

Celarius stared at her, dumbfounded—until he laughed out loud. "Forests, she knows not. But give her open air!"

"Is that from a poem or something?"

"When I have finished writing it, perhaps." He smirked. "Una, the Lunar Mystic. I do want to know where you are from, after—"

She grabbed at the sleeve of his jacket. "*Look!*"

At the edge of the forest behind them, she saw an *ollodon* poking its head out of the woods. And then another. A screeching wail came from somewhere—and then she saw that the massive beasts were entering the glade from several other points around its perimeter.

"They have us," Celarius shouted. "The tree!"

As creatures thundered into the clearing, she and the woodsman made a break for the tree. The trunk, as big around as *Enterprise*'s command well, looked like it was shrouded in dark chain mail. Arriving at the foot of it seconds before Celarius, she found they were overlapping sections of bark, each one taller than she was.

"Hurry!" she yelled. Chin-Riley grabbed at the nearest chunks of bark, searching for a handhold—only to have the massive plate snap off the tree in her clutches. She turned with it, only to see Celarius running toward her, flanked by a stampeding *ollodon*. She screamed at the monster, gaining its attention—and then raised the fragment before her like a centurion's shield and braced for impact.

The beast slammed into her hard, smashing her body against the tree. Staggered, she rebounded—and saw that the *ollodon*'s horns had driven through her makeshift shield, catching it. It was stuck, obscuring the creature's vision—and more important, its teeth.

"Now!" As the *ollodon* was blindly thrashing, Celarius grabbed Chin-Riley by the waist and yanked her off the ground. She grabbed at a plate of bark on the tree and found it had a more solid hold. She scrambled up several meters—and looked back to see Celarius dodge the behemoth again before leaping onto the tree himself.

Evolution seemed to like trees, but they weren't the same everywhere, she knew. Climbing this one was like scaling an upside-down pinecone. She worked her way across the interleaving panels—and every so often ripped one off to hurl down at the *ollodon* below. By the time the creature's slower companions arrived, she and Celarius were ensconced in a natural perch eight meters off the ground.

Whatever hatred the fur-covered giants had for other species in the forest, they apparently didn't mind one another's company at a prospective feast. One slammed its forelegs against the trunk, shaking the rotted hulk. Another battered it with its shielded carapace. Each hit resulted in more shards of bark falling, the dead tree's defense system.

She finally took a breath. *Up a tree again. Great.*

"That's a lot of *ollodons*," Celarius said, watching the assault below.

She looked to Celarius. "Is there a term for them as a group?"

"An inconvenience."

"An inconvenience of *ollodons*?"

"That wasn't what I meant—but it is as good a name as any. I'll make it official."

"You're the naturalist. Where'd they all come from?"

"I expect others came upon the *kuuko* carrion and got it in their minds there was more prey about."

"Yeah, I don't imagine your species-control efforts have kicked in yet."

"As your people say, Rome was not built in a day."

The expression surprised her, but it wasn't the time to ask about it. It didn't seem likely to Una that they'd be able to knock down the tree, but neither did they appear to be going away, and she had to sleep sometime. She expected Celarius did too—but he didn't seem agitated. "What now?" she asked.

"Look up."

She did, half expecting he was alerting her to an attacker from the air—or maybe her avian annoyance from the day before. But she saw only puffy clouds and the moons above. "I don't think we'll be able to reach any of those."

"The moons are relevant. But that's not the only reason to watch."

Chin-Riley didn't mind keeping her eyes on the skies if it meant she didn't have to look at the worrisome pounding and gnashing below. Feeling the shaking was bad enough. But then she heard something else: a sonorous hoot, like a foghorn.

She looked this way and that but couldn't tell where it was coming from.

"Hey, ho!" Celarius shouted. Bracing himself between two branches, he released hold of the tree and cupped his hands to yodel.

Another blare in return, so loud the commander nearly fell out of the tree herself. Steadying herself, she turned and saw the reason: a massive white airship descending through the clouds.

It was a dirigible, but like none she'd ever seen. The largest portion was pie shaped, an inflated dish of some kind. Attached port and starboard below amidships and extending backward were two similarly inflated tubes, giving the impression of nacelles; a gondola stretched horizontally between the two, attaching them to the main saucer. It reminded her of an aerial version of the *Nimitz*-class starship, if one missing the class's upper pair of nacelles. Admiral Brett Anderson had gone down in one, the *Europa*, at the outset of the Klingon War.

The dirigible was smaller and constructed of something akin to silk—yet it was large enough to scare the hell out of the *ollodons* below, who bolted in panic when the vessel sounded its horn again.

Celarius laughed. "Right on time!" He looked to Chin-Riley, who was haphazardly trying to cover her ears without falling. "Just minutes from the conjunction. Or that other thing you said."

"*Appulse*," she shouted in return, but right into another trumpet blast. It was just as well the tree hadn't any leaves, because it would have lost them now. "What is that?"

"It is *Zersa*—and it is here for me." He looked at her. "And you, unless you prefer it here."

She slumped against the branch, exhausted. "I'm done with trees. Take me away. Anywhere but here!"

CHAPTER 13

THE RONDURE

It felt like a Spanish mission.

Christopher Pike had seen a couple of those in California. Old World buildings, around which the structures of the New World clustered. Here, in what he perceived to be the geographical center of Havenbrook, was something similar—and something dissimilar to everything that surrounded it.

On a piazza between the blocks of wooden buildings, a marble dome rose over an octagonal structure. That Pike hadn't seen it owed to the tall conifers lining either side of the plaza. Within was a well-manicured courtyard, where those in town for the Jubilee chattered happily.

"This place certainly doesn't fit," Pike said.

Jennie agreed. "Our people didn't build it. It was here before us. The town grew around it."

That made sense to him. Many of the landmarks that survived Earth's wars didn't match anything that had later been built nearby.

Pike figured a hundred people were in the plaza, all decked out. There was the man whose drink he'd spilled; there was the family they'd encountered riding into town. Sharply dressed and smiling, Garr was greeting everyone at the door to the stone edifice. *This must be the church he was talking about.*

Deputy Garr tipped his hat when they approached the doors. "Glad to see you."

Jennie gave an exasperated sigh. "You told me an hour ago I had to come."

"And I'm glad you listened—but I was directing that at Mister Pike." Garr looked him over. "Feeling better?"

"I guess," Pike responded.

"That's good. Glad you're getting to see how we do it here in Havenbrook!"

"It is something." He didn't know what that *something* was—but he expected that would soon change.

"I need to talk to Jennie for a moment," Garr said. He nodded in the direction of the entrance. "Go on ahead."

As Garr and Jennie stepped aside, Pike found himself outside the great doors. Several greeters stood there, handing something out. Hymnals or programs, he assumed. But the kindly old woman handed him something much different. "Your *zazic*, sir."

It was a crimson-colored wand, shiny like glass—tough, but impossibly light in his hands. Half a meter long, one end of it split into two curlicues that came to smooth, rounded ends. It looked a lot like the astrological symbol for Aries, he thought. A yoke or maybe a divining rod. *But why did he have it?*

The old woman and her companions had more to distribute, and he hated to bother her. But before he could ask, a familiar voice called out. "Here I am!"

Pike turned to see Mochi, his barber, hurrying in his direction. She'd had time for a wardrobe change, he saw: a lilac frock complementing her purple skin. "You made it," he said.

"I did!" She noticed the object in his hands and nodded to the old woman. "It's okay. I'll share his *zazic*." She looked to him. "Is that all right?"

"Sure," he said. *I don't even know what the hell it is.* He looked in vain for Jennie as Mochi walked him inside.

It was a theater in the round, with something spherical floating in the air at the center. It looked almost like a polished ruby, except it was a little over a meter in diameter. It appeared to be made from the same stuff as the object he'd been handed—and so did the circular base that it levitated over. A sunburst of red rays inlaid into the stone floor emanated from the circle, leading to spots in the audience. Other townspeople were already here, sitting cross-legged on the ground.

Mochi led him to an open spot, where she encouraged him to sit. His attention was still on the floating jewel, if that was what it was. It couldn't be magnetism holding it up, but he had no idea what was. When he looked down, he noticed that one of the ruby rays on the floor came to an end before him, punctuating with a notch in the floor.

Mochi looked to the *zazic* he held, puzzled at his inaction. "You're the guest. I figured you wanted the honors."

"Oh, no," he said. "I don't mind." He did not object as she took the thing from him. Putting a hand around each of the *zazic*'s curls, she inserted the base of the wand into the notch and pushed hard, hard enough that Pike thought the handles would break. But the *zazic* was not fragile, and it went in with a thunk.

She moved her hands to one side of the yoke, such that she was only gripping part of it. She nodded for him to do the same on the other side. He did—and saw as he did so that others seated all around the great orb were doing the same.

"The rondure always looks so beautiful," Mochi said, her eyes on the sphere as she clutched her half of the *zazic*. "It speaks to me, even when it says nothing."

"The rondure? Uh, yeah."

Pike had questions upon questions—but held off on them when he saw people he knew walking toward the center. Garr entered holding a taller version of the *zazic*, more like a staff. He escorted Jennie and Joe Magee to the front, where they were seated by a *zazic* that had already been implanted.

The deputy stepped to a spot just outside the central circle and declared, "It's time." Then he turned and implanted the staff into a notch in the floor.

Behind him, the large orb began to rotate—and glow. Its dull red turned a cloudy orange, with darker patches almost resembling the continents Pike had seen from orbit. Burning light from within soon overpowered those features, leaving a globe shining as yellow as the planet's sun. But rather than blinding the audience, the rondure, as the barber had called it, had a hypnotic effect on those watching it. Hearing Mochi gasp with excitement, Pike wanted to look away, but found that he couldn't. How could he, when the rondure was growing smaller every second—

—*no, it's not*, Pike thought. *It's the room that's growing.* The people seated on the opposite side of the rondure from him appeared to shrink as the far wall of the building receded farther into the distance. The domed ceiling above the sphere disappeared into the heavens, leaving nothing but the sky.

The rotunda that had seated a hundred now seemed an open-air arena, seating a thousand—and in the next instant became a coliseum holding tens of thousands. *A hundred thousand?* Pike couldn't tell. He just knew that *he* hadn't receded back from the rondure; in fact, he felt closer to it. His middle row was a ringside seat.

Yet he could also see the others—and in detail. As he looked from one section of the coliseum to the next, he found he could focus on the audience there just by concentrating. Here were people who looked like Mochi did. There, more humans—and people who looked like humans, but with subtle differences. Here the Akaali, there the Menk—and were those Denebians?

And there were more that he didn't recognize at all. A group of massive, gray-skinned brutes with fangs like walruses looked so naturally fearsome that seeing them so close in his mind's eye made him want to recoil. But on a closer inspection, they seemed to be doing as all the others were: clasping their hands together.

Not clasping, Pike thought. *They're holding.* Holding *zazics*, just as he was—only the objects could not be seen. This was no optical trick, he realized: it was all playing out in his mind, somehow, a dynamic created by his physical contact with the *zazic* and its connection to the rondure.

He was wondering to what end when the masses began chanting.

He found that just as he could visually focus on others far away, he could also listen in on them. He did not initially understand the languages that the others spoke, but as he listened more closely, the words turned to something his mind could comprehend.

"Save us. Save us. Save us."

Pike shook his head. They could all be chanting about somebody or something named Savus—but he knew that wasn't it. They were chanting for rescue, all of them, even as most had smiles on their faces. He drew back his mind to take in the whole coliseum and heard the chant loud and clear.

"Save us!"

The rondure paused its rotation—and the glow receded. Above, the daytime sky turned to night. The aurora appeared more brightly, and beyond it, he could see the planet's two moons in close proximity. He knew from earlier that they weren't overhead in his location, but he also knew that it didn't matter.

The rondure was now a shimmering gold, and an older man emerged from behind it. He wore not the ornate robes of a pontiff, nor the decorated uniform of a military leader. Rather, he wore the apron, gloves, and hat of a gardener.

He looked up. "The moons are in conjunction," he said in a voice that was both craggy and comforting. "Two bodies, brought together, as *we* were all brought together, in the First Days. This is Epheska telling us all: deliverance has arrived."

Cheers went up—and the man straightened. He removed his hat and basked in the light from the moons, revealing bumpy red protrusions above each eyebrow and in front of his ears. With pride, he shouted to the heavens:

"I am General Drayko of the Skagarans. And I welcome you to your Jubilee!"

CHAPTER 14

THE SKAGARAN

Christopher Pike had been a child when he had first seen a Skagaran—and the tales she told had excited him endlessly. Her stories appealed to both his interests: space travel and the Old West. Taliyah was from the Old West in space. How could he resist?

It made sense that she would visit the Bar T Ranch. Its owners were Luddites, who'd thrown themselves into experiencing life as it had been lived in the past. Taliyah was an old woman who was born on another planet where the past still existed. In the mid-1800s, her Skagaran ancestors visited Earth, abducting an entire town from the American plains: people, livestock, and buildings.

No one would have known, had the captain of another *Enterprise* not happened upon a nameless world in what was then the Delphic Expanse. Jonathan Archer discovered the remains of the crashed ship that had abducted the humans. In a town called North Star, he found the old ways still thriving three hundred years later. He'd also found that the humans had turned the tables on the surviving Skagarans, mistreating them for centuries.

Archer sought to put both groups—which were merging into one anyway—on a better path, one that he hoped would lead the survivors to a better future. Taliyah had been present, then, and had been one of the first to venture off-world, when her people were ready. She visited Earth several times, including the Bar T, where she spoke to members of the Luddite colony—and a visiting Pike—of what it was like to live between two worlds, between past and present.

Pike had started to tell Jennie about it earlier, but there was part of the story that neither he—nor Taliyah nor Archer nor anyone else—had ever learned about: who the Skagarans were, and what had happened to them.

And here was one of them standing in front of him, so to speak, ready to give him all the answers.

"I am the thirty-third conservator general of the most important project in the history of sentient life," Drayko said. "As caretaker, it is my duty—and privilege—to share with you again the miracle of its founding. For the young among you, who will learn it for the first time. And for the others among us who may wish to recommit themselves. Here is our—*your*—story!"

With an audible whoosh, the ground fell away beneath Drayko. Pike could swear he felt wind blowing. He didn't know if it was an illusion or if he was on some astral plane somehow, but the experience was completely immersive.

A new world rose around the Skagaran leader. "Our home planet was a paradise like this one," he said. "But our people were restless and wanted more from Skagara than it could offer."

Pike saw mountains and trees give way to mines, factories, and power plants.

"They used it. Polluted it. Defiled it." Drayko looked around sadly at the surroundings, which rotted as he spoke. Skies went black with smoke. The general shook his head. "You can guess what happened next."

The audience certainly reacted, gasping in horror as a tidal wave washed into the scene, carrying their leader away. Pike heard crying—and cries of "Save him!" But the leader emerged from the water, perfectly dry. Drayko then walked upon the new sea, showing off the extreme weather events racking the world. Lightning, high winds, floods—all ravaging the world-city.

"The planet tried to fight back. Millions of Skagarans died. Millions more were displaced. Yet, our people kept up their assault—until they finally broke the world. And when nothing more would grow, they left it—for dead."

The arena went black. Silent, but for whimpering.

"But there was hope," Drayko said, a voice in the darkness. A light appeared. "Some who left the planet understood what they had done, what they had left behind. They felt regret."

More lights appeared, a flotilla in the night. Pike realized they were colony ships—ones, he supposed, like the one Archer had found wrecked.

"Those in *our* movement refused to bring harm to another world," Drayko said. "And when they learned there were other peoples in the galaxy, they sought to share their story. To warn others of what consequences awaited them."

One after another, Pike saw scenes of Skagarans visiting other planets, and other peoples. But he also saw Skagarans leaving in disappointment.

Drayko lingered nearby in all these scenes, looking grim. "No one listened to us," he said. "Too many societies had already tasted the blood of their planets. They would not rest until they, too, killed their hosts." He walked away from the final scene, and the space around him again went black. "We sought to withdraw, entering a nebula to hide from the galaxy and its ruin."

When Pike saw the Bullseye Nebula appear, he knew there could be no trick. Drayko, or whoever was casting this illusion, had been to space, knew what the system they lived in looked like from the outside. *What primitive culture could say that?*

"Again, there was hope!" Drayko, meandering into the nebula, gestured to a light ahead, which grew into a globe with two bright moons. Pike knew immediately what it was: Epheska.

Drayko paused for cheering, which only rose when he spoke again. "Epheska! A world where the hateful spark is stilled. A world where fire itself will not be enslaved. A world that fights back, as ours did—only without harm to those who live here. Epheska loves us—so long as we love Epheska!"

The hateful spark? Pike's eyes narrowed. Of course, the Skagarans would have to know about the effect preventing the use of technology here.

For them, it was a selling point.

For nearly a minute, Drayko simply meandered the hills, valleys, and shores of Epheska. Pike could hear others reveling in the beauty, some applauding with recognition as they saw natural features they knew.

"We had to share this great discovery," Drayko said. "But not with everyone. Those who already tortured their own planets would never appreciate this place. No, it could only be home to those who had never tasted from the sinful cup."

He gestured around him—and scenes from Epheska were replaced with overlapping views of pastoral settings on other worlds, populated by other species. Simple scenes, with little machinery in sight.

"Epheska could only be home to those who remained in a state of grace," Drayko said. "People who practiced craft, rather than industry. Who sought to serve themselves and their nearest neighbors, but who had no further designs. Neither beyond the stars—nor beyond the horizon."

A stump appeared in the middle of the multiworld view, and Drayko sat. He spoke gravely. "Finally, the most important thing: in order to protect Epheska, we could invite no one to join us whose departure would be noted. Fortunately, we had the ability—and patience—to do just that."

In the scenes around him, various disasters threatened. A great wave rose against long-legged seafarers. Cyclones endangered humans. A volcanic eruption imperiled people who looked like Mochi—the Avgana, Jennie had called them. Pike could feel his part of their shared *zazic* shaking in his hands as she shouted, "Save us! Save us!"

More shouted. And Drayko waited—until it was a din, until things were darkest everywhere.

Then he stood and pointed at Mochi's people in the image. "*Saved!*" he declared, and a massive Skagaran starship screamed down from the heavens, beaming the Avgana up. The barber began to swoon, and Pike had to remove one hand from the *zazic* to keep her from fainting. He still remained in the illusion, as Drayko theatrically pointed at other endangered peoples, repeating his shout.

Pike's first thought on seeing a town saved from destruction by tornadoes was that he was watching the removal of the humans of North Star—or perhaps those of Havenbrook—from Earth, four hundred years earlier.

His second thought was that he was wrong about Drayko not being a religious leader. This unassuming gardener could run a revival meeting better than anyone.

CHAPTER 15

THE WARDEN

I wasn't the one living in a nightmare, Christopher Pike thought. *It's everyone else. And the Skagarans saved them all.*

That was certainly Drayko's message, as the scenes of destruction before Pike's eyes disappeared one by one.

"All of you we delivered here," Drayko said. "And not just you. Your lives, as you knew them. Your homes. Your structures. Your animals. Even some of your crops and insects. We brought you to places similar to what you had left behind, because we knew Epheska was a planet of endless variety."

One by one, the rustic scenes reappeared, just as they had been before.

And then, in the center of the vision, the rondure came back into view. Pike wondered if it had ever been gone at all.

All around Drakyo, the others in the audience became visible. Drayko stepped beside the rondure and threw his arms apart. "We brought you together with us—and everyone on this world—via the fantastic rondures which link our minds now. Distance and language are no barrier when it comes to sharing our passion for this planet, and our way of life."

The old man chuckled. "More importantly, that is *all* that we share. For there's one thing my ancestors saw on every planet they visited: Orderly communion promotes harmony, but nothing good comes from haphazard connections between people half a world apart. That way lies envy, and misunderstanding."

Pike got the message. The Epheskans were a global community, but only at functions like the Jubilee. Their current joining seemed something short of a mind-meld, but he really didn't know enough to say. He wished he could get Spock's opinion on it.

Spock! It dawned on the captain that he might be able to see if he, Number One, or Uhura were in the audience anywhere. Quickly, he looked around the coliseum, focusing quickly and then moving his gaze.

He soon realized it was no use. Too many people—and Drayko seemed to be wrapping up.

"We are in this together," the old man said, "ensuring that we can enjoy life as it was—and always will be. And now that a new cycle dawns, it is time for me to wish you well."

Pike heard wails of disappointment, which Drayko waved off.

"No, no," the conservator general said. "As always, I leave you in the best hands of all: your local lookouts, who will share advice important to all."

The announcements before the benediction, Pike thought. Some things were the same everywhere.

"Take care of one another," Drayko said, "and take care of Epheska. Until the moons meet again, farewell." He bowed—and was gone.

Reality returned slowly to Pike. In place of the stands far away, he again saw the dozens seated in the rotunda on the other side of the rondure. No longer a glowing sun, it slowed to a stop, motionless in midair over the disk below.

He unstuck his hands from the *zazic*. They were sweating. Mochi, to his left, was flushed, her skin a bright burgundy. "No matter how many times I see it," she whispered as she dried her tears, "I always feel it when they show what happened to the Avgana."

"Your people?" Pike asked.

She nodded. "Somehow he shows what happened to us almost every time."

Pike wondered if that was intentional. He'd seen humans from Earth. Did the rondures microtarget Drayko's messages?

The big bruiser with the nervous stomach that Pike had bumped into stepped before the rondure. His hat off, he spoke. "Wonderful, wasn't it? I'm so glad we could have some visitors here for this one."

He smiled at Pike, who nodded back.

"As y'all know, I'm secretary here—and there's a bit of business, like the general said. First off, Cyrus—I'm afraid the answer on your rigging that sema-phore link to Greenfield is no. I think you can keep that broadsheet of yours filled without people needing to find out what's going on there every day. I mean, they're nice folks and all . . ."

Laughter from the audience. Pike located the face of the dark-skinned human the secretary was facing. Cyrus was nodding along with the laughter, though not joining in.

"Next up, about the tin mine. We've got our allotment out of it for the year; ain't nobody gonna need any more. It's for the best."

Pike sat through several such announcements, all town council stuff. Livestock feeding areas, notes on items available for trade with other settle-ments—there was something communal about it, but he suspected that "Gen-eral Drayko," wherever he was, might be tipping the scales here and there. *He did call it a project*, Pike thought.

Just as he and the others around grew restless, the secretary closed with an introduction. "Now, I know you've been waiting to hear from our new warden. She's gone from a lookout to a deputy to a warden in no time at all—shows what good regard the folks uphill hold her in. And you know she raises some good mutton." He stood to the side. "The warden!"

A woman stepped before the rondure. She had long auburn hair with a streak of silver under her brown cowboy hat—and while she wore no badge, she carried herself like a country sheriff. No swagger, just the sense that she could go where she liked, even if she was in no hurry to do so. And even though the rondure wasn't working, Pike heard the sandy scratch of her voice in his mind before she said a word.

When she did speak, he heard it again. He covered his mouth.

It can't be.

"Really fine Jubilee, folks," she said. "We'll have another one in a few weeks, as the moons go. But first, I'd like you all to share a moment with a brother of ours." She gestured. "Come on up, Joe."

Joe Magee rose from where he was seated with Jennie and hobbled toward the warden. He had a new piece of wood for a prosthetic leg. He looked terrified to be the focus of attention, but the woman tried to put him at ease. She placed her hand on his shoulder.

"Now, we all know Joe—and his daughter, Jennie—and many of you knew his wife." She looked to him. "I'm real sorry not to have met her. Everyone speaks highly of her."

Joe shrank a bit.

The warden looked to the crowd. "Now, I guess you all know Joe likes to fiddle with gadgets—and you know what it's cost him."

Pike knew. But his eyes were on the warden. That face—and that voice.

It can't be. It can't be.

"You may have heard what happened at the mill last night," she said. "I've been in back talking with Joe all morning about it. I've told him, the Sorry doesn't care how good a person you are or your family or what your intentions are. The Sorry is Epheska protecting itself. It was here before we got here, Joe—and with your help, none of us will ever have to see it." She looked down at the slouching miller. "Will you help us, Joe?"

He let out an exasperated sigh. "I guess," he muttered.

"That's all right." The warden looked up. "And I'd like the rest of you to help too. Help show Joe the way. Can you do that?"

Loud approval from the crowd—but not Pike. He said under his breath: "*It can't be.*"

Not noticing him, the warden guided Joe back to Jennie's care. "I want to thank you all for that—and for making a newcomer like me feel at home. If you have any questions about *anything*, just ask." She tipped her hat and smiled—a smile that Pike knew. "Lila Talley will be sure to help you."

The others rose from their positions, moving to greet the new warden, and to pledge their willingness to aid Joe and Jennie in the aftermath of the fire. Pike could only see her intermittently through all the bodies—but now he knew. "*It's her.*"

Mochi, rising, looked back to him. "I thought I heard you say something. Do you *know* Warden Talley?"

"You could say that. She taught me how to ride a horse."

Part Two
OLD FRIENDS

Matayan River

OM MATAYA

Merv

Heiyan

Valqua

Wellspring

The
Grandwood

Olan

Gorm
Tigah

oldmeadow

CHAPTER 16

THE REUNION

Lila Talley loved a Jubilee as much as anyone. She'd even gotten to where she could tolerate public speaking, something she'd never figured on. It helped that she believed what she was saying. But she had no love for crowds of any kind, and where Seb Garr thrived on glad-handing, she couldn't wait to get outside after her speech—and back home to the flock.

She thought she'd made a clean break until she heard someone calling out after her by Wright's Run.

Nope, she thought. *I'm out for the day.* She prodded her horse into a gallop. Garr and his lookouts could handle any problem, she knew; they'd been doing it since long before she arrived. And nobody could catch Buckshot once he let loose. The stallion raced over the bridge and made for the opposite hillside.

Whoever it was, he was still yelling. "*Lila! It's Christopher!*"

She slowed Buckshot to a trot just before the crest. She knew several Christophers in Havenbrook; it was a good, solid name from the First Days. But this one belonged to someone she hadn't seen in half a lifetime or more.

She said it just as he yelled it: "*Christopher Pike!*"

Without thinking, Lila wheeled and turned. She raced back down the hill. The man on the far side sped toward her on a black horse. Lila didn't go to the bridge crossing this time. She drove Buckshot straight into the creek, spraying water everywhere. Pike met her halfway.

The two horses stomped past each other. Both riders pulled up and dismounted into the shin-deep water. Lila threw her arms around him. "What are you doing here?"

"What are *you* doing here?" Standing in water to his knees, he beamed as he looked down at her.

During the time she'd known him, Christopher Pike had grown from a gangly kid to a strapping teen; this man was old enough to be the father of either of those boys. But the smile she knew was there. She embraced him again. "I can't believe this!"

"You and me both."

She caught her breath and found Buckshot's reins. They led their horses onto the land—and with a million questions to choose from, she could think of no better topic as they walked than the one that had brought them together, years earlier. "This is your horse?"

"Shadow. He belongs to the Magees," Pike said. "I guess you could say I'm staying with them."

Still dazed, Lila connected the dots. "*You're* the mysterious brother-in-law?"

He chuckled. "No, that's something Joe told Garr."

She started to ask why Joe would say that, but then she remembered the miller's inebriated condition when he was brought to her attention. He might well have said anything. "But you *are* staying with them."

"Yeah, I woke up at their place yesterday. When I arrived here, whatever happened must have knocked me cold. Joe found me."

The implications of his presence dawned on her, and she looked about. "You didn't bring all of Starfleet with you?"

"Here, it's just me. There was an accident."

Lila remembered the light she'd seen while leaving the Magee place the day before. She described what she'd seen, adding that it had been very high above.

"That was probably our shuttle," Pike said. "We were transported off—at least, I *hope* we all were."

"'We'?"

"I have three other crewmembers to find. If I'm here, they might be too."

Lila listened as he described his three companions. Pike looked at her. "Would you know if anyone else had seen them?"

"Haven't heard a thing."

"Nobody said anything over that communication system back there?"

She didn't know what he meant for a second. "What, you mean the rondure? No."

She stopped walking and smiled at him. "I just can't believe we're here, having a conversation."

He paused as well. "A long time since the Bar T Ranch." He lowered his voice. "I heard your parents passed some years ago. I'm sorry."

She nodded. "Thanks. They liked you."

And they had, for a while.

It had been a long time since she and Pike had conversed on *anything*. He'd gotten his own stable and had stopped coming to ride—and then had started hanging out with a different crowd. The way of teenagers.

After that, he had set his sights on Starfleet Academy. If ever there was a path leading away from the Talleys and the simple life they favored, that was it. Her father, James, had hated the notion.

"Someone told me you made captain," she said. "But that was the last I heard."

"I did. *Enterprise*," he added. "Pure exploration vessel."

"That's a relief." She lowered her voice. "I was afraid you were in . . ."

"What, the Klingon War? We missed it, in fact—we were trapped somewhere else." He looked about. "And now I guess I'm trapped here."

Lila nodded. *Yes, you would be.* "It's called the Baffle. Nothing technological works."

"You've found that out?"

"I had to get here somehow."

He shook his head. "I'm sorry—I'm still shocked you're here. Your dad, rest his soul, would have moved heaven to keep you on the Earth."

"Nice way to put it." They began to walk their horses again, and she explained. "I'm here *because* of how I was raised, because of what I knew how to do. I was brought in to help an anthropological expedition."

"Don't tell me. The *Braidwood*."

Lila gawked. "You know it?" She looked down and put two and two together. She slapped her forehead. "Don't tell me you're here to find *us*!"

"That's what we do—sometimes." Pike regarded her. "I can see it was a landing you could walk away from. Are *your* crewmates here?"

"On Epheska? Sure. But not nearby." She added, "I kind of went my own way."

"That sounds like you. Still, I can't believe you signed on."

She had an explanation. "It's funny you mentioned *Enterprise*. You know I was always in love with the story of the people of North Star, right?"

"We both were. I remember when Taliyah visited."

"Do you know why she called on us in the first place? She found she had a human ancestor who descended from the abducted settlers. Last name Talley."

He laughed. "She's a cousin?"

"Far removed, but yeah. That was the only time Dad ever let any of us have our DNA tested!" Lila's smile faded, and she looked to the side. "I talked to her again over the years. She was dead set on finding out where the Skagarans had come from—what they had originally intended." She glanced at him. "You were at the Jubilee?"

"I saw it. The whole story."

"What'd you think?"

"Quite a production." He scratched his head. "There were parts that don't add up."

"How do you mean?"

"Miss Bethany—the schoolteacher Archer met—said the Skagarans who took people from Earth did so because they wanted them as slaves, to work a colony they were founding. Hoshi Sato's log translations from the Skagaran wreck said the same thing."

"I know that, Christopher. I've read those records—thanks to Taliyah, I could read Skagaran before I ever came here. I'm not sure anyone ever had the whole picture."

She turned and gestured back down the hill they were climbing. There were fishermen much farther up the creek, and back at the bridge a family was crossing in a wagon.

"Tell me, do these people look like anyone's slaves?"

"I don't guess they do."

"There's nuance neither Bethany nor Hoshi caught," she said, approaching the top of the hill. "You probably heard the ship's directive was to deliver the humans to a place where they would be 'bound to work the soil.'"

"I remember that."

"It actually said they would be *bound to the soil they worked.*' Very different!" Atop the hill, she showed him the valley—and the beautiful patchwork of farms populating it. "People here *are* bound to the soil, Christopher. Everyone on Epheska feels that way. The planet owns us."

"But the humans *were* enslaved. The sheriff that Archer met—"

"MacReady."

"—MacReady told him that the humans were in bondage until they revolted."

"I looked into that," Lila said. "And I asked the Skagarans here about it. They don't really know, but they suspect their rescue party went off the ranch."

Pike's brow furrowed. "Somebody wanted to set up their own colony?"

"Maybe. They didn't come back here, at any rate. The Delphic Expanse existed then—you know it was nobody's idea of a place to settle. It *was* a place for a bad actor to hide."

"And get stuck." He nodded. "Interesting. So North Star was a mutiny before it was a revolt."

"You're sharp, Christopher. You always were." She stopped walking and put her hands on her hips. "Why would anyone with the ability to cross light-years and transport an entire settlement need to bother with manual labor?" She snorted derisively. "Aliens didn't build the pyramids and the Skagarans didn't take slaves. Why else have we never found the species—or any other colonies?"

He seemed to take it all in. "I've always wondered that."

"Taliyah wondered too. She'd been looking into it herself. Remember, after the humans revolted, the Skagarans weren't allowed to educate themselves. Theirs was an oral history. That, and a judgment call made by Hoshi—a talented translator who had never seen the language before—is what got you the story you knew."

Pike nodded. "Drayko's version does make sense."

"I've been here nearly a year in your reckoning, Christopher. They're in earnest. Nobody is a victim." She gestured behind her, in the direction of town. "The worst trouble anybody ever gets in is what you saw with Joe Magee. Nobody put him on a rack. We just talked—and downed a lot of what they call coffee around here." She sighed. "They use tree bark. By far, it's the worst thing about the place."

"I had some."

"Then you know. I give 'em credit for trying."

Pike raised another matter. "What about the floating fire? Garr called it the Sorry."

"That's what the Skagarans call it—*sah'ree*, the traveling flame. I don't know what it is. Nobody does. But we know what it doesn't like, and we don't have any problem with that." She looked at him. "Joe said you were with him when it struck. Do *you* know what it is?"

"I don't know—but I've been around. Intelligent planets that try to keep people from leaving is not the craziest idea. It might even have something to do with—what did you call it? The Baffle."

"You're reaching, there."

"Yeah, it's one reason I depend on my science officer. He's better with theories."

Lila saw Pike's expression change when he thought of his crewmate.

"I do need to find my people and leave," he said. "Would the Skagarans help? I ought to be able to approach them now with the whole story, given the Prime Directive."

"What's that?"

"Starfleet used to call it General Order One. It's our noninterference doctrine. I should be able to tell them where I'm from, since I know they are warp capable."

"*Were*. They're done with all that—including bringing anyone new to the planet. That phase of the project ended long ago."

"Why is that?"

"Dunno. You'd have to ask them."

"That's what I'd like to do. They might know something that could help. They gave you a title, so I assume they're okay with offworld visitors."

She crinkled her nose. She knew about her own case but couldn't say what the Skagarans would make of arrivals from Starfleet. She paused while she considered how to respond.

"The locals here will help you find your crew," she finally said, "just like Joe taking you in when he found you. They're good people. But the part about being from space—Christopher, it just doesn't matter. The Skagarans can't help you leave. Everyone here was from somewhere else, at some point—and they're all here to stay. That includes them, and me—and now you. And your crew."

Pike looked about. "Much as I like this place, I can't let my responsibilities go. Or let my people down."

She expected that. She was a warden all the time; she knew Starfleet's officers had the same level of commitment. "Well, take a few days," she said, climbing back aboard Buckshot. "It grew on me." She nodded to the south. "My spread's that way. Sheep and pigs, descended from the ones the humans here had in Dry River."

"Dry River?"

"That's the Earth town the humans of Havenbrook were originally from. Eastern Colorado, before the Civil War."

"You've moved light-years to raise pigs from Colorado."

"Some Epheska critters too. You should come check it out."

Pike looked behind him. "I took off with one of the Magees' horses. I really should get him back to them." He climbed onto Shadow and stopped to stare at her. "It's great to see you, Lila. You look good."

"I look like I was up all night trying to talk sense to Joe Magee. Not the easiest thing to do!" She cracked a smile. "I'll see you again, Christopher."

Starting for home, she knew she'd told no lie. *Neither of us is going anywhere.*

CHAPTER 17

THE AMBUSH

While Christopher Pike loved old Westerns, he'd also sampled stories set in other times. He'd noticed something: even as technological progress improved the lives of fictional characters, it had made the jobs of the storytellers who created them more difficult.

Not the physical act of writing, of course. That had gotten easier. No, he thought more about the dilemmas that made drama. Hamlet didn't need to see his father's ghost; he needed to see his father's toxicology report. Rick Blaine could have found Ilsa Lund's marital status if only he'd had a computer to ask. And secret agent Lanie Sundergard could have simply transported into General Quarto's headquarters, saving a whole lot of ammunition.

Comedy had particularly suffered. Missed connections were the mother's milk of farce. How many story ideas had writers been forced to reject, simply because of the invention of the telegraph, portable telephone, and communicator?

It was thus inevitable that Pike's unplanned foray into rustic life would confront him with obstacles that otherwise would never have troubled him. He had one of Joe's horses but didn't know how to get back to the farm. He knew the way back to Havenbrook, and how to reach the Magees' place from there—but he had no idea where Joe and Jennie were. He figured he needed to reach them before night fell—and before they judged him for racing off right after the Jubilee. Pike had a responsibility to them, and he was riding it.

There's nothing worse than a horse thief.

The ride back to town gave him time to think. He was still reeling over Lila's presence. The *Braidwood* sponsors had never supplied Starfleet with a crew list, and Pike doubted he'd have thought *his* Lila Talley aboard.

He wasn't sure how she remembered the end of their friendship. Looking back, he didn't feel good about it. He'd started hanging out with Evan Hondo, a future Starfleet washout who'd introduced him to a souped-up hovercraft: high speeds for high spirits. The simple pleasures of the ranch had faded in his teenage mind before the thrills technology could offer, and his rides with Lila had grown less frequent. Her family didn't want her hot-rodding around and she thought his new friend childish. She felt the same way about his growing interest in Starfleet.

There was no confrontation that caused them to part company; instead, his visits petered out. It happened. New friends and interests replaced old ones. The grapevine had it that she'd criticized his enrollment in Starfleet Academy, but he'd never heard that from her. The Lila Talley he knew didn't own a comm unit.

Yet here she was, enticed to leave Earth's embrace by the mystery of the Skagarans. *That would do it*, he thought. It certainly had amazed him.

Her theory about the refugees Jonathan Archer discovered was novel, Pike thought, but not implausible. The lack of technology on Epheska made it less of a stretch. If the Baffle—*now there was a double entendre!*—were present four hundred years ago, nobody here would have known what happened there. The Delphic Expanse wasn't a favorable place to transmit from. He and *Enterprise* had spent a whole year in the Pergamum Nebula, another place where conditions were such that he might as well have been in another universe.

All these people were here because Skagarans had "saved" their ancestors. It was certainly possible. Eastern Colorado before the Civil War would have still been the Kansas Territory, and threats abounded there. Wildfires or tornadoes easily could have erased settlements. People vanished all the time on the frontier.

And Pike had some related experience. Michael Burnham's mother, Gabrielle, had rescued a church full of people from destruction in World War III, relocating them to Terralysium, a planet where her heroics had been worked into their religion. Pike had visited it with Burnham before either knew Gabrielle was at the center of the refugees' deliverance myth. The fact fascinated Pike, while also reminding him what the Prime Directive was all about. Whether from the stars or from the future, no visitor should aspire to godhood.

Drayko and the thirty-two previous conservator generals of the Skagarans' project had certainly leaned into their role as saviors, but he hadn't yet seen any signs that they were abusing that status. The Jubilee had seemed as much a thanksgiving for the Skagarans as it had for the people he'd seen in the astral arena. They'd found a nice planet, one that had a peculiar built-in tendency to stay nice. What was wrong with that?

The "here to stay" part, Pike thought. He could easily see Lila Talley finding her nirvana here. He, on the other hand, had crew to find and a ship to rejoin.

The Jubilee celebration was winding down as he approached Havenbrook. A sole cookout remained, and while the workers couldn't say whether Joe and Jennie had left for home yet, they did provide him with a late lunch. It settled his stomach, even if knowledge of the menu might unsettle M'Benga. Whatever other things the Skagarans preached, a low-fat vegetarian diet wasn't among them.

Pike was finishing up when a dark-skinned human in his late twenties approached him. Wearing a tan suit, a bowler, and spectacles, he carried an armful of newsprint. He tipped his hat with his free hand. "Mister Pike?"

"That's me."

"I'm Cyrus Hodge. I saw you at the Jubilee."

"Pleasure's mine." Pike recognized him. "You run the newspaper, right?"

"The *Post*." They shook hands, and Cyrus handed him a paper off the stack.

Pike spread it before him: a single broadsheet, still warm. Its headlines spoke of the day's fête, with notes about the local announcements at the end. "You wrote this up awfully fast."

"It's a Jubilee edition. The services don't change much. I just move the paragraphs around!" Cyrus smiled broadly before continuing. "Deputy Garr told me what you did for Joe Magee. Mighty brave, sir. Mighty brave!"

"I barely knew what I was doing." *That was no lie*, Pike thought. "No offense, but I'd rather not be interviewed. It was nothing."

"Oh, I won't be writing about that. You'll see I didn't mention it there."

Pike studied the paper. "The fire wasn't news?"

"The Sorry was involved. I never write about that. The lookouts feel word of mouth is good enough, and they don't want to scare people. What I wanted to tell you is Joe Magee is back at my office, looking for you. He pointed you out to me after the service—right as you were taking off. That's how I knew who you were."

"He went to the newspaper?"

"In case you came looking for *him*. I'm kind of the lost and found for the town. Everybody knows Cyrus." He pointed past the gazebo. "I can show you the way, if you'd like. You can leave your horse tied up here until we return."

"Much obliged." Pike rose to follow Cyrus, hoping that if Number One, Uhura, or Spock were around, they might gravitate to such a place too.

As they walked the well-trodden streets, he noted the nameplate atop the newspaper. "How come it's not the *Havenbrook Post*? It's a common name."

Cyrus chuckled. "Well, there is another *Post* over in Sawgrass—maybe more, for all I know. But none of those papers would ever make it here, so there's no confusion."

Pike remembered now the edict after Drayko's speech. "You wanted to set up a signal system with another town."

"Just for the paper. It'd fill some inches," Cyrus said. "I have a cousin in Greenfield—we'd been talking about setting up a code using flags on some of the hills."

Pike was going to say that light or smoke might make for a better signal system, but he remembered the locals' testy relationship with fire.

"It was a bad idea anyway," Cyrus said. "Somebody'd have to ride out to change them." He shook his head. "The general knows best."

Pike sympathized with the publisher—and remembered his thoughts from earlier. Here was an occasion where an advance in technology would have meant *more* stories, not fewer. But the ruling tracked with what Drayko had said about "haphazard communications."

Still, he thought as they rounded a corner, there had to be other options. "I assume you're already getting dispatches from the other papers by post, right?"

Cyrus looked confused. "Pardon?"

"By mail. You get letters from other places, right? A postal service?"

"Oh. No. I mean, we get messages, but nothing formal."

No post office; no Pony Express. That seemed to typify everything about society here, Pike thought. His opinion was reinforced when Cyrus described some of Havenbrook's connections to the larger world. Intercity travel, when it happened at all, was occasional and at random; there weren't any scheduled stagecoaches. Even Cyrus's newspaper was not published at set times; it came out whenever he filled a page.

It reminded Pike, of all things, of the Klingon monastery at Boreth, where time had little meaning to the residents. Time here was entirely measured in natural increments of days, nights, and seasons, with the only pertinent schedules coming from the needs of animals and plants. Even the Skagarans' Jubilees were tied into lunar cycles.

Pike did his best to respond to Cyrus like an out-of-towner and not an offworlder, but he couldn't help but be fascinated by this long-lost twin culture, separated at birth and by four hundred very different years. The town's infrastructure was the work of volunteers using donated goods. Want, when it existed, lasted only as long as it took for word to get around—at which point neighborly charity would kick in, drawing upon the surpluses from a bountiful world.

Pike wasn't a knee-jerk skeptic, but neither did he take things at face value. Yet what he'd seen so far had impressed him. Maybe Lila was right.

There are people who would kill to live here, Pike thought as he walked the dusty street. *And here I am, trying to leave.*

Just as he had the thought, several happy children ran past, excitedly shouting and pointing to something above. Pike looked to the sky, above a row of buildings—and gawked as he saw a white shape soaring lazily over the highest wooden rooftop.

"*A blimp!*"

Cyrus saw it—and dropped his newspapers in the street. He grabbed Pike's arm. "Come on!" he yelled, pulling the captain toward an alley.

Pike didn't want to go. "What is that? Who is that?"

"Get out of sight!"

Pike reluctantly acquiesced and allowed Cyrus to guide him into a narrow path between rows of buildings. When he stopped to look back, the structures obstructed his view of the airship, but he did see the children—along with some adults now—in the street, excited but not agitated.

An airship could certainly come in handy to his search, Pike knew—and Cyrus had led them into a dead end. It was time for reason. "Listen, Mister Hodge, I want to go back and—"

"Now!" As he shouted, Cyrus threw himself to the ground.

From either side, Pike heard a loud springing noise. Something firm struck his left side, and a length of rope wrapped around him. Metal weights on its ends caught one another, pulling it taut. The captain had barely registered it when another bolo fired from a spring-loaded wooden contraption set up to his right.

"What the—?" Before Pike could say another word, another noisy *sproing* interrupted him. He looked to one side, and then the other—but this time, the attack came from above in the form of a weighted net, falling from a building above.

And then another.

And another.

Still standing, Pike struggled against the weighty mass of ropes. "Cyrus, what are you—"

No mechanical sound in response this time: just a burlap bag thrown over his head from behind, followed by panicked voices rasping, "*Get him! Get him! Get him!*"

More ropes. His attackers bound him like a maypole—and yet he continued to stand. Hands tried to push him over, to no avail. After thirty seconds, Pike was still on his feet, and his attackers had gone quiet.

"Can I help you with something?" Pike asked.

"The chair!" a high nasal voice said. "From the office!"

"Seriously," Pike said, "there's no need—"

"Hush, you!" said a deep voice. And then: "No, not that one! The chair that rolls!"

It was another minute before Pike heard wheels squeaking toward him. By that time, he had already concluded that it was the stupidest ambush ever. But it beat being shot.

CHAPTER 18

THE SENTINEL

Una Chin-Riley knew propulsion systems. It was why Pike had chosen her to pilot the maiden—and, it appeared, the final—flight of *Eratosthenes*. Starfleet didn't have anything in service that she couldn't fly, and you couldn't fly without understanding how thrusters, impulse drives, and warp engines worked. She'd seen it all.

Or so she'd thought. Propulsion-by-priest was a new one on her.

The forward section of the wooden gondola beneath *Zersa* hadn't surprised her. The compact compartment served as bridge, galley, and barracks all in one, and what it lacked in spaciousness it made up for in view. Windshields forward and on either side and a glass-bottomed area provided ample views of the countryside.

Weirder was what passed, in her mind, for main engineering. A door aft led to a catwalk that straddled the space between the two connected gas envelopes stretching under and behind the main blimp. She didn't know much about ballooning on any world, but even on this planet with its peculiar physics she'd expected to see equipment: valves, pipes, burners. Instead, two figures in burgundy cloaks and hoods stood at either end of the catwalk. They faced rearward, gesticulating with staffs topped by what looked like ram's horns.

She'd only had a few seconds to see them up close. The rope ladder *Zersa* had lowered for her and Celarius led to the catwalk, and she'd glimpsed the monk-like figures as she'd boarded the vessel. Inside the main compartment, she saw four others wearing the same attire but without the staffs. Two of the clerics, if that was what they were, were stationed forward, calling out in a strange language what she assumed were directions. Two more stood aft, repeating commands via speaking tubes to the staff-wielders, who responded with more gesticulations.

Portholes allowed her to vaguely see them going through their motions. "Who *are* they?" she asked.

Drinking from a small water cask, Celarius looked back idly. "Who do you mean?"

"Those people in back, with the staffs. What are they doing?"

"Their job."

"Are they praying for good weather?"

"All this beauty below, and you're looking at *them*."

"I'm interested."

"I would take you back there, but it's exposed, and it's going to get colder as the sentinel ascends."

It was the first time she'd heard him use the term "sentinel," and it suggested to her that *Zersa* might be one of a class of ships. Chin-Riley couldn't easily ask about that without giving her origins away, but she could investigate on her own. "They don't seem to mind the weather back there." She looked about. "Are there more of these cloaks around?"

He chuckled. "Not for you. Besides, that part of the craft is their domain. They're possessive."

That rang familiar to her. Whether they stayed in the post for a week or a year, past *Enterprise* chief engineers from Grace to Barry to Louvier had treated main engineering as holy ground, a domain where they communed with the transcendental powers of science to achieve magical results. Hemmer was no different, even if he was quicker with a complaint. The people aft almost seemed a satirical version, taking the next step by dressing the part of miracle workers. Chin-Riley made note of the costumes, in case there ever was an *Enterprise* comedy revue.

She stepped forward. The others aboard had greeted Celarius but had paid no attention to her, and that had not changed. He handed her a cask and approached the large pane in the middle of the floor. He plopped down on it and sat cross-legged, apparently not fearful his bulk would strain the glass. He invited her to sit closer to him. It didn't look safe to her, so she positioned herself on the wooden area.

"Come on," he said, rapping on the pane with his knuckles. "There is nothing to fear, and it is a unique sensation."

With trepidation, she scooted forward—and tried to get comfortable with the sight of the countryside rolling past hundreds of meters below her on all sides as she sat.

A farm appeared, then houses. Soon a village came into view. "Una, do you recognize that place?" Celarius asked.

"Should I?"

"It's Gorm Tigah, your alleged home."

"I thought we'd already established that it wasn't."

"Yes, but you never told me which settlement you *were* from—or where this party you got separated from was heading."

"Nowhere, exactly. You could say we're explorers."

"*Explorers!*" He clapped his hands together. "I begin to see. Was this undertaking cleared beforehand?"

"Cleared? With whom?"

"You're really going to act like you don't know?"

She shrugged. "I have no idea."

"You realize the rules exist for a reason, right? Regions have been set aside for their own protection. Behind every explorer is an exploiter." He scowled. "Whoever was behind your expedition—what did they hope to accomplish?"

We came in peace, she wanted to say, before remembering that he believed she was a native explorer, rather than one from another planet. She decided there was a tack more likely to be favorable with him. "My friends and I love animals. *All* animals. We wanted to find out more. To see them."

"Not to hunt them?"

"You said yourself I was unarmed. We wanted to make drawings. That's all."

Celarius took that in for several moments—until his posture relaxed. "I see it now. You and your companions *did* appeal for permission and didn't receive it for whatever reason—and then you went anyway. And that's why you won't tell me what village you're from. You don't want to return to trouble."

She felt she'd stumbled into a smart solution. "Something like that," she said, looking down. "And I didn't expect the forest animals to be quite so dangerous."

"That's another reason such visits are discouraged." His tone turned sympathetic for the first time since she'd met him; it was clear he liked this explanation. "No one on Epheska ever gets in much trouble, Una—and while I would rather not have the wild spaces overrun by tourists, you meant no harm."

Epheska. So the planet has a name.

She tried to look more closely at Gorm Tigah, only to see that it had been left far behind. *Zersa* traveled with a speed that surprised her. Several minutes passed before she began to see more indications of intelligent life: cultivated land, first, but then the odd trail, leading to another small settlement.

Now that he knew her cover story, Celarius pointed out more creatures below. When a black herd came into view, he spoke to the others, who quickly complied by bringing the airship down far enough for her to see the six-legged ungulates below. Whoever the hooded people were, he seemed to command them.

"This is certainly a good—and safer!—way to see the animals," Chin-Riley said. "Do you go on a lot of aerial safaris?"

"I prefer to study them up close. But this is a unique privilege, for which I am thankful."

He didn't say whom he had to thank, she noticed. Either way, Celarius seemed to assume she'd never ridden in an airship before. That posed an opportunity, as she could ask other questions without giving away her alien status. Some he even answered.

"See the temple?" He pointed down to a stone structure in the second settlement, its central dome a jarring contrast from the wooden structures surrounding it. "What do you see flying above the tower beside it?"

She squinted. "It's a windsock. And some flags."

"Both are conveying information to our spotters," he said, gesturing to the two cloaked figures forward. "I would argue that the air is like the forest, or the sea—a place in which to lose oneself and exist amid nature, cut off from annoyances. But this information is necessary for operating the sentinel—which is itself a necessary evil."

"Necessary for rescuing fellow explorers from wild herds, you mean."

He laughed.

They were too high to clearly see the people milling below. She imagined many were looking up at the passing airship. If so, they did not see *Zersa* long. Its heading changed, and it was on its way again. She realized that like Earth aircraft of old, it was following a zigzag course, taking it past one populated area after another, and grabbing some information while on the way.

By the third village, she had come to expect that the styles of architecture varied greatly from one settlement to the next. The only commonality to each: buildings like the one Celarius had called a temple, with signal posts erected on the turrets alongside them.

Stone temples, check. Mystery monks, check. Starfleet didn't have a standardized typology for different kinds of pre-warp societies, but quite a few seemed to fall into this particular bucket, she thought. She decided to look on it as good news. Finding her crewmates—and anyone from *Braidwood*—would be challenging enough without the help of *Enterprise* or any of her technological tools. A religious order that both spanned the globe and could cross it by air made for a good source of information.

Hillier country followed, and *Zersa* pushed onward. With light beginning to wane—and greatly tired from her busy day, night, and day—Chin-Riley found she was able to see less detail as time went on. But what she saw near the temple in the fourth village ruined every theory she'd been developing about Epheska.

"*That's a pagoda!*"

"Eh?"

"That building!" She pointed to the lines of the structure. It looked like it belonged in medieval Asia.

Celarius regarded it mildly. "Yes, that's Shimao below. The people like that style. It's not an original feature—the structure's too big. It was likely something they remembered."

"What—" she began to ask. That statement was too much to take in, and she didn't know how to craft a response. And there was something else, running wild in the fields outside town. *Were those horses?*

She had read her Hodgkin, like anyone else in Starfleet, but this was ridiculous. Feeling undone by the exertions of the day, she didn't trust her eyes anymore. She stood. "I think I've had enough sightseeing."

"No matter," he said. "There is but one sight left, and you'll want to be forward for this." He accompanied her to the front of the vessel, where they leaned against the glassed-in ledge and looked ahead at the approaching mountain range. *Zersa* climbed as it advanced, and she sensed the air getting thinner. The compartment might be warmer than the outside world, but it wasn't airtight.

For a time, the sun dipped behind the mountain, and she felt a chill—until the airship found the pass its operators were looking for. Beyond, she saw the brilliant return of light: a mountain sunset, illuminating a gorgeous valley.

A glistening river wended its way between steep slopes festooned with garden terraces. It took her a moment to see that most of them were rooftops. Structures had been built into the walls: chateaus, almost, except of a style no builder had ever employed on Earth.

Avian creatures filled the air—and they were not alone. Many airships were here, making their way in or out of the valley. They were all smaller than *Zersa*: one she saw pass nearby had only two occupants, including a single gesturing priest aft.

The whole setting looked like something out of fantasy. "It's magical." She said it aloud, without meaning to.

"It's Om Mataya," Celarius said. "It has that effect on people." He chuckled. "Yet I can never wait to leave."

The airship cruised toward one of the mountainsides and gently descended. It came to rest on a terrace. Celarius gestured toward the exit. "We disembark here."

She was expecting a ground crew, especially in a windy valley. "Don't they need to tie it down?"

"The sentinel is going from here to the shelter. And the minders have full control over it, in any weather."

Indeed, Una and Celarius had barely stepped onto the surface when *Zersa* lifted off again and glided away. The terrace backed up to one of the chateaus on the mountain, and she saw several cloaked figures approaching from it.

The air crew had never addressed her or Celarius, but this greeting party had more to say. Their cloaks were lighter in color—a muted lavender—and at center was an old woman.

Celarius addressed her. "*Ahao*, Zoryana."

The woman responded in a foreign tongue. She looked him up and down, before doing the same with Chin-Riley.

"This is Una," Celarius said in Standard. "I found her lost in the forest. Speak so she can understand."

"Zoryana welcomes you to the Garden House." She curtsied. Her voice was crisp—and her words had an edge too. "I was told to expect Celarius, Una, but you appear to have brought with you one of the beasts of the wild."

Celarius ran his hand through his voluminous hair. "You don't like the new look?"

"Nor the smell." Zoryana put her hand before her nose. "You will have time to prepare before dinner."

"He's working late again."

"And anxious to see you." She gestured to Chin-Riley. "My attendants will see that you and the heritor general are properly attended to."

"What did you call him? *Heritor?*"

"One who inherits. Of course, you would not recognize him: he is not a public figure. But somewhere beneath all that hair is the son of your leader, Conservator General Drayko." Zoryana gave him a scornful look. "At least, that is my theory. Only soap will tell."

The *Enterprise* officer looked at Celarius, who shrugged. "I guess she told *me*," he said. "See you soon."

He made for the house, with Chin-Riley trailing behind, accompanied now by two attendants. She shook her head.

The mountain man is a prince. Now I've seen everything.

CHAPTER 19

THE MENDERS

What is it with this planet and kidnapping people?

Christopher Pike had wondered that several times during his ordeal in Havenbrook. His attackers—who included Cyrus and three others, from the voices he'd heard—had forced him into a rolling chair so they could move him. But they hadn't advanced a meter when the nets covering him got tangled in its wheels. A haphazard attempt to carry him, chair and all, then began. That had been interrupted when another of the spring-loaded bolos, which apparently had not activated on schedule, suddenly went off, its weights belting one of his would-be captors so hard he yelped.

There was nothing for Pike to do but wait. And he had waited, until they finally got him inside, apparently seconds before another pass by the airship he'd spied earlier. Cyrus didn't want any of them to be seen. Pike understood that. Being spotted in the middle of a criminal act was bad enough without people also finding out how incompetent you were at it.

Hours of commotion followed, including a stretch where the net trailing the chair had gotten snagged on Cyrus's printing press. Finally, they got Pike to where they wanted him. Either that, or they'd gotten tired of arguing with one another.

Hearing a break in the confusion, Pike asked for the tenth time: "Can you take this bag off my head?"

"Don't do it!" the high voice he'd heard earlier said. "Remember his eye beams!"

"My *what*?"

"He doesn't *have* eye beams," Cyrus replied. "He's human, like me."

"That's what you think," High Voice said. "He might have the ability to mimic other species. Besides, we don't want him to know who we are!"

"I know who you are," Pike said. "You're Weedaw, the blacksmith."

"*Wrong!*" shouted his shrill captor. A beat. "Wait. How did you know?"

"He's a spaceman," the female voice responded. "They can read minds, you know!"

Pike explained that he had seen Weedaw earlier in town. "And you've said his name a lot, Vicki—just like he's said yours. I expect you're the gunsmith. Vicki Whitehorse, if I remember your shop's sign correctly."

"What?" the woman sputtered. "Where do you get that idea?"

"Because when you were trying to get the netting out of the chair's casters, you sent Weedaw to get your sprue cutters from atop your bench vise. Those are things I'd expect to find in a nineteenth-century gunsmith shop. And earlier today, I saw your place was next to his. I'm guessing you share the same forge."

"Well, that's just great," said the fourth voice he'd heard, much deeper. "I told you all to stay quiet."

"And from what I heard, *you're* either a carpenter—or that's your name," Pike said. "Which is it?"

Silence. Then a sullen response: "Both."

Another argument ensued. It continued for a minute until a bell rang. Everyone suddenly went quiet.

"Is that the end of the round?" Pike asked.

"Hush!" Cyrus whispered. "I'll be back."

Pike heard footsteps, locks being worked, and a door opening. Shortly after, he heard the *clack-clack-clack* of wood on the floor presaging the approach of someone he knew. "What have you idiots done?" It was Joe Magee's voice.

"How's it going, Joe?" Pike said, unruffled as he could manage under the bag.

"*That's Chris!*" Joe shouted. "Y'all let him go!"

Weedaw objected. "What makes you think it's safe to let him go? He's from outer space. You said so."

"We're *all* from space, you idiot! Did you sleep through every Jubilee we've ever had?" Joe sounded thoroughly disgusted. "Get him some water, Weedaw."

"Did you bring the thing?" Vicki asked, expectant.

"Check our saddlebags," Joe replied. "Carpenter, go with her and make sure we weren't followed."

After Joe's commands, Pike heard people on the move. Seconds later, the bag over his head was tugged off. "Thanks," he said. "Getting a little stuffy."

Beside Joe, Cyrus looked remorseful. "I don't want you to get the wrong idea about hospitality on this planet, Mister Pike."

"Why would I do that?"

"They're *all* sorry." Jennie approached from behind Joe and whipped out her pocketknife. She went to work on the netting binding Pike.

While she did, Pike saw that he was in a broad, high-ceilinged warehouse stuffed with junk. Gas lanterns lit the room, including the one that Joe held while Jennie worked.

Pike got a whiff of the lamp. "You shouldn't burn those indoors."

"I'm not afraid of fire," Joe said.

"No, but the smoke from it is bad for you, and if your kerosene's even a little impure, you won't need the Sorry to get a blaze going."

Jennie smiled at the others, all standing out of sight behind Pike. "I told you. Spacemen are smart."

"Not smart enough not to get caught," Pike said.

"At least you were caught by the right people," Joe replied. "I never wanted Jennie to bring you to town. After I told Cyrus who you were, we knew we needed to get you out of sight."

Pike stared. "You told a *newspaperman* I was from outer space."

Cyrus put his hands before him. "I'm a friend. I promise."

Joe shook his head. "The only spaceman we've ever seen falls from the sky into our laps." He stamped his wooden leg on the floor. "I finally get set free, Chris, and you run off after Warden Talley, herself!"

"Why did you do that?" Jennie looked up at Pike, hurt. "We took you in."

"Did you speak to her?" Cyrus asked, agitated. "You didn't tell her you were from space, did you?"

Pike's eyes narrowed. "No, I didn't say that." If he was the only person from space they'd ever seen, it meant only one thing: Lila hadn't shared her origins with them.

Jennie smiled at her father. "You see? I knew he wouldn't tattle! He's still our secret." Her smile faded. "But why did you go?"

Pike didn't want to lie, but he didn't want to speak out of turn about Lila, either. "I was hoping to learn more about this place. I'd really like to find a map."

Joe chortled. "I bet I know how that conversation went."

"I didn't get a map, if that's what you mean." *Again, the truth.* "Do you have one?"

"I've drawn a few," Jennie said. "Just of the valley. That's as good as it gets."

"We barely know what's two settlements away," Cyrus explained. "Most people never go farther than a village away in their lives. That's why people like you—and the warden, for that matter—cause a stir. You're from somewhere else."

Pike cautiously asked a question of his own. "What . . . do you know about the warden?"

"Rode in here from out east," Joe said. "Nice enough, I guess—but very much a hard-ass."

Cyrus concurred. "She's very committed to the project. She wasn't here any time at all when she was named a lookout—and she made warden so fast that old Garr's head spun. She's a good talker, and Drayko likes that."

Pike wondered what it meant that the others didn't know they already had a recent arrival from space in their midst. He tried to remember what Lila had said about *Braidwood*. Had the Skagarans known about the ship at all?

He decided it didn't matter. She apparently wanted to blend in, and she'd suggested he try to do the same. Maybe she figured her status as a recent arrival clashed with her authority as warden somehow. If so, he thought, it wasn't his place to say anything. Whatever her reasons were had to be good ones.

Freed from the chair, Pike rubbed his neck and rose, joints aching. His eyes, adjusting to the light, registered what he was seeing. It looked like a transporter accident in a historical museum. By intent or accident, someone had stuffed the area with more material than the space should serviceably hold.

There were recognizable things, like a carriage, the guts of a large clock, a ginormous wooden treadle lathe, and a hydraulic drill press. Intermingled—and far outnumbering them—were other things, some of which merely aspired to be something.

A penny-farthing with three large wheels in place of one. A Swiss Army-knife version of a shovel, with a hoe, a spade, and a rake on a pivot. An analytical engine, recalling the works of Charles Babbage and Ada Lovelace—but grafted, for reasons unknown, to an iron plow. And propped against the walls and stretching to the ceiling were tall gridwork lattices. Pike didn't know what to make of those.

His captors didn't know what to make of him, either. Pike turned to see Weedaw enter through a sliding wooden door. The blacksmith advanced slowly, his skin and stubby horns a bright orange as he stepped into the lantern light. He held a glass of water and was trembling so hard he had already spilled half of it. "I hope you're not upset with me, Captain."

"No hard feelings," Pike said, taking the drink and downing it. He squinted, trying to remember what he'd said to Jennie earlier. "Wait. Did you just call me 'captain'?"

"It's right here!" Vicki said, entering. A middle-aged human in dingy overalls, the black-haired gunsmith held a bundle in her arms. "It's printed right inside your spaceman suit."

Pike looked to Jennie. "I thought you hid that."

"It's what we went home to fetch," Joe replied. "After you took off, I assumed we'd see lookouts searching the farm."

Pike understood, though he didn't know why bringing it here was any safer.

Vicki swept her arm across a crowded worktable to make room for the environmental suit. She ran her fingers across the breastplate and gasped. "A thing from another world!"

"The other world smells awful," said Weedaw, at her side. "What do your people breathe?"

"Jennie was cleaning the stable in it," Pike said, shooting her a look of mild annoyance. She shrank a little, and he grinned gently. "It's survived worse."

"Hey!" It was Carpenter's voice, calling out from the entrance.

Pike looked over to see a large figure emerging from the shadows. Carpenter was a rugged, square-jawed titan—and his jaw was all that could be seen of his face. He could only get the fishbowl over his head as far as his nose. He peered at Pike through the faceplate. "I don't think your war helmet's working!"

"It's not a war helmet," Pike said. "And it goes fully over the head. A head of the right size."

"Sorry." Carpenter removed the headgear with an audible pop, revealing a gray face with black hair. He walked with the helmet to Pike, who only stood up to his shoulders. "I'm of the Zoldaari," Carpenter explained preemptively. "My people live in the northern ice."

"And you're here because?"

"I hate the northern ice."

Pike thought that was a good reason. He reclaimed his helmet. "You're a carpenter?"

"I've been told my name is hard to say. It was simplest to take the name of my job." He added in an even lower register, "I've regretted it."

"It's okay," Pike said. "I'm named for a fish. Or something you can hit a fish with." He looked about again at the panoply of equipment. "What is this place?"

"Over the years, Havenbrook has attracted people who think like us," Vicki said. "This room is the reason."

Weedaw's and Vicki's shops were on the other side of the block from the newspaper office, Pike learned. The space he was in had been an empty alley, inaccessible—until Carpenter put up a roof overhead. Vicki gestured to doorways, which Pike presumed led to the two smiths' shops.

"I put a bird coop on top," Carpenter said, "so if the sentinel sees it when it flies over, they won't think much of it."

"The sentinel? Are you talking about the blimp?"

"The what?"

"The dirigible." More blank faces. Pike pointed in the air. "The balloon!"

"Yeah, it's how Drayko and his people keep tabs on the world," Joe said. "The sentinels see something they don't like—and later, you get a remedial lesson from the lookouts."

An airship could solve a lot of problems, Pike thought. "Where do they land?"

"Nobody's ever seen one do it," Carpenter said. "I don't even know if they can."

"I could have sworn I saw one pass by during the millhouse fire," Pike said. "Is that why Garr and the lookouts came to the farm? Did the airship call them?"

Joe shook his head. "Don't know how they could, unless they got one of them rondures up there."

Pike was going to say the big orb had looked too heavy, but then again, the one he'd seen was floating on air, so all bets were off. "So this room—you're running a club here?"

"It's more than that," Cyrus said. "It's a movement of the like-minded."

"Of which we have exactly nine like-minded in the whole town," Joe said.

"I'm number ten!" Jennie said.

"You shouldn't even be here, squirt." Joe gestured. "There's a few groups like ours in various villages, Chris. We call ourselves the Menders."

"Why not the Makers?" Pike asked.

"Making things on Epheska is a good way to get hassled," Cyrus said. "Fixing things—and making them a little better each time—is safer. That way, you don't come up against the Book."

Pike blinked. "There's a Book?"

"Oh, there's no Book," Weedaw said.

"Nope, definitely no Book," Carpenter added.

Vicki nodded. "They always say there's no Book, and that means there's definitely no Book."

They held their expressions for a few moments, before smiles appeared. "So, Captain," Jennie said, "would you like to see the Book?"

CHAPTER 20

THE PRINCE

Celarius actually loved Om Mataya. Short of everyone living deep underground, he couldn't imagine a better coexistence between a sentient population and a natural area. Built into the mountainsides of an Epheskan gorge using no outside materials whatsoever, the city took its sustenance from its own gardens and the river below. Terraces atop structures mimicked natural areas so loyally that the animal population of the valley continued to traverse them.

It was court that he hated, even considering the fact the Skagarans put no pomp into their peculiar brand of monarchy. As Zoryana, his father's aide and counselor, had told Una, most of the planet's population didn't even know the conservator general had a child—or that his successor was already chosen. They only knew there had been peaceful transitions for centuries, giving no thought to where the replacement leaders came from.

Skagara's next-to-last government had been pluralistic and egalitarian—noble in intent, but vulnerable in practice when there were so many competing commercial interests vying for resources. The Epheska project, once launched, had gone with a monarchial system for the reason that it was simple, taking ambition out of play.

But while there was no intrigue about who would come to power after Drayko retired, Om Mataya had many people vying to become the next Zoryana. It was as close to power as any of them could get. That meant toadies constantly warming up to Celarius, wanting to be his best friend and advisor—disregarding the fact that he was his own favorite company.

He also had to deal with prospective consorts hoping to become a part of both a historic family tree and a household that had been underpopulated since the death of his mother, decades earlier. Drayko's obsession with his work and Celarius's love of the outdoors had kept both men bachelors, a fact that had only increased the drive of others to work their way into the Garden House.

Om Mataya's place as the philosophical and administrative center of the project meant Celarius saw people who had been invited in from all over Epheska. He didn't mind those who were being trained to operate the sentinels. It was the others that annoyed him, full of the ambition that had earned them the chance to work in the capital. Most of them arrived with nothing interesting to say—and an urgent desire to prove it at every opportunity.

But not Una. When the refugee from the forest spoke, it was always with care, seldom an ill-considered thought. He'd initially figured that had to do with her fear of being punished for her unsuccessful nature tour, but since then he'd found her cautious and deliberate on many other subjects. And while Celarius occasionally encountered someone who wasn't an open book, it was rare that he took enough interest to read any of the pages.

It helped that she was attractive, for a human. Since freshening up, they were both new people. She looked marvelous—and glad to be in the gown she had been provided, a modest blue calico dress with about a million buttons up the front.

"Not a style I was expecting," she said of it as he met her outside the dining hall. She adjusted her big, ruffled sleeves. "To be fair, I'm not sure *what* I was expecting—"

"We keep some clothes here from the human collection. Just be glad they didn't whisk you off to the novice barracks. The cloaks aren't really designed for indoors—or comfort."

"That's what the person who helped me said." Una looked him over. "I barely recognize you."

Celarius had trimmed his beard and pulled his hair back into a tail, an act that revealed his facial ridges. "You probably couldn't even see these, could you?"

"Not behind the hair."

"I don't mind. I like being anonymous."

"Enjoy it while it lasts," echoed a voice from down the long hall. Una and Celarius turned to see his father approaching, several books under one arm and a bunch of scrolls under the other.

"On Jubilee days," Drayko said, "I see half the people of the world. Then when I try to get some work done, the half that I missed comes to my door."

Celarius grinned at Una. "It's why I flee."

Drayko called out, "Harjon!"

A young aide hustled up from behind him. "Yes, General?"

Drayko piled his books and scrolls into the youth's waiting arms. "Take these to my north study. If you attempt to reshelve them again, I will send you back to where you came from. You will be the first person in history ever exiled from Om Mataya for an inability to alphabetize."

Celarius watched the child's mad scramble away. His father burned through assistants like the *sah'ree* through metal.

Drayko regarded his companion. "Is this the person I was told about?"

"Una." She nodded. "You're his father, I hear."

"And he needs no introduction," Celarius said.

"You're being rude." The older man took her hand. "Conservator General Drayko." He guided them into the dining room. "You both missed a fine Jubilee."

"I make it a policy," Celarius said.

Drayko smirked at Una. "You think he's joking, but no. My son flouts our most noble traditions like a child rejecting vegetables."

Celarius countered, "I eat vegetables."

"And the odd thing you kill in the wild."

"For sustenance, not sport. And only when I have to."

They arrived at a table already set, with candles burning. Celarius knew that others on Epheska considered firelight a danger, but the occupants of the Garden House certainly didn't. Several of Drayko's sycophants filed in behind, taking the other seats at the table and nattering pointlessly. His father, at the head, sat between Celarius and Una—and between courses, he peppered her with questions.

"Celarius tells me you were exploring as a sort of vacation," Drayko said. "What is your *vocation*?"

Una appeared to think about how to respond. "I guess you could say I keep things—and other people—organized."

"A rival for Zoryana! And perhaps a more polite one."

Celarius looked about. "Careful, she'll hear you."

Drayko pointed an eating utensil at him. "You could use an organizer, for certain." He looked to Una as he cut his food. "My son and I share a love for Epheska and all its glories. But he likes to wallow in soil that I merely tend. As a child he used to dig his hands in my gardens, to see what worms and insects he could come up with."

Una grinned gently behind her wine glass. "There's nothing wrong with that."

Drayko harrumphed. He put down his knife and reached for his napkin. "You have seen my son in the forest, Una. Does he really leap from tree to tree, interfering with the social lives of animals?"

"He would call it population management."

"I have the affairs of an entire planet to manage, and he looks after one beast at a time!"

Celarius had been hearing this for years. "What my father does not say is how much time *he* spends dealing with animal-control issues. When you have the livestock from dozens of worlds milling about on the same planet, you begin to see why humans invented fences."

"*Dozens of worlds.*" Una gave him that cautious look again. "How did they all get here?"

Drayko laughed. "You would know this if you'd been back home, attending your local Jubilee today instead of running about in the forest." His father looked down the table to the others. "I'm not telling the story again. I swear, half the people who come here just want me to repeat it in person!"

Laughter, from people who'd been barely listening before now. Celarius knew the dynamic well. He was a little surprised by Una's question, though. It was impossible to live on Epheska and not know how one's ancestors got there. The Skagarans made sure of that, every time the moons aligned.

He figured he knew the answer. "You're tired."

"This has been nice," she said. "But yes."

"That's okay." He waved over an attendant. "They'll get you a room in the chateau. I'll see you tomorrow."

"You're not going back out to find more *ollodons* to work on?"

"I'll stick around. Maybe I can help you find those friends of yours."

"I'd appreciate that." She let out a sigh of exhaustion, rose, and stepped away. The attendant led her off.

Drayko watched her leave. "You found this one in the forest," he said in Skagaran. "You are forever picking up strays."

"She needed help."

"Hmm. At least you seem to discriminate in whom you save. She is fetching."

"She's more than that," Celarius said. "She stood up to an *ollodon*—and then a whole herd."

"I'm not impressed by anyone who would expose themselves to such a situation in the first place. That includes you."

"You've made that clear."

Drayko rose, and the gathering broke up. Father and son walked out to one of the outdoor terraces. The air was crisp, and the nebula was bright tonight, a placid layer of color above the more active aurora.

"How am I to do it?" Drayko asked.

Celarius knew this tone. "Here we go."

"They will bring my deathbed to the rondure, and I will be forced to tell the people of Epheska that the person I have entrusted with *their* future has become breakfast for a beast. And we will be back to another interregnum where a class of people who have never been asked to think beyond the harvest will have to learn how to keep order from chaos."

"You could fix that by occasionally delegating responsibility to someone."

"I am trying to do it with you."

Celarius snorted. "You'd make me like that kid back there—Jarhon?"

"Harjon."

"Whatever. I'm an adult and I'm not your apprentice. I support the goals of the project, and I understand the challenges. I'm just going to deal with them in my own way as long as I'm able."

"You mean as long as *I'm* able."

"I may have to take this job of yours someday, for the good of the planet. But I'm not running into the fire."

"On this planet, the fire is not so hot." Drayko shook his head and waved his hand. "But as you wish, as always." He looked up. "Did I hear there were more members of Una's party missing?"

"Three other people, yes."

Drayko saw Zoryana approaching from the house. "I should ask her if there have been any other foundlings."

"I already did," Celarius said. "The canopy in the Grandwood is thick enough to walk across—there's no seeing them from the air. We'll have to wait until they come out."

"If that's where they are."

Zoryana arrived at their side and cinched her cloak tight. "If the two of you aren't frozen to death yet, I have news of the incident."

Celarius squinted. "What incident?"

"There was a vessel that fell from the sky," Drayko said. "While you were playing in the woods. I was standing right here when I saw it. And not too long after the last one. Very worrisome."

"It has been found," Zoryana said. "Lookouts from Nerathos encountered the wreckage."

"Nerathos Island?" Celarius asked. "That's a long way from here."

"It was traveling at quite a pace. I would have guessed even farther away." Drayko questioned Zoryana. "What was found?"

"An empty shell, burned to a crisp. Much worse than the other one."

"A probe," Celarius guessed.

"It was large for that," Drayko said. "I had the lookouts searching for something like it earlier."

While no Skagaran on Epheska had flown a spaceship in hundreds of years, the conservator generals maintained some records of what they looked like. Celarius had seen some of them as a child; they resembled things out of fantasy.

Drayko made up his mind. "Tell the warden at Nerathos to search the entire island. If there were occupants, they must be there."

Zoryana nodded and turned away. As she parted, she looked back. "I suggest you two go inside before we must send a party to chop you out of the ice."

"Good night, Zoryana," Celarius said. He'd always found her more amusing than aggravating, but then he didn't have to spend all his time here. *Yet*.

Drayko frowned. Turning back toward the house, he paused and put his hand on his son's arm. "I don't suppose you'd like to take *Zersa* out to Nerathos?"

"Why? You've already said, it's an island. The lookouts will do fine." Celarius looked back at the chateau. "Besides, I have a search to do around here."

"On behalf of that woman. Human, is she?"

"I think. Human, Strooh, Tigan—what of it?"

"You just need to consider—"

"We just met. I'm helping her out. That's all." He started to walk away, only to grow angrier with each step. He stopped and turned. "And even if it *was* more than that, what difference does her species make? Our people don't care about racial purity—we never have. Devotion to the cause is all that matters."

"And you know nothing about what she is devoted to. Indeed, you know nothing about her at all."

"Well, that makes her more interesting than anyone else I've ever met here."

Celarius left his father and walked back inside. He didn't know whether Drayko was right to worry or not, but he was pretty sure of one thing: people like Una didn't just fall from the sky.

CHAPTER 21

THE BOOK

If Christopher Pike was expecting a single volume upon which Epheskan society was based, he learned otherwise when Cyrus trotted over with his first armload of bound volumes. Indeed, it took half an hour for the journalist to find them all. "The Book" would not fit on a shelf, nor in an entire bookcase. There was a whole alcove devoted to it.

"Heavy reading," Pike said. "This is something the Skagarans wrote?"

"No, it's a record of everything they've told the wardens and the lookouts that people can and can't do in the centuries since we got here from Earth." Cyrus gestured. "Read any one of them, and you'll get the idea."

Pike cracked open one of the leather-bound editions and went to a random page. "Three hundred and sixth year, ninetieth day: On the matter of slide fasteners." He looked at the image on the page. "Zippers?"

He drew blank looks.

Well, here's something that'll still function. Book in hand, Pike walked over to the spacesuit and turned part of it inside out. There was a small pocket there, sealed by a simple mechanism. The others gathered around as he worked it open and shut. "They're called zippers."

"Ooh, nice," Vicki said. "Fine metalwork."

Weedaw agreed. "Look how it does that!"

Pike let them marvel over it as he paced with the book. "It says here someone in the three hundred and sixth year invented something like a zipper. But there weren't any in Dry River as of the abduction." He scratched his head. "I guess they came along soon afterward on Earth."

Jennie's face contorted. "You mean we just missed them?"

"I don't know. I guess."

"How would you not know when an invention like this came along?" Weedaw ran the zipper back and forth, eyes wide. "It's the greatest thing ever!"

It's so great I never thought about it. Pike flipped some pages and found another passage. "'Lariats to be made of fiber or horsehair, not rawhide.'"

"Oh, yeah," Joe said. "That one."

Pike looked up. "That doesn't make sense. They were braiding reatas in California and Mexico long before the Skagarans visited."

"But the Skagarans didn't go to those places," Cyrus said. "Read on."

Pike did. The historical section bewildered him. "The residents of Dry River, Colorado, knew about reatas, and someone knew how to make them. There just weren't any in the effects the Skagarans brought from Earth. So when somebody after the First Days tried to make a lasso out of rawhide, the lookouts were told that constituted an advance in technology."

Joe ran his finger across his throat and made a cutting sound.

"But you've got other things made from rawhide. Saddles, boots, whips!"

"Nobody said it had to make sense."

Cyrus rummaged through the books. "That one's even a case where the Skagarans forgot the rule for a while."

That startled Pike. "Don't they keep their own record of decisions?"

"We don't even know where they live. But there was a conservator general under which the four-strand reata was okay, but nothing more. Then her successor said six strands were in. Then all rawhide lassos were out."

"New pope, new rules." Pike heard his own remark—and raised something else he'd been wondering about. "What happened to the religions that came from Earth?"

"The Skagarans didn't do anything about them," Vicki said. "Dry River had two churches and people from three or four different faiths. They left them alone. After a long enough time, they either faded out—or merged into the soap that Drayko is selling."

Carpenter spoke up. "It was the same with my people. The Skagarans didn't tell the Zoldaari *not* to believe in the Nine Overlords—but the idea became that the Overlords sent the Skagarans to save us from destruction." Broad shoulders shrugged. "Eventually the deities faded out of the story."

Pike recognized that. It had worked that way on Terralysium. Here, Garr had called the structure surrounding the rondure "church." The people of Havenbrook and other settlements didn't know what the rules were, just the rulings—handed down as if from on high. "How do the lookouts get these rulings?"

"Through the rondures."

"So Drayko can call individual ones."

"Seems so."

That could definitely come in handy, Pike thought—and it further explained how society had evolved. The communal rondure conversations must have felt not unlike prayer for some. He walked around the stacks of books, still amazed. "How is it that you have this, Cyrus? Did you print this for the lookouts?"

Laughter from the Menders. "Oh, no," Cyrus said. He patted a pile of books. "This is a journalistic record. Going all the way back, the editors of the

Post kept a log of what people were told by lookouts—and what had brought on the Sorry."

"A crime log. But I thought you couldn't write about such events."

"I can't publish them. Nobody can stop me from writing. And even editors with no connection to the Menders—or whatever people like us were called in other days—wanted a record of things."

"So you've reverse-engineered the Ten Commandments." Pike looked to another alcove. "What are those with the different covers? More edicts?"

"Of a kind," Cyrus said. "The Skagarans call them Harmony Notes."

"Sounds innocent."

"They deal with how our communities interact. There are tools and resources in other settlements that we don't have. Even some skills that some species have that others don't."

"Specialization."

"The Harmony Notes are how Drayko rules on conflicts. But they also limit who can trade with whom, and for what. And what workers can do, outside their home settlements."

"Like that woman you were sitting with," Jennie said.

Pike looked back at her. "Mochi? The barber?"

"She was free to move here and practice hairdressing. But she wouldn't have been permitted to work as a herder. Her people have an inborn connection with animals—she could probably run three times as many sheep as the warden can."

Weedaw nodded. "I can be a smith here, but not, say, in Veeney. The residents there have no thumbs. Even here, I wasn't able to bring the metalworking tools of my people. Back home, I could shoe twice the horses I can here."

Pike sensed that frustration was part of what motivated them all to join the secret society, such as it was. "The books must come in handy."

"It didn't stop Joe from building his damn engine," Vicki said.

Joe slapped his chest. "I'm not taking orders from books, or blimps, or whatever you call them." He frowned. "I work all day, Captain. I can't read all of this to see what I *can* do."

Cyrus said that not everyone felt that way. "We get visits by Menders from other towns. They're looking for printings of their own."

Pike raised an eyebrow. "I'd guess they don't go home happy."

"You'd guess wrong." Cyrus led Pike around the warehouse to where a massive printing press awaited. It had more metal in it than Pike had seen in all of Havenbrook, and it looked relatively new. "Weedaw and Vicki helped me with the metalwork."

"I helped move it," Carpenter said.

Cyrus demonstrated how it functioned. "It's a rotary press. Dry River only had a hand press, like I've got out in the print shop. It was old when they brought it west. But rotary drum presses had been invented elsewhere on Earth, and they were described in the journal of Dry River's newspaperman." Cyrus smiled. "I stole the idea."

Skagaran logic, at it again, Pike thought. The press existed on Earth, but not in Dry River, so it was forbidden. He smiled to see Cyrus's excitement as he turned the crank. "It's something," Pike said.

"How do you think I got my special edition out so fast?" Cyrus poked his temple and winked. "It's also how we make books available for the others."

"Drayko doesn't know about your interests—but does he know about the books? The lookouts must stumble over them occasionally."

"They don't bother you unless you've broken a rule. It just so happens that breaking the bigger rules also tends to bring down the Sorry—and you know fire and books."

The sinful thing is destroyed—as is the tome that says it's sinful. Pike shook his head.

Carpenter slapped Pike on the shoulder. "Come see my new lathe!"

For the next half hour, the Menders trotted out inventions, hoping to elicit reactions from Pike. He felt like a visiting grandparent whose grandchildren were showing off their toys—but these were grown people, strivers who'd built things they were proud of. Some devices neatly predicted things that came later; some were trips down dead ends abandoned by humanity centuries before. And some were things he deemed useful, which nobody had ever thought of.

"An air-conditioned stagecoach?" Pike asked, regarding the centerpiece of the room.

Jennie claimed credit for it. "There's a gearbox attached to the wheels that operates a fan in the compartment. Perfect for hot summer days."

Joe beamed at his daughter's ingenuity. "She got the idea from my grandpa's windmill blades, over there," he said, gesturing to the tall structures lining the walls. "They'd be running my well today, if only someone in Dry River had put one up—or if I'd been born an Avgana. They had 'em." He swore. "Buncha tyrants, Captain!"

"They aren't tyrants," Weedaw said. "The general says they're doing the right thing. And they did save us, all those years ago—"

"Stop it, Weedaw," Cyrus replied, irritated for the first time. "That shouldn't be permission to run our lives now."

Pike walked over to his spacesuit and picked up the helmet. One of the problems with his job was that he was always on to some new discovery, some new adventure—when the complexities of the planets and populations he encountered couldn't be grappled with in a decade, much less a month or a week.

Starfleet had second-contact vessels for that. But here was a case where he had no choice but to stay. Stay, and deal with the whole problem—without making it worse.

Again, he remembered Jacob, the citizen on Terralysium who had so wanted to leave the planet. The captain had preserved his duty to Starfleet's regulations, but he hadn't felt good about it, and he'd long wondered if he should have done something different. Jacob had just been one person, longing for a better way.

What if there had been ten Jacobs?

Or a million?

Pike had to start somewhere. So he began with an admission. "I understand what Drayko has to deal with."

"You do?" Jennie asked.

"My people have what we call the Prime Directive. We don't change the worlds we find—and if their people aren't ready for what our knowledge might do, we don't even visit."

Joe didn't like the sound of that. "Who decides who's ready?"

"There are guidelines," Pike said. "But it comes down to the people on the scene. In my case, here, it's me." He gestured. "I shouldn't have even shown you the zipper."

"A fine thing!" Joe glared at him. "You've judged us. Been here a day and have barely met anybody, but you've judged us, just like the Skagarans!"

"It's not like that, Joe. We look at the big picture. At everyone."

"That's just great," Carpenter said, riled as well. "Anybody looking at my people would see a bunch of muscle-bound idiots. And because of that, you'd say that I don't deserve to have the secret of a zapper!"

"Zipper," Weedaw corrected.

"Shut up!"

Jennie raised her finger. "The captain also brought a zapper."

Joe's eyes bugged. "A zapgun?"

"He threw it down the outhouse."

"Awww!" several shouted at once. Bickering began.

Pike raised his hands, appealing for quiet. "Okay. I understand—it seems arbitrary and capricious, just like what's in those books over there. I admit it. We just do the best we can. We don't want anyone to get hurt."

Cyrus nodded. "We appreciate that."

"I don't want my crewmates to get hurt either. I need to find them—and the best bet for that is for me to get off this planet." He walked around the inventions. "But to do anything, I need to contact my starship, and do it in a way that doesn't draw attention. I don't want to get any of you in trouble."

Joe waved his hand. "Hey, I don't mind a little—"

"Those of you who don't *live* for trouble, I mean."

Pike stared at the windmill blades for several long moments—and then the ceiling. He snapped his fingers.

"I know how to do it. But I'll need help—presuming any of you want to help me."

The Menders looked at him, and then one another. They stepped aside and entered a huddle. After hearing muffled voices for a minute, Pike saw them break.

"We'll help on one condition," Joe said.

Pike preempted him. "We are *not* sending you zapguns."

CHAPTER 22

THE RAISING

On Earth, circuit riders had brought the gospel to people in the hinterlands. Those who were too far from any church to visit, or whose lives were too hard to allow them to escape, even for a morning. Not everyone had a large family or hands to work the land.

One of Lila Talley's distant and storied ancestors had been a circuit rider, and while she wasn't of his faith, she'd always liked the idea. It was a way of meeting members of the community without having to live in town, which she could do without. It also helped to put people on the right path, before she had to be the one to counsel them after they made mistakes.

Normally, she wouldn't have made one of her rides in the aftermath of a Jubilee, when the story of Epheska's founding was still fresh in people's minds. But the job of the warden entailed additional duties. That included checking in on the regularly wrong-footed, making sure they weren't straying—and the recently chastened, making sure they weren't suffering. The Sorry might not have much compassion, but she and the Skagarans did.

Joe Magee was both a recent offender and a repeat offender, and that led to her second visit to the farm in a week. That, and the fact of a certain guest staying there. Christopher Pike was an old friend, but he was also a Starfleet captain, which meant his ship was probably somewhere up there between the moons and the nebula, circling like a vulture.

There was no reason to fear it, of course: a planet with its own immune system against technological contamination was proof against anything Starfleet could throw at it. Some news she'd received that morning also held the promise that *Enterprise* was likely to be on its way soon. But until Pike came to grips with his situation, he could be a wild card—and possibly a bad influence on Joe, who already had trouble accepting reality.

When Buckshot approached the millpond, Lila realized she needn't have worried. Joe and Pike were both atop the damaged mill, hammering at timbers. Carpenter was up there, winching up more lumber—and while his presence was predictable, she was surprised to see Vicki Whitehorse and Weedaw lending a hand on the ground. The gunsmith and the farrier rolled a barrel off a cart for placement in a maze of construction materials on the ground.

Knowing the activity would rattle Buckshot, Lila dismounted near a post and tied him up. Pike hadn't seen her yet.

"Morning, Warden."

She turned to see Cyrus, the *Post* editor. Strolling amid the supplies, he made notes in a small booklet. "Writing this up for the paper?" she asked.

"And keeping track of what goes where," Cyrus said. "I guess I'm part of the story."

"I won't tell."

Cyrus went back to his ciphering, and Lila saw Jennie emerge from the mill.

"I didn't know you were doing this," Lila said. "I don't see Carpenter's usual crew here today."

"Oh, they brought out all the wood and stuff," Jennie said as she picked up a board. "He sent 'em back when our friends got here."

"Neighborly of them to help."

"Well, you did ask people to."

"That I did." *I just wasn't expecting them all to listen.* "I'll give you a hand."

Lila helped Jennie move planks to the side of the mill, where Carpenter had set up a gantry with a pulley and rope. It was an old technology, and permissible. Lila was surprised how quickly she had internalized all the nuances in human society here. It helped that her family had tried to live by the old ways, even on Earth—but there were things even she hadn't considered. Like the way Cyrus was taking notes. He could use shorthand, but only the kind that the *Dry River Post* editor used in the 1850s. And as sensible as using a clipboard might seem, those were from half a century later.

When Lila had secured the load to go up, Jennie gave a shout and then went back into the mill. Above, Pike peeked over the side. "Lila!"

"Howdy!"

"Just a second." He rode down on a rope, slowing himself with his boots on the side of the mill as the lumber acted as a counterweight. In seconds, Carpenter and Joe had the load on the top floor.

Pike released the rope and examined his hands. "This planet needs more gloves."

"I'll take it up with the Skagarans."

He took a rag from his back pocket and wiped his face. "Sorry I didn't see you when you rode up. That's a ways up there."

"That's okay." She grinned. "You've just arrived, and you've already found yourself a barn raising."

"More of a roof raising. They say winter comes quick around here." He stepped over to get a drink from the well.

Lila followed—and cast a look back at the work area. "That's a lot of lumber."

"The top floor was gone. That's what I've been doing most of the morning. Just about got it done." He chuckled. "I guess that's not exactly what they mean when they say 'officer on deck.'"

"Nope." She didn't favor the Starfleet jokes, but she figured it wouldn't be too long before he'd find other expressions to replace them.

She couldn't get over what she was seeing. Pike had been a part of her life that she thought was lost forever. Just like the Bar T Ranch, where her ancestors and other like-minded Luddites had settled after World War III ravaged the planet. The Mojave Desert was one of the few places on Earth that looked the same before and after devastation—and she'd felt connected there to the distant past. Epheska had that place beat in that department, but it didn't have the same people. It never could.

Yet Pike was here, wearing jeans and a plaid button-down shirt like any worker in the autumn, drinking from a tin scoop. All those years in the stars, all that travel—and here he was living the life of an Epheskan.

He predicted her first question. "I didn't tell anyone where I'm from, like you said. I didn't tell anyone where you're from, either."

"Thanks. You've done the right thing." She looked up at the people on the roof. "They just wouldn't understand, and there's no need to complicate their lives, or yours." She squinted at him. "You look better than when I saw you last."

"Sleep helps. And most of the pain's gone."

"The unhappy landing, I guess."

Pike flexed his wrist. "I'm working it out. I owe Joe and Jennie for the hospitality."

She looked at the mill and smiled. "I have to say, I like your way of not interfering with things."

Pike wiped his mouth and looked up. "It's something to do. I want to find my friends, but *Enterprise* will be looking for all of us, and it has far more chance of finding them than I do." He gestured to the farm. "In the meantime, I don't want to stray far. This is near enough to where I arrived."

"Makes sense." She walked back with him to where Buckshot was tied. She didn't mind Pike waiting, and him doing it where she could keep tabs on him was even better. She already knew it wouldn't come to anything.

She'd known since that morning, when she dropped into the church at Havenbrook to see if there were any notes from the Skagarans. It was one of the regular duties of wardens. She'd learned the unidentified flying object from earlier had been discovered on the island of Nerathos, which was as isolated as it got. The vehicle was shattered, with no occupants. That hadn't surprised her. *Braidwood*'s approach a year earlier had been gentler, but just as uncontrolled. It was a crash she'd been lucky to walk away from.

Enterprise was probably up there right now, wondering where Pike was and considering all the ways it might interfere with the population below. She expected they'd make another stab at approaching the planet, if they hadn't already; they'd learn it was futile. The important thing was that their vaunted tools had probably already detected the destruction of Pike's shuttle. She didn't give a hang for the Federation's word when it came to noninterference, but she doubted they'd send parties looking for crewmembers that were already dead.

He was here, for better or worse, and she'd need to keep an eye on him. But then again, that might not be so bad.

"You're making progress," she said, untying Buckshot. She looked to the rooftop. "First steps, anyway."

"Yeah, we're not going to finish today. These people have shops to get back to."

"I don't expect any rain. You might hear some of the weird rumbles tonight, but it's just how the air gets when the seasons turn." As he stared at the skies, she climbed aboard Buckshot. She stared down at him—and decided. "What time are y'all thinking about wrapping up?"

"Not sure." Pike faced her again—and caught her looking at him. "You have something in mind?"

"Had any mutton lately?"

He smirked. "The ship's galley is plumb out."

"You'll love it. Besides, it'd be nice to talk." She looked to the side and sighed. "This place is paradise, and all, but—"

"You want someone who can listen to you complain about tree-bark coffee."

"I guess." She smiled. "I live to the south. Jennie can give you directions. Say, a bit before sunset?"

Pike chuckled. "That's some precision scheduling, there."

"You'll get used to it." She tipped the brim of her hat and nudged her horse into motion.

CHAPTER 23

THE PORCH

The dog was a mutt, if ever there was one. The people of Dry River had been carried skyward by the Skagarans along with their belongings, buildings, and livestock—and approximately thirty dogs of various breeds, which had given rise to every canine that followed on Epheska.

But while the humans that had been relocated to Epheska had never discovered DNA, they did understand breeding—and the dangers of a limited pool. With the encouragement of the Skagarans, the refugees put that knowledge to work, trying for centuries to preserve and promote as many different traits as they could in their animals. If the lineages really did hide Shire horses, Great Danes, or Choctaw hogs somewhere in the distant past, some breeder would find them.

Rufus, however, was everydog, and undisturbed by it. Christopher Pike watched from Lila's porch as the hound rolled in the dirt. The Bar T Ranch: Epheska Edition was significantly downsized from the place Pike had known in California, but it had a lot going for it. Lila's sheep and pigs were healthy and numerous, and Pike also got his first look at *hennigars*, the humans' name for a native fowl. Fat and flightless, but blue. The egg she'd served him with dinner was almost worth a trip back for breakfast.

The house was modest, built a hundred seventy years earlier in local reckoning; it had been vacant for a decade when Lila moved in. Pike didn't know how she managed to arrange the house, keep her flock, and see to the behavior of the people of Havenbrook, but she seemed not to mind the challenge. She was living her best life.

Lila called to him from inside the house. "Making friends with Rufus?"

"He's been showing me around." Pike turned to see her approaching with a couple of jars. "Did Dry River have any cats?"

"A few. They took a bad attitude about the whole thing and ran off."

"Typical feline. I guess that was that."

"No, there's a forest region down south with half a million of them. We think. People are kind of afraid to go there."

"No one wants to get mugged by cats." Pike took one of the jars from her. They looked like they held tea. "What, no ice?"

"You learn to live without it."

He took a drink—and realized it was something else when the gulp resulted in his eyes bugging. "*Moonshine?*"

"Corn whiskey, but we sub in a local plant for the corn." She took a swig. "They call it *gormil*. It's where you get the color from."

Pike was still getting over the taste. "You could call it gold lightning."

"Lightning's kind of weird here. Something to do with the Baffle."

"Is it anything like the Sorry?"

She shook her head. "I see you're still playing Starfleet." She took another drink and walked to the other side of the porch.

Okay, I get it. Pike had thoroughly enjoyed dinner with her, catching up on old times. Of her intervening years, she'd said nothing at all—and whenever he quizzed her about the Skagarans and their capabilities, she'd gotten downright prickly. He needed to finesse things, find out what he needed to know without seeming an inquisitor.

Another sip told him what to ask about. "I'm surprised the Skagarans let the Earthlings bring their vices."

"It's not a matter of them *allowing* anything," she said, finding a seat on the porch swing. "People retained the cultures they brought with them. The Skagarans were cautious not to interfere with that."

"Even if they're dangerous?" He took a seat beside her. "Come to think of it, I haven't seen any cigars around."

"Oh, there were cheroots in Dry River. But nobody had any tobacco plants, and nothing native to Epheska or any other species' homeworld here is similar." She rolled her eyes. "You already know they can't fake coffee."

Pike looked at the jar. "Still, there's this stuff. Joe Magee seems to have a problem with it."

"You seem to think they're a bunch of social engineers—or that everything's frozen in place. Neither's true. You saw all the women running businesses. Nobody's riding sidesaddle here. The people decided that, not the Skagarans. Folks are free to make their own decisions."

"But not with technology."

"Because that affects more than them. Factory pollution was the original secondhand smoke."

He laughed in spite of himself. "It's like we're back on the Bar T. We were having these arguments decades ago."

"Well, you always did have a foot in the past." She twisted a lock of her hair. "Some of us were there with both feet."

As the sun closed in on the horizon, the aurora, present all day, really got going. Fronds of orange and silver framed by pillars of purple cloud. "Wow" was all he could say.

"That's what it's all about."

Lila explained that the Skagarans had found the planet so wonderful, they had to share it—but not with just anyone. They wanted people who they knew would preserve the place, even as the world preserved their ways of life.

"That trip to Colorado four centuries ago has given rise to ninety-one different human settlements."

Pike's eyes widened. "Ninety-one?"

"The population in the American West was doubling every thirty years—although that was with immigration. It didn't keep at that pace here, but it's enough that the Skagarans okay a new settlement from time to time."

Parts of that didn't make sense to him. "I knew there was oversight involved with people migrating, but you need permission to found a new village?"

"The Skagarans know the good places better than we do," she said. "They make sure there's a temple with a rondure waiting."

Pike still didn't understand. "When they approve these new towns, how do they make people move to them? They don't sweep people up and carry them away again, do they?"

"No, they make it more like an adventure. Some move out of civic duty, others for a change of scenery, or because they want better weather or a better well."

So it's not as Soviet as I thought, Pike thought. *More Oklahoma Land Rush.* He just hoped there wasn't already someone living where the Skagarans sent people to.

With the sun gone, the light show had picked up an extra player: the Bulls-eye Nebula, which looked nothing like a bull's-eye when you were inside it. The aurorae danced before it in colorful conversation. Together, they eliminated the need for a lantern on the porch. *Not that many people use lanterns here anyway.*

He was admiring the display—and tasting the last of his drink—when she broke the silence. "My mom always said you were in love with me."

Pike nearly choked.

Lila laughed. "You okay, there, chief?"

"Captain," Pike said. He shook his head. "That *does* sound like something your mother would say." He took a breath. "I was more in awe of you. You were older, Lila. Three years is an unbridgeable gap at that age."

"Yeah, I used to tell her you were in love with our life."

"You're not wrong." He thought back. "But I also liked that you treated me like I was older. You called me Christopher, took me seriously."

"Well, I'm a serious person."

She was. Their dynamic had always stupefied him—and here it was, back again. Pike was more accomplished and farther traveled than nearly anyone else in the Federation. Yet by virtue of her position in his life story, Lila Talley still seemed to be on the next level, removed from his existence.

Her drink finished, she dismantled him again. "You were serious too. Then you started hanging out with *Evan Hondo*." She ridiculed the name as she said it. "Wild man with the hovercraft. What happened to him?"

"He died."

"I didn't hear." The mocking tone was gone. "How?"

"Using technology to mess with nature, actually." Pike explained that his friend, the bad influence, had met with a fatal accident. "It's part of what got me straightened out. And off to Starfleet." He looked to her. "What was *your* life like after I left? There were a lot of years there."

"For Luddites, one year's like another."

"I'd have thought you would have connected with someone from one of the other families, maybe. What was that guy your age that used to come around—Eddie?"

"Eduardo."

"Lopez, right."

"No." She glanced to the side. "No, there's no one." She stood abruptly, causing the swing to rock backward. She put her jar on the porch railing and walked to the porch steps. "How about you?"

"Me?" Tables turned, he rose to follow her into the yard. "Well, the job doesn't leave a lot of time. But I have someone I'm seeing."

"I'm sorry." His eyes widened a little at her remark, and Lila was quick to amend it. "I don't mean I'm sorry you're seeing someone. I'm sorry you won't be able to get back."

"That remains to be seen. She's another captain. Maybe she'll come find me." He looked up to the nebula. "No, really, my family is *Enterprise*. Two-hundred-or-so strong when I took over."

"I hope you had more than one outhouse."

"She's *Constitution* class. We thought of everything." He smiled. "They're great people, Lila. A lot of them are young, so I'm part teacher and part parent. Every day brings something different." He looked about into the shadows. "I guess it's the opposite, here. Always the same."

She shook her head. "We had this argument before, too. When you were getting restless with riding. I told you that variety is there, every day, if you just pay attention. The weather brings you something new. Or one of your animals does. Or one of the folks you're looking after. They're not planet-shaking events, for sure. But who wants to measure their life in catastrophes?"

"Avoided—or otherwise." He nodded. "It does all kind of run together sometimes."

She reached down to scratch Rufus. "The Epheskan way is the Luddite way. What my parents and grandparents were searching for, what they promised me. When I accepted I wasn't able to leave here, I finally saw it. You'll see it too: you could have been just as happy back there in California on that horse." She looked up at him. "Give this place a chance, Christopher, and you'll find it answers some of your questions. And not the ones you've been asking."

Pike was still figuring out how to respond when she picked up the dog.

"Zeeter bugs are starting to bite," she said. She nodded in the direction of his horse. "You'd better get back to Joe's before the really big varmints come out."

"Good advice, as always."

"It sure is." She gestured toward the house. "If I let you stay overnight, by morning the whole planet will know, technology or not."

CHAPTER 24

THE SIGN

"Good-bye, my love."

Doctor M'Benga pressed the control and watched the child disappear. A tear formed in his eye. The transporter hadn't sent her away; indeed, it hadn't sent her anywhere. But unlike whatever had happened to Captain Pike and his companions, this was no accident. It was on the orders of a doctor—and a father.

M'Benga's daughter Rukiya suffered from cygnokemia, a merciless disease that had left her with a few months to live. The malady was incurable, but he intended to change that, employing the systems of Starfleet's greatest research vessel. To ensure that his efforts would not be in vain, he had used the emergency medical transporter to keep her stored in stasis, allowing her to materialize only very briefly on days such as today.

He had not shared the knowledge of Rukiya's presence with the captain. He trusted in Pike's humanity, but he was certain Starfleet would never have approved of his actions. The transporter existed for the benefit of the crew, not for his personal use—even in so important a cause.

Enterprise's initial approach to the mystery planet had knocked out systems across the ship, and M'Benga counted it as a miracle that Rukiya's pattern had not degraded during the outage—or, worse, disappeared. He'd studied transporter technology enough to employ it in the first place, but this situation had exceeded even the understandings of Hemmer and Kyle. *Enterprise* might survive another trip to a place where physics did not obey. Rukiya might not.

If only there was a way to convince others, while keeping the secret. And M'Benga knew there was one person he needed to convince most.

He saw her in the turbolift. La'an looked as if she hadn't gotten a lot of sleep. "Hello, Lieutenant."

"Doctor."

"I understand you are considering taking *Enterprise* closer to the planet."

"More than considering, Doctor. We can't remain on station out here forever. We have to do something to find out if our captain and crewmates are alive. Once confirmed, we must help them."

"Of course I agree—" The turbolift stopped, and La'an stepped out. It was not his destination, but M'Benga followed her. "I was saying, I agree. But I thought Lieutenant Hemmer's team was working on options that would not risk the entire ship."

"That's one track he's working on," she said as she walked. "But this isn't spacedock. We're not going to be able to construct a vessel that can land and return to orbit without any electronic components whatsoever. Our people are clever, but they don't have the materials."

"And so—?"

They arrived at an observation port, and she paused. At this distance, the planet was larger than the Moon from Earth's surface: the brightest thing outside by far. La'an pointed to it. "We know we can employ momentum and gravity so *Enterprise* can make a close flyby and exit from the zone without any need for electronic assistance. Hemmer is preparing a variety of different instruments, some with hardened architecture, others using alternative power sources. We'll activate them as we go to see which ones function properly."

M'Benga's brow furrowed. "I thought we were doing that with probes."

"We have been. This will be a more robust examination."

"How many of the probes went without faults?"

La'an went silent for a moment. "None," she finally said. She began walking again.

M'Benga shook his head. La'an was a capable officer, but she was young, and he could imagine the pressure on her. It was one thing to have the conn when disaster struck. It was another to be left in charge for days at a time when one's captain and first officer were missing.

He hurried to catch up with her. "I understand you want to do something," he said. "But there are risks to those aboard when our systems fail."

"I'm aware of that." She stopped and turned. "I've read your reports. They also say that sickbay is now empty, and the medical experiments you've documented that may be imperiled are frankly worth the risk."

You're not aware of everything, he wanted to say. But he could think of nothing to add.

"Like it or not," she said, "it's my call. Main engineering is my next stop. I'm giving Hemmer until the top of the hour to finish his preparations. Then we go." She watched his response. "There's nothing else I need to know about, is there?"

M'Benga scowled. There was no way around it. He was going to have to come clean, or deal with what came.

He let out a deep breath. Of course, he knew the answer.

"La'an, I need to tell you—"

"Bridge to La'an."

M'Benga stopped talking as La'an stepped over to push an intercom control. "This is La'an."

"We've found something."

"I'll be right there. La'an out." Without saying good-bye, she made immediately for the turbolift. M'Benga followed.

"Commanding officer on the bridge," an ensign announced. Ortegas rose from the captain's chair as La'an approached.

She did not sit. "What do we have?" she asked as M'Benga entered and lingered by the turbolift door.

"We've been running the lidar scans," Mitchell responded from navigation. "We've resolved the surface down to a resolution of half a meter." She pointed to the main viewer. "There's a structure being built. It wasn't like this on the previous pass."

La'an shrugged. "We know there's intelligent life there. Structures are being built all the time."

Mitchell looked over her shoulder to the science station, where the xeno-anthropologist was staring into Spock's viewfinder. "Sam?"

"Right." Sam Kirk moved over to the adjacent console and punched buttons. "You had us running everything new through the computer, looking for anything that might be used as a beacon."

La'an nodded. "Captain Georgiou once traced a Starfleet chevron into a surface to alert *Shenzhou*."

"Well, this is in that ballpark." Two images came up on the large screen, side by side. "Here's before-and-after shots of a location in the temperate zone, not far from the descent path of *Eratosthenes*."

The lidar image was a relief map, in a sense, measuring elevation. M'Benga watched with interest as Kirk toggled between two images.

"Since yesterday, it appears that workers have brought materials out to this construction site, putting a new roof on an existing building." He left the "after" image remain up and pointed. "You'll see there are barrels and large piles of lumber outside—and then on top of the building, you'll see the roof is incomplete. It's been like that for hours—deliberately or not, work stopped."

As Kirk focused the image, M'Benga could see there were four gaps in one side of the roof where decking had yet to be mounted.

"Looks like some piano keys are missing," Ortegas said.

"More like ribs," M'Benga said.

La'an glanced over her shoulder at him. He imagined she had forgotten he was there. "What's the significance?" she asked.

Kirk counted them off. "Viewed from this side, we have two slats, then a gap. One slat, then a gap. One slat, then a double-sized gap. One slat, then a gap. And one final slat."

M'Benga stared. "I don't get it."

"11010100101." Kirk smiled. "If Lieutenant Spock were here, he could probably do the binary in his—"

"One thousand seven hundred one," La'an said.

"And the other side is here." This side had gaps, too, but it also had five rows that only went halfway across the roof. "Don't bother with the binary. *It's Morse.*" He tapped some keys on his console, and typewritten letters appeared, superimposed on the roof:

NCC-1701

M'Benga gasped.

La'an crossed to Kirk's terminal. "The computer caught *that?*"

He showed her what he was working on. "It wasn't just that—there's more. It was one of a thousand candidate images planetwide that it selected to send to the decryption algorithm." He widened the image on the main viewer. "Remember the supplies all around?"

M'Benga and the others watched as the stacks of lumber and barrels came back into view. They had looked randomly placed, before—but now they seemed less chaotic, even to his eye. Woodpiles for dashes—and barrels for dots. Shankar at communications read them even before Kirk applied the text to the screen: "*Code 710.*"

"Code 710?" La'an knew immediately what it was. "That's the Starfleet alert warning ships not to approach."

As the bridge buzzed with response, M'Benga let out a heavy breath. *Thank you,* he mouthed.

And in the next instant, he knew whom he had to thank. "Check out the other row," Shankar said. "*P-I-K-E.*"

Ortegas clapped her hands together. "*He signed it!*"

La'an stared at the imagery. "How far was this from the crash site?"

"It's a *long* way uprange," Mitchell said. "But it's almost directly below the entry path. Just a few kilometers away."

The turbolift doors opened. Hemmer emerged. "My experiments are ready. If you insist on going back to Engineer's Nightmareland, I'm prepared."

La'an walked under the image on-screen. "I regret to inform you the mission has been scrubbed." She looked back at Hemmer—and M'Benga, on the other side of the door. "We're not going anywhere. *Captain's orders.*"

CHAPTER 25

THE GIFT

Christopher Pike had heard howling on his ride back to the farm, but nothing molested him or Shadow, apart from the insects Lila had mentioned. He did regret coming back so close to midnight. His hosts had worked hard on Pike's gambit, bringing the mill to the purposefully half-finished state he had suggested earlier in the day. It was a lot of work to put into a long shot, and given farmers' hours, he expected the Magees had long since retired.

He wasn't expecting to find Jennie outside to meet him as he rode up. Wearing nightclothes and holding a glowlight lantern, she looked beleaguered. "I can't find Pa."

Pike let out a deep breath. *Now what?*

She'd seen no sign of Joe in the mill. "I checked the barn. One of the mares is missing. Did you see him riding out on the way here?"

"No, but I didn't come from—" Pike stopped. He heard motion some distance away. "Is that your cornfield?"

"We don't—" She turned. "That's not corn, it's *gormil*."

"Whatever it is, your horse has found it." Something large meandered between the tall stalks. The mare emerged into an open spot, allowing him and Jennie to barely see the unconscious figure of her father, slumped over on the horse's back.

"That's Honey—and Pa!"

The two hurried over in the nebular light. Fearful something bad had happened, Pike grabbed her arm to slow her as they approached. "You'd better let me see to this."

"I already know. He's fine, if you can call it that."

Pike discovered for himself when he stopped the mare. A halfhearted attempt had been made to rein the horse, but she had no saddle: just the burden she carried. He evaluated Joe's condition. "You make whiskey out of *gormil*, right? He seems to have jumped ahead a few steps."

Jennie swore. "There's a woman in town who runs a still. I wish she'd stop leaving samples."

Joe woke up. "Get away," he murmured. "This is Erin's horse."

"Honey was my ma's," Jennie said. "Pa gets like this."

"Is it an anniversary or something?" Pike asked.

"He don't need a reason." Jennie steadied the mare while Pike worked to slide Joe to the ground without injury.

"Lemme go," Joe muttered.

Pike thought the man stank from more than liquor. "I think he's fallen off a time or two in the wrong spot."

"They're all the wrong spots." Lantern in one hand, Jennie led Honey toward the barn. "See what you can do with him."

Joe didn't struggle as Pike helped him hobble toward the house. The farmer did try to resist when they reached the horse trough, but he couldn't avoid a dousing. Pike didn't make out any of the epithets Joe said as he leaned against the trough, dripping and wheezing in the night.

Pike knelt beside him. "What's going on, Joe? I thought we had a good day."

Joe spat out water. It took a few moments for him to form words. "Got thinking about your ship—and Erin."

Pike didn't see the connection. "What happened to her?"

"She died giving birth to my son. Jennie's brother. Or he would have been."

Pike rocked back. *Both, then.* "How long ago?"

"Years. Jennie had just finished school."

"People talk about Erin like she just passed."

"Time ain't nothin' here."

Pike ruminated. He knew how dangerous childbirth was in bygone days, and particularly out on the frontier. *But this wasn't exactly the frontier, was it?*

"Those rules the Skagarans have. Do they extend to medical advances?" Pike asked his next question carefully. "Joe, could the Skagarans have helped Erin?"

"Could have. Didn't." He glared, eyes full of tears. "She ain't here, is she?"

Pike shook his head. It didn't make sense to bring people across the stars and let them die out. But something about what Lila had said hadn't added up. Ninety-one settlements descending from the Dry River humans *sounded* amazing—but math had told him there ought to be a lot more.

He looked down at Joe's peg leg. "Do they *ever* use any of their advanced knowledge to help people once they're here?"

"At the start." Joe wiped his face with his sleeve. "They took care of some bad things in the beginning. Something called TB, cholera, dip . . . dip . . ."

"Diphtheria."

"Whatever. They didn't set us up to fail. But for the most part we're on our own." Joe reached for his shin. "When the Sorry got me the first time, it burned through the rope holding the engine I was workin' on. I nearly died when the doc took my leg."

Pike began to understand. The Skagarans would have known they were bringing not just their refugees' animals, but also their germs and viruses. They'd have gone after the big things, the maladies that could threaten one or more of the species on the planet. But the small things, they let go.

Small things—and sometimes their mothers.

Pike helped Joe to stand. "Easy, now."

"You see why I try so hard," Joe said, wearily looking behind him. "I don't want this for her. For Jennie."

"I understand." Pike saw the girl emerge from the barn. "It's late. We need to get you to—"

Jennie saw it first. "*Look!*"

From near directly overhead, an object lit the night. Joe pointed and shouted, "Falling star!"

That's close! Pike's eyes widened as he saw the white dot grow larger. He pulled both the Magees back just as it slammed hard into the fallow field directly south of the *gormil*. A plume of ejecta rose high before showering the ground with black rain.

"Bring the lantern," Pike said.

"Take it. I'll get a shovel." Jennie handed him the light and hastened away.

Pike found a good-sized pit near the edge of the field. Something was down there. He scrambled in and illuminated the hole. "Have you ever heard of meteorites, Joe?"

"Maybe."

"Well, I don't think this is one." Pike looked up to see Jennie offering the shovel. "Much obliged." He began digging.

"There ain't gonna be anything left of that thing," Joe muttered.

"There sure is," Pike replied as he pulled up a dark canister. It was already cool to the touch, as he expected it would be. "It's duranium."

They gazed at it in silence for a moment—until something disturbed the insects in the field nearby. Jennie looked back. "Is something else out there?"

Pike remembered what Lila had said about wild animals at night. "Back to the house."

They brought the object into the kitchen and closed the door. As Jennie pulled the shades and brought out another lamp, Joe yanked the tablecloth and all the evening's dishes off the table, creating room for Pike to place the mystery thing upon it.

"What is it?" Jennie asked. "Looks like a big bullet."

"It is, sort of," Pike said, examining it in the low light. "On Earth, they used to send canisters through tubes pressurized by air."

"There's an idea," Joe said. "Whatever for?"

"Sending messages." Pike tested the rim of the cylinder and found that it unscrewed with moderate effort. He tipped it over, allowing several round packets to fall onto the table.

Jennie picked one up. "Biscuits?"

"Rations. High-protein wafers."

"They must think we're awful, not feeding you!"

Pike grinned. "I didn't have enough room on the roof to tell them I was getting fed. No, even if they guessed I had help, they wouldn't know what I had here was palatable to me."

She pawed at the packet. "What do they taste like?"

"Probably not palatable to anyone. Rations haven't changed much." Pike sifted through the other pouches. "Water treatment tablets too. And these are emergency medications."

Joe grinned at Jennie. "I told you he was worth bringin' home. That's the future in this tube." He held the cylinder up to his eye. "Something else in there." He pulled out a sheet of paper. "It's got your name on it."

"Mail call." Pike had a look. "It's from La'an, my security chief. She was left in charge."

"A message from space. Let me read it!"

Pike couldn't see why not, especially as the excitement seemed to be sobering Joe up.

"'Captain Pike: Your message received and understood. *Enterprise* will not approach, per instruction.'"

That's La'an, all right. "Try it with a British accent."

"What?"

"Never mind," Pike said. "Go on."

"'Electrical disruptions prevent planetary approach in any event. *Era—'*"

"*Eratosthenes?*"

"'*Era-who-bah* destroyed on entry. Chin-Riley, Spock, Uhura remain unaccounted for. Scans continuing. We will remain on station. Regret we are unable to render more aid, but contents may serve you.'" Joe put down the letter. "Is that it? They're not coming for you?"

"Not with the Baffle doing what it's doing. They could all get stuck here." Pike gestured to the canister. "This is what they did on short notice."

Jennie took hold of the container. "Hey, there's something else rolled up in here." She pulled out a curled-up document. "It's a map!"

Pike wasn't surprised. It would have been the first thing anyone on *Enterprise* would have thought of. He flattened it on the table and brought the light closer. The map combined visual imagery with glistening contours for elevation. It was absolutely crammed with information; Pike imagined a magnifying glass would bring a lot more out.

"Look at the colors on this thing!" Jennie said.

"And the detail," Joe added. "This printing would make Cyrus weep. What's this of?"

"That's Epheska." Pike glimpsed the expressions on their faces. "That's right—you've never seen what your own planet looks like." He pointed. "This is north."

"What's this 'V' here by this one dot?" Jennie asked.

Pike examined it. "You're looking at it upside down."

She recognized it. "That's the symbol from your suit!"

"I suspect it means 'you are here.'" He didn't remember much about the planet when he'd seen it from space, but he knew its landforms were divided by oceans of significant size, with icecaps near the poles. Now he knew where he was relative to them.

He'd known there were many population centers just from *Enterprise*'s initial survey. Seeing them now, knowing what they were, brought home to him just how big the Skagarans' project had grown. He also noticed that the settlements tended to appear in locations that didn't conform to the land. Some places were near the banks of a river or a seacoast, but by no means all. Pike imagined people settled more or less where the Skagarans deposited them, but the haphazardness surprised him.

Jennie traced her finger. "What's this line with the arrowheads?"

Pike knew when he saw the name printed on the island at the arrow's end. "That's the path my shuttle took."

"Your ship! We can go get it!"

He shook his head. "That's far—and there's probably nothing left of it anyway." He didn't mention that Lila had already confirmed that.

Pike flipped the sheet over to find a second map. This one was mostly land, but it had another Starfleet chevron beside a curvy blue line.

"What is this, the other side of the planet?" Joe asked.

"No." Pike jabbed his thumb toward the kitchen window. "I think it's your stream."

"And that glob there must be Havenbrook!" Jennie said.

The map appeared to cover a forty-by-sixty-kilometer area, the territory that would be most relevant to Pike. He pointed to the other villages one by one and was pleased to learn that Joe knew what they were. Pike didn't know what his next steps were, but he could at least plan knowing what was around.

While the Magees focused on the map, Pike took one more look at the container. On a hunch, he rapped the closed end of it—and watched as a black disk fell out. He knew immediately what it was. "Way to go, La'an!"

Jennie looked up. "What's that?"

"A present from a friend of mine. They went into my office to get it." Pike pressed a clasp on the outside of the disk, and the clamshell snapped open. One side held a piece of gray material, barely two centimeters across. In the other side of the lid was an inscription:

To Chris. May the lost be found.
—Katrina Cornwell

Pike laughed.

Joe stared. "What is it?"

"I don't know if I can tell you. It might be classified."

"Might be *what*?"

Pike smiled. *Okay, let the Federation Security Agency and Section 31 come and get me. I could use the ride.* "The outfit my friend worked for has a lot of unusual things. Anyone from space who knows how to look for this patch can find it, even from far away." He held it between his fingertips. "It's called viridium."

Jennie couldn't believe it. "It's so small!"

"The admiral once told me she'd tracked an officer from light-years away by putting some inside his tooth."

"You don't have to put that in your mouth, do you?"

He laughed. "Here will be fine." He put it in his pocket.

"That's a nice case it was in," Joe said. "What's it made of?"

"The only substance known that could block the signal from the patch, or so I was told. But it kind of defeats the purpose." He closed the circular case and put it in his other pocket.

Pike yawned. He saw there was no tearing Joe and Jennie away from the map, where they were still excitedly pointing out landmarks. "I'll make plans tomorrow. I'm turning in."

Feeling the disk in his pocket gave him confidence as he walked. The only reason viridium wasn't standard issue everywhere was that it was incredibly rare. On this planet, in this situation, it might be even more valuable.

Katrina had predicted such a need all along. After he returned from being lost in the Pergamum Nebula, she had made a gift of it to him. Her untimely passing had made it an important keepsake, but in the days to follow, he expected it might do a lot more for him.

Here you are, saving me again. Thanks, Admiral.

CHAPTER 26

THE SEARCH

Enterprise had missed the Klingon War on account of being in a war of its own, but in the time since, Una Chin-Riley had gotten the chance to visit a rare thing: the wreck of a Klingon warship. Its occupants having earned their glory—or just deserts, depending on one's point of view—the hulk provided insight into the lifestyle of Klingon warriors aboard ship.

The spartan conditions hadn't surprised her. Crew quarters were indistinguishable from storage areas, with bunks nothing more than metal shelves. She had tried one. While the discomfort was predictable, what she saw when she looked up surprised her: Klingon graffiti, etched into the bottom of the upper bunk with a blade.

She knew enough Klingon to understand she wasn't seeing names or insults. Mostly she saw quotations from Kahless the Unforgettable, founder of the Empire. Others were from T'Kuvma, who had sought the recent destructive conflict with the Federation. The etchings overlapped, suggesting they'd been added to across time. Near her feet, more quotes appeared; someone apparently used to sleep in the other direction.

The practice confirmed for her that inspirational material for night reading was a phenomenon that crossed even the widest cultural gaps. She'd stayed in Vulcan homes where Surak's teachings were provided in guest quarters; some on Earth had even resurrected the ancient practice of placing religious texts in hotel rooms.

The Garden House in Om Mataya was neither a barracks nor a hotel, but it did receive visitors who spoke her language—and the book in her bedstand drawer had told Chin-Riley more about her situation than any intelligence analysis could have. She had read, the first night, the story of the Skagarans and their despoiled homeworld, and how they'd left in search of a new start. She'd learned of the discovery of Epheska and its technology-defeating Baffle, the miracle they'd hoped for. She'd seen the accounts of rescues of primitive peoples from other planets—and how they'd been transplanted here. And she learned about the job of the conservator general, communicating through the amazing rondures to ensure harmony. Harmony among the planet's residents, and between them and Epheska itself.

The undisturbed pages suggested she was the first reader of that copy of the book. For individuals visiting Om Mataya, it was probably assumed to be common knowledge. The commander had devoured it, even though it meant she got even less sleep the first night in the luxurious chateau than she had in the forest. Fortunately, her wilderness ordeal provided ample excuse for staying in, and she had relaxed while absorbing the history and its appendices.

Reading it was part of her job, but it was not without guilt. Wherever the captain, Spock, and Uhura were, she doubted they were able to order room service. But Chin-Riley knew she was doing it for their sakes. Her research meant that when she emerged that morning to join Celarius to begin an aerial search for her friends, she was able to credibly pose as the person she'd presented herself to be: a member of Wellspring, one of the human settlements populated by descendants of the refugees from Dry River.

She thought her strategy was pretty good. On learning of human settlements on all sides of the Grandwood, she decided to claim that she and her three missing friends each hailed from a different one of them. Any of them might be destinations for Pike and the others, and the four sites were logical choices to search.

The attendants provided her with traveling clothes—no skirts this time, thankfully—and Celarius dressed for the trip in his backwoods attire. She chuckled when she saw the clash between the rustic clothing and his clean-and-coiffed state. *Prince Sasquatch*. Celarius decided against *Zersa*, employing instead a smaller and faster sentinel with room for two in an exposed passenger cage and a single wand-wielding cleric behind. It couldn't soar as high, but it was fast.

She felt that speed as they flew over the Grandwood. In less time than she expected they reached Wellspring, near the forest's northern edge. She marveled at the frozen-in-time aspect of the village. Celarius did not land, but that barely mattered, as the low flyover had brought what seemed like the whole population out to gawk. Hundreds of people in cowboy attire were something she never expected to see on a foreign planet.

What she did not see, however, was Pike, Uhura, or Spock.

"Sorry your friends weren't there," Celarius said. "Are you sure you don't want to visit your home here?"

"Thank you, but I'd rather keep searching."

Celarius eyed her. "There will be no repercussions from your trip, Una, if that's what you're concerned about. The locals may not know me by sight, but the warden will listen."

"That's not the problem. I'm just afraid time is running out."

She had other reasons not to stay. She'd never met any of the humans Jonathan Archer encountered, but as interesting as meeting descendants from an

Earth abduction four centuries past might be, she had no house in Wellspring, and nobody there would recognize her. It was better to save those explorations for later. She named the other nearby settlements, resisting the urge to joke that they all sounded like retirement villages.

"We'll check out Sunny Valley, then around to Goldmeadow," Celarius commanded. "West-by-southwest."

Behind him, the ship's mysterious monk went into motion. If it weren't for the staff in his hand, Chin-Riley might think the guy was pretending to be a bird.

She watched below as the flags atop the Wellspring temple were changed. Celarius took notes. She understood what was inside the identical buildings, having been shown the rondure in Om Mataya by Celarius earlier that morning. That one had been inside the same kind of stone temple, down the slope from the Garden House closer to the river. She'd really wanted to see the device in operation, but just seeing how it levitated told her it was worth learning about.

"How do the rondures float? What's the principle?"

"The principle is we don't ask how they work," Celarius said, scowling. Then his expression melted into a smile. "Isn't that what your local warden always told you?"

"Just curious. Did the Skagarans invent them?"

He laughed. "My father would have you believe we put the moons in the skies in addition to putting the ground beneath your feet. I like that you don't take everything at face value."

That wasn't an answer, she thought. But there were more pressing things to learn. She wanted to ask whether a call made by a rondure could be detected via subspace, but she couldn't figure out a way to ask that. On the other hand, there was something she *could* ask about. "I was reading the history book by my bed—"

"I'm surprised you woke up at all!"

"I was interested in the part where the Skagarans brought all—er, brought *us* to Epheska. Are the ships you used still around?"

"I have no idea. Why would anyone care?"

"And if this Baffle thing was working even then, how did you get people to the surface? How did you call out to begin with, so you could send for more settlers?"

"You keep saying 'you,' as if I had anything to do with it."

"Didn't you? Your family, I mean."

Celarius sighed with exasperation. "I can't believe you read the book. I've never understood how people abide the Jubilees. But some people go again and again." He turned away and looked over the railing at the forest passing below. "All such a bore."

She watched him. The Jubilees, she now knew, were going to be his responsibility someday. "You don't want the job."

Celarius gestured aft. "Don't let that guy hear you say that. Their faith in the project—and its leaders—runs the planet."

"But maybe someone else would do the job." She stepped to the rail beside him. "Maybe they'd be better at it."

"No," he said, shaking his head. "I would be *outstanding* at it. I have been raised to think of ecosystems, and how to balance competing interests when they overlap. I may not know all the details of *how* my father runs Epheska's affairs, but I understand everything else. That land below is committed to my memory. Every rock, every tree."

"Then why—"

"Because the job will last every day until I die."

She saw fatigue in his eyes just from considering it.

"Okay," she said, "forget it." She looked at the notepaper in his hand. "What's that?"

"The signal I got from the temple at Wellspring. It's a message sent through the rondures from my father. Apparently, there is no distance I can go without being harassed."

"Is it bad news?"

"He thinks it's fascinating, whatever it is, and he wants to see me immediately."

She sighed. "So we're turning around?"

"We have more settlements to visit. Let's just say I missed that message—and the next three." He crumpled up the paper. "Onward!"

CHAPTER 27

THE HARVEST

"*nuqDaq 'oH Qe' QaQ'e'?*"

"*Ogda novara-to shah olagah Hindiwah.*"

"*Kripya restaurant ley chaliye?*"

"*Gehen Sie immer gerade aus.*"

"*Excusez-moi, Monsieur. Est-ce que c'est possible d'avoir une table pour deux, s'il vous plaît?*"

Nyota Uhura's conversations with herself had started on the morning of the third day of her walk, and by the afternoon she had populated the barren landscape around her with a vibrant and diverse imaginary cast. It was the sort of world where you could ask for a restaurant recommendation from a Klingon, who'd tell you in Tellarite to ask the constable in Hindi, who'd respond in German.

Now, approaching what should be dinnertime, she imagined a nice French restaurant. "*Est-ce qu'il y a un plat du jour? Non?*" She looked over to the floating empatherm. "They don't have any specials, Empy."

The fire creature curled into a flaming knot.

"Well, we're not going anyplace else." She gestured to the black hills all around. "We won't get a table at this hour. Where do you think we are, anyway?"

The empatherm fascinated her. Sometimes it was a puff of flame, rolling around. At other times, it was an orange zephyr, wafting about with no more direction than the strands of the aurorae above.

Sometimes it reacted to her emotions, as it had before, getting more animated when she got excited about some find. When she slept, it settled nearby, continuing to meander on the ground but emitting much less light. Once when she woke up in the night, she thought it was on the verge of dissipating. But it flared up as she grew more aware of it.

"Why have you latched onto me?" she had asked more than once. No answer came, but she thought she had figured it out. There just *wasn't* anyone else. She'd won by default. In three days, she hadn't seen a soul. The hopeful moment earlier when she'd exited the volcanic field had dissipated when she discovered her path fraught with even more stretches of wasteland.

Uhura wished she'd spent more time—frankly, *any* time—studying the surface scan of the planet while preparing for her mission. Her attention had been solely paid to the geography of the living. She knew the sun set here in the east, a fact which muddled her sense of where she was heading. There were only hills and more hills. And for every trickle of water with edible foliage, there was another active volcanic feature. Wherever all the people on the planet were, nobody in their right mind would go near a stinking seam.

Even before she reached the ridge to the north, the smoke had told her to expect the worst place yet. Topping the hillside, she beheld a steaming, bubbling lava lake. Beings like Empy rose from it here and there and returned, almost like porpoises leaping from the sea.

Her hand over her nose, Uhura knelt and watched for a few moments, wondering what she was seeing. To her side, the empatherm shimmered. "Is this your home? Or are these friends of yours?"

Uhura watched as Empy lingered near her. As strange as it felt personifying a waft of plasma, she was sensing something. Tentativeness, perhaps.

"It's okay," she said. "I can make it alone. Go ahead."

The empatherm bobbed for a moment and started tumbling down the slope. Uhura sighed. She'd need to make her way around the rim of the crater and hope to get someplace that smelled better.

She'd worked her way to a large black boulder when she saw the wisp's progress had halted. Empy sat just at the edge of the lake.

"What are you waiting for?" she called out. "The lava's fine!"

And then it was not fine. She'd ascribed playfulness to the elementals in the crater; now she saw movement she could only interpret as panic. Some beings dove for the lake, splashing lava, while others started making their way in her direction.

Her first thought was that they were after her, and she hustled back toward the boulder. But she soon saw something new, rising across the northern ridge.

A balloon!

Uhura stopped her retreat. Blimp-like, it appeared to carry a pair of riders, exposed in a cage beneath.

"Hello! Hello!" she shouted, waving her arms. "I'm here! I'm here!"

It was no use. The balloon turned sideways, drifting over the lake. Whoever was aboard wasn't looking in her direction. She'd need to risk running toward the edge, where she might have a better chance of being seen.

But then she saw something else. Empy, streaking in her direction, far ahead of other elementals that were likewise on the move. The empatherm reached her and spiraled around her body, a disembodied spirit stopping her progress. She took the hint and headed back for the shelter of the rock formation.

Looking down, she saw the airship had changed its aspect. A figure aboard gestured with a reddish staff—and below, the other fire beings stopped their flight. One by one, the creatures were ripped from the surface of the lake. They rocketed upward, passing the balloon and arcing high into the sky toward the western horizon.

She watched, spellbound, as what she could only consider a harvest continued. "Who are they, Empy?"

She looked to the empatherm—and saw that it was elongated. The being seemed to be straining. One end rooted to the spot behind the boulder, the other stretching toward the lake and the harvester. The being's color changed, too, growing whiter as it fought whatever was influencing it.

"Don't go," she implored. Uhura had no idea what was happening, but she had every sense that it was against the creature's will. Without thinking, she reached out for her fiery companion. "*Empy, stay here!*"

The fire had no form, but she was able to bear-hug it anyway. While it had not burned her before, she began to feel heat as it struggled, as if whatever protection she had from immolation came from the creature's will—a will now being disrupted.

"Stay!" Uhura shouted, yanking backward. Ignoring the pain to her hands and face, she pulled the varying streaks of flame toward her, gathering it into a ball. Only when she was fully behind the black rock did the empatherm relax.

Uhura peeked around the side of the rock. The western sky was lit with flames racing over the horizon, while to the north, she saw the airship heading back where it had come from. They hadn't noticed her, she decided.

She knelt and examined her face and hands. She wasn't burned, she realized; she'd just *felt* like she was burning. The empatherm had still tried to protect her, somehow. Now, she saw, Empy had no desire to head toward the lava lake.

"I wouldn't want to go there either after that," she said. But she would head north. Whatever the air travelers' intentions, they were the first people she'd seen. Civilization lay ahead.

What *kind* of civilization, she'd have to deal with when she got there. Beggars couldn't be choosers.

CHAPTER 28

THE RAID

Being in Starfleet called for a lot of sacrifices, most of which Christopher Pike was willing to make. Committing an act of betrayal wasn't one of them—even when he knew for sure it was for the greater good.

He faced that unwanted prospect now. It began after he spent the morning poring over the map, deciding on his next steps. La'an hadn't provided any suggestion of a rallying point, which made sense as she hadn't detected Una and the others yet. The wreck of *Eratosthenes* was also clearly out.

That meant staying, but he felt he couldn't impose on the Magees any longer. The Menders had done what he'd hoped by helping him contact *Enterprise*. Every day he associated with them made it more likely one of them—probably Joe—would do something unpredictable, possibly getting in even worse trouble. None of them needed that. He had to leave them first.

The smart thing to do, he'd decided, was to throw himself on Lila's doorstep. Her joke about gossip aside, he expected she'd be more than willing to shelter him—and he knew the Menders would come nowhere near a warden. She'd understand and even approve of his reluctance to interact with others. At the same time, he expected she'd be able to update him on any information the Skagarans got about his crewmates. And while there was something tempting about just finding a horse and riding off to search, being near Lila might give him the chance to find out what had happened to *Braidwood* too. His original mission.

But the Menders would hate it. And Jennie would be crushed.

He'd already decided what he was going to do as he worked that afternoon with Joe and Jennie on the mill. His secret message having done its job, there was no reason to leave it in its unfinished state, and while he wasn't able to complete the roof without the Menders there, the loft was mostly rebuilt. After dinner, Pike had ridden to Lila's to wheedle an invitation. When he discovered she wasn't at home, he turned back for the farm, figuring one more night spent there wouldn't hurt.

The Magees weren't home either. Pike found two horses missing from the stable. It seemed awfully late for a jaunt to town. It was only when he entered the house that he understood. Jennie wrote adequately given her limited education, and he got the gist from the note she left. In Pike's absence, Joe had taken off to see the Menders. He hadn't left empty-handed.

The map!

Pike kicked himself for showing it to Joe. Of course the map would have been irresistible to him. It wasn't something Cyrus was going to be able to re-produce with his printing press, but the editor surely would have found some-thing to do with it. And while the Prime Directive's governance of any actions surrounding these people had grown complicated given the nature of their origins, suddenly having a view of their planet from space was likely to stir things up.

Besides, Pike thought, *I want my map!*

The sun setting behind him, Pike mounted the gelding and rode west for Havenbrook. Jennie's note had said she'd followed her father. How long ago had she written it? He didn't know.

After a couple of kilometers, the trail led through the woods for a stretch. He emerged from the trees and pulled up when he saw a roan horse munching on grass along a ridge to the north. Pike guided Shadow back into the trees and sat silently, watching. The roan's rider, apparently having answered nature's call, ascended back over the ridge, adjusting his belt.

Reedy. Pike recognized the kid from the other night. What was he doing out here, with night falling?

Pike decided to abandon the trail and keep to the thicket, which would get him to Havenbrook slower but allow him to remain out of sight. He spied another lookout from Garr's group posted along the way. And that wasn't all: he saw an airship cruise over, heading away from the town.

They're out tonight for some reason.

In contrast to earlier evenings, clouds obscured Epheska's nightly display, making the fall of night more oppressive—especially going to town the hard way. When he arrived in Havenbrook, however, he saw more light than he was expecting.

Fire!

Pike rode up to find half the town out in the street. He was still trying to get his bearings when a familiar face looked back at him, sobbing.

It was Mochi, the barber. "The Sorry! The Sorry!"

Pike dismounted and tied Shadow in a safe spot. He hurried to her. "Mochi, are you okay?"

She was in hysterics. "The Sorry never bothers the town!" She looked to what Pike now realized was the barber shop, fully ablaze. "What did I do? What did I do?"

He shook his head, trying to register what was going on. Citizens were running a bucket brigade in what he could already tell was a futile effort. The way the flames were moving, it clearly wasn't a natural fire.

"I was using a new shaving brush made of horsehair," Mochi said. "Maybe the Sorry didn't like it!"

Pike wanted to tell her it wasn't that—but there was no time. Releasing Mochi to the care of another villager, he walked up the way and realized the two smithies were afire too. *It's the whole block.*

He cut through the throng and ran around the corner, eyes always on the tower of living fire. He knew the Menders' alleyway sanctorum backed up to those businesses. When he reached the side street the newspaper office was on, he knew what had happened. The Sorry had struck the secret workshop and was taking out everything surrounding it.

Pike found the door to the office smashed open. He entered. The peculiar flames wouldn't hurt him, he hoped, but the whole structure was afire, with all the dangers that entailed. It was the mill all over again—only this time it was worse, as he found when he reached the secret sliding door. It was already open, and through it he saw an inferno.

Like orange ghosts, tendrils of plasma leapt frantically from place to place, immolating the contents of the hidden warehouse. Part of the ceiling had already come down.

Pike squinted. Whatever the fire might or might not do to him, the smoke it created was hot and real. "Joe! Cyrus!"

He heard a high squeal from across the room.

"Jennie? *Jennie!*" Pike dodged a falling timber and entered the maelstrom. He looked around. "Where are you?"

"In here! Help!"

It was the air-conditioned carriage he'd been shown the other night. Debris had fallen from the rafters above, closing off the only door not blocked by junk. Pike navigated the mess, pausing only to grab a handy mallet on the way. He scaled the pile.

"Jennie, stay back!" He smashed through the window and heard coughing in response. He cleared as much glass as he could in order to give her a place to exit. "Come on!"

She scrambled out and tumbled onto the ground. She looked up, teary eyed and bewildered. "You came!"

"Is anyone else here?"

"Everyone *was.*"

"What?"

"Not now. They were!"

Pike saw nothing but chaos—and more of the roof caving in. No time to linger. He threw her over his shoulder in a fireman's carry and worked his way out, wending around one ill-fated brainstorm after another.

Cyrus's presses—both the newfangled one, and his original one. The windmill parts. And the books—all the books.

And likely somewhere in here, his spacesuit and map.

He got Jennie back to the still-abandoned street and instinctively headed up it to another alley before stopping. It took them both time to catch their breaths.

"I know it was the Sorry," Pike said. "The others, Jennie. Where are they?"

Jennie leaned against a wall and panted. "Pa knew the others were meeting tonight, so he brought your map. But he was followed."

"A raid?"

Lit by the still-towering firelight, Jennie nodded. "I hid in the carriage when they came in. I heard it all. Garr's had lookouts posted near the farm the last two nights. One of them saw your message land!"

The sound we heard. "So they went to the farm tonight—and tailed Joe here instead. Who all broke in?"

"It was Garr and some men. I couldn't see, I only heard."

No Lila, then. "Did they hurt anyone?"

"They just yelled a lot. This place has been under their noses forever—it made 'em pretty sore." Pike saw that Jennie's eyes were red from tears. "Weedaw was so scared he told them everything." She looked at him. "*Captain, they know about you!*"

The air went out of Pike.

Okay, he reasoned, *the person in charge is in the same boat with me.* Maybe Lila would help sort it all out. "Where are they now?"

"They were taking them to the church—to that room in back, where they held Pa. They took that metal thing—"

"The canister?"

"Yeah. And your map, and some of the other inventions here."

Evidence, Pike guessed. He patted his pocket, reminding himself that he still had the viridium container. "What about the fire?"

"Nobody set it. It burned through the ceiling first, and then it kind of exploded. It was everywhere, destroying everything. The stuff that fell trapped me in here."

Pike wished he understood how things worked. At what point did a fire become the Sorry—or was it the Sorry from the start? And did it mean to torch Mochi's shop, too, or was it just collateral damage from its proximity to the sanctum? He put the questions aside. Hiding back in the carriage wasn't the best of moves for Jennie, but she'd survived. He offered her his hand. "Are you okay to move?"

"I think. Where are we going?"

"We're going to get you some water and find our horses. We have to stay out of sight. The lookouts were watching the way to the farm when I saw them. If Garr hasn't sent the whole troop down there looking for me, he will."

Jennie snapped her fingers. "Captain, if they're all gone, we can check the church!"

"The church?"

"We can break Pa and the others out!"

"A jailbreak at a church?"

It didn't sound like anything from any movie he'd ever seen. But it also didn't sound necessary—not if Lila would listen to reason. He wasn't going to let anyone else get hurt because of his presence, and he'd already disrupted enough.

Whether he was going to break his friends out or turn himself in, either path took him to the same place.

"Okay," he said. "It's Sunday somewhere. Let's go to church."

CHAPTER 29

THE BREAKOUT

A science teacher who taught comparative religions, Christopher Pike's father had made sure his son visited several places of worship. Not all had survived to the twenty-third century with congregants. But seeing the different buildings had helped a young Christopher understand the often-complicated historical relationship between faith and science.

The two were not always in direct opposition, he had learned; not everything was a case of Galileo versus the Inquisition. Still, he had distinct feelings of familiarity when approaching the church, whose attached outbuilding held Havenbrook's only equivalent of a jail. It was a place for those who'd sinned with science.

While Pike clearly had a preference—*Enterprise* had no shuttles named for Pope Urban VIII—he tussled with his responsibilities as a Starfleet officer. He didn't want to interfere, but the Menders were suffering because of him, and that was enough to require action. He didn't have to undo the entire society; he just had to make sure his friends were treated fairly.

The plaza before the stonework structure was abandoned this evening, with everyone over at the fire. Nonetheless, he and Jennie had brought three horses—theirs and Joe's—to the shadows off to the right of the main entrance. Emerging, they spied someone standing on the portico.

"She's one of the lookouts," Jennie whispered.

Pike didn't recognize her as one of the ones from the mill—and that, he realized, could be used to their advantage. "Play along."

He tucked Jennie's hands behind her and walked her up the steps to the entrance. "Is Warden Talley here?"

"No." The woman in her twenties assessed him. "What's going on?"

"She escaped the fire," Pike said, nodding to Jennie. "This girl is Joe Magee's kid."

That clearly meant something to the guard, who snatched Jennie by the arm. "Everyone's looking for her!"

Pike stared. He hadn't lied yet—and he still held hope that Lila would be helpful. But the speed with which the sentry had laid her hands on Jennie struck him wrong. He made up his mind.

"Did you say *everyone's* out looking for her?"

"Yeah. This is the worst crime in the town's history!" She eyed Pike. "Who are *you?*"

"I'm a lookout, same as you—from Pleasant Ridge. I can take care of her. You're needed at the fire."

"What? Why?"

Pike wrested Jennie from her hold. "There's more people involved in this thing. Garr needs all the help he can get."

The woman looked at Pike and then back inside the church. "I don't know if I should—"

"I had dinner with Warden Talley just yesterday. She was talking about you. You want to make a name for yourself, tonight's the night to do it."

That got the sentry moving. Pike walked Jennie toward the entrance. The guard was halfway down the stairs to the plaza when she looked back. "Wait. You don't *know* my name!"

"*Jones,*" Jennie whispered.

"Jones is on the job," Pike said loudly. "That's what I'll tell the warden. Get to it!"

The sentry vanished, off to fulfill her ambitions.

Pike and Jennie entered the circular arena surrounding the rondure just as they had during the Jubilee. The skylights in the dome above didn't help much on this cloudy night, so instead chemical lamps like Garr and the lookouts had wielded illuminated the scene. Their emerald light made the hovering globe of the rondure look black and ominous.

Jennie pointed to the door Joe had been marched through during the Jubilee. "There."

Whereas the structure containing the rondure was stone, the attached outbuilding was wooden. And sealed. "I thought nobody locked their doors around here," Pike whispered.

"Except for cellars holding spacesuits," Jennie replied. She pulled a chain of lockpicks from her vest pocket and set to work. "My uncle—my real uncle—was a locksmith. He didn't have much to do."

"Looks like he taught you a thing or two."

"Yeah. Before he passed, he got Pa into the Menders." She smiled at Pike as they both heard a click. "We're in."

A wider room, with more of the same lighting. Pike picked up one of the lanterns. He realized it was the Menders' warehouse in microcosm: smaller, but more organized. "What is this, an evidence room?"

"I don't know what that is," Jennie said. "But some of this is ours." She gestured to a wide front table where items from the sanctum had been haphazardly piled. "This is the stuff they took out before the Sorry hit."

Pike found his helmet and the spacesuit. "I don't see the map."

"Look under that," she said, pointing to a bulky contraption. "But be careful shifting it."

"What is it?"

"That's one of the net weapons the Menders invented. Like the ones they used on you."

Pike gave it the respect it deserved in moving it. "Nothing."

In the more orderly section of the long room, many things were labeled with a short description. But some of the items had clearly been there for a while, judging from the dust and cobwebs.

"Why would they keep this?" Pike asked. "I'd think they'd destroy it."

"Rumor is, every few years when there's enough to fill a cart, the warden has it dumped somewhere. I think the Sorry gets it then."

"And the Skagarans trust the lookouts not to use any of this stuff in the meantime."

Jennie called out from before another table. "Look at this. An optivator!"

Pike had never heard the term. It appeared to be a brown box with a lens and hand crank.

She was amazed. "Pa told me about this thing. It takes pictures—and you get them right away."

Pike's eyes goggled. "Someone invented the Land Camera?"

"You can take pictures of more than just land."

"No, I mean the person who invented it— I mean, on Earth—" Pike gave up. "Never mind." So far as he could recall, the automatic camera was about a century in Dry River's future. Somewhere in the past four hundred years, someone had figured it out.

But the presence of it—and everything else here—surprised him. "If the Sorry hates technology, why wouldn't it come after this place?"

Someone unseen called out from the side of the room. "Y'all gonna jaw or you gonna let us out?"

Pike looked over to see a door. "Pa!" Jennie called out. She found the door locked, and immediately went to work on it. "Hang on!"

"What happened to you?" Joe asked. "Are you all right?"

"This is Christopher Pike," the captain said, holding the lantern close to Jennie's work. "I found her. I'm afraid the Sorry struck your warehouse."

He heard several muffled voices respond, talking over one another.

"Having some trouble here," Jennie said.

Pike looked at what she was working on. He decided it couldn't be that secure a door. *It's a church, not a Klingon prison.* "Step away." He set down the lantern, faced the door, and put his boot through it.

The Menders burst forth from the shattered doorway. Vicki glared up at Carpenter. "Why couldn't *you* do that?"

"Spaceman thinking," Joe said. "*I like it.*"

Carpenter looked at the busted frame, sheepish. "The Skagarans can fly. I expected a better lock."

Pike recognized the people he'd seen the other night but was surprised to see more people filing out, all average looking. In all, nine had been imprisoned. He looked to Cyrus. "Who are all these people?"

"Even the part-time Menders wanted to see the map," the journalist replied.

No wonder the secret was blown, Pike thought. "Where *is* the map?"

Joe stamped on the floor. "Rolled up in this leg of mine. It's a trick one that Carpenter made me. They ain't gettin' it!"

Pike was glad that this prosthetic didn't get burned up like Joe's previous one had. "You need to get out of here. Everyone's looking for me—or is over at the fire."

"*The fire.*" Weedaw looked at him, face fraught. "What was struck, Captain?"

Pike hated to say. "The whole block."

The others rumbled with shock. "*Everything?*" Vicki asked.

Jennie nodded. "The Sorry took it all."

Joe swore. "Funny how everything we got that they don't like ends up getting hit."

Pike had noticed that. "You think there's a connection?"

"You've seen how the rondures work. If they could create devices like that, who knows what else they could do? The whole damn Baffle is probably their doing!"

If so, Pike thought, Skagaran power could be beyond anything the Federation was capable of. Manipulating the laws of nature and the ability to connect the world in a psychic gestalt would put them well above many other civilizations.

Then again, the wooden door was just a wooden door.

"All those books," Cyrus muttered. "And my presses." He looked to Pike, sorrowful. "What will people do for a newspaper?"

"Same as they'll do without a gunsmith—or a blacksmith," Carpenter said.

"Or a barber," Jennie added. "Mochi's shop went up too."

"No!" Vicki blurted. She put her hand over her mouth. "She didn't have anything to do with us."

"I don't think the Sorry knew that," Pike replied. "To the extent it knows anything." It felt strange to discuss fire in that way, but he couldn't linger on the thought. "You all need to go, now!"

"Not empty-handed," one of the Menders that Pike hadn't met said. The white-haired man grabbed the optivator. "Let's take something back!"

Raiding the temple was not something Pike had in mind, but after his third objection he realized letting the others grab what they wanted was the only way to get them moving.

They had all filed into the main room with the rondure and were discussing next steps when Weedaw dropped what he was carrying. He stared at the rondure, seething. Then he gave an angry yell and leapt into the circle surrounding the floating sphere.

Vicki gasped. "What are you doing?"

"What someone should have long ago!" The normally meek blacksmith laid his hands on the giant ruby-colored marble and shoved.

Cyrus's eyes bugged at the act of sacrilege. "No one has ever touched it!"

Carpenter looked to him. "What are we waiting for? Come on!"

They went for it, as did several of the other Menders. Joe lifted his wooden leg over the circular basin and joined them at Weedaw's side.

"I can't push it off," Carpenter said, straining against the orb.

"Harder," Joe shouted. "We'll roll the damn thing out of here!"

"And then what?" Pike called out. "Go bowling?"

"*Heave!*" Carpenter said, veins bulging. But the rondure simply sat, motionless on its meter of air.

The group collapsed around it, winded. Weedaw looked deflated. "I couldn't even get it to spin." He waved his arm in the space underneath. "There's nothing here holding it!"

Pike wanted to tell them there were forces they did not understand—and ones his people didn't understand either. But there was no time. "Forget the rondure. You stay here, and the lookouts will be back."

"The lookouts," Joe snarled. "I'm willing to shoot it out with them. The Skagarans—everyone!"

Carpenter nodded. "Yeah, I'm about ready for a fight."

"With what?" Vicki asked, helping Joe to stand. "Your guns are all at home—which they're already searching. And the Sorry probably melted every gun I had!"

Pike gestured to the gear they'd dropped. "All you can do is get out of here."

"To where?" the white-haired man said, frantic. "Where, Captain? Are you going to take us to space?"

Pike put up his hands. "Nobody's talking about that—"

"We might as well," Cyrus said. "There's nothing for us here now!"

This was more than he'd bargained for. "We can't decide this now," Pike said. "Is there somewhere safe that you can go?"

Vicki and Cyrus looked at each other. "The livery yard," she said.

"Is the owner a Mender?"

"No, but Max is sweet on me. He'll take us in—and hide our stuff."

Weedaw sputtered. "B-but what about our homes?"

"Weedaw, I work next door to you," Vicki said. "If you spent more than ten hours a week at that house, I'd be stunned."

Carpenter, chastened by his failure at the rondure, was already gathering up the gear he'd dropped. "We're wasting time. Let's go!"

Pike breathed a sigh of relief as he watched most of the others exit. Only Joe and Jennie remained. Joe reached for his leg. "Let me get you your map," he said.

"No time." Pike would just have to stick closely to him.

"Look," Jennie said. A fiery orange glow filled the room. "The rondure!"

Pike saw that the giant ball had started revolving, seemingly of its own volition. He remembered that it had done that before, just before the Jubilee began. "Do you think it's an incoming call?"

Jennie nodded. "That is how it starts."

Joe gritted his teeth. "Drayko!" He hobbled toward a nearby container and took a crimson *zazic* from it. "Dammit, I'm gonna give him a piece of my mind. He's meddled in my life enough."

Pike's eyes widened. "Joe, that's not a good idea."

As her father approached one of the slots on the floor connected to the rondure, Jennie put up her hand. "Pa, don't!"

"Stay out of this, Jennie. From what the captain says, your mother could have lived. Your brother, too—if the Skagarans had let us learn something!"

She looked to Pike. "Is that true?"

There was no answer *but* the truth. "Yes. But this isn't the time." Pike shook his head and advanced toward Joe. "They could be back at any second." He started prying Joe's hands off the *zazic*.

Joe released his hold on the object's other horn—and in the process it slipped down just a centimeter, such that the other end of the staff lodged in the notch in the floor while Pike still had hold of his side.

Pike thought for a moment he was blacking out. But the rondure was there, shining yellow before him—and as its glow waned, he could see a figure walking toward him.

The old gardener smiled and spoke in a craggy voice he'd heard before. "Christopher Pike of *Starship Enterprise*, I presume. My name is Drayko." He bowed. "Delighted to make your acquaintance."

CHAPTER 30

THE AUDIENCE

"General Drayko," Pike said.

"It's *Conservator* General. Nothing martial about my role, I assure you." A chair materialized near Pike. "Sit. I know it is later there than it is here."

"I'll stand." Pike knew that the motion was only in his mind's eye anyway. He saw that Jennie and Joe weren't in the vision. He hoped they had sense enough to leave.

There were no special effects in this call. Just a canvas, blank but for the chair. "I was at your Jubilee. Interesting show. Seems different today."

"I can attend to that." Drayko looked to one side and spoke a word to someone unseen—and the two were suddenly in a solarium, surrounded by plants. "The setting is not from this instant, of course, but is a genuine location in my home. I take pride in things that grow."

"Looks nice," Pike said. "How do you project it?"

"My tireless assistant operates my rondure with me, and aids with the visual impressions. She does fine work." He looked up. "What do you think of our planet?"

"It's been full of surprises."

"Not bad ones, I hope?"

Pike was diplomatic. "It's quite a place. You've been able to do a lot."

"It's been the work of all Skagarans—and the other residents of Epheska— for nearly a millennium, to use your reckoning on Earth."

"Cultivators of worlds."

"Singular." Drayko's lip curled slightly. "One world only. You have seen far more planets than I, Captain." He looked up, and stars appeared.

"I take it you know my name from the people that were detained."

"Something like that." Drayko looked up. "A ship called *Enterprise*. What a marvel it must be, traveling in the heavens."

Pike knew Weedaw had told the lookouts about his origins. "Were you surprised to learn I was here?"

"We detected your vessel as it crashed. Sudden arrivals are not unprecedented." Drayko turned to examine a flowering plant. "I understand you have missing friends."

Pike watched him cautiously. "That's correct."

Drayko turned from what he was tending and opened his hands wide. "I will help you find them. This planet has many dangers, as I expect you have heard."

"I have." Pike's eyes narrowed. "You don't mind helping us? I've been here long enough to see you have a closed society."

"For its own protection," Drayko said, walking past the whirling rondure to another table. "I'm sure you understand it's not in our interest to have uninvited visitors. It upsets the balance of our civilization."

Pike's brow furrowed. "As has happened here in Havenbrook, you mean."

"Just so." Drayko took up a pair of cutters and began snipping at what looked like a tiny tree. "You've been here three days, and you see what has happened already."

"I didn't mean to cause any of this. The Federation doesn't believe in interfering. It's codified in our Prime Directive." The Skagarans *had* been starfaring and there was a chance Lila had explained her origins to them, so Pike didn't see any harm in mentioning that the Federation was an association of planets. "Places your people may have heard of. Tellar, Andoria, Vulcan." He peered at Drayko. "And I know you know Earth."

"Ah, yes. Home of the humans."

"You came to 'rescue' people from our planet." He thought of the residents of North Star. "More than once, in fact."

"There's no need to thank me."

"*Thank* you?"

A slight grin crossed Drayko's face. "From what my predecessors have written, few races were happier to leave their world and join our project. You must have seen the delight expressed at the Jubilee. I do not see every face when I project my little talks, but I see enough to know the humans are satisfied."

Not all of them. Pike watched as Drayko kept snipping away at his little tree. "The people who helped me," the captain said. "I don't want them to get in trouble. It was their misfortune they found me."

"From what I understand, they had been up to mischief well before your arrival—and quite a lot of it. And we have known of the acts of some individuals for many years." The Skagaran waved with indifference. "But these are minor infractions. They will be forgotten, and the world will return to normal."

"To stasis, you mean." Pike nodded to the plant. "Like your tree there. Frozen in size."

Drayko looked back at him in mild surprise. "You know horticulture, Captain?"

"On our world, plants like that are called bonsai. They're pruned and tied back to prevent growth."

"Ah. Here it is called the *yawfa* method. There is more involved, of course—but it allows us to preserve the characteristics of the original in a size that is supportable." He clipped off an entire branch. "When the past works, there is no reason to change it."

"And if some want to?"

"That's a discussion that must take place within our own society." Drayko put down the clippers and faced Pike. "Surely you must respect that, if your beliefs are as you describe."

Pike nodded.

"I do not think Epheska will ever seek relations with those beyond the nebula. I abhor the idea, in fact. But should it ever happen, it will be *our* decision. Is that acceptable to your Federation?"

"Of course. That's all anyone ever has to say."

"Good. Then let me help you find your friends." He removed his garden gloves. "Tell me about them."

Pike thought carefully. He needed to inquire about *Braidwood* as well as his own people, but he didn't want to betray Lila, knowing that she had chosen to stay. He also wondered how invasive this gestalt was. *Was it even possible to lie here?*

Then again, Drayko was asking a lot of questions. Pike decided if the general was able to read his mind, none of them would be necessary.

He started slowly. "First, there's the matter of *Braidwood*. It was an exploratory vessel which arrived here a year ago."

"Ah, yes. I did say we had visitors from time to time. We detected that crash site, just as we found yours."

"What can you tell me about it?"

"Very bad. Tremendous wreckage. I can't imagine people wanting to travel at such speeds." He focused on Pike. "Which brings us to your ship. I can tell you no one was found near its wreckage—and it is far from where you are now. How is this possible?"

Not knowing whether he should mention the existence of transporter technology, Pike hedged. "I was able to escape. My friends may have too. There were three of them."

He gave their basic descriptions. He didn't see any harm in that now.

"Two females and one male," Drayko recapped. "Human in appearance."

"Mostly."

"Their names?"

Pike paused. "Sorry to interrupt, but I have a question."

"Anything."

"Finding my friends is just the first part. We also need to find our way off your planet. I expect *Enterprise* is considering options, but I wanted to see if you had any."

"Are you asking if we have a secret rocket that defeats the Baffle?"

"Do you?"

Drayko chuckled. "No, and it is just as well. I might sneak aboard it and slip away when my duties tax me." He shook his head. "No, ironically, the one transport we had with the capacity to deliver settlements to the surface vanished on a trip to Earth."

Pike's eyes widened. "I believe my people found that vessel. It crashed, almost four hundred of our years ago."

"As we always suspected. A shame, but we were near our limit here anyway. Epheska is vast, and there are many places for our peoples to expand to. But the phase where we populate the world from the outside is long past."

Pike was still struggling with the news. "That really was your *only* transport?"

"The Epheska project was not some massive movement, involving all Skagarans. It was as you saw in the Jubilee—a last-ditch attempt to salvage a better way, drawing upon the few hundred people who would agree with us."

"And the thousands of people you could appropriate from elsewhere."

Drayko raised a white eyebrow. "You make it sound as if we weren't doing them a favor."

"You didn't exactly give them a choice, did you?"

"We saved their lives. More importantly, we saved their *ways* of life. Those would have been ruined soon enough, just as on our world."

"Technological development doesn't have to cause harm."

"Yet it does. For example, take the people from Dry River."

You already did, Pike wanted to say.

"Those humans told us they feared a conflict was looming in the lands they had left behind. That it might even break out in a war that could last as much as a year."

"Or four," Pike recalled. "It happened."

"Tell me, did the technology of war advance during this conflict?"

Pike's mind went from ironclads to Gatling guns to submarines. "Yes. Yes, it did."

"And were there even greater wars to follow, in which the weapons grew even more destructive?"

Pike expected his face showed the answer.

"And that is simply war, and not the everyday demands that regular life places upon a poor, defenseless planet." Drayko shook his head. "Oh, no. The people of Dry River were already refugees, my dear captain. They were already in flight. We just took them the rest of the way."

It seemed a place for debate to stop. Pike had made what little case he could for the Menders. He was the intruder here. He needed to play by the rules. "What will happen now?"

"I'll have you brought here to Om Mataya. Your friends, as well, when they are located."

"And we'll wait there for *Enterprise* to find a way to rescue us."

"No, you will remain with us forever. Your presence suggests that even *Enterprise* is no match for the Baffle."

"I expect they'll find other ways."

"I expect them to leave." Drayko snapped his fingers, and the greenhouse was replaced by darkness, lit only by the rotating rondure. He crossed his arms. "They must leave, and never return. We learned from the Strooh blacksmith that you had crafted a message seen from space. You will send another one, ordering them to depart."

The message too? Weedaw had certainly spilled his guts, Pike thought. "My people will not give up on us."

"If you send the right message, they will. Perhaps if you tell them that others will suffer if they don't depart."

Pike froze. "Why would I send anything like that?"

"For the same reason. These friends of yours, for example. My forgiveness is bountiful, but there can be other outcomes."

"Their businesses have already been destroyed. What more—"

Pike stopped. Eye to astral-projected eye with Drayko, he understood what kind of person he was dealing with.

He remembered Kiley 279, where he'd been forced to play hardball. "Threats won't work with me, General. There are things my ship can do—"

"Against the Baffle? Nonsense. A *Constitution*-class ship has no more power against it than any other sort of vessel we've seen." Drayko scowled. "*No. Power.*"

Pike took a step back—and reflected on what he'd said to the Menders. "Wait. How did you know *Enterprise* was *Constitution* class? That's not on the spacesuit emblem—and I never told the others here."

A new voice: "You told *me.*"

Pike turned. "Lila?"

She stepped out of the blackness and into his mind's eye.

"Welcome to the call, Warden." Drayko bowed and watched as Pike's childhood friend stepped to his side. "I take it you two are already acquainted."

CHAPTER 31

THE TURNABOUT

When a chair appeared this time, it looked more comfortable. It was Drayko who sat in it. "I thank you for alerting me to this situation, Warden Talley. Are things in hand in Havenbrook?"

"Getting there," Lila said. "I came back to the temple with some lookouts." She gestured to Pike. "You shouldn't have come in here, Christopher. This place is special."

"I was helping my friends," Pike said. His eyes were locked on her—and full of disbelief. "*You* told him?"

Drayko clasped his hands together and smiled. "It's as I said, Captain. The people we rescued from Earth were only too happy to join our project. That extends to a recent arrival, the warden here."

Pike understood. "So he knows you're from *Braidwood*."

"And he knows I believe in what we're all doing here."

"Are there more survivors? Did they go to work for him as well?"

"You've got it all wrong," Lila said. "I'm not working for him. I'm working for everyone."

As she spoke, Drayko waved his hand—and at once they were surrounded by thousands of cheering people. A replay, Pike figured, of the Jubilee.

Lila walked about the rondure, facing the crowd. She took off her hat in respect. "This world *works*, Christopher. Maybe not for some, but it works for most. I can't let you mess it up."

"'Mess it up'?" Pike walked over to her. "I told Drayko I was leaving, as soon as *Enterprise* could figure out a way. How does that mess anything up?"

She spun and spoke into his face. "Word up there is going to get out. Someone will come. Maybe prospectors looking for easy pickings, if they can only figure out a way to beat the Baffle. There'll be no gold rush on my watch."

"I won't let that happen, Lila. Starfleet and the Federation—"

"Don't control a damn thing." She took a breath, and her anger dissipated. She reached out for his hand. "I gave you a chance earlier, Christopher. Here's another. You're on Epheska to stay. You, and your crew. But it's okay. Do as I do, and you can be a part of it."

Drayko gestured amiably. "That would be acceptable. As you can see, Captain, I have already accepted it once." He nodded toward Lila. "Warden Talley's title was no bribe, I can assure you. She has earned her position with her devotion. She sees our project for what it is."

Pike studied Lila, wondering what had changed in her. It wasn't like her to cross the stars to begin with. And now this.

He squeezed her hand. "I'm sorry, Lila. But I've already been to a planet where I was expected to stay, living the life they wanted for me. I didn't like it then, and I don't now."

Her imploring look turned to an angry glower. "That's your old life talking. It's done. It's over. It's—"

Lila vanished.

Pike looked at his hand. He'd squeezed her wrist, sure, but he wasn't expecting her to disappear.

Drayko clearly wasn't, either. "Warden Talley?"

"What happened?"

"I do not know. Her contact with the *zazic* must have been interrupted."

Really? "Is that all it takes?" Pike smirked. "In that case—hailing frequencies closed."

In the real world, he released his hold on the *zazic* he'd wrested from Joe. The coliseum disappeared, to be replaced by the green lighting of the church. The rondure, before him, abruptly stopped spinning and went dim.

Darker, but not quieter. His eyes adjusting, Pike looked at the commotion surrounding him. The Menders had all returned—the ones he knew, and the others—and a group of them were in the process of trying to relocate a mass of writhing individuals, tangled in multiple nets.

Pike had to look at the mob for several seconds before he understood. There were three individuals in the mass of netting—including, he thought, Reedy, returned from his reconnaissance. "Are those all lookouts?"

"You bet!" Joe said, triumphant. "Our people were hangin' about outside—and saw 'em come in. The stinkers tried to grab me and Jennie—but the Menders got *them*!"

Pike squinted. "The net launcher?"

Joe hooted with glee. "*Twang!* We caught 'em!"

"Christopher, make them stop!" Lila shouted from behind him.

Pike turned to see her struggling, her arms pinned by the muscle-bound Carpenter. It made sense: she'd found the captain beside the rondure and joined the astral conversation. She would have been an easy target to grab. "Let her go, Carpenter."

"Not a chance. She's a warden!"

"You're all in big trouble," Lila said. "You know that, don't you?"

Joe blew a razzberry. "I've had my fill of the lot of you! Grab her keys, Jennie!"

Pike turned to see the gaggle of Menders forcing the bound lookouts through the open doorway to the evidence room. Jennie, who'd picked that door's lock once, left the group. She passed Pike and reached for the key ring on Lila's belt.

Lila spoke to her as she went for it. "Don't do this, Jennie. You're ruining your life."

"No disrespect, Miz Talley—but save it for your sheep." Jennie plucked the keys off and examined them. "It ought to be one of these."

Carpenter lifted Lila off the floor and began walking toward the open door. Pike moved along with them, trying to make the passage less rough for her. It had all gotten out of control, and the Menders weren't listening anymore.

But *she* might.

"Lila, I didn't mean for this to happen," he said. "But they need to leave—and so do I." He had a thought. "*Come with us!*"

"Where? To space?" Fury flared in her eyes. "It will *never happen*, Christopher. I wish I could find a way to get that through your thick skull."

"You'll have time to think about it," Carpenter said. He toted her into the evidence room and set her down.

There was no changing anyone's minds, Pike saw—at least not at the moment. It couldn't be helped. He called out, "Lila, I'm sorry about this. I'll find you again and we'll sort this out!"

He heard her swearing but did not see it. Carpenter backed out, blocking the opening until Jennie closed the door.

After she found the correct key, the Zoldaari tested the door. "At least this one's made of better wood!"

At the entrance, Cyrus signaled. "Coast is clear. We've got a few minutes at most."

The others went on their way, heading for the rendezvous at the livery yard. Pike and Joe were the last to leave—and were almost to the exit when their shadows appeared on the wall before them. Behind them, the rondure was spinning. "Here we go again," Joe said.

"It's just Drayko, calling back to see where Lila went."

"Who's Lila?"

"The warden. You don't remember her name?"

"We ain't friendly!"

Pike's impulse was to leave it alone. But it occurred to him that Drayko might be putting out an all-points bulletin—possibly in another concert setting that showed how many more wardens there were. Knowing how many settlements existed and how many groups of lookouts might be arrayed against him would come in handy. He'd only have to pop in for a second or two.

"I might as well see what I'm up against," Pike said, walking back to where the *zazic* was still stuck in the floor. "This will just take a moment."

Pike touched the device—and was back again in the astral plane, black except for the warm glow of the rondure. He looked about, unable to see anything. *Prank call*, he thought—or, worse, some mental trap he wasn't aware of. It was dangerous to linger, in any event. He was about to release the *zazic* and complete his escape when a voice called out from behind him.

"*Captain!*"

Pike stopped. It wasn't Drayko's voice. He turned.

Spock emerged from the darkness. "It is agreeable to see you," the science officer said. "I am aware of your situation, and may be able to offer a solution. . . ."

CHAPTER 32

THE PLEDGE

It was late at night before Celarius returned with Una to Om Mataya. He'd done his best for her, checking all the approaches from the settlements to the forest. Her friends were nowhere to be seen below. A roadblock had been her reluctance to give him their names; he could simply have sent word via the rondures to the towns, to see if anyone had seen these people. No matter his assurances, however, she was still afraid of getting them into trouble.

It didn't matter to him. It just meant more time with Una—and Celarius was already certain that her companions had perished in the forest. It was the answer that made the most sense. She seemed brave and resourceful, and it was no surprise that she had been the one to survive. But he hadn't wanted to raise that possibility with her. It was already hanging like a pall over her, especially on the chilly ride back once the sun had set.

A cold trip across the terrace to the Garden House and a warm meal later, they were in the library's map room. Like the day's venture, it had been at Una's initiative. It wasn't *the* map room in Om Mataya, of course, but he doubted his father would admit a newcomer to that. This one had the more ancient drawings, those from Epheska's discovery and from the various First Days of all the arriving refugees here. It also had exceptionally comfortable chairs and a ready supply of relaxing drinks, both of which Celarius welcomed.

"So many settlements," she said, paging through large sheets while sitting at a broad table. "Have you seen them all?"

"I doubt any Skagaran has, even after the development of the sentinels." He poured himself another ale. "The world is vast—many unseen places. That's why I like it."

"You use the rondures to tie it all together. Could I use it?"

It was the fourth time she'd asked, although never so directly. "The rondures are how my father talks to you, the people. He is here. What could you need it for?"

"I'm just curious. A communications device—one that works here, despite the Baffle. I'm wondering who else it could reach."

Celarius shook his head. She had been wonderful company, but her questions sometimes confounded him. "I suppose we could ask my father."

"Ask me what?"

Celarius and Una looked up to see Drayko entering the library. His father appeared a little tired, to be expected at this hour. Una started to get up to bow; Celarius waved for her to keep her seat. "She had a question for you," he said.

"Actually, I have one for her," Drayko said, approaching the table. "Una, you said there were three others you're missing?"

Celarius sighed. "More than once, since you've met her." The man was so preoccupied, he never listened for very long.

She intervened before he could say anything else. "Yes, three others."

"I thought so." Drayko glanced at the maps Una was looking at, and then stepped over to the service table to pour himself a drink. "It's the most amazing story. The other day, I saw a spaceship in the sky."

That got her attention—and also that of Celarius. "You told me about this already," he said. "The thing that crashed on Nerathos."

"Where's that?" Una asked.

"An island far to the east," Celarius said. He peered at his father. "You told me it was completely destroyed. That no one could have survived the crash."

Drayko nodded. "There are apparently more ways out of a space vehicle than we thought—even one going that fast."

Una looked puzzled. "You, uh, found someone?"

"We did indeed. I even spoke to him, just a short time ago via the rondure. His name is Christopher Pipe."

Celarius saw his father staring right at Una as she responded. "What was that name again?" she asked.

"I'm sorry. I meant *Pike*. Captain Pike from the *Starship Enterprise*." Drayko watched her. "I hope I got *that* name right." He raised an eyebrow. "Did I, Una?"

Struck dumb, she stared at Drayko.

Celarius didn't understand the whole exchange. "She's not one of your wardens you can make uncomfortable, Father. What's this about?"

"I was hoping that Una would tell *us*. Especially as Captain Pike has been in communication with *Enterprise*." Drayko saw a response from her this time—and cracked a smile of his own. "I apologize for my bit of fun. But you match the description the captain gave. Can I tell him I have found one of his friends?"

Una blushed a little. "I guess there's no need to pretend." This time, she did stand up. "*Enterprise*'s first officer Una Chin-Riley, at your service."

Drayko brightened even more. "Glad to make your acquaintance."

Celarius goggled. "What goes on here?"

"Our friend here arrived in the forest the hard way—from above."

"You're from space!" Celarius said. He was seldom caught off guard, but this was one of those times. Now he stood up too. "When were you going to tell me?"

She put a hand before her. "I am sorry. I'm not supposed to reveal my origins in certain circumstances."

Drayko nodded. "I heard about it from the captain. The Prime Directive. It's about protecting the peoples they're visiting from the shock of an alien arrival." He offered his hand to her. "I approve of it—and also of the care you took."

She accepted the handshake. "Thanks for understanding. I had your people's well-being in mind."

"Not everyone would have taken such care," Drayko replied. In a lower register, he added, "Someone else might have made a dreadful mess of things."

Celarius was still on the earlier revelation. "You're from space." He looked to the window facing the night. One by one, her more unusual questions from the past few days made sense to him. "That's why you wouldn't tell me their names. You knew if I called the settlements, they'd say they never heard of your friends."

"There would have been more questions then. And I needed to search."

"Some naturalist I am. I can't even tell what planet someone's from!"

Una shook her head. "Don't feel bad—or be angry. I'm trained to adapt to new situations. You could say it's in my blood."

He let out a breath. "You *did* adapt." He chuckled in spite of himself.

Drayko continued with his disarming ways. "You needn't be embarrassed, Una. If you have learned anything about us, you know none of us are from this planet."

She nodded. "It is an amazing story. I'd like to know more, now that I can just ask about things. But first—"

"You wish to know about the captain. I have ordered that he be brought here to Om Mataya as soon as the winds are right."

She seemed excited to hear that. "Can I speak to him? Over a rondure?"

Drayko pursed his lips. "He's not near one. Not anymore. But you are not alone here—and we will help you find your other two friends . . ." He appeared to reach for their names.

"Spock and Uhura."

"Just so. I am terrible with names, you see. In any event, I don't think you should go out flying yourself again. From here I can put the whole resources of Epheska into the search, and you can help organize it." He grinned at her. "Ah, I understand that now. As a first officer, you organize things!"

She beamed at him. "Thank you both very much. Once we've found my friends, we can work on getting out of your hair." She bowed. "I'll see you both tomorrow. Good night."

Celarius watched her exit, more amazed by Una—he still preferred to think of her by that name—than ever. *From outer space. Imagine it!*

Then he saw Drayko had watched her go as well. He knew the gleam in his father's eye. "What's it all about?"

Drayko stepped over to pour himself another drink. "What can you mean?"

"You aren't terrible with names. You've memorized the family trees of everyone who's ever annoyed you."

"It's as you learned the other night. We've been following up on the spaceship. Tonight, I got the information I was looking for—and Una just provided even more."

"Is this connected to that other spaceship crash a while back?"

"That is unclear." Drayko took a seat across the table from his son. He glanced at the maps Una had been poring over before pushing them away. "Her group is from Starfleet, the military arm of an organization of several planets—one of which was Earth."

"Home of the humans." Celarius stared. "Is that why they're here? To find the earlier ship?" He had a more distressing thought. "Or are they after the humans who live here?"

"I don't care. I told her the truth. I will have Pike delivered here." He sipped his drink. "But there are complications. It might take a little longer."

Celarius didn't mind that idea.

"Yes, I definitely want her staying around," Drayko said. "The way to get all four of them here is to have one of them here already."

"You're talking about her like she's leverage or something."

"Perish the thought." He raised his glass. "To the project!"

CHAPTER 33

THE MUSTER

They had dispersed from Havenbrook the night before, most finding their horses and riding away in different directions. Some Menders had returned to their homes briefly, as there weren't enough lookouts to check on all their residences at once. By dawn, however, word arrived that there soon would be reinforcements, called in from Pleasant Ridge and some of the surrounding towns. The law had come to Havenbrook.

True to Vicki's word, Max at the livery outside town had taken her friends in, albeit a bit nervously—behind the closed doors of a complex of barns and stables large enough to hide not just the Menders, but their horses. By midafternoon, Christopher Pike estimated the number in hiding had reached thirty, as various spouses and relatives had been contacted and persuaded to sneak out to Max's yard. The cover story for several families had been a picnic, which explained the large baskets they were carrying. Had the lookouts searched any of them, they would have found firearms and other hastily collected personal items.

The Menders of Havenbrook were clearing out. The *Enterprise* captain was both cause and catalyst—and the destination was something he'd gotten from yet another spaceman. Pike commenced one of the stranger briefings he'd ever given: standing under the high roof of the stable, beside the precious map held by Cyrus's young daughters.

"I didn't have long to speak to Lieutenant Spock," Pike said. "I didn't find out why he was at another rondure. But Drayko put out a bulletin about me being at Havenbrook the second after our call ended—and Spock happened to be at another rondure then. That's when he called me up directly."

"How does he know how to do that?" someone shouted.

Pike shrugged. "He's Spock. That won't make sense to you now, but it will. Trust me." He paced toward the chart. "Spock doesn't have a map like mine, but he described a place he thought we should meet up at. It's on the tip of a peninsula—shaped, he says, like the boot of Italy."

"Boots we got!" The shout came from Cabrini, one of the other Menders the lookouts had swept up. "But what's an Italy?"

"Something that looks like this." Pike pointed to a small spot on one of the coastlines on the map, well to the southeast of their current location. "There's nothing else that looks like it. The problem is, we'll have quite a ride ahead of us. But Spock says he can accommodate all of us and get us to safety."

"Where?" Carpenter asked.

"I didn't have time to ask."

The listeners buzzed. "Maybe they've gotten to him," Weedaw said.

"Like they got to *you*," Joe muttered.

"I was scared!" The blacksmith appealed to Pike. "How do you know this Spock was telling the truth?"

"Again," Pike said, "he's Spock. You'll see what I mean."

Pike looked down. This was a difficult ask for these people. They weren't the settlers of the Old West. They were the settled—or resettled—and the lives of their immediate ancestors were all here, within a small radius.

"I understand you're concerned," he said. "I don't know what awaits us either. All I know is I believe Drayko when he suggests harm will come to you if I don't surrender." He looked up. "That leaves me with two choices. I can turn myself over, or I can take you someplace where he can't get you." He placed his hands before him, palms upright. "It's up to you. But it's got to be unanimous, or it won't work."

"I already know," Joe called out. "You heard what I heard. They already took all my animals, 'cept the ones we rode here. They've taken my farm. I say we ride!"

"I need to hear from someone besides Joe," Pike said.

He spoke with the listeners, one by one, hearing their concerns—but also hearing commitment.

Finally, it came to Weedaw, the one person Pike was least sure of.

"What's it to be, Weedaw?"

He put an orange finger tentatively in the air. "Can I look at that map?"

"Sure." Pike watched as Havenbrook's former blacksmith approached. "The other side's a close-up view."

Weedaw looked at both sides before speaking. "I thought as much. Our route would take us near Iklik, where I'm from."

"You know the way, then."

"I know my brother and my sister. And I know they and several of their friends are Menders too." He clasped his hands together and swallowed. "I will do this—but I would like the chance to bring them with us."

Joe growled, disgusted. "Weedaw, we don't got room!"

Pike blinked. "Why not?" He gestured to the vehicles they'd been loading. "It's a wagon train. They just follow along." He looked around. "That is how it works on this planet, right?"

The others laughed. Pike took out a pocket watch he'd been given that afternoon. "We'd better get underway. Time's a-wasting."

Pike exhaled as he saw the others rush into action. Cyrus's daughters gingerly presented him the map.

The loading began. Pike was no Number One, but he organized as best he could, attempting to get riders and gear into as few wagons as possible, trying to make sure food and feed were available for the journey. The work was hard, but it had the benefit of taking his mind off what had happened.

They'd considered reaching out to Mochi—possibly offering her a place among them. But it was too soon, too raw, and they'd already heard that the barber blamed her sinful neighbors for all that had happened. There was no way to fix that now.

Another problem was Lila. If Pike left her here to live on this planet, he didn't want to leave things as they were between them. The only good thing about the end of their earlier friendship had been that there had been no ugly argument to look back on. Now that was gone, because of a philosophical conflict light-years away from their original homes.

At last, the Menders and their families were ready to go—and someone else had something to present to him.

"Got something for you," Joe said. "For what you've done. Beller over there worked it up, just while he was sittin' here this afternoon—he's the clockmaker."

Pike recognized the elderly man as the father of one of the Menders he'd broken out of the church prison. "You already gave me the watch. That's plenty."

"Just look," Beller said. The contraption he held had apparently been cobbled together from various spare parts—and included clamps gripping something familiar.

"That's the container for the viridium," Pike said. Joe had asked to borrow it a couple of hours earlier, but he hadn't said why. The captain had seen no urgent need for it and had agreed.

"Watch this," Beller said. He pushed a spring-loaded lever, and the clamshell package snapped shut. Toggling another lever brought it back open again. He did it quickly in sequence.

"Wait," Pike said. He fished the viridium patch out of his pocket. "I put this in there—" He placed the item in the small container and watched as Beller triggered it open and shut.

"It was Jennie's idea," Joe said. "Since that box prevents the valium—"

"Viridium," she corrected.

"—validium from being detected by your spaceship, she figured maybe you could make someone notice that the thing was there one second and gone the next."

"In a pattern. Like sending a smoke signal," she said. "But using a box and a weird little patch."

Pike was beside himself. He shook his head. "Jennie, you've just invented an alternative to subspace."

"Oh," she said. "Is that good?"

Pike laughed. "I'll say. I can send extended messages to *Enterprise*. Without all the lumber, that is." He placed it safely aboard the lead wagon—and then helped Jennie board it before opening the barn doors.

"Everyone mount up!" she shouted. "It's a wagon train to outer space!"

Not exactly how I would have put it, Pike thought, but it would do in a pinch. "Let's move 'em out!"

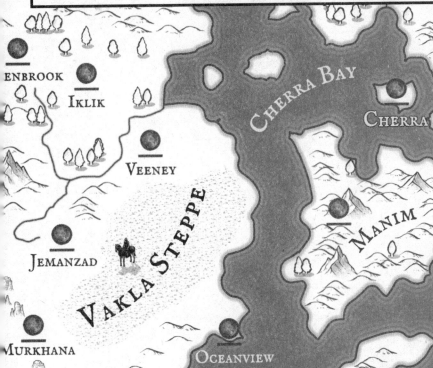

Part Three
OLD SOLDIERS

ENBROOK

IKLIK

VEENEY

JEMANZAD

VAKLA STEPPE

MURKHANA

OCEANVIEW

LEEJO

LEEJO PT.

CHERRA BAY

CHERRA

MANIM

OKUA SEA

ZEVAYNE

AGAR

CHAPTER 34

THE HUNTERS

"Come on! Where are you going?"

It had been days since Lila Talley had left her flock and hound in the care of another local shepherd, but she felt like she was herding again. A rider passed her, angling away in another direction. Lila wheeled Buckshot around and spurred him on. She rode expertly along a slope, passing the panicked rider and beating her to the notch in the valley.

Lila felt she shouldn't have to head her own people off at the pass, but that was what was required. "What's going on?"

The purple-skinned woman on the palomino was ragged and breathless. "I'm leaving!"

"You're a lookout, right? You're not one of mine, but I'm still a warden!"

"I'm going home." The Avgana female pointed to the southern horizon. "It's crazy up there!"

"What happened?"

The fearful rider took a breath—and kicked her horse, charging over the rise. Lila followed her to the top of it, only to see the two other lookouts she'd already lost track of heading away.

"*It's that damn Christopher Pike!*" Her father used to say it when the kid repeatedly came around, looking to ride. James Talley had been joking. Lila wasn't. Not now. She gritted her teeth and turned back south.

It had only been a few days since the chat on the porch with her old friend, sipping whiskey and swatting bugs under a sky from a dream. That was how life was supposed to be, could be, on Epheska. It had been a good evening. Lila wasn't in the market for a permanent companion, and the two of them had never been like that anyway, her parents' playful paranoia notwithstanding. Christopher seemed to understand that. As long as he did, the prospect for more nice evenings existed, and she'd have welcomed them.

That was before he lied to her.

The construction work at the mill was a lie, a signal of some kind to his ship. He'd entered the confidences of the local trouble seekers. He'd given them ideas and gotten them out of custody. And now he had taken them all out on—*what?*

A getaway to nowhere? It was an exercise in futility, and it had left poor Haven-brook shell-shocked with many of its established citizens on the run.

For all Lila knew, his purported arrival in search of the *Braidwood* crew was also a lie. Where Starfleet explored, exploiters followed. Pike's kind of people simply couldn't accept that a planet like Epheska existed, defended by magical fire and the miracle of the Baffle. No, they would insist on figuring out how those things worked. What caused them. Whether they could be replicated for their own weaponry—and whether they could be defeated.

And then they'd move in. In six months, Havenbrook would be host to a Tellarite strip mine. But at least there'd be an imported coffee vendor nearby.

Pike's wagon train—and it was surely his idea—had left at dusk the day after the Havenbrook fire, exactly when her exhausted lookouts returned to the church to debrief the first reinforcements from out of town. Word had later gotten to her of the gathering at the livery yard, whose owner—Max, loyal to Vicki—continued to play dumb about what had happened to fourteen of his horses, several wagons and coaches, multiple rifles, and an indeterminate amount of feed and supplies.

Christopher hadn't tried to cover his tracks in the beginning, opting instead for speed. She didn't know what he sought to the southeast, but that was clearly his direction. Her problem was a posse of lookouts couldn't form up and just go, like in a movie. Not with the harvest coming in, and animals to tend. It required preparation. She'd been forced to begin the chase with the riders with the fewest local responsibilities—and that meant the young and the green, when it didn't mean the dim and the unreliable.

She judged that many of the fleeing pursuers she'd met, like the Avgana woman, belonged to the latter population. The main body of her force encountered one advance scout after another in full retreat—or showing signs of having been completely undone by Pike and his so-called Menders. Reedy, when they'd found him, was naked in a creek, trying to scrub off the "space jelly" he'd supposedly been doused with. To hear him explain it, he'd gotten close to the trailing wagon when Pike's cohorts lobbed a bucket of something at him. It sounded like bacon fat, but there was no telling him that.

The fugitives had cannibalized fences to make caltrops, loaded shotguns with rock salt to keep riders at bay, and had devised several ingenious traps when the chasers got too close. Several of the covered wagons had served as miniature versions of the ill-fated Mender warehouse, cooking up nefarious surprises for the pursuers.

Their behavior had been even worse when Drayko tried to bring a couple of the sentinels into play. The winds were coming up, presaging an early winter, and on the Vakla Steppe the airships couldn't stay on station at all. But even when they got close, Pike's cohorts had fired warning shots with rifles, keeping the sentinels at least a kilometer away. It was hard for Lila to believe that anyone would take a shot at the guardian angels of Epheska's population, but nothing surprised her now.

What havoc the retreating Menders had been able to wreak was minor mischief, however, compared to what her more seasoned riders were contending with now. She saw some of them up ahead, riding in ragged formation, as if from a rout.

As the others passed her, Garr pulled up. He looked grayer than usual. "Warden," he growled.

"What's happening?"

"Don't you know? I thought you knew everything."

A charmer on a Jubilee day, Garr had tried her patience lately. At her request and in the name of societal stability, Drayko hadn't shared the fact that she was from off-planet. It had made her normal life possible, while increasing her acceptance by the other lookouts. But Garr had chafed after she leapfrogged over him to become warden.

Now, instead of seeing her demoted due to Pike's breakout, Garr had to cope with the Skagarans' decision to place her in charge of the overall hunt. It was no reward, she knew; Drayko understood she had a better handle on Pike's thinking, and what he might be planning, than anyone. But if Garr wasn't counting on serving a warden twenty years his junior, field marshal was an even bigger blow.

She shook off his hostility. "Tell me what you saw."

The older man coughed and shook his head. "Pike skunked us."

Lila knew Epheska had no skunks, but the word had stuck around. "What happened?"

"We'd come upon the wagon train when this *thing* came down from the sky. It was a little ball, moving fast."

Oh, no. "Did it blow up?"

"No, about a mile up, it let out this big cape, and floated on down. Like my kitchen tablecloth."

A parachute. Lila frowned. Yes, Pike's people would have figured out that clockwork timers could be used to trigger manual effects. "What then?"

"So it's in front of us. Some of the lookouts start taking target practice at it. And I don't know if one of them hit it, because there was this big *snap*." He coughed some more. "The next thing you know, there was this orange smoke coming from it."

"Smoke?"

"Yeah. It was like the Sorry, I guess. It didn't hurt none of us who rode into it, but we couldn't see a thing, and the horses couldn't wait to turn around."

Lila put her hand over her forehead. *A smoke bomb.* Somehow, the people aboard *Enterprise* were tracking Pike's movements—and had a good idea of what kind of trouble he was in. She wondered if the starship could even see the pursuers. It didn't seem possible from such an incredible distance, but Starfleet's capabilities were something she'd never cared to learn about.

And despite the Baffle and its constraints, the starship had managed to interfere several times, lobbing down targeted gadgets designed to block, distract, and unnerve her teams. One object had even made it rain. The items had been necessarily primitive in nature, running on windup timers, pressure-sensitive hydraulics, and other mechanisms that functioned without electricity. And some consumed themselves, leaving no leftover remnants—zero artifacts from outer space.

Yet she knew they were all pale shadows of the chaos Starfleet could wreak. A blessing of Epheska was the fear that the Sorry had put into people about using incendiary devices; rifles and shotguns were the limit. Mines that required blasting were too big to exist anyway. But offworlders might have no fear about sending down machine guns or hand grenades—or flat-out bombarding pursuers. Did *Enterprise* have the resources to send down something large, like a steam-powered vehicle?

One thing was clear: the so-called Prime Directive didn't mean anything to Pike now, if it ever had. Whoever was running things for him up in space had thrown the whole crew toward coming up with methods to help their wayward captain, no matter the cost to the world below. It was a nightmare waiting to happen.

Garr looked up. "You say them people are out beyond the moons?" He shook his head. "If they get any closer, there's no telling what they can do."

"They *can't* get any closer. And I already got word from the rondure back at Veeney. We've got lookouts coming in from a half-dozen settlements in their path, human and otherwise. If we do it right, we can pinch 'em together."

Garr let out a deep breath. "What are we supposed to do then? They ain't shot at us, other than to keep us back. And ain't none of us has fired on another person ever. You know that. We ain't Zoldaari."

"Watch that, Seb. They're just like us."

He spat. "Carpenter grabbed you like you was a sack of feed."

"I wasn't hurt. And I can take care of myself. Everyone has a part to play."

"Human and otherwise," he muttered. Garr set his horse in motion. "Not looking forward to it."

It's already happening, she thought as he rode off. One of the Skagarans' miracles was that they'd gotten the people of many different planets to live in peace and brotherhood, with no differences that couldn't be settled by a Harmony

Note. Pike's disruption was just a few days old, and already Garr felt comfortable mouthing off about the planet's most physically imposing sentients.

But there were no humans and no Zoldaari—only Epheskans.

She started back on Pike's trail, growing angrier as she rode. *Haven't they messed up enough planets, Christopher? What can you be thinking?*

CHAPTER 35

THE HUNTED

What could I have been thinking?

Christopher Pike had wondered that a half-dozen times a day since the wagon train left Havenbrook. It occurred to him again as he looked back to see another wave of lookouts racing toward them.

The first day had been almost pastoral. They'd hurried, for sure, but for him it recalled what the migrations of old must have been like. That time, when all they had to contend with was a scout or two, had long since passed. Drayko's minions were onto him now and had been for three days.

He'd brought the trouble upon his friends by suggesting the drive in the first place, but he'd compounded the danger by agreeing to pick up the Menders at Iklik. The train wasn't about to enter a settlement, but he had agreed to a looping path toward it to allow Weedaw to find and return with his relatives. That had led to another Mender asking for the same chance at another town, and another—and now Pike found himself feeling responsible for fifty souls.

Fifty who could only go as fast as the slowest horse or wagon. People who had mostly never been part of a wagon train themselves—and who were looking for advice from someone who'd gotten his education from John Wayne and Ward Bond.

From behind the column, he heard warning shots. Nobody had fired at the Menders; it was all psychological, trying to get the train to stop or break apart. The fact that Drayko was able to call upon aerial reconnaissance was even more decisive; the Skagarans only needed to contact the rondure of a settlement to send yet another batch of fresh riders into the fray. Every one forced Pike to think of something, or the Menders to build something, to remain on course.

That was becoming harder all the time. With every hoof that hit the grass, his mind was on the maps in his vest. He knew roughly where he was. *Enterprise* had dropped more care packages in their path, including another map with an update on his location. Of more help was the star chart that La'an sent down—a view of the nebula from the inside, along with a tool that made him feel like a true ship's captain: a sextant. He didn't know whether these things were being fabricated, or if he had an aficionado on board. But he'd done his best with it.

They just needed another kilometer or two to make one of Epheska's few permanent river crossings: a bridge *Enterprise*'s sensors had said was still there. That was as of the last message they'd dropped to him; they couldn't tell him if anyone was lying in wait there.

He rode up to the lead, where Weedaw, a most able equestrian on his gray Welsh Cob, was keeping himself as far as possible from the pursuers to the rear.

"What do you see?" Pike asked.

"They're there all right!" Strooh eyes were better than any scope the humans had, and Weedaw called out the number of riders he saw waiting at the bridge.

Carpenter rode alongside on his enormous draft horse. "Another sentinel coming in. Gonna be hard to keep these guys at bay."

"Don't shoot the balloons," Pike yelled. "And keep going forward!"

He looked back. The chasers had hit the soft marsh they'd crossed, and he could see the noon sun reflecting off the water their horses were kicking up. *We're going to cut this close*, Pike thought.

"Up there!" Weedaw shouted, pointing to the sky.

Another special delivery. Pike knew there was something planned for the bridge—a natural choke point—but not what. He waved his hat at the lead wagon. "Keep going!"

The silver comet came down, a dead weight directly over the bridge. But it did not strike it, nor land at all. A kilometer up, it blew apart in a clockwork-timed, spring-loaded explosion that sent smaller projectiles rocketing horizontally from it in all directions. They were clear, almost transparent—

—until one exploded. There was no fire, just white smoke and violence—and noise, plenty of noise. This was no smoke bomb. He knew what he was seeing—and he knew it posed no danger. "Keep riding!" he shouted, waving again. Seeing Weedaw readying to veer off, he rode alongside and grabbed onto his reins. "*Keep riding!*"

There was no question of Weedaw hearing him by then, because every one of the projectiles responded to an internal trigger, snapping off like popcorn kernels hundreds of meters in the air. At the bridge, the epicenter of the cluster bombing, Pike saw riders fleeing in panic, while those without mounts dove into the river.

"Keep going!" Pike and Weedaw raced as one, bisecting the fleeing riders and pounding onto the bridge, even as fountains of white came down all around. Weedaw averted his eyes and yelled—but he did not change direction. Nor did the wagons, which thundered over the wooden bridge, going right through the curtain of crystals.

On the other side, he let loose of Weedaw's pony and looked back to see who had made it. It appeared everyone had crossed—and better, the pursuers were not just far behind, but running madly away from the display. A display that was gone after a few seconds, as if the explosion had never happened.

Carpenter shouted, "What the heck was that?"

"Dry-ice bombs," Pike said, pulling up his horse. Simple nonincendiary explosive devices, the combinations of solid carbon dioxide and water created extremely loud shockwaves, propelling fragments at high speeds. There was no shrapnel; he imagined the containment vessels were extremely thin, or possibly even made from ice.

Enterprise had helped—almost a bit *too* much.

"One of them nearly hit that sentinel over there," Weedaw said. The airship was heading away as quickly as whatever powered it could manage.

Pike didn't like hearing that, any more than he liked hearing Carpenter's next question. "We crossed the bridge. Should we burn it?"

"What? No!"

"I'm not afraid of fire."

"That's not why." Pike shook his head, not believing. "We're not doing it. We're across. That's all."

He nudged the gelding into a trot and eased away, watching the train pass. Pike had to get control of the situation before it got any worse. He didn't want the Menders hurt, but he also didn't want them to hurt anyone else. When he'd found out what the wagons in the rear were doing with the rock salt and caltrops, he'd put his foot down. Meanwhile, *Enterprise*'s clever science projects were hampered by a lack of real-time information—as well as some questionable judgment calls.

That, at least, he could do something about. Pike rode up to the coach he'd dubbed his communications station. Riding along beside it, he matched its speed.

Cyrus, seated inside, opened the door and called out. "What's the good word, Captain?"

"I have quite a few words, and they're not good. Take another message to *Enterprise*."

Cyrus already had his pad at the ready. His daughters sat beside him with the makeshift viridium telegraph. He hadn't gotten his semaphore plan approved, but Cyrus was broadcasting at last.

"Pike to La'an," he said. "Do not, repeat, *do not* send down further counter-measures unless I've requested them. We're not able to target smartly. And it doesn't matter if the chemical agents you employ disperse, or if the mechanisms are designed to consume themselves. The simple act of using them is an addition to these people's knowledge."

Cyrus transcribed what he heard. "Got it. Anything else?"

"Remind La'an that under the Prime Directive, *I am expendable*. My actions to get the Menders to safety are an act to undo my earlier interference, not to make it worse."

"Odd things to debate in the middle of a chase, Captain."

"I have to keep a lid on it, Cyrus. I'm on the outer edge of several general orders and regulations. Some I've blown past entirely." He guided Shadow around a pothole and returned to the carriage's side. "La'an is my security chief, and that colors how she's thinking: she's looking for ways to help me that are possible given the Baffle, and unlikely to be misappropriated. But she's got to be more careful."

"Looks to me like it doesn't make much difference. We know you're from a space civilization. The lookouts know. And we all know *we're* from somewhere else. Why do these worries apply?"

"There are rules."

"Like all the ones the Skagarans have been laying on us? How many books' worth do *you* have to memorize? And do they make any more sense?"

Pike understood what Cyrus was saying very well. Every new situation was a negotiation with guidelines that were based on past experiences. They couldn't cover everything. That was where captains came in.

He was pinning his meager hopes on a later section of General Order 1, which held that if exposure to an advanced civilization had already happened, a Starfleet crewmember could engage with a society after gathering extensive information on its laws and cultures. Even then, the officer wasn't to interfere and had to stay within the confines of the culture's restrictions. But it wasn't clear to Pike which culture mattered more here: that of the Skagarans or those of the peoples they'd kidnapped.

"I'm up to my neck in it no matter what," he said. "One more thing—tell her we could use some era-appropriate medical supplies. Some people have gotten hurt keeping the train moving."

"Sending alcohol and bandages isn't interference?"

Pike shook his head. "I'm rendering aid to people who wouldn't have been harmed but for my previous interference." He waved his hand. "Cyrus, you can keep all the notes as evidence for the court-martial. Just send it."

The newsman grinned. "We'll get this right up to La'an." He paused. "How do you do the apostrophe again?"

CHAPTER 36

THE CONTROLLERS

"Sentinel One-Nine moving southeast along the Gelm Corridor. Sentinel Eight-Eight checked in above Lashta, reports no candidate travelers. Sentinel Two-Oh-Two, high winds at Oceanview, returning."

The round crystal pavilion sat near the much smaller stone temple by the bank of the Matayan River; Una Chin-Riley had earlier looked down on them both from the terrace at the Garden House, high above. The day after Drayko and Celarius had learned of her interstellar origins, they'd made good on their word by allowing her to see what the larger building held.

It turned out to be the nerve center for the planet. One of the largest traffic-control facilities *Enterprise*'s first officer had ever seen—and by far the strangest.

"Sentinel Seven-Seven, reroute to Murkhana to investigate lookout report," said a blue-cloaked human controller to a note taker. "Sentinel One-One-Five, observe Harmony Note Two-Eight-Triple-Four compliance at Snow Falls. And we need an equine count on Ellawa Plain, per general's orders."

It was the same chatter she'd heard in similar locations in space, except the controller spoke barely over a whisper. A prayer to be passed along. Where most of the others spoke in Skagaran, the controller had switched to Chin-Riley's language when she approached, a courtesy for their guest. She stood back as the listener, wearing lavender robes like Zoryana's, rushed past her and out the doors, headed for the temple.

Earlier, Celarius had again taken her to see the amazing thing that stone structure held: the floating rondure which allowed Zoryana and her compatriots to psychically commune with members of other settlements. Chin-Riley still wondered if she could use it to somehow reach *Enterprise*, but the magic ball was constantly in use. Many of the calls were about locating Spock and Uhura, so she couldn't really complain.

The glass pavilion known as the Care Circle housed a colossal relief map of Epheska in gnomonic projection, which made sense to her, as it depicted aerial routes as straight lines. This map covered the Northern Hemisphere; a smaller round deck on a platform above them held the south, which, while populated, had more ocean and fewer settlements.

Yet both maps had things in common. One was the blue-cloaked controllers, who were uniformly slight in build and who stepped gingerly around in silken socks. She guessed they were selected for the duty so as not to damage the map. Another feature was what looked like rubies, suspended above the map of the north by silvery strands from the upper platform. Hanging meters above, they gave the appearance of stars in the sky. Every settlement depicted below lay beneath one of the gems, but there were many more of them than there were villages.

"The jewels are rondure stations, right?" she asked Zoryana, her guide for the hour. She was glad to be able to ask a simple question. "Are there temples in all these locations?"

Zoryana glanced idly at the hanging gems. "The project is always thinking ahead. We locate new settlements near the rondures, not the other way around."

The vacant areas appeared to include a gnarled, jawlike landmass ringed with archipelagoes; no settlements at all appeared there. Celarius had suggested it was another place like the forest she'd arrived in. Wild and untamed, a perfect nature preserve.

A large number of the gems that Chin-Riley saw hung over bodies of water. She pointed them out to Zoryana. "Are there water-breathing species here too?"

"They were either not known to our ancestors," the Skagaran woman said, "or deemed to be in no danger, either from immediate or ecological disasters. This is common. The sea is just as vulnerable to destruction by its inhabitants, but the land dwellers tend to have more weapons at their disposal."

"But you built rondures there anyway. Are they floating, or—?"

"They already float." Zoryana gave her a courtesy nod and stepped away to confer with someone else.

Chin-Riley realized Drayko's attaché hadn't really answered her, but she supposed it did make sense to have coverage in the seas, given how rondures were employed in sentinel navigation. For a planet that was forcibly medieval, the Skagarans clearly had hung on to some Information Age thinking.

Perhaps that was why Zoryana, like her hosts, had come to terms with Chin-Riley's alien origins with seeming ease. *Knowing the big picture prepares you for a lot.*

She glanced at the youth Zoryana was talking with. She had seen members of a half-dozen species here amidst the Skagarans of Om Mataya, and from her conversations with them, they were all just as devoted to the cause. But she'd realized that while landing a position here was considered the pinnacle of achievement for adherents to the project, it was also a permanent assignment. Nobody ever went home.

Then again, nobody ever *wanted* to leave, from what she'd heard. She couldn't blame them. The Skagarans had put a thousand Standard years into crafting a paradise to replace their ruined home, and they appeared to have done it while creating refuges for other species as well. Managing it all had kept them busy day and night for centuries, and by now they operated with practiced precision.

So why is everyone over on that *side of the map so agitated?*

She watched as Zoryana walked over to a gaggle of attendants in blue. She heard them conferring in Skagaran, quiet but still louder than the prayerful whispers all around. They paused their debates every few moments to admit a lavender runner from the rondure. Seconds after, they dispatched another messenger back to it. At one point, two of the pages slipped in their socks and nearly collided, threatening to take out an entire mountain range when they stumbled.

Chin-Riley studied the map. The commotion was far to Om Mataya's southwest, a considerable distance south of where Pike was said to have been found. She'd just spent days listening to false starts coming from Drayko. *An airship was heading for Pike. No, it had to turn back. An airship had arrived, but he was off riding somewhere.*

Nothing about the delays screamed obfuscation—yet—and her hosts remained gracious as ever. But since her revelation, the evasion indicator had gone in the opposite direction. Instead of Celarius trying to pry information out of her, she'd found the people she met more reticent. If it wasn't in her bedside book, she wasn't likely to get a straight answer about it. Celarius seemed as defiantly sincere as ever; the man couldn't be bothered to lie. But there was still no Pike, no Spock, and no Uhura—and she was stuck in Om Mataya.

On the other hand, Zoryana's preoccupation meant that for the first time in days, Chin-Riley was without a babysitter.

She casually strolled around the circumference of the map. There was no sense listening in to the chatterers, as she didn't know all the lingo—but she could see what was happening at the speakers' feet. Markers were being moved toward a dagger of land, jutting into the sea.

That was all she could gather, but it wasn't her destination anyway. Far to the "west" was the side of the pavilion abutting the mountain. She'd seen various individuals going back and forth behind an arras, and she wondered what the divider hid.

She entered a hallway—and walked right into Celarius. "Una!" he said, ebullient. "Lost?"

"I left you on the terrace. How'd you get down here?" She gestured behind her. "There's a million stairs out there."

"Magic." He winked and headed into the map room.

She figured she'd better follow. "Do you have a secret turbolift back there?"

"I don't know what that is. But as winter comes, you will find the stairs less refreshing."

"I'm about there now." She looked back to see the huddle at the peninsula was still going. Zoryana looked back, saw her and Celarius, and returned to her conversations. "Something is happening over there."

"If I know Zoryana, she is complaining about my father's latest arbitrary edict, whatever it happens to be. Vexing her is his favorite sport."

"And speaking of me behind my back is yours," Drayko said from behind him. He emerged from behind the arras and smiled at Chin-Riley. "We meet again."

Her eyes went wide when she saw him. She'd left him dozens of meters above, as well, and she *knew* Drayko didn't walk down all those stairs. He was far from feeble, but by no means young—and she had never seen him in this place. She reached for something to say. "Reviewing the troops?"

"I keep telling people, I'm not that kind of general." He spotted Zoryana's gaggle. "But a peace conference is in order. Excuse me."

Celarius offered her his hand. "Let me show you over here where I took my last safari. The landforms seem unique to me, but I'd like your opinion—as a judge of planets."

You'd also like to hold my hand. She had his number by now. The standoffish man of the forest was, at court, tamer but not harmless. At least he didn't come across as a presumptuous lothario. Despite the busy world around him, he seemed a little lonely.

In her world, of course, there was a time and place for everything—and this wasn't it. He'd realize that, she hoped.

Celarius was in the middle of a disquisition on equatorial avians when she noticed more raised voices speaking Skagaran back at the peninsula. At one point, she saw Drayko stamp his foot. He wasn't wearing the visitors' socks, and the force of his stomp caused several markers on the ground to topple over.

He saw her looking at him. Chin-Riley tried quickly to turn away, but Drayko broke from the confab and quickly approached her.

"Now what?" Celarius said.

Drayko peered at her. "Your *Enterprise*. What would it be able to deliver to the surface?"

She wasn't ready for the question at all. "What do you mean?"

"Could it land here?"

She shook her head. "It's not that kind of ship. I mean, one section of it did land a few years ago, but it was a miracle it ever lifted off again. And there was no Baffle there."

"Of course." Drayko waved his hand. "It's clear they can't send down a shuttle safely. But smaller things would be possible."

She thought she knew where he was going. "Again, anything they'd send down for me wouldn't be able to get back. Even if you could put down a rocket that had no circuitry at all—just a brute-force lifter—it'd have to be enormous to get escape velocity from Epheska. And *Enterprise* is not a floating shipyard. They wouldn't have the parts."

"I expected that. I mean smaller. What other objects could they put down?"

This is getting specific, she thought. "You mean, like impactors?"

"Yes. Could they fire down weapons?"

"They wouldn't. Why would they?"

"Humor me. The ancient Skagarans knew energy weapons—and they certainly knew bombs. Could your ship employ them, even at their current distance?"

Chin-Riley looked to Celarius, who seemed flabbergasted. She figured she'd better put his mind at ease. "If they're as far away as I think they are, phasers wouldn't be practical. And our missile weapons have so many compartments holding circuitry it's practically surgery to get to them all."

"Yes, but a simple explosive charge would work, wouldn't it? Or have there been gases or germ weapons which have been developed during the time we have been—"

"Father!" Celarius interposed himself between Drayko and Chin-Riley. "Stop interrogating her. She's not an enemy."

Drayko's mouth hung open—and he let out a deep breath. "No. No, of course she isn't." His expression changed. "I apologize, Una. My job is to consider all possible things that might impact Epheska."

You said "impact" again, she thought. It was better not to mention that. "It's nothing. I fully understand."

She did not, and it was not nothing. But as they exited from the Care Circle, she cast a glance back inside, wondering what the hell was happening out west.

CHAPTER 37

THE MARSHALS

Christopher Pike had seen worlds with weird weather before, but nothing prepared him for being out in the open in the middle of an Epheskan thunderstorm. This was his third, and it was more intense than the ones from two days before. Skies darkened and wind blew—and the electrons in the clouds tried to get something going.

Only whatever was going haywire with electromagnetism on the planet was at least partially at work in the atmosphere as well. Tiny tingles would sparkle and chain together only to fizzle out, like fireworks. Sometimes a thunderhead would rev up, beginning to glow—only to have all the juice drain out at once, producing a sound like a cat's hiss. Energy that had to go somewhere found a willing partner in the wind. It had forced him and the others to dismount and walk their horses.

It was costing time he couldn't afford to lose. The people chasing him probably weren't going to slow down, no matter the weather. Pike grew more certain when one of the Menders loaned him a pair of makeshift field glasses. He was barely able to make out who was leading the lookouts.

Lila was on her way.

She hadn't just taught Pike how to ride a horse; she'd taught him how to race. Countless times, they'd circled the Bar T, hellbent for leather. But even as kids, Lila had never let him win, not even to make him feel better. It was for his own good, she'd said. "When you do beat me, it'll mean more."

He hated to admit it, but Lila had him beaten again. Gone was any hope of misdirection, or a choice of routes. His column was making a beeline for Leejo Point, which was a name he'd gotten from one of the Menders he'd picked up along the way. The Leejo peninsula did indeed resemble the boot of Italy, if on a smaller scale; the heel narrowed to a knife's point. Pike was glad Spock had mentioned that specifically. He didn't want to accidentally go to the tip of the toe instead.

This storm wasn't subsiding. It was where they were, he knew: winds whipping across from one body of water to the other. The rain was coming in too. He squinted through it to see his advance riders returning from the south.

"Meteor Express," Jennie said. She carried a hefty satchel, so large he was afraid she would fall. Pike steadied her as they moved both their horses away from the procession.

After dismounting, he found a large metal drum in her bag. He knelt over it, working the mechanism. "These *Enterprise* drops are getting bigger."

"I wonder if they could send people down next. Maybe an army."

"We don't have an army—and La'an knows better than to send anyone down here. We won't entrap anyone else." He looked inside the container and exhaled with relief. "Medical supplies. Good job, M'Benga."

He waved over one of his companions to start distributing the bottles and the bandages. Some riders had fallen off their mounts in the chase; others were just saddle-sore. Several Mender defensive contraptions had proven as dangerous to their operators as to the pursuers. And very few had the constitution for cold beans in cold rain.

"Looks like another note," Jennie said, pointing at the bottom of the bin.

"From the doctor?" Pike wasn't expecting that. He read:

> *My best to you, Captain. We are standing safely out of the area, as you*
> *ordered, but never doubt your crew seeks your return most fervently.*
> *—Doctor M'Benga*

The captain folded up the message. "That's a little strange."

M'Benga had just reiterated his own order to him. Was there a hint here about a disagreement on the ship? The doctor wasn't someone likely to go around channels and inform on La'an, and he hadn't done so here—not in so many words. But the effect was that Pike was likely to reiterate his command on the next send. Whatever experiments M'Benga had running had to be pretty important to necessitate such a note.

From behind, a rider raced alongside the column toward him. Vicki pulled up just before reaching him. "*This is it!*"

Pike looked back. "How bad?"

"It's the end," the gunsmith said. She pulled her rifle out of her scabbard. "They've formed a line miles wide, moving down the peninsula. Warden's bringing all of 'em."

The captain scowled. *Yes, this is where I'd do it.* The isthmus was narrowing. No room for surprises anymore; no other directions open but one.

"Everyone, mount up! South, south, south!"

Lila Talley led the charge, heedless of the wind and rain. She'd never been to this part of Epheska before, and the coastal weather was angrier than she'd expected. But that wasn't going to stop her.

She pulled Buckshot up when she realized how far she'd gotten ahead of everyone else. She turned about—and looked in awe at the force she'd brought. Gathered behind her were the humans of Havenbrook and several other settlements, but also representatives of many other peoples, all dispatched by towns they'd passed along the way.

Garr approached her, flanked on either side by wardens. He gestured to one of the newcomers, a tall golden-eyed Jemanite. "Warden, this here's—"

"No time," Lila said. She rode up and down the line, reviewing the leaders. "Do you understand the job?" she shouted. "We're not going to hurt them, but we *are* going to stop them. They're misguided, that's all."

"What do we do with them?" a Strooh warden asked.

"We'll break up the train and take them home peacefully," Lila said. "Everyone goes but one human. Christopher Pike."

"What'd *he* do?"

Drayko must not have wanted to get into it, she thought. She certainly didn't have the time. "The conservator general wants to see him, that's all. We'll take him back to the nearest rondure and await a sentinel. You will not—repeat, *not*—hurt him, or anyone else. These are your families."

"That's what you think," growled the Jemanite warden, clearly annoyed to have been called out into the rain. "Nobody in my family would act this dumb."

"Dumb they ain't," Garr barked. "You're gonna see for yourself."

"He's right," Lila said. "You need to be ready for anything." She tipped her hat back and looked up at the clouds. "And if you notice anything coming down from the sky, you need to ignore it, you understand? It's just a trick."

"Sky. Ignore. Right." The Jemanite looked away.

Lila ignored his arrogance. "You know this country. Is there any way off this peninsula?"

"Not unless humans have gills." He looked around. "You don't, do you?"

She rolled her eyes. Lila turned Buckshot about. The tail end of the column was just barely in sight. She had to assume that Pike knew he was trapped. Maybe if she got to him first, she could defuse this before there were any unhappy accidents.

Come on, Christopher. You say you're in charge of people. Do what's right!

CHAPTER 38

THE ABANDONED

Starfleet Academy prepared its students for a lot. If you wanted to know what it felt like to be under fire, to have a core breach, or to enter the Neutral Zone without authorization, there was an appropriate simulation for you. Nyota Uhura's studies had additionally included pretend encounters with a wide range of other speakers, both in person and over comms. She thought they'd done a good job.

What Starfleet's survival training couldn't simulate was time, and how its passage took a physical and mental toll. She'd seen enough sunrises to account for more than a week, although with the planet's shorter days she'd lost track of what that meant in her reckoning. Several days earlier she'd found gourds that doubled for sustenance and water containers; since the encounter with the airship, that had been the only event of note.

The balloon was long gone, but she'd kept to a route heading in the direction it had taken. It hadn't been easy, as the terrain often forced her along a different path. But she'd doggedly returned to her bearing, leaving the volcanic rifts behind once and for all. After that, it had been one valley after another, with yellowing grasses and the occasional clump of shedding trees indicating both the turn of the seasons and her latitude. She'd seen some small animals, but still none of the population FGC-7781 b was supposed to have.

The empatherm remained. For whatever reason, it had stayed near her. The ardor with which it danced on the air seemed to have cooled, and it was more often compact and near the ground. "Fetal position," she called it. She didn't know whether it was because it was cold and tired—or because she was. *Probably a combination of both.* Uhura had assumed the same posture when sleeping, and Empy had lingered near her. It provided warmth when she shivered; additional light when she grew fearful. Whatever it really was, it seemed to sense she needed a guard dog.

Uhura had awakened late that morning feeling awful and unwilling to take another step. Howls on the horizon got her going. *All this and predators too.* By afternoon, the winds picked up and the sky grew dark and threatening, moving shelter to the top of her list. So she climbed one more rise, thinking as she did that it might well be her last.

A farm!

She rubbed her eyes. It wasn't a mirage. Turquoise fields lay ahead, with a cluster of buildings beyond. She forced her legs into motion and nearly stumbled down the hill. Recovering, she made her way toward the crops.

Uhura felt life returning as she walked between the rows of plants. Blue puffs on the stalks gave the appearance of cotton bolls, and they felt as soft to her. The stands were ragged and unkempt, and a lot of it had gone to seed—but that didn't matter. Here was intelligence, and there had to be more around. She emerged from the overgrown patch just behind the barn. Tall, it obscured her view of the buildings beyond. "Hello!" she called out. "Is anyone here?"

When she rounded it, her breath caught in her throat. There, beyond a few intact shacks, was the burnt skeleton of a wooden two-story farmhouse.

Uhura approached it, realizing with every slowing step that whatever had happened here had transpired long ago. There was no one in sight. Just a mound of windswept debris, rotting in the elements.

This hurt. She climbed the stoop and entered what had been a kitchen, given the evidence of a basin and a table. Something humanlike had lived here. Maybe there was something she could use.

For an hour, she worked her way into the shell, looking for anything. She'd concluded four beings had lived here, and shreds of blue cloth led her to believe that they'd grown their crops for textiles. Further investigations found cabinets. One held what looked like a hairbrush. A fanciful inlay decorated its handle. She resisted the urge to use it. This was someone's home—and they had left without it. *Why?*

She found no answers until late in the day when, with the sky rumbling, she located a curious object. It appeared to be a small table, half burnt; its legs had snapped off when the ceiling fell in. With effort, she dragged it out into an open part of the floor. She realized it had been a desk when she saw the drawer. The ornate finish suggested something Earth-like to her, but she knew that was impossible.

It was no more impossible than what she found when she cracked it open. Old parchment, on which were written numbers and various notes. *In Mandarin.*

"How is that possible?" she said aloud.

She flipped through the crinkled sheets. Crop estimates. Weather recordings. Notes about what was planted where. And diagrams—many diagrams, including schematics for something.

She rushed through the stack, hoping for anything that would shed more light: a map, anything. She found it at the very bottom, a memoir written by someone long since departed:

We have moved from the village. We have gone as far as we can from the round things and those who speak through them, and those who speak for them. The family will be happy here, and we will be able to work on the machine in the shed. We will grow the chaltaka, *and the machine will separate the seeds from the bolls, and there will be something else to our days.*

She read it again. She didn't know the word *chaltaka*, and she didn't know what "the round things" were. She only knew the writing was all by the same hand, and the notation on some of the drawings suggested the author was named Wei.

"There's a shed," she mumbled, taking the letter with her and extricating herself from the wreckage.

The empatherm had remained outside the ruins, morosely wafting about on the wind. She passed it on the way to the small outbuilding behind the house. She opened the creaky door—and watched it fall off its hinges, landing on its side inside the hut. The façade was all that existed intact. The shed beyond was worse than the house, with debris collapsed onto a central pile.

Uhura moved rotted timbers away, hoping to find any clue as to what Wei had been referring to. She found metal jutting out here and there. More work revealed a mass of iron slag, melted beyond all recognition.

Looking back in confusion, she spied another bit of parchment, nailed to the inside of the fallen door. It was in Wei's hand:

They have found us. They know of the steam gin. The watchers from the air will send the menace. They will take us, but we will not bend. This we promise.

"Gin." She looked behind her. *Steam gin. Is that like a cotton gin?*

She knelt on the floor of the erstwhile shed and fought back tears. This had been someone's life—and it had been dashed to bits, along with the machine.

The wind swept through where walls had been. She remembered the barn—intact. For all the destruction, it was shelter, and it was a farm. She couldn't eat cotton—or *chaltaka*, if that was what it was—but she had to imagine there was something edible out there somewhere. She'd felt on the verge of getting sick for days. Even lying in hay would be an improvement as long as there was a roof over her.

She exited the wreckage and walked slowly to the barn, almost worried she might upset some ghosts. Empy lingered nearby, motionless. "Just let me take a look," she said as she forced up the bar that held the door fast.

Uhura pulled the door open—and gasped.

Carcasses of animals, all around. Large and small, but all familiar in shape. *Horses!*

There was little smell, so long ago had it happened. But she knew what had transpired. Wei and his family had died, fled, or worse—and the animals here had starved to death. Locked away and abandoned.

"*No!*" Uhura fell to her knees and threw up. A place of death—inhabiting the only hope she'd seen. She cried with abandon. "*No! No! No!*"

Gasping for breath, she opened her wet eyes and saw her shadow, long and stark in the terrible place. She wrenched her head around and saw the empatherm behind her blazing bright, rising in height as if in response to her anguish.

"Empy, no!"

The fire elemental shot over her, a zephyr seeking the thing that caused her emotional pain. It lanced from one carcass to the next, touching off independent fires—nonliving, but still destructive. Uhura stood, shouting—but to no effect. She scrambled back and away, withdrawing as the entire barn went up.

Cold rain pelted her. The sky had finally opened up, but it could do nothing for the barn. With a sickening creak, the roof collapsed. "Empy!"

She fell to her hands and knees, weeping.

The rain was pouring when she looked up and saw tendrils of plasma emerging from the embers. Unhindered by the water, the empatherm collected itself and wobbled toward her location.

Uhura wiped her nose. "Are you okay?"

There was no response. It remained still as she spoke.

"Empy, that place hurt me to see. But I didn't want it destroyed. Can't you understand?"

Again, no response. But then, what was she expecting? There was no way she could ever expect a fireball to comprehend anything on a planet where she'd understood nothing at all.

Uhura realized she still had the papers in one hand—their ink now running. She shoved them into her tunic and stood. The sun was setting, and the rain felt as if it might turn over to snow at any moment. It didn't matter.

"I can't stay here." She found what she supposed was north and began walking. And whether or not the empatherm was capable of understanding her decision, it followed her.

CHAPTER 39

THE CAVALRY

The wagon train ran out of things, one by one.

First it ran out of tricks. After a shallow river proved no barrier to either the column or its pursuers, the Menders had used every ploy they had. Everything that could be dumped in the lookouts' path had been. Every net had been launched. Even the rock salt was gone. Short of Pike calling on *Enterprise* for another ploy, which he refused to do, the only defense remaining lay in the few guns the Menders carried.

Then it ran out of land. The end came up quickly, as Christopher Pike first saw dark water to the west—and then the sun setting over the ocean to the east. It had been visible only briefly, because no sooner had the storm vanished than merciless fog rolled in. He was surprised at how abruptly they came upon Leejo Point, which stuck into the air like a rocky sundial. An angry sea raged below the outcropping; beyond it was nothing but darkness and haze.

From atop his horse on the promontory, Pike knew he was out of something else. Time.

Several of his allies arrived beside him at the precipice. "Storm's back," Joe said, listening.

Pike shook his head. "That's hooves."

Weedaw shook atop his pony. "My friends and relations—the ones we brought from my town—they've fled."

"Took their ponies and made for the lookouts," Joe said. "Cowards."

"They're not!" Weedaw shouted. He looked around in anguish. "What did we *do* this for?"

"My lieutenant said to come here," Pike said. He faced the sea. More quietly, he repeated: "He said to come here."

"*Vaguely,*" Carpenter replied atop his stallion. "You were just *guessing* this was the place."

Yes, I was. "It was all we had."

They turned back. The wagons had made two concentric semicircles around the outcrop. Beyond them, Vicki had assembled a picket of a dozen armed Menders, facing north. "Keep that line formed," she said.

Pike rode up to her. "I don't want you to shoot anyone. Drayko just wants me."

"It's too late for that." Vicki looked to her companions on the line. "They get to choose."

Carpenter dismounted and took a position. "Might as well."

Joe called over for Pike to help him down off his horse. "Thank you for trying," the miller said. "You gave me something for a while."

"Joe, I'm sorry."

"You just make sure Jennie stays safe."

Somber, Pike nodded. He looked up to see the lookouts approaching from the north. They came at a canter, evenly spaced and deliberate. Most were not armed, but he saw a few rifles and shotguns—and some of the members of other species carried poles. They stopped a hundred meters from Pike, whereupon he saw the ranks behind the line filling in.

It's a horde.

A gap appeared in the middle, and even in the dwindling gray light, Pike could make out Lila riding through it, flanked by two others. One was a member of Weedaw's species; the other had ruddy skin and glowing golden eyes Pike could see even at a distance.

"Looks like a parley." Pike glanced back. "Weedaw, Jennie. You're with me."

Near the first line of wagons, Weedaw gulped. "Me?"

Jennie rode up beside him. "Don't you get it, Weedaw? He's taking us with him so we can cross." She glared at Pike. "You don't want us to fight."

"You do what he says," Joe shouted. He clenched his teeth together. "Please, Jennie."

Reluctantly, they left the others and rode alongside Pike into the neutral ground.

Lila stared coolly at him as he approached. "Warden," he said.

"Christopher." She nodded to her companions. "This is Warden Areet from Murkhana and Warden Zem from Jemanzad."

Zem looked Pike over and smirked. "Yep. No gills."

Pike didn't know what to make of that.

Areet, one of Weedaw's species, studied the blacksmith. "I'm surprised you would do this," she said to him.

"That can wait," Lila said. She looked behind Pike to the ring of defenders. "It's over, Captain. The cavalry's here."

"Normally the cavalry is what saves people."

"From my point of view, it has." She sighed. "You say you're in charge of folks in your old life. You need to protect *these* people by letting them go back to their lives."

"They're not happy with their lives," Jennie spouted.

"That's why we wear chaps, Jennie. Life isn't always easy. But our lives here are as close to perfect as you're gonna find." Lila glanced away. "Believe me, I've looked."

Pike wondered what that meant, but he had the sense she was done talking. "Take me. Let them go."

"Not happening," Lila said. "The Skagarans need to undo what you did."

Jennie's temper flared. "He didn't do—"

Pike gestured for silence.

He got it—only to have it broken. He looked up. "Is the storm back?"

It was not. But a screaming something pierced the fog—and struck the territory halfway between Lila's crew and her forces. A colossal explosion rang out, and dirt shot sky high. Everyone's hands were on their reins then, struggling to hold their horses.

Lila looked back. "What was—"

Another blast, and then two more—both just meters ahead of the lookout ranks. Pike's ears were still ringing when Zem shouted at Lila. "Ignore the sky, you said!"

She looked up, searching. "Damn it, Christopher! I don't know how you're doing it, but call off *Enterprise*! These are primitive people!"

"They're not doing it!" Pike looked to Jennie. "Go back!"

She did as he said. Weedaw was already halfway there, Pike saw. They had left just in time, as a fifth explosion showered the conference with dirt and ash.

Pike leapt from his horse before he could be thrown off. "Lila, you'd better—"

She ignored him, focusing instead on her companions, who were taking flight. "Stop!" Another impact struck even closer, causing Buckshot to rear violently, overturning and slamming his rider into the muddy ground.

Pike dove and covered her as best he was able to, pulling her clear as the stallion regained its footing and bolted away.

He knelt beside her, watching in amazement as the orderly lookout ranks went into rout. Nothing had hit them yet, which he realized owed to the fact that the shots were clearly being targeted. "It's cannon fire!"

Lila shoved his hand off her. "Get away!" She tried to stand—and faltered with a yelp of pain.

"It's your ankle," he said. "Don't move."

Tears of pain and fury filled her eyes. "Christopher, what have you done?"

"I swear, it wasn't—"

Pike stopped midsentence and froze. He saw a sail approaching from the east. It was fanlike, similar to a Chinese junk.

No, he realized. *It is a Chinese junk.* And more emerged from the fog. Lila was seeing it too. On the other side of the isthmus, more arrived from the west.

He stared. "You didn't tell me there were—"

Oh, my God.

To the east, the fog dissipated, revealing the last inkling of the sun on the ocean horizon—and the mammoth structure riding before it: a British ship of the line. Three masts. Two gun decks—what would have been classified a third-rater on Earth, he figured.

And a flag—of course, a flag. Pike squinted, expecting to see the white ensign of the British Royal Navy. Instead, it appeared to have a pair of circles and a triangle.

He looked to see if Lila had seen it, too, but she was doubled over her ankle, wincing in pain. Pike worried that her injuries were more severe than he'd noticed. In a daze, she asked, "Did you get your cavalry?"

"No," Pike said, unable to believe the words he was about to speak. "*It's the Vulcan navy!*"

CHAPTER 40

THE MARINERS

Spock's arrival on Epheska, days earlier, had left something to be desired. Nearly drowning had little to recommend it. His first encounter with intelligent life on the planet was not much better.

He'd ridden the marine trap he was clinging to all the way to the surface, only to be struck by a blunt object soon after he broke the water. He suspected the weapon was the hook which the owner of the snare used to tend her contraption. Shocked by Spock's sudden appearance, she'd clubbed him over the head under the mistaken impression he was there to steal her catch.

That was conjecture, as he'd fallen unconscious seconds later—but his awakening in a metal cage on the beach suggested he was not far from wrong.

The pink-hued sea people grew animated as they gathered about him, but they had no spoken tongue that he could hear and did not respond to his words. They did, however, bring him a book in an attempt to communicate with him through writing. Its style was archaic, binding single-sided sheets; Spock inferred from the characters that it was a phrasebook, connecting their language to several others. Unfortunately, he didn't know any of them.

But they had allowed him to keep it—as well as their writing utensil, which he used to begin his own log on the backs of the pages. During a previous mission in which both he and Captain Pike had been separately stranded, they had communicated over subspace about an Earth literary work featuring a castaway. There was no such option here, but Spock had felt he could at least keep a record, as Robinson Crusoe had.

Granted, his third entry seemed to offer little promise of any to follow, mentioning they had moved his cage to below the tide line. "It appears I have become a sacrificial offering to the sea," he'd written, before going back to work at the seals of his prison. Spock hadn't gotten anywhere with that when the next surprise occurred.

He witnessed the arrival of a small vessel that appeared much like something found in the fleet of Zheng He early in Earth's fifteenth century. Of even greater surprise was the fact that those operating it were Vulcans. Their attire somewhat recalled an older style used by his planet's defense forces, but the sailors wore it in a utilitarian manner, some eschewing shirts altogether as they worked their oars. The trappers' intent was benevolent, Spock realized; they'd assumed he belonged to their number and had placed him where the sailors would notice him.

The seafaring Vulcans were as startled to see him as he was to see them. Assuming they were either castaways from *Braidwood* or an earlier incident, Spock had identified himself as a Starfleet officer. They seemed not to know what that was; one, in fact, accused him of being a runaway.

"A runaway from what" was answered when Spock was taken to the open sea, where he saw many more of the Chinese ships, many much larger—and the greatest shocker of all: a colossal British warship from Earth's eighteenth century.

Hauled aboard, he was brought before an aged Vulcan woman, T'Var. Seeing no Prime Directive impediment, Spock had shared his origins with her, hoping that would encourage some reciprocation. Instead, it produced arguments between T'Var and her companions over his veracity. It was only when Spock displayed his defunct tricorder and comm that she took it upon herself to initiate a mind-meld, which he did not resist. His log entry, written that night in the quarters she then provided, was a parade of astonishing information:

> T'Var's transport visited this planet nearly a Standard century ago. Ensnared, it crashed near an archipelago, where its occupants survived until their discovery of a sailing vessel from Earth, abandoned in a harbor. They also located a building with a mysterious spherical object which offered mental communion with those who purport to rule this planet, evidently from a land far away. It was a society the Vulcans determined they wanted no part of.

A hundred years in a paragraph that seemed to hold an even larger number of mysteries—and yet Spock believed the Vulcans had, since crashing in *Xen'tal*, gotten an admirable handle on what was going on.

They were well aware of the Skagaran abduction of humans from Earth which Jonathan Archer had uncovered in the Delphic Expanse; it was one of the last pieces of intelligence they'd learned about before their entrapment. By using the so-called rondure to lurk during the lunar conjunction celebrations over the years, they'd further formed a detailed picture of the rest of the planet the Skagarans called Epheska. Those experiences also helped them overcome the reluctance of Vulcans from their era regarding mind-melds, which Spock considered fortunate.

Xen'tal's survivors had already given up on escape from the planet and its neutralizing Baffle, but they'd determined there was no good to be had in joining Epheskan society as they understood it. Fortunately, they had an option. Even though some temples with their rondures were present, the Skagarans had left the landmass known as Zevayne and its surrounding islands alone. That seemed logical to the Vulcans, as the place was overrun with jungles teeming with dangerous wildlife. That life—either large or microscopic—may have led, they surmised, to the abandonment of so many ships in the area.

By far the largest was *H.M.S. Thunderer*, launched in 1760 according to the records T'Var found aboard. The ship was foundering in a massive hurricane in the West Indies when the Skagarans arrived, wrenching the ship and six hundred crewmembers from the storm—and from Earth altogether.

While it was evident from the rondures that humans existed elsewhere on Epheska, the Vulcans had never encountered anyone associated with that vessel or any of the Chinese ships they'd found. Somewhere in the intervening centuries since arriving here, their occupants had left their ships behind. Perhaps they had failed to find anyone else and died out; perhaps they'd left to join one of the Skagarans' planned settlements. It intrigued Spock that Epheska might be home to descendants of the explorer Captain Cook, whose son the ship's records had said was aboard.

His greater interest, however, was finding a different captain—as well as Chin-Riley and Uhura—and a way off the planet. He found a ready ally in the Vulcan commander, who gave him access to a rondure her people controlled on an island. The alert from General Drayko of Pike's presence both gratified and concerned Spock; while glad to hear of his superior officer's survival, it was also clear he was in dire straits. The fleet made all speed to Leejo Point, bringing its cannons to bear just in time.

And now, a human again stood on *Thunderer*'s deck, treading the boards of a ship that last saw its home planet during the Great Hurricane of 1780. Pike marveled at the masts and rigging in the morning sun.

"Amazing." Dazzled, he looked to Spock, seeing him for the first time since the shuttle disaster. "You know, you made quite the entrance."

"Theatricality was not my intent."

"No, of course. It never is." Pike smiled. "Good to see you, Lieutenant."

CHAPTER 41

THE EXILED

As surprised as Christopher Pike had been at the fleet's arrival, he'd been even further mystified when the first occupant to land was a Vulcan who was not Spock. The young messenger had handed Pike a journal, which had brought the captain up to speed even before he was invited out to *Thunderer*.

"I believed it would be an economical record," Spock said as he strode the great ship's deck. "My hosts expected me to assist them in sailing, and I thought it right to agree."

Pike chuckled. "I guess you've gotten an education. Do you know your shrouds from your stays yet?"

"To the extent required," Spock said. "It has, at a minimum, given context to Starfleet's proclivity for human maritime history." He looked over at the Vulcans working the ropes. "T'Var's people and their descendants have learned their craft as well as any people from a desert planet might. They have had the time."

"Are you sure this is *Thunderer*? I always thought she was at Trafalgar," Pike said. "That was after 1780."

"It is the practice of Earth's navies to reuse names of vessels, lost and otherwise."

Pike nodded. "Yeah, I guess Starfleet should start noting that somehow in its names." He looked out at one of the junks, an equine ship that was taking aboard the Menders' horses. "Do those ships mean there's a Chinese equivalent to the Dry River culture here too?"

"I presume so, but the planet is large enough that—"

"Commander on deck!" called a Vulcan in Spock's mother tongue.

Pike turned to see the elder that Spock had gotten to know well over the last week. Aged at least a hundred forty, she wore a uniform that mixed elements of frayed and patched Vulcan attire with handmade additions. "Captain Christopher Pike, this is Fleet Commander T'Var."

She touched her cap. "Lieutenant Spock's introduction is both accurate and inaccurate," she said in a creaky voice. "I am commander of a fleet, and I am of Vulcan. But I was never a fleet commander *for* Vulcan. My terminal rank was subcommander." She looked up at the standard. "But technically I have never left service."

She strolled the deck, and Pike and Spock followed. "My lieutenant says you arrived a hundred years ago," the captain said.

"In your accounting. The number in Epheskan years may confuse the matter." She looked up. "What do you think of our ship?"

"She's amazing," Pike said. "How did the Skagarans manage to carry off anything this large? The ship Archer found wasn't anywhere near big enough."

Spock had a theory. "On that, the commander's staff and I have reached agreement. They must have had a transporter far superior to ours—with the ability to hold its patterns for the duration of an interstellar voyage."

"Holding someone in a buffer." Pike shook his head. "Novel and dangerous."

"It solves the matter of how abductees reached the surface here," T'Var said. "Although I understand that even your advanced transporters had difficulty."

Pike and Spock looked at each other, appreciating the understatement.

T'Var glanced back at Pike. "I am sorry you became trapped, but my experience may save you some difficulty. Everything you might attempt to depart this planet, Captain, we have considered many times. We have run every experiment, every test we are capable of. There is simply no explanation for the Baffle, and no way to defeat it. But on learning you were here, I could not ignore your plight."

"I appreciate it." Pike looked to Spock. "Leejo Point was a good idea."

"I theorize the name reached the locals from the Chinese mariners," Spock said. "They would have known the Leejow Peninsula, which abuts Hainan."

Pike remembered the area. "This formation looks more like the boot of Italy."

"Which the mariners had never seen," Spock noted. "They used a name they were familiar with."

T'Var shook her head. "This is life, my young friends. We all look out from the limited perspectives of our times and our surroundings. You either choose to expand your perspective—as you have done—or you act as the Skagarans, keeping everyone blind. It is the definition of a game. Lives lived, but to no end."

She reached a railing and looked out at the land. Work was continuing all along the shore, bringing the Menders, their equipment, and animals aboard.

When Pike and Spock were at her side, she spoke again, solemnly. "I cannot carry you from Epheska, but I will deliver you from your tormentors. It may be no great military victory—but it will be mine."

Pike nodded with appreciation and stepped aside as T'Var was called to the quarterdeck. He edged closer to Spock and spoke quietly as he watched her depart. "Remarkable person. How did she come to be out here?"

Spock knew. "The commander is reluctant to say because Vulcan today would consider her an outlaw, leading a fugitive faction."

Pike's eyes widened. "You don't mean they're logic extremists?"

"I do not. She attempted to withhold it from me in the mind-meld, but I now believe they were part of the faction that supported the war against the Andorians."

"That's a blast from the past."

"Indeed. Her ships were part of the forces massing for a strike against Andoria when Captain Archer's intervention brought an end to the effort. By the time they knew what had happened, the Syrannites had come to power, establishing peace and logic as the core principles of the Vulcan state."

"So they fled?"

"They wandered for some time, deciding what to do. They considered this nebula a place to settle."

"And the Baffle decided the rest."

"Correct."

Pike shook his head. "We're doing fine as detectives—just not so well as astronauts." He looked over at T'Var and spoke more quietly. "Spock, if they are throwbacks to the bad old days, they wouldn't know about the Federation—or Starfleet. They might not like us."

"She saw it all from our mind-meld—and would have seen how both our societies have flourished in alliance." Spock studied T'Var from afar. "She is, above all, logical—and her desire to help others avoid her fate is sincere."

"So not a dead-ender."

"She has lived at a different dead end for decades. I trust her."

"That's good enough for me."

T'Var returned with an officer Pike recognized as the medic who had evaluated him. "Your injured friend sleeps in the orlop, Captain Pike."

"Lila Talley," Pike said for Spock's benefit. "How is she?"

"Her injuries were not life threatening," the physician said, "but you were right to bring her to us. She has been sedated."

"Her people left her behind," Pike said. "They're not coming anywhere near this place while the ships are here." He addressed T'Var. "When Lila is stable, I'd ask that you return her to them. She won't want to be with us."

"Impossible," the commander said. "The Skagarans brought these sailing ships here and know that someone has put them into operation again. But we have prevented them from learning more by avoiding populated areas and firing on sentinels whenever they appear."

"Warning shots, to drive them away?"

"We are warriors, Captain. We do not warn when our existence is at stake."

Pike didn't like it, but he didn't pursue it.

"From what my spotters tell me, Warden Talley was the only individual harmed last night," T'Var said. "We can heal her and will provide better care than she will receive at any settlement on the planet. But she cannot go back."

Pike looked down. "Role reversal, I guess." He glanced back up at the commander. "Thank you."

He made his respects and stepped away with Spock—who had his own question for once. "Who is this Lila Talley? If you will pardon the curiosity, your concern seems to suggest a longer acquaintance."

"I have a lot to explain to you as well," Pike said. "Afraid I didn't have time to write a book."

"Few do."

CHAPTER 42

THE ORLIGHTS

"Get out!" Drayko yelled. "*Get out, now!*"

The flowerpot he threw did not hit Harjon, but it smashed against the shelving unit beside him, sending shards and soil over the young page's robe. The boy impulsively reached down to pick up the pieces.

"I don't want you to clean. I want you to go!"

Drayko glowered as the boy stumbled all over himself trying to retreat. Harjon came close to colliding with Zoryana, who was on her way into the arboretum.

Her face barely registered the youth's panic. "It's all right," she said mildly. "He has never struck anyone. The general is only a danger to things with stems—and to his own stomach."

Drayko was no happier to see her. "Why are *you* here? Haven't you sent me enough bad news today?"

"I'd have sent a messenger, but they are all too afraid to come." Zoryana stepped to an alcove and collected a broom and dustpan. She walked toward the shattered pot—only to pass by it and place the cleaning items in Drayko's hands. "I am the last one in Om Mataya with courage."

"Then we are truly damned, because no one else on Epheska has any sense." He glared at her. Then he went to work sweeping the shards. "This one had never produced a bud anyway."

Getting information from out west had been difficult. Firearms had been permitted to humans and a few other species who arrived on Epheska with them; they were strictly for animal control. But they could also neutralize the sentinels as an observing force, keeping them well at bay. That and the weather were limiting his updates from the pursuit of Pike.

What had arrived over the rondures since had been a cacophony of confused statements about bullets from the sky and tall phantoms emerging from the dark to protect the wagon train. Most recently, he'd heard Leejo Point had been retaken. But the only indication the fugitives had been there was what their horses had left behind. Drayko had used the Skagaran word for that many times since.

His greatest fear was that *Enterprise* had somehow picked them up. Anything suggesting the Baffle could be thwarted meant the end for Epheska and all their dreams. He fully expected Zoryana's next news to be about the sighting of a vessel lifting off. There was no sense dreading any longer. "Tell me."

"No starship saved them. The lookouts across the bay confirmed it. It's the Orlights."

Drayko dropped the dustpan.

Damn.

In Skagaran mythology, the Orlights had been bogeymen—half machine, half monster—who haunted the seas, rising to attack shipping before disappearing under the waves. The Skagarans buried that fear by draining their oceans. The Orlights of Epheska, meanwhile, were clearly mortals: people operating sailing ships which had long since been abandoned.

Whatever communities they came from, they seemed to have no morals at all when it came to the project. From the first fragmentary reports of them in his grandparents' time, they had fired their weapons willingly on sentinels, preventing any attempt to locate them.

"Mother always said we should have destroyed those ships," he said, rising.

"We preserve the past. The people who abandoned the ships might have changed their minds."

"Too late now. The Orlights can no longer be ignored. Not if they've thrown in with these 'Menders' and Pike."

He frowned as he put away the broom. The Okua Sea was vast, its winds capricious—and the renegades haunted the waters near Zevayne, an area with no active settlements and no aerial coverage. There was only one thing to do—and he had delayed it too long. "Is my son still in the Care Circle?"

"Where else, but by Una's side?" Zoryana responded. "I have never seen him so taken with anyone."

"He'll find someone else."

Drayko went down to the pavilion the back way, reserved for the privileged few. He found Celarius at the perimeter of the great map, gazing stupidly at Una, many meters away. Drayko surprised him.

"Here twice in one week?" Celarius asked. "Did you banish all the runners?"

Drayko took him aside and spoke out of earshot from Una. "It is finished. I know where Pike is."

"You do?" Celarius looked out at the activity on the floor. "The last I heard was something about—"

"I know. Quiet." His son knew about the Orlights, but even in the command center, little was spoken of them. A rebellious force outside the Skagarans' control was a dangerous entity, and the mere news of its existence was a threat. "There's only one way to flush Pike out, and that's to tell him we have her." He pointed at Una.

"You don't *have* her. She's our guest."

"*Your* guest. But she's about to be my guest."

Drayko realized he should have done it right away. He would invite Pike to a peace meeting over the rondure, whereupon he would reveal he had Una in his clutches. She would acknowledge she was his hostage. Pike would surrender himself and the Menders, and the crisis would end. Perhaps he might even yield up the Orlights too.

It all hinged on one woman—who had just spotted them, and was walking excitedly in their direction, holding a sheaf of papers.

"General, we've done it!" she said.

"What is it, Una?"

"*We've found Uhura!*"

Celarius took her arms. "Is it the drawings?"

"Yes!" she nearly gushed. She showed Drayko a series of hand-drawings, made by observers flying sentinels over the last week. "The characters have been marked on the ground. Sometimes in sand, sometimes mud. Now it's in snow. In some places, the grass has been burned to form the characters; the snow likewise looks melted away."

Drayko looked at the top image. "It is the letter *Y* in your language."

"No," she said. "It is the Cyrillic letter У—from the Russian language on Earth." She leafed through the pages in his hands. "This one is a *U* from Federation Standard. This letter is in Swahili—and this one, in Vulcan."

"Vulcan?"

"Another Federation member. Klingon, Andorian, Tellarite—they're all the first letter in her name!" She took the pages from Drayko and led them onto the colossal map. "No sentinel has seen more than one—that's why we had trouble realizing that what we had here was all in a path." She smiled. "We call it the Georgiou Gambit."

Drayko studied the markers she'd placed below—each labeled with a letter and a day of detection. "Would *Enterprise* be able to see these?"

She concentrated. "Doubtful. It's far away, and they're too small. Lidar mapping is more sensitive than visual, but these impressions aren't deep enough to detect. Even we've probably missed some of these because of the weather wiping them away."

Celarius knelt. "She's made it all the way from the hot seams of the Sah'Redah. Not a straight path, but there's a direction here. She's not far."

"You're the tracker," she said.

"Let's go!" Celarius rose. He grasped his father's shoulder. "Whatever you wanted can wait. We'll continue our conversation later."

Drayko thought to object, to order that Una remain—but there was no stopping them. Celarius and his new companion dashed, even as Zoryana entered from behind.

"It's starting to snow out there," she called out. "Don't run so fast!"

Drayko's mind was racing when she arrived at his side. "So much commotion," Zoryana said. "What now?"

"A gambit of my own," he said. "Two hostages are better than one. And even Celarius is unlikely to be infatuated with both of them at once."

She sighed. "These are the statements that make me wonder if you have ever actually met your son."

CHAPTER 43

THE STARGAZERS

Christopher Pike squinted at the pocket watch in the nebular light. "Any time now."

Along *Thunderer's* railing, Menders and Vulcans alike pointed scopes at the night sky. They had suggested both the time and the location for the event, and now it was just a matter of patience—and hope.

Carpenter had gotten bored. "This is silly."

"Keep looking," Pike replied.

"*Yes!*" Cheers went up from the Menders on the line. The Vulcans nodded to one another, their version of celebration.

"That little twinkle?" Carpenter asked, putting his scope down. "Was that *it*?"

"That's it," Pike said.

"It is not a small thing," Spock said, stepping back from his spot on the railing. "As we suggested, *Enterprise* responded to our latest message by emitting a deflector pulse for half a second. They are attempting to harden the ship's EPS conduits against the Baffle's intermittent expansions anyway, so it serves secondarily as a test of those efforts." He clasped his arms behind his back. "The simple opening and closing of a container here set off a chain of events leading to the release of many megajoules of energy in space."

That produced oohs from the Menders. They were really doing something now.

"Why didn't they try this before?" Vicki asked. "I mean, when it wasn't day, or when there were clouds or moons out."

"We were running like hell before," Carpenter said. "Who was looking up?"

The Menders had looked up a lot more lately, Pike thought. With the aid of Spock and a group of Vulcans who were not too far removed from space travel, the hobbyists' simple clockwork communications device had been upgraded significantly. The lids of the viridium's protective case had been separated and attached to gears that went past one another, creating a shutter effect that toggled much faster. The openings and closures were also of more precise duration, which allowed a secondary channel of information.

Pike congratulated Spock, who, as usual, credited others—and said more that could be done. "The crew has a small steam engine they wanted to bring to bear," he said, "but some of the Menders were unwilling to see it used."

"Some of them fear fire." Pike shrugged. "I've explained, but you'll just have to see it to believe it."

"Your friend Joe Magee showed no fear."

"If they have a steam engine, they may never get Joe to leave."

Pike saw T'Var was on deck. She hadn't missed a chance to use her own telescope. "What did you think, Commander?"

She nodded serenely. "Three of my original signals experts yet live," she said, voice betraying a little emotion. "You could say they have lived for this moment."

Pike hoped there'd be more to come, but he didn't know how he'd make that happen. Presuming *Enterprise* could generate more frequent bursts without damaging or depowering itself, there could be actual exchanges of information. They could only come at certain times, but at least it was something. Their previous method, receiving handwritten notes from the sky, was hit-or-miss when the fleet was on the move.

T'Var had chosen the heading, getting them all away from land overseen by the Skagarans as quickly as possible. But they had not determined where to go next.

"There are islands I could deliver you to where you could await retrieval," she said. "Now that *Enterprise* knows where you are, you could wait in such a place. I could provide arms to keep the sentinels away—and could visit to resupply. There are races like the Chone, who found Spock, that trade with us without Drayko's knowledge. You would be another stop."

Pike didn't like the idea, but before he could object, someone stumbled behind them. He looked around to see Weedaw, who had tripped. T'Var called for a chemical lantern.

He helped the blacksmith up. "Are you all right, Weedaw?"

"I am. Sorry!"

"You were listening?" T'Var brought the lamp before him—and held it there for several seconds, staring at him.

"Again, sorry." Weedaw wiped his hairless brow. "I—I—"

"Speak. We are friends."

The timid blacksmith found his voice. "I just thought you said you were taking us to space, Captain Pike!"

Pike had heard that a lot. "I don't even know if we can get *me* to space, Weedaw. The commander here has been trying for a hundred of my years."

T'Var peered at him in the light. "You . . . are Strooh."

Weedaw nodded. "I am. Glad to meet you." He looked behind him. "I'd better go."

Pike glanced at T'Var, who seemed spellbound. She handed Weedaw the lantern. "Take this. We will talk again."

Surprised, Weedaw took it and used it to light his way back to the hold.

"I have seen his kind," she said to Pike. "He has a settlement?"

"One of several. There were others with us, but they fled. But Weedaw has been with us all along."

"I must visit my sailing master," she said. "There may be a destination for us after all."

Pike puzzled over that. His eyes followed her—and then went to the hold. Weedaw was already gone, but someone new was emerging.

"Lila." Pike approached her as she stepped off the stairs with her cane. He offered his hand, but she ignored it. "You're looking better."

"Yeah, well, it's dark out." She pushed past him.

He saw there was a Vulcan sailor behind her, acting as escort. T'Var considered her a prisoner. Pike gestured that he'd be responsible for Lila.

She hadn't been on deck during her convalescence. "Where's Buckshot?"

"We brought him."

She looked about. "I want to see him."

"He's over there." He stepped to the port railing. She hobbled over and looked out on the low silhouette of a fan-sailed vessel, riding the waves. "It's an equine ship, designed for horses."

She stared at it. "Huh."

"Yeah, the Chinese mariners traveled with a full complement of different kinds of vessels. It looks like the Skagarans picked up a whole flotilla."

"I wondered. There are pagodas out east of the Grandwood. I saw them on the way to Havenbrook."

"That's good to hear. That they survived, I mean." He looked back at the sails. "There doesn't seem to be any sign of the people who originally ran this ship anywhere. They just vanished."

She glared at him. "I see what you're doing. You're trying to tell me the project failed them."

"No, but even the Skagarans aren't infallible. What are the chances you'd get a long-lasting, stable population by relocating a ship that held only men?"

She stared at him—and then laughed a little. "I'll allow that." She looked out. "Where are we?"

"We've just been heading further to sea. But I think the ship commander's got a lead on something."

"I don't want to hear about it." Then her curiosity got the better of her. "They're all Vulcans."

"Crash-landed here a hundred of our years ago. They've been trying to stay out of the way of everyone else."

"Nice that *someone* tried that idea." Lila started to turn away—and winced, beginning to falter.

"Careful, there." Pike helped her back to the railing.

Lila gritted her teeth. "Me, falling from a horse. Hasn't happened since I met you."

"That's funny—that day was the first time it happened to me." He grinned. "I tried to go down to the orlop to see you. I saw they put all the children there."

"It's encouraging me to heal faster, so I can get out of there. Jennie's got them all building gadgets."

"It's a way to pass the time."

"They'd be happier on a horse."

"You're saying it's a few steps from building wind-up toys to designing computer games."

"And photon torpedoes." She looked directly at him for a second and turned. "I'm not going to do this, Christopher. We're not going to be the way we were again. Our old arguments—they're not theoretical anymore."

"I understand." He looked down. "I'm sorry about what's happened."

"Me too." She caught the attention of her Vulcan minder. "I'm ready to go back in now."

She limped away, leaving Pike standing alone. Alone, between one ship and another high above.

CHAPTER 44

THE SAVIORS

Nyota Uhura knew it was time to give up when she realized she could no longer remember how her name was spelled in any language.

She had made the markings on the ground countless times on her winding path from the volcanic region. Sometimes with her feet, sometimes with a log. Empy had even cooperated by following her through grass and snow, clearing the path. It was a silly gesture, but it had been something to do.

But the weather had grown colder since the incident at the farm, and her remaining fruit ran out after she reached a rocky region. Snow fell often, and between the clouds and the colorless ground she no longer had any sense of direction.

Empy, too, had burned lower, growing smaller every day. He had given up too much heat, she supposed. Or maybe the being was reflecting her hopelessness. Perhaps it was both.

She didn't know anymore. The day before—*or was it a week ago?*—she had seen another hut, a small shack in the snow. Again, an airship appeared, with a wizard aboard waving a wand. Flames descended from the clouds and consumed the house. She'd looked for occupants but had seen none. Their work done, the flames and the flier vanished into the heavens.

Had it even happened at all? It was hard to tell, and there was nothing left of the hut when she reached it. All she found was a lantern lying in the snow. She took it, as proof to herself that she had not lost her mind.

Starvation, malnutrition, exhaustion, infection—so many Standard words ending with the same letters. One of them would take her, she knew. It had always been a matter of time. That time had finally arrived.

She had crossed her millionth hillside when her legs gave way. She rolled down, tumbling in the snow. Cold and wet, she looked up to see a dark shape in a nearby wall.

A cavern.

A place to curl up and die.

She staggered into it. It wasn't big, just a crevice large enough to keep her dry, but not warm. That was okay. "I have my Empy for that." She waved the creature over, and it settled near her. *Burning as low as I am,* she thought. *But at least we're not alone.*

She had started to drift into a sleep when she heard a horn.

Hallucination. Another I-O-N word.

Another blat.

Blat. Spelled блат. *A form of corruption in ancient Russia.*

Another, louder.

Corruption. I-O-N. Go away!

Empy flared brightly—and she woke up. She rolled over and saw an airship sailing past outside. Larger than any she'd seen before.

Uhura got to her hands and knees in panic. "They saw the light!"

There were voices out there somewhere. It was landing.

"They're coming for you!" Not even thinking about what she was doing, she thrust her hands into the empatherm and kneaded the creature like flaming dough. Her hands were stinging from the cold anyway; what difference did it make? Yet it did not burn her as she compacted it into the lantern. Trading volume for luminescence, Empy sizzled brightly.

"Shhh!" she said.

"Don't shush a commanding officer," said another voice she was sure was a trick of the mind.

She turned. "Commander!"

"Uhura!" her friend called out. Chin-Riley hurried in and embraced the cadet. "We thought you were a goner!"

Uhura couldn't believe it. She watched, bleary-eyed, as the older woman fished out a canteen for her. This was no Starfleet uniform she was wearing; rather, it looked like the garb of a Lapland adventurer.

Chin-Riley started rubbing Uhura's hands together. "You're shaking. No surprise there."

Uhura looked past her outside, where the airship had settled. "The balloon. Don't let them take Empy."

"What are you talking about?"

Uhura fell to her knees and grabbed the lantern. She drew it to her body, protecting it. "You can't let them take him."

"Your lantern?" Chin-Riley exhaled, her breath crystallizing before her. "It's okay, Nyota. I know you've been through a lot."

"We have to keep him. Keep him safe!"

"Okay, Lucky Lantern. We'll take it." *Enterprise*'s first officer paused and looked kindly upon it. "I guess it saved your life."

CHAPTER 45

THE SURVIVORS

The island was tiny. The hut was smaller. Round, with a straw roof barely able to keep out the elements. But the cove it sat near was a brilliant blue, and fruits and flowers were all about.

Christopher Pike had initially thought this was the island that T'Var had intended for them all to retire to. As it turned out, she had already used the place for that purpose for someone else: an acquaintance she saw only once every few seasons when the fleet came by to deliver supplies.

An acquaintance who looked like no being T'Var had ever seen before—until she met Weedaw on the deck of *Thunderer*.

The ship sat in the natural harbor as the commander's sailors dragged the launch onto the beach. She walked toward the hut first, followed by Spock and Pike, both flanking a very nervous Weedaw.

"I met Jaddak not long after I arrived here," T'Var said. "He is from a place in the interior of the northeastern end of Zevayne. I never spoke his language, but I could easily understand he lived in fear." She gestured around. "This place, which I brought him to, may be the only safety he has ever known."

Pike remembered how long ago the Vulcans had arrived and wondered how long members of the Strooh species lived. It was only on stepping into the hut that he realized that whatever the life span was, Jaddak was well past it. The shriveled being lay in bed, moving only to sip at a shell full of water now and again. He paid his visitors no attention at all.

T'Var spoke. "It has been too long," she said. "I hope I am not too late for you."

Jaddak stirred at her voice. He lifted his head a little and mumbled something.

Pike looked to Weedaw.

"Do you understand him?"

"Yes. It's the old tongue of the Strooh. Not many speak it now."

"I thought Drayko and the Skagarans wanted their settlers to protect their original languages."

"My people have been here a *very* long time," Weedaw replied. "We have evolved the farthest from where we were. But my grandmother remembered, and I remember her."

Pike nodded, and Weedaw spoke some words to the old man in a chirpy language.

Jaddak focused hazily on the other orange face in the room—and rolled over on his side, facing away from Weedaw.

Pike glanced at Spock. It wasn't going well.

Spock addressed T'Var. "You told us some of his history. How did you learn it?"

"I mind-melded with him when he was younger," she said. "I wanted to know what he feared—and also to give him peace."

The science officer concentrated on the figure. "Would another mind-meld now be appropriate?"

T'Var shook her head. "You do not want to be in a dying mind."

"I am not afraid."

"I admire your commitment, but your youth speaks now. The mind-meld is no shortcut to knowledge."

"You performed one on me."

"My *age* spoke. I know when to use it and when not to." She looked to Weedaw. "It is up to you. When I saw you, I could not think but to bring you here. You are our last chance to learn what he has to tell us."

Weedaw shrugged. "He's not listening."

Pike put his hand on the blacksmith's shoulder. "Tell Jaddak who you are. Tell him where you're from. Where you live." His eyes narrowed. "Tell him about the Skagarans, and what you think of them now."

Weedaw gulped. Then he did as asked, speaking to the old man nonstop for twenty minutes. Pike was ready to give up when Jaddak's eyes opened wide. He began to speak. Weedaw listened.

"He says the Strooh from the First Days—"

Weedaw paused.

"Why'd you stop?" Pike asked.

"I'm not sure I understand. He says the very first Skagaran mission on Epheska was on Zevayne—and that it was failing. The continent was too wild, too dangerous. My people were made to help clear the land—and the countryside."

Pike looked to Spock, astonished. "They *were* slaves!"

Weedaw's eyes were wide. "I don't believe it. But, yes, that is how he says it was in the beginning."

Jaddak spoke some more.

"The Skagarans chose poorly with us," Weedaw translated. "We were builders, not hunters." He listened to more. "That is why the Skagarans later went to Earth, to get the fan ships. The Skagarans used them to relocate to safer areas."

Jaddak growled something.

"And they left many of the Strooh behind." Weedaw looked to Pike. "Jaddak's ancestors. They weren't happy about it."

Pike didn't blame them.

Something had been unleashed in the old man. Jaddak spoke in a nonstop stream of consciousness and Weedaw tried his best to keep up.

"Over the next several hundred years, the few remaining Strooh of Zevayne fought every day for survival. Disease. Disaster. Everything had come for them. Every day was a battle against the elements. And while the Skagarans spoke with them through the rondure, they did not offer to help them. They were told to make their settlement work."

T'Var breathed out. "They would have said so. Zevayne is very far."

If they weren't going to take them along, they weren't going to help them, Pike thought. It was a tragic story. But it didn't become something else until Jaddak spoke again.

"His people understood the rondures. They understood the Baffle." Weedaw stopped and looked at Pike. "They know how the Baffle works."

Spock, Pike, and T'Var looked at one another.

"*They know how to control it,*" Weedaw said. "And he says they are still there, deep in the jungle . . ."

Lila Talley watched from the deck as the pinnace was loaded aboard. She was feeling better, but still not well enough that the sailor watching her had any need to worry.

She noted that the commander had immediately ordered full sails. *Thunderer* was signaling the other vessels of the flotilla when Pike walked toward her.

"Still playing explorer?" she asked.

"You could say that," Pike said. He gestured to the sails. "We're heading for a place on the far end of that big landmass on the horizon."

"If you say so."

"In the interior, way in the jungle, there's a settlement. It sounds dangerous— and the Vulcans aren't much for horses or cross-country travel." Pike looked directly at her. "We need a tracker."

Lila did a double take. "You want *me*?"

"*Braidwood* hired you as a scout. No reason why we couldn't. We even brought your horse."

"Not interested."

"See," Pike said, "there's this lost city. Wonderful lost-city name, too: *Agar.*"

"That doesn't sound inviting."

"Yeah, it's the stuff bacteria feed on in petri dishes. Hopefully not a sign. We think it might be the very first place the Skagarans brought anyone to." He paused. "There's a rondure there."

She froze. "There is?"

"Yes. We expect it's still connected to the network."

Lila looked back at the island they'd just departed—and then back at Pike. "What happens if I help you?"

"We'll find out what we need to find out. Then you can call Drayko and have someone come to get you, if they say they're capable of it. T'Var will leave you with all the food and water you need." Pike gestured behind him. "Someplace nice like this, maybe."

Lila didn't know what to think. "They fired on my people. I don't trust them."

"I had to twist T'Var's arm, Lila. The Vulcans value their privacy, their independence. Releasing anyone who's seen them to the Skagarans is the last thing they want to do. But they're going to make an exception for you."

"Why would they do that?"

"Because I told them you were the best." He tapped his temple. "Logic."

Lila clasped her hands together and looked down. Her ankle still smarted, but she figured she could still ride. And being on Buckshot, anywhere, was just as good as being set free. Nobody would capture her again. But she still had a question.

"Why do they want to go to this place?" She stared at him. "The truth."

"We think it has something to do with the origins of the Baffle."

Oh. The ulterior motive.

Pike kept talking. "Maybe you're right that it's permanent. That we're all stuck here. That nobody up there in space is ever going to see us again. But I'm not going to rest until I find out *why* this thing exists. I can't live someplace where I don't know that."

"You won't stop, will you?"

"No."

"And if you find out what's causing it, and there's nothing to do about it— what? You'll apologize to Drayko and settle down with a nice homestead somewhere?"

"Seems to have been done before, yeah."

It wouldn't be the first time she'd taught him something. Maybe this trip— all of it, from the wagon train to the jungle—was what he needed to finally let go of his old life. If that was the case, then it was worth it.

"When do we leave?" she asked.

"As soon as we get there."

"Fine." She hobbled past him and punched his elbow. "You'd better be ready to ride, Pike. I don't wait for stragglers."

CHAPTER 46

THE REUNITED

Uhura's gone again!

Una Chin-Riley charged through the halls of the guest section of the Garden House, opening door after door. Desperate to find the cadet that she'd brought to safety the night before, she had interrupted the repose—but thankfully never the activities—of several visitors to Om Mataya, with no luck.

She couldn't fault the nurses that Drayko and Celarius had appointed for Uhura. They'd tended to her immediately, getting fluids into her and treating her exposure and blistered feet. After Uhura had slept for twenty hours, whoever was responsible for attending her had been called away to aid another guest. How were they to know that the young woman would choose that hour to rise and escape?

Chin-Riley circled back to Uhura's room twice, fearful of alerting anyone higher up of the cadet's disappearance. Celarius she trusted, but the others she wasn't sure about. She was preparing to surrender and ask for help when it dawned on her to check her own quarters.

She heard a muffled voice through the door. This was what she was worried about: someone searching her room. She was considering what to do when recognition struck. She opened the door and saw Uhura sitting on the bed, hunched near the lantern on Una's bedstand.

"Sorry," Uhura said. "We're talking."

"To the lantern?"

"Uh-huh."

Chin-Riley stared quizzically for a moment before stepping inside and shutting the door quietly behind her. "You're AWOL, Cadet."

"I was looking for him."

"For whom?"

"The pronoun is of my choosing—laziness, I guess." Uhura patted the top of the lantern with her hand. "I just know I couldn't have made it alone."

The commander sighed. *Still fixated.*

Uhura had turned out to be in relatively good physical shape, despite her days of deprivation. Chin-Riley had been expecting some kind of mental breakdown, as well—but even she had been surprised by the extent to which the cadet clung to the rusty old lantern.

Whatever Uhura had found to fuel it, the thing had given her light and warmth, and the commander understood what that meant. It was important to her. But Uhura's behavior aboard the airship had been something else. First, she'd panicked on seeing the staff-wielding figure aft. Then, once the sentinel lifted off, Uhura had curled into a fetal position around the lantern, chattering to it nervously.

"Calm down. Calm down. Don't go!" she'd said, in between cooing to the lantern like it was a baby. Focusing on the fast retreat to Om Mataya, Celarius hadn't seen much of the spectacle, and Chin-Riley was glad of that. She was also happy that Uhura hadn't set herself on fire. How she hadn't smothered the flame, Chin-Riley still didn't know. Once in Om Mataya, she'd been forced to peel Uhura's fingers from the handle.

The lantern had sat in Chin-Riley's room ever since, during many hours while she was sitting vigil with Uhura. The commander assumed it had burned itself out, many hours before—but the cadet had apparently gotten to it. "What did you fill it with?"

"Nothing."

"I mean, what's it burning?" Chin-Riley couldn't imagine anyone giving her access to any kind of oil.

"Nothing." Uhura gestured to the lantern with pride. "I would like you to meet *Flamma motus*, my first life-form!"

"Your what?"

"I thought about it a long time—I had a long time to think, anyway. I was going to tack an *uhurus* at the end for a subspecies, but we'll have to see if he has friends."

"Friends."

"I know I haven't had all the experience with encountering new species that you have. Empy's my first."

"Empy?"

"He's an empatherm."

The commander decided she needed to sit down. She found a chair across from the bed and dragged it over. "Did they give you anything? Any medication?"

"No."

"Eat any wild fungi on the way here?"

"Mushrooms would have been lovely. But no."

"You think the fire is alive."

"Of course." Uhura looked at her sideways—and brought up her hand to speak confidentially. "I'd ask him to prove it, but it seems rude to get someone to confirm that they're alive."

Chin-Riley didn't know how to respond. She decided to avoid the matter entirely. "Someone else is alive, you'll be glad to hear. Captain Pike."

"Great!" Uhura smiled broadly. She put her hands to her chest. "I was so worried."

Chin-Riley squinted at Uhura—and then realized why she was squinting. The lantern had, in the last few seconds, glowed more brightly: a soothing, brilliant blue.

"Oh, *there* he goes." Uhura chuckled. "I was hoping he would do that. Like I said, it felt rude to ask."

Chin-Riley stared at the flame. "How'd it do that?"

"I'm happy. It's happy for me."

"Do it again."

"Do what again?"

"Make the flame jump."

Uhura pursed her lips in judgment. "I don't think you should do that, Commander." She placed a protective hand on the lantern. "It doesn't like being manipulated."

"It doesn't?"

"By those people with the cloaks and the rams' horn staffs in the balloons. They're making the empatherms do things."

"What things?"

"I'm not sure. But they don't like it." She looked at the lantern like a puppy. "Do you, Empy?"

The fire pulsed orange.

I definitely saw that, Chin-Riley thought. "Was that why you were talking to the lantern aboard the airship?"

"Yes! Empy kept trying to get out of the lantern. The people with the staffs, they might do something to it."

The commander stared at the container—and considered all the strange things she'd encountered. "Open the top."

Uhura's expression grew fretful. "He might leave."

Chin-Riley couldn't see how that would happen. "Indulge me. It'll be okay."

Reluctantly, Uhura loosened the lid from the lantern. For several seconds, the fire continued to burn. The flame reddened and rose a little higher, licking over the top of the open container—

—and then left it altogether. The flames swirled and coruscated, expanding in volume and size.

"What the hell?" Chin-Riley sat back in her chair as the wisp whirled around her, a glowing ghost on the air.

"I told you. It's alive." Uhura smiled. "It's okay, Empy. She's my friend."

Chin-Riley froze as the flames whipped past her face. "Uh—yeah," she said. "I'm Uhura's friend. And she's yours."

After a moment, the flame creature—for that was now what Chin-Riley had to agree it was—cooled to a friendly blue. It left the space around the first officer and wafted up to explore the ceiling.

"Well, we've established that it knows the associative property." Chin-Riley looked up. "Won't it set fire to the room?"

"I don't think it would do that." Uhura looked up. "Would you, Empy?"

The commander didn't know whether the thing answered or not.

"We clearly have a lot more to talk about, Cadet. A lot more. But we'd better get you to your room, before you're missed." Chin-Riley glanced up. "By chance, could you put the cat back in the bag first?"

Uhura responded with a playful frown. "He's not a pet."

"Just do . . . whatever you do. I'm late. They're expecting me at dinner."

The cadet held her midsection. "Please don't tell me about it. I'm hungry, but the idea of food makes me queasy."

"Don't worry," Chin-Riley said. She glanced up at the elemental. "This time, I think I'll be going for the drinks."

CHAPTER 47

THE EXPEDITION

As captain, Christopher Pike wasn't supposed to lead landing parties. Expeditions were for junior officers. He hadn't lived by the letter of that rule, even when events, such as on Talos IV, demonstrated he absolutely should have. He frankly didn't know many officers who would go through everything it took to lead a mission across the stars, only to sit at a desk and say, "I'll read your report."

Number One was on Epheska somewhere, he hoped, and every five minutes since waking up on the planet, he'd longed to run into her around a corner. They could debate the wisdom of him taking a look at the planet from *Eratosthenes*—which, he'd successfully argued, did not constitute a landing party. But what she couldn't object to on regulatory grounds was the four-person expedition heading into the interior of Zevayne.

For Pike was not leading the expedition at all. Lila Talley was.

That wouldn't have stopped his first officer from pointing out the incredible dangers he was subjecting himself to by going. Seven times since entering the jungle, they'd been attacked by creatures that even Lila hadn't seen before. Some running or slithering on the ground, some bounding from the trees, some diving through the canopy. But Number One probably wouldn't have handled the situations any differently. Lila had fired her rifle into the air sometimes; other times, she'd fired it at something. On two occasions the party had come to a full stop, then headed another way.

The most recent encounter had been the "run like hell" time. He trusted Lila to know the difference, just as he'd trusted her to know a rattler from a garter snake when he was young. The thing that had pursued them for three kilometers before giving up was something she hadn't seen before, but it was close enough to something she *had* seen that she'd played her hunch. Whatever an *ollodon* was, Pike was glad he hadn't met one on the range.

Their long, winding journey into the Zevaynian uplands had started in the bedroom of a dying Strooh, with a pause to consult higher powers. *Enterprise* had generated another lidar map, taking a closer look at their target area, and had sent coordinates for a suitable harbor via a series of highly energetic flashes which had almost certainly made Chief Hemmer rend his uniform. A care package with the map itself was waiting on the beach when they arrived.

A path decided upon, they'd made their way through the brush in single file, with Lila in the lead and Pike in the rear. They weren't going to get Weedaw on anything larger than his pony, but at least he was an experienced rider.

That wasn't true for their fourth, whom Lila seemed to watch with eyes in the back of her head. "You're too close, Spock. Didn't you have horses on Vulcan?"

"Clearly they were kept where I could not see them," he replied.

"I said you needed to wear the hat," Pike said. "It conveys competence."

Lila shot back, "Yeah, you're not watching Weedaw's gait either, Christopher. You're bunching up on the transitions."

"Yes, Mom." Pike smiled in spite of himself. She was fully back on the Bar T.

"Horses will tailgate," she added, "but they don't like it being done to them."

"Is the tailgate another kind of gait?" Spock asked.

"I'll ask you not to confuse my lieutenant," Pike said. "He's still working on 'riding shotgun.'"

They'd needed the banter. It had taken hours of intense cajoling during *Thunderer*'s voyage to convince Weedaw to even look at the map of the jungle region. Putting him on the ground had been accomplished only by promising that T'Var would send her entire platoon with them. That had slowly been whittled down to just Pike, Spock, and Lila as the time approached and it became clear that the only way two horses abreast could make it through the foliage was if they had disruptors mounted on their heads.

But Weedaw had agreed, ultimately, understanding that somewhere in the jungle lay the secret past of the Strooh. Their history before Epheska had never been depicted in any of the Jubilees, and after meeting Jaddak, the blacksmith seemed to feel he represented all his people on the mission. That was literally true, given his relatives' desertion from Leejo Point. Maybe, Pike thought, Weedaw dared to hope for a little redemption. The captain wanted to make sure he got his chance at some.

Most of all, Pike had been pleased by how Lila had taken to the assignment. The saddle was where she was happiest; he'd been glad they'd saved her stallion for her.

They kept climbing, all noticing that the wind had picked up. Pike was going to say something about the weather when Lila gave her hand signal, slowing them to a walk. That usually meant she'd noticed something ahead and didn't want to attract its attention. Pike quietly drew the rifle he'd been given. T'Var had insisted they go armed, and not because she thought Lila was a threat to bolt. The commander had been right. If Jaddak was correct, this place didn't just kill people: it had killed *everyone*.

"We're good." Lila nudged Buckshot ahead. One by one, the four riders trotted into the open.

There's your lost city, Pike said to himself. *Just to complete the experience.*

"Agar," Weedaw said, mesmerized.

Like the other settlements Pike had seen on the planet, either from the trail or on the ocean, it had the prototypical Epheskan stone temple, presumably to house its rondure. But it was unlike them in that the temple was half demolished. Even from a distance they could tell a third of the rotunda was missing, shattered away—and the attached portico had cleaved completely off, the ground beneath it having sunk a meter and a half.

It was more than erosion, Spock said. "Structural damages suggest tectonic activity."

Quakes. Pike shook his head. It wasn't enough that everything above ground had tried to kill the Strooh who had remained. Epheska itself had turned against them.

They entered the village, wary of any creatures that might be in hiding. What they hadn't counted on were the ghosts. The rest of the surrounding village only evoked silence from Spock—and horror from the others.

"Everything's gone," Pike said. Mounds of rubble barely suggested structures anymore. Rot had taken the wood, and a blue moss had covered everything. Every so often, they saw a shaft of metal poking out from the ground, part of something that had existed long before.

Pike thought Weedaw would break down. He lamented all that he saw. "Attacked by the ground itself. Could anything have saved this place?"

People in San Francisco figured it out, Pike wanted to respond. A glance at Lila suggested that it wasn't a good time to bring that debate back out.

Spock surveyed the ruins. "If Commander T'Var is correct about the Skagarans having used their form of transporter to deposit the colonists onto the surface, there is little point seeking a vessel."

"I wonder why they chose this place to start with," Lila said.

Pike thought he knew. He rode to the southern edge of what was only barely a clearing anymore. Stone stairs led down into a maze of green. To the left, the stream providing Agar's eastern border plummeted down in a brilliant waterfall, only to vanish in the foliage.

The four dismounted and looked down together. "The map suggested this," Pike said. "Temple on the hill, population on terraces below."

Lila nodded. "This was probably nice once."

Weedaw agreed. "People joke that the Skagarans put their rondures in some of the ugliest places they could find, hoping we'd gussy them up."

"This appears to be the exception," Spock said. "Or it once was."

An evil zephyr cut up from far below, shaking the trees and causing an evacuation of bat-like avians. Weedaw stumbled back, and all four horses had something to say about it.

"We'd better get the horses to that water, and then back to the temple," Lila said. "If T'Var's weather report is right, this place after dark could make the blow at Leejo Point look like a Mojave dust devil."

"They weren't all small, but I agree," Pike said. He kept to himself that T'Var's warning had been fortified with observations from *Enterprise*. "Let's go."

He stepped up the pace and walked alongside her. "You doing all right?"

"You can stop asking me now."

"Just concerned."

"As long as nobody fires a cannonball at me, Buck and I should be fine."

They had found some luck at the stream, which had a rivulet that fed into a trough near the town. It had probably once been part of an aqueduct, Spock surmised. Lila didn't judge the water dangerous, so it had suited. Finding a secure place to tie the horses, on the other hand, was easier said than done.

"Weedaw and I tied up over there," she said to Pike.

He and Spock had only found a gnarled metal post in the ground that didn't seem to be going anywhere. They were still working to secure to it when Lila pushed past them and took over.

She looked at Pike as she secured the leads. "Who taught you to tie like this?"

"She was brutal. It was terrible."

One by one, the four scrambled across the wrecked portico and up into the shattered temple. Late afternoon light from the cloudy sky illuminated the central room. The rondure sat inside, hanging in midair just as Pike had seen in Havenbrook—and amazingly, it appeared to have survived a direct hit from debris from the ceiling.

"The granite shattered on impact," Spock said. "Incredible."

The surrounding circle and its rays on the floor appeared intact, as well—if covered by rubble and dust.

"Too bad we didn't bring a broom," Pike said. He reached into his pack. "Torch time." Since leaving the coast, the Sorry hadn't even been a consideration, but he still didn't expect he'd get Weedaw to carry one.

"Look here," Weedaw said. The circle ringing the rondure had something different to it. Black marble tablets were affixed to it, spaced equally around its circumference.

"Looks like twelve of them," Pike said as Spock began dusting. "Have you seen anything like these?" Pike asked Lila.

She seemed entranced. "Most people wouldn't attach anything near the rondures. It's kind of—"

"Desecration?"

"They're afraid they'd get in trouble with their wardens. I'd certainly yell."

Spock looked up. "There are etchings on these tablets. It does not appear to be the Skagaran type I found in the book my rescuers provided me."

It was what Pike had hoped for. "You're up, Weedaw. Do your thing."

CHAPTER 48

THE GUESTS

The denizens and guests of Om Mataya woke to an early snow, which, if anything, made the hidden valley even more beautiful. It also made it feel more secluded, Una Chin-Riley thought. And since her rescue of Uhura, she'd come to feel the Garden House's comfortable embrace a little too tightly.

There were no more airship jaunts with Celarius for her to search for anyone, even though Spock was still unaccounted for, and her visits to the Care Circle had ended altogether. "We have a new class of novices in," Zoryana had told her; she didn't want to crowd the floor. The commander had certainly seen the green-cloaked newbies moving about on the grounds, and they always moved as a group, like a scout troop. But they couldn't be in the pavilion *all* the time.

Pike's reported transit to Om Mataya had been interrupted nine times and counting, including four weather diversions, three cases of mechanical difficulties, and two side trips to visit natural wonders. *And a partridge in a pear tree*, she wanted to add.

Enterprise's first officer had not just fallen off the nearest *kuuko*, and she had cornered Celarius about it at the chateau when he came to lunch with her and a recuperating Uhura. The scion had been kept busy lately by Drayko, whom she had not seen at all, and he had been oddly evasive. But at least he seemed to feel bad about it.

The empatherm was still burning in the lantern in her room when she and Uhura returned from the meal. "He's starting to like you," the cadet said.

"I figured it was better to keep it in here for the time being. I'm Celarius's special guest, and they're less likely to mess with me." Chin-Riley closed the door behind her and stared at the plasma being. "In another circumstance, we'd definitely have our tricorders out right now."

"I know," Uhura said. "I had elementary astrobiology, but this is a case for Sam Kirk."

"Have you given any thought to asking what it wants? It's been following you for days, right?"

"I wondered about imprinting or pair-bonding. But I don't even know how it's sensing me." She thought for a moment. "It seems to control when it's hot or not. Maybe it's something thermal. It's reading my emotional state by sensing changes in my body temperature. If I had my environmental suit, I might be able to test that. But it melted."

"I threw *my* helmet at a bird."

Uhura laughed.

"And this concludes the science portion of our mission." Chin-Riley had to get back to functional Starfleet equipment before she lost her mind.

Uhura crossed to look out the window. She, too, was clearly taken by the place's natural beauty. The cadet shook her head. "Commander—" She stopped without finishing.

"What is it?"

"Oh, nothing."

"Permission to speak freely."

Uhura shrank back. "No, I really shouldn't."

"I insist."

She turned. "It's just that while I've been starving and walking across half of creation, you've been here."

"Pampered in a warm bed, eating wonderful food, and being romanced by a wild man turned prince."

"There's a prince?"

"The guy from lunch."

"That was *him*? I thought he was just the pilot. You've got a prince that flies balloons?"

"You should see what he gets up to in the forest." She laughed. "My arrival was pretty awful, too, Nyota. And while I've been in Om Mataya for a while, I haven't just been wasting time. Secure that door for me."

While Uhura did so, Chin-Riley reached under her bed and pulled out a stack of papers.

"Maps," Uhura said.

"Lifted from the library. Then when I was in the Care Circle—that's the pavilion with their command center—I'd memorize what I saw and mark it back on these." She paged through the documents, stopping to display her notations. "After they told me the captain had been found, I noticed they had forces out west chasing something. Then it all suddenly broke off, and next thing I knew all the attention was at the shorelines of the sea."

"Captain Pike is out there somewhere?"

"I know where he isn't—on an airship heading here." She pulled a book from her hiding place. "That's the other thing. I've been learning Skagaran at night. This is a Standard-to-Skagaran dictionary."

Uhura reached for it. "May I?"

"If you're ready to get back to work, by all means. Here I am a guest at a palace, and I'm spending my nights conjugating irregular verbs." She put up her hand. "And before you make a joke about the prince—"

"I wasn't going to."

"That's fine, because I was going to. He's a brilliant naturalist and entertaining to be around. But he's also gotten his way on every small thing since he was born, and he seems to have gotten to what you and I would consider forty without getting up the nerve to leave the house for good."

"He's *forty*? He looked—"

"Younger. You should have seen him in the forest. I thought he was primeval." She smiled and shrugged. "Anyway, even if I were stuck on this planet forever, I wouldn't want to waste my time waiting for him to decide what he wants to be when he grows up. No matter how good the imported seafood is here."

Uhura winced, a hand on her stomach. "I wish you hadn't said seafood."

"Sorry. I hope you saw that I had the porridge in solidarity with you."

"I'd kill for crackers."

"I'll kill if I don't get out of here." Chin-Riley put away the maps and looked at the window. "Let's try something. Tell Empy to hang on."

The commander turned the handles to the balcony doors. The doors cracked open loudly, admitting a cool breeze and frost particles into the room. The balcony had steps leading down to the terrace, from which the rest of everything on her bank of the Matayan River could be accessed. She and Uhura walked outside.

"We're not really dressed for this weather," she said, heading down the steps.

"I'm having flashbacks," Uhura responded.

"Don't worry. We won't get far."

Indeed, the two were barely on the bottom step when a large, cloaked figure confronted her. The commander had seen his kind before. A Zoldaari, Celarius had called them, by far the planet's most imposing-looking sentients.

This one was kind and proper. "The terrace is closed, my friends."

"Why?"

"The snow."

"We've walked in snow before," Uhura said.

He switched gears. "Tile maintenance."

"Under the snow?" Chin-Riley asked.

"I'm sorry, but you're not allowed to leave. Please stay in the chateau's luxury guest chambers." He crossed his arms and did not move until they returned upstairs.

"*Please stay in the chateau's luxury guest chambers*," Chin-Riley parroted. "Words of a tyrannical regime if I've ever heard them." She closed the balcony doors tight behind her.

Uhura warmed herself by Empy, who glowed extra bright for her. "I guess this is what they call house arrest."

"In any language." Chin-Riley pursed her lips. She thought about what she'd seen, about the schedules she'd noticed everyone keeping. There were ways around the complex that they hadn't shown her, but she knew they existed and had a good idea how to find them. "I'm done giving these people the benefit of the doubt," she said. "It's time for you and me to go on offense!"

CHAPTER 49

THE THINKERS

Even without the Sorry to worry about, Christopher Pike still found himself contending with rebellious fire. Angry winds outside whipped through the openings in the temple, creating sudden updrafts through the gaps in the dome above. Gusts either extinguished their torches or sent their flames licking chaotically. The temple at Agar was well stocked with *zazics*, but he'd seen none of the chemical light fixtures that had been in Havenbrook.

I guess they never planned on an open-air ceiling here.

The best news was that after a frightening first night with the others in the ruins, Weedaw had been able to use the light he had to make some headway. The etchings on the tablets were too shallow for Spock to take rubbings of, but he had knelt beside the blacksmith, transcribing his interpretations on a pocket diary that T'Var had provided.

The first tablet largely bore out Jaddak's recollections, but he had either not known or not revealed the rest of the story, Weedaw said. "Some of the Strooh did leave with the Skagarans when they relocated off the continent," he said. "But not all. Those who remained here were the educated, the wise."

"The wise stayed *here*?" Pike asked. Given the dangers of the area, it didn't seem very smart to him.

"That is what it says."

Spock looked up from his notes. "Perhaps the Skagaran project did not begin in its current shape."

Lila, who'd been wandering about clearing debris as she waited, asked him what he meant.

"Perhaps their prohibition on nonelectronic technologies was not present at the start," Spock said. "It might have come about as they determined that workers who embraced them would grow more restive, and harder to control."

"Please," she said. "Have you even been to a Jubilee? They've showed us how it happened. They weren't trying to control people. They were trying to help them."

"I believe they think their intentions are noble now," Spock said. "But theirs would not be the first society to ascribe their current values to historical founders whose motivations were different. On Vulcan—"

Pike gestured for him to stop. Lila wasn't being combative, but the last thing he needed was a war between his guide and his science officer. "Weedaw, this split that happened—was it violent?"

Weedaw read some more. "No. There was conflict, but fighting is not the Strooh way."

"So it wasn't like the human revolt that Jonathan Archer found. I told you that story, right?"

"You did. And no—from what I read here, only the 'thinkers' wound up remaining." He looked up. "They sound like Menders."

"How do you know *what* they were?" Lila asked. "Anyone would *say* they were the smart ones."

"Yes, but these people wrote it," Weedaw said. "Writing is not widespread among the Strooh, even now." He gestured to the other panels. "And then there are all these calculations."

Pike and Spock looked at each other. "Calculations?" Pike asked.

Weedaw nodded. He moved to the next panel. "It's what most of the tablets are, in fact. Explorations into the origins of the rondures."

"That shouldn't require much space," Lila said. "The Skagarans built them."

Pike looked to her. "They've said that?"

"Of course."

Spock stared at the floating sphere. "This technology is unknown, even to us. You are certain of this?"

She thought for a moment. "Never in so many words," she said. "The Baffle was here when they got here, but the rondures are different. The Skagarans placed them."

"That's what I was always taught too." Wide-eyed, Weedaw tapped the glyphs he was reading. "This says otherwise."

Lila rolled her eyes. "Now you're going to tell me it says the great Strooh inventors made them."

"No. They were all here when the Skagarans found the planet. Just sitting there, all around."

Pike stepped up to look over his shoulder. "You mean the rondures are just like the Baffle? Artifacts?"

"I think so. The Strooh here called this the 'planet of orbs' long before the other rondures would have been placed elsewhere. The people who landed here just kept finding more of them."

"But no native race." Pike looked to Spock, who was quickly scribbling away in his notes. "Another case of abandoned technology."

"They're *not* technology," Lila said. "At least, they're not supposed to be."

Pike watched her walk to an upturned stone. She sat down on it, fixed her eyes on the ruby sphere, and frowned. It was a hard thing, having one's belief system challenged. He was glad that she'd only been here for months rather than years.

Weedaw went on. "I don't understand it all, but I think it says the temples were here, too, already constructed. The *zazics* were inside, like you see over there. Just sitting there. It was after the Skagarans found the second temple that the Strooh figured out you could use the *zazics* with the rondures for mental communication."

"The *Strooh* figured it out?" Lila asked.

"And then taught the Skagarans. But I may be misreading."

There go all the history books, Pike thought, before remembering he hadn't really seen one, beyond what the Menders had cobbled together. But it all made sense.

On other worlds, people tended to form communities near natural features—rivers and coastlines—that afforded them benefits. But he'd noticed from the map and from his observations that that was rarely the case on Epheska. The best spot for Havenbrook was actually closer to Joe's farm, next to the actual brook, rather than farther west, where there was no easy water source. Now he understood. The Skagarans settled people by the rondures, and controlled migration so no one moved too far away from one.

Excitedly, Weedaw moved from one panel to the next. "The Strooh continued studying the rondures, even after the Skagarans left in the boats. They believed the Baffle itself was connected to the rondures—"

"*Yes,*" Pike said. It was what he'd been hoping to hear. "Go on."

"—and that there might be a rondure that controlled the entire system."

"You mean . . . ?"

"The—" Weedaw paused, struggling for a word. "What do you call a center, governing but not in the middle of something?"

Pike smirked. "A bridge?"

Spock had an answer. "Nodal."

Weedaw accepted that. "Okay. The 'nodal rondure,' as they call it, can bring the Baffle's strength down to zero, like reducing the fire in a kiln." He looked back at Pike in shock. "Your devices would work then!"

Spock nodded. "It could be deactivated."

"*Deactivated*?" Lila blurted.

Weedaw nodded. "That is what this says."

She got up from her seat. "Have you thought what that will mean?"

"Certainly," Spock said. "It means that whatever is interfering with the natural interplay of forces on this planet would be removed, and the—"

She cut him off. "Have you thought about what it would mean for someone other than you?"

"I believe the same results would obtain for everyone."

Lila shook her head. "The answer is no, then." She turned to face Pike. "What about *you*?"

CHAPTER 50

THE NOVICES

Nyota Uhura knew that the commander had been investigating Om Mataya's secrets for days. But something they discovered together would have made all their efforts easier: a turbolift.

It was not a turbolift, of course. Neither Uhura nor Chin-Riley knew how the thing was powered. But it functioned more or less like one in that it was a car on a track that combined diagonal inclines with short horizontal and vertical stretches, and it connected the Garden House with buildings on several of the lower terraces. All done with gears, gravity, and pulleys—and, she supposed, some kind of animal or hydrostatic energy driving the motion. You could do a lot without electrical power.

"I knew Drayko wasn't taking all those stairs to get around," the commander said. She added that she'd nearly caught him using the thing days earlier.

The two officers had secretly ridden on top of the car, which was less frightening a prospect than the equivalent experience in a turbolift or mine elevator would have been. The alpine lifter rode a route that passed through one successively higher building after another, and they'd needed to listen to the speakers below to have any sense of what they were arriving at.

Uhura and Chin-Riley both recognized a word that they'd been hoping to hear: *barracks*. The novices were at their training sessions at this hour, and it had been a small matter for the women to steal out—and purloin a couple of green cloaks. Then a return to the lifter, where they tested their robes out.

"You two are late," said the Zoldaari car driver in Standard, after deciding they were human. "You won't stay here long that way."

Uhura played the clueless cadet. "We won't tell if you won't."

"Hrm."

Whether the driver accepted that or not, he did convey them to the place Una said she had wanted to go all along: the tier where she'd seen several of the airships enter a hangar facility. Once there, they followed a long hall until they saw a gaggle of green cloaks just inside a broader room.

Looks like we just made the lecture, Uhura thought. The novices were fully focused on the speaker before them, which made sneaking into the back of the large group child's play. She glanced at the commander. *It can't be this easy, can it?*

The hangar held several airships of varying sizes. The vessels' main envelopes full, they were all at anchor. Uhura noticed all had additional gas bags aft that hung empty. Over in the middle of the facility, large doors were open to allow vessels to exit both horizontally and vertically; they admitted a snowy wind, which nipped at the crimson-cloaked workers moving gear back and forth.

But the teachers had provided for their listeners' comfort. The novices formed a half ring around a large brazier, burning warm and bright. It reminded her of her fiery friend, which Una had locked in her room, his lantern hidden away in her closet. If Empy minded being cooped up, the creature had not made any moves that suggested it. Uhura was happy he was under lock and key. She didn't know if he could be extinguished, but she didn't want any housekeeper making the attempt.

"Feels like Christmas," Chin-Riley whispered to her as they noted the red-clad Skagaran about to address the students in green.

"Where's the cocoa?" Uhura whispered back.

She hadn't had time to learn much Skagaran; Chin-Riley's primer had been Uhura's reading the night before, and she could only call herself a second-year student at this point. Fortunately, the teacher's three companions were present to repeat things in Standard and two other languages. It made for a bit of a cacophony, but Uhura was good at managing those.

"I am Saachi," the purple-skinned lecturer began. "Some of you may be selected by Zoryana to work the rondure. You may be given the chance to work in the Care Circle. You may even get the opportunity to serve the general himself in the Garden House, administering Epheska's grand plan."

There was a buzz from the listeners at that.

"But in my view, the Sentinel Service is the most exciting way one can serve the greater good." She gestured beyond to a departing airship. "You have grown up seeing these vessels. Learn well, and you may be selected to fly them yourselves."

Happy chatter, now, as Saachi ticked off the various positions aboard ship. Pilot. Navigator. Communications. Uhura glanced at Chin-Riley to see if she was experiencing the same flashback. It was Starfleet Academy all over again, only with funny clothes and a lecture hall that needed only marshmallows to be complete.

"The most important position," Saachi said, "is stoker. Without the stoker, the sentinel has no direction. No speed. The stoker makes everything work."

Uhura hadn't recognized "stoker" in Skagaran and had to catch it in Standard to understand. It struck her as odd. She hadn't had time to read the text that sat in her bedroom nightstand; she'd been too busy learning the language. But the commander had told her enough for her to know that not only did electrical equipment not work here, but steam power was frowned upon. *Environmental reasons*, she figured. What kind of fire were these people supposed to stoke?

She found out when an aide brought something to Saachi. It was one of the crimson-colored ram's-head staffs she'd seen back at the caldera. Holding tightly to the end without the horns with both hands, Saachi thrust it skyward—

—and the listeners gasped as a tongue of fire licked out from the brazier, reaching for the staff. It circled around the staff's horns, almost caressing it. Saachi turned and strode forward. More flames came off the pyre, spooling around the end of the staff.

Saachi led a parade of wearers in green, carrying the fireball high like a Roman standard. She entered the wider hangar, where winds gusted from outside. They did nothing to dislodge the flames.

She faced the students. "You see, my friends. The *sah'ree* is the living will of Epheska made manifest. It serves those who would care for this planet. You have all used *zazics* during your Jubilees. These taller ones, we have found, amplify the desires of the user, allowing the *sah'ree* to be manipulated. Any questions?"

Uhura had many. This made what she saw make sense, but there was so much more she wanted to know. Fortunately, those in front were eager to know as well. "Is the *sah'ree* really alive?" one asked.

"Yes. It comes into being and it dissipates. A beginning and an end. But it is not intelligent—and it cannot feel harm. This we know."

Another questioner, more tentative, asked, "Doesn't the *sah'ree* hate people? We have seen what it does to sinful things."

"The *sah'ree* hates sin. It never hurts people." She put the bottom of the staff on the floor and took one hand off it. Saachi thrust it into the flames, above her. "You see?" she said over a chorus of oohs and aahs.

Uhura was about to burst. *The sah'ree are empatherms.*

And before she knew it, she found her mouth moving. "Do you get them from volcanic rifts?" she asked.

Saachi looked around—but could not see Uhura directly. Chin-Riley had quickly moved in front of her. "An intelligent question," Saachi responded. "Yes, we do find them there—and they retire to the sky. Sometimes when you think you see aurorae, you are actually seeing our magical servants."

Saachi hoisted the post back into the air and snapped around dramatically. "And this is how they may serve!" She brought down the staff as if pointing a sword and closed her eyes. At once, the flame-being uncoiled from the horns and curled toward the waiting airship. Tenders in red held the sides of one of the deflated envelopes open. The empatherm dutifully entered it—but it did not set the silk on fire. The bag inflated, and was sealed.

Another tender bearing a *zazic* repeated the process—and the floating vehicle turned about, revealing an exhaust tube with a propeller just visible inside.

"I've thought they were hot-air balloons," Chin-Riley whispered as the others applauded. "It's an engine."

"But they shouldn't use them like that!" Uhura said.

It was louder than she'd intended and occurred at that moment in the party when everyone suddenly had gone silent. This time, Saachi did see her. "What is your name?"

"I—"

Chin-Riley had her arm. She was already taking a step back. "I apologize. My friend is excited to be here."

"And what is *your* name?"

Another step back.

"*Una*," someone else said. The students turned, all in shock at a voice they seemed to know.

"General Drayko!" Saachi declared. She smiled broadly. "Students, this is a treat. A visit from—"

"A visit from Una," the older Skagaran interrupted, stepping into view. "And . . . Uhura, is it?" He glanced to either side. "Call the Zoldaari."

The first officer turned Uhura about. "Cadet. Run!"

CHAPTER 51

THE AFFECTED

In the temple in Agar, Christopher Pike took a deep breath. If, as Weedaw said, there was a way to deactivate the Baffle using the rondures, it could be the miracle he was looking for. If only there weren't another alleged "miracle" already in the way: the entire Skagaran project on Epheska. Lila had made damned good and sure he remembered it.

"It's a big step," he finally said.

"A step?" Lila walked around the circle, gesturing at the panels. "Your big discovery here is a set of instructions for destroying civilization on this planet. There are hundreds of thousands of people here—at least. You're going to tell them the world they understand is over?"

Spock was moved to respond. "The proper functioning of electrical activity does not necessarily lead to a negative outcome."

"Ask the people of Skagara that. Or of any planet destroyed by pollution—or nearly destroyed." She looked to Pike. "Christopher, you and I came from one!"

Pike nodded with reluctance. "We'd be taking the safety locks off the cabinets."

Weedaw seemed not to understand the allusion but did get the drift of the discussion. He clearly didn't like what he was hearing. "Warden, if there's a way to turn off the Baffle, we have to do it. The captain is stuck here. Mister Spock is stuck here. *We're* stuck here!"

Lila frowned. "Speak for yourself, Weedaw."

"In Drayko's political system," Spock said, "Weedaw cannot."

She turned and appealed to Pike. "Turning it off. Is this what you call non-interference?"

Spock countered. "The Prime Directive may not be in force, Warden. The population of this planet—"

"Spare me. We know." She gestured to the broken ceiling, and the darkening clouds above. "It's not just about what would change here. Other people would come. There'd be nothing to stop them."

Pike nodded. "I know."

His agreement with her seemed to startle Spock. "Captain?"

"Spock, the civilizations of this planet are pre-warp. They may have been brought here by people who weren't, but even the Skagarans chose to leave modernity behind."

Spock stood. "Do we know it was a matter of choice? The Baffle is what is enforcing pre-warp status here—on the Skagarans and all those they settled here."

"We don't declare other societies warp-capable just because some of their members would like to go to space." Pike looked to Weedaw. "Sorry."

The blacksmith shook his head. "I just want to be able to read at night."

Spock took it as evidence. "Aspirations here have been artificially limited by a third party, Captain. You know the regulations in that case call for the removal of previous interference."

"That's if *we* did the interfering," Pike said. "The Federation, or any of our people."

In a sense, he thought, that had made his decision to leave the power supply behind on Terralysium more palatable. Gabrielle Burnham, who had brought the human refugees to *their* timeless world, had been a Federation citizen. But while humans had been abducted in this case, as well, the Federation had no complicity in it. "This might not be our problem to repair," Pike said.

"It isn't a problem," Lila said, only to look at him, surprised, when she realized he had been taking her side. "*Thank you.*"

Pike shrugged. "These are the kind of discussions we have, Lila. Nothing is done carelessly, if we can help it."

Spock explored the position. "Do you suggest that deactivating the Baffle should be put up to a vote?"

"And how is *that* not interfering?" Lila asked.

Weedaw didn't like that idea. "We're already at the mercy of the Sebastian Garrs of the world. I'd rather not give them the power to tell me—"

"Enough." Pike put up his hands. "We're getting ahead of ourselves. Where *is* this nodal rondure?"

Weedaw returned to his translating. "It took decades for them to figure that out," he said. "But they think it is a place they saw on the map the Skagarans brought with them when they landed. It's atop a mesa, far to the northeast, beyond the sea ice. It is impossible to reach."

Pike opened his pack and removed the map. Opening it, he scanned the features until he found a suspect point that matched Weedaw's description.

He traced his finger on the map for Spock and Lila to see. "We'd have to go all the way to the end of this sea. Then it's all ice and glaciers."

"This imagery is from days ago," Spock said. "The seasons change quickly here."

Pike kept tracing. *Ice, ice, ice*—until a great mesa at the tip of the most severe mountain range on the planet. No other approach seemed possible, and the topographical feature itself appeared daunting.

"That's some elevation," Lila said, a trace of relief in her voice.

He nodded. "I don't have any idea how we'd get there, much less get to the summit. I guess we could fly up."

Spock sounded doubtful. "Even if an airship could be obtained, I would question whether they could operate in that environment."

"Spock, could *Enterprise* put someone there?" Weedaw asked.

"The transporter was unreliable in our case."

Pike agreed. He didn't relish the thought of materializing at the right elevation but in the wrong location, or vice versa. "I guess they could land a team the old-fashioned way."

Spock didn't think that was possible. "So far, they have sent down only small landers, without crews and with no onboard electronic equipment. A landing in such a place would be hazardous without the proper systems. Done entirely manually—"

"Yeah," Pike said. "Not to mention it's a starship up there, not a starbase. Building an unpowered shuttle large enough for a team would be next to impossible."

Lila spoke calmly. "That's it, then. We go home."

Weedaw's head jerked back. "Go home?"

"There's nothing to be done. This is a secret that people were not meant to know. We leave it here."

"Not a chance." Pike shook his head. "Not until I know all the options." He gestured to Weedaw. "There are more panels yet. Let's see if there's something closer."

As Weedaw worked, Pike looked to Lila. He hadn't meant to shut her down and was afraid he'd spoken too firmly. It had occurred to him when he saw the *zazics* that she might try to use one to activate the rondure and call her former allies.

But while she'd debated her position vigorously, she hadn't ever made any move in that direction. Now, she retreated to a far wall and knelt, her back against it as she watched the others. It seemed like the wind had gone out of her.

"Are you okay?" Pike asked. "I'm sorry, I know this is heavy stuff."

"Just missing my sheep. Forget it."

Pike nodded gently and turned to approach Spock. He took the officer aside. "You used one of these rondures to contact me."

"Correct. It was one that Commander T'Var controlled, on an island to the north."

"Does it have any kind of system to it? I mean, can you hack this one to make it do what the nodal rondure does? To turn off the Baffle?"

"I am not certain computer terminology is the correct metaphor," Spock replied. "But were such a thing possible, is it not reasonable to expect the ancient Strooh would have attempted it?"

"If they had no way to get back to space, it might not have been priority one. They might have found a way here to bypass the system, but never bothered to do it."

"A reasonable hypothesis." Spock held up the book he'd been writing in. "I will look for that as I assist Weedaw."

Pike let out a deep breath as the lieutenant stepped away. The trip hadn't been for nothing. They were closer than they had been to an answer, and even if they wound up not deactivating the Baffle, it would be good to know how to do it. Perhaps a middle position might be turning it off and departing, allowing the Skagarans to turn it back on, bringing their society back into accordance with their—

He glanced at the wall—and then all around the room.

Lila was gone.

CHAPTER 52

THE DEPARTED

Lila Talley watched the shadows grow long in the ghost town. They came and went, disappearing as dark clouds alternated with white as they soared overhead.

It was strange. Beyond the temples, Skagaran and Strooh architecture had few similarities with that found in the Old West. But burnt, smashed, and rotted cities all looked the same. Every so often she saw some tiny reminder that this place had been something to someone. It was no more.

Cracking trees announced an incoming gale. The Skagarans had done right, choosing to leave this place centuries before. There were countless better locations around—and rondures to settle near, if that was how it had happened. She didn't like the idea that the Skagarans hadn't built them but was willing to accept it. If the supposedly smart Strooh had chosen to stay in this village, that was on them. There was no paradise to be found anywhere in Zevayne.

Thunder sounded. She looked up. The light show she often saw out on the range looked different here. The sparks here were persistent, tumbling slowly from the sky like so many falling stars. They weren't reaching the surface, but she could imagine the result if they did. *Was the Sorry born here?* she wondered.

She had reached where Pike's and Spock's horses were tied up when she felt the first raindrops. Shadow and Ember whinnied unhappily as the wind whistled past. There was no safer place to move them to. No safe place anywhere. She fumbled with the lines securing them.

"No safe place," she said, placing her hands on their heads as the rain began falling in earnest. She closed her eyes. "I'm sorry."

"*Lila!*"

She didn't look.

"*Lila!*"

She heard footsteps and opened her eyes. Pike, out in the downpour in the main street, looked in all directions. He spied her and ran toward her. "Where did you go?"

She gestured weakly to the tie-off. "No safe place," she droned.

Pike looked up at the sky—and got pelted with rain. "They'll be okay," he said. "We need to get back inside. We'll be safe there."

When she didn't move, he reached for her wrist. No sooner had he touched it than she swatted him away.

"Hey! What—" was all he was able to get out. He reached toward her again—

—and she struck him in the face. "*Get away!*"

She averted her eyes from him. She saw him again only when he entered her view, having circled her. Massaging his jaw, he kept his distance this time. "Lila, what—"

"*There is no safe place!*" she screamed.

Pike looked around, seeing only the storm. "Inside—"

"Not inside. Not outside. Not anywhere!" She looked up at him. "Epheska was safe. But you're going to turn it off!"

"What, the Baffle?"

"Of course the Baffle! Why do you think I'm here?"

"Here—this village?"

"On Epheska!"

Pike's eyes fixed on her. "You said you were investigating the North Star refugees."

"There had been rumors the Skagarans had found a planet where technology didn't work. A paradise," she said, tears starting. "*Braidwood* got a lead on where the Skagaran ship that crashed was supposed to have gone."

"And that brought you here," Pike said. "I gathered that." He took a careful step toward her in the rain. "But I never understood *why* you went."

She turned aside. "I never wanted to leave Earth. I never wanted them to leave."

"Who?"

Her tears mixing with the rain, she looked back at him. "Have you been back to Earth?"

Pike nodded. "I have a place up north, in the mountains."

"I'm talking about Mojave, California. The Bar T. *The colony.*"

"The Luddite colony?" He shook his head. "I'd heard a lot of people moved away."

"The whole colony relocated. Earth is getting too crowded, they said. My neighbors—they all packed up and moved to another planet three years ago. Livestock and all."

"I hadn't heard. I was away—"

"They said it would be better." She winced. "They said it would be a *safe place!*"

Pike took another step toward her, his eyes focused. "Where did they move?"

She couldn't say it.

"Where did they move, Lila?"

No.

"Where did they—"

"*Kelfour VI!*" she yelled, throwing her arms before her.

Pike stepped back as if struck. But only the words had hit him. "No."

"Yes!"

"Kelfour VI." Pike finally appeared to get it. "The Klingons."

"Yes."

He moved toward her. "Oh, Lila—"

"Don't!" She balled her fists and raged at the sky. "Just don't! Your Federation sent your Starfleet into space—and they provoked the Klingons. And the Klingons went to Kelfour VI and *burned the damn atmosphere off!*"

Pike nodded. "I heard."

"Then why didn't you *do* something?"

"I wasn't there, Lila. I told you. I had missing crew that I was searching for in a different nebula."

"You're always losing people. Going places you never should have gone!"

Pike put up his hands. "I'd have helped if I could."

"You could have helped by never going, Christopher. Any of you."

"The Klingons would have come anyway."

Hair blowing in the wind, she shook her head. "T'Kuvma started his war because of your movements, all of you. I heard the reports—what those Klingon prisoners said he said. 'They are coming. Atom by atom, they will coil around us and take all that we are!'"

"Yes, but—"

"And now you've come for Epheska. For the only safe place I've ever known."

Pike pleaded with her. "Lila, the Klingons would have attacked anyway."

"They wouldn't have attacked here. They wouldn't have been able to! The Baffle protects us!"

"The Klingons are just as happy dropping dumb bombs from a distance," he replied.

"So you're saying no place is safe. Which is what I was telling you!"

"The war is over."

"Until the next one." Lila leaned over, panting and overwrought as the wind whipped around her. Pike kept his distance. When she looked up, she saw beyond him that Spock had emerged from the temple. He was searching for them in the rain.

"There it is," she said to Pike in a small voice. "He's going to tell you he's got some fancy way to turn off the Baffle—and Epheska will be over. The temples will all become pizza places. But hey, maybe they can plant gardens outside. It'll *look* natural."

Pike was speechless. More thunder above.

Spock arrived beside them, clearly unaware of what had passed between them. "I have a report of vital importance."

Pike looked at Lila. She wasn't moving. "You'd better give it now. Then we need to pack up and get back to the coast while we can."

"We found a final panel on the far side. Weedaw translated it." Spock wiped rain from his forehead. "It was a warning."

More horrors. Lila looked away and closed her eyes.

"The same mechanism by which the Baffle can be dialed down to zero may be utilized in reverse."

Lila's eyes popped open. "What?" she heard Pike say.

"The radius of the affected area can be made to increase," Spock said.

She looked to them. Pike's voice rose with alarm. "How far could it reach?"

Spock spoke gravely. "*Everywhere.*"

Pike's shoulders sagged—and then tightened. "That's it, then. We don't have any choice."

"I concur, Captain. It is too dangerous to exist. Were it accidentally triggered—"

"Yeah. This is bigger than Epheska. We've got to disable it. *Permanently.*"

Lila clung to the post the horses were tied to. Around them, the wind suddenly intensified, shattering branches in the trees surrounding the site. She knew what she had to do.

Thunder. The horses, straining against the maelstrom, reared back—and came loose.

"Whoa!" Pike shouted. Another crash of thunder, and Shadow and Ember were off, running toward the woods.

"After them," Lila yelled, boots splashing through puddles as she began to chase them.

"Lila, you'll scare them even—" Pike said. He didn't finish the sentence. His and Spock's horses were to the treeline, beyond which lay the arduous descent through the jungle. "Come on, Spock!"

She ran along with them to where the foliage began—and stopped, letting them continue.

Lila Talley had just thought of a safe place.

Part Four
OLD WOUNDS

ANDRUS ICE SHEET

GOLARAAD

KRYKANDER

SNOW
FALLS

PELLA STRAIT

OM MATAYA

Z'NEV

NDWOOD

SAH'REDAH

OKUA SEA

CHAPTER 53

THE MISSING

"*Lila!*" Standing at the edge of the jungle, a drenched Christopher Pike shouted into the rain. "*Lila!*"

The sun had sunk behind the trees, turning the downpour from tepid to cold—and it had made their job finding the horses extremely difficult. At last, he and Spock had found them. But on working their way back to the clearing, they'd discovered Lila was missing.

She'd been with them at the start of the chase, only to turn back. He'd assumed she had taken refuge in the temple, and that was the first place he and Spock checked. Weedaw had been absent then as well, but that hadn't come as a surprise, as his nervous stomach had sent him out back of the temple several times already.

The fact that Weedaw's pony and Buckshot were also missing didn't immediately set off any alarms. Pike expected Lila would have tried to find someplace more sheltered for them. But he'd found no such place in the ruined village, and Spock's expression on emerging from the temple was decidedly non-Vulcan.

"When I brought you my news earlier," he said, "I did not want to carry outside the book I was taking notes in."

Pike, soaked, didn't need to ask why.

"I left it with Weedaw," Spock said. "It is gone. So are our maps."

No.

The two hurried inside for another look.

The torches they'd mounted in the room had burned nearly down. Removing one from its sconce, Pike checked the area around the rondure. It floated there, immobile as always. But now that he looked in the light, he noticed something.

"The tablets mounted around the circle on the floor. They're wet."

Spock arrived with his own light. "This is a boot print."

"Someone tried to put their foot through the thing." Another panel was the same. The slabs were too strong to break. But something else was not.

Pike knelt and came up with a gnarled crystal horn. "It's part of a *zazic*." He saw other parts nearby. The rondure itself might have been impervious, but the yoke was not. "Someone smashed this."

"They are *all* destroyed." Spock led him to the side of the chamber, where the container of *zazics* had been overturned.

"Smashed—in a hurry." Pike looked around. "This doesn't look like the work of one person. Was there someone else here?"

He and Spock searched the ruined building. Emerging outside, they checked all around it. They met again, unsuccessful.

"Analysis," Pike said, staring into the woods.

"Our companions are hostages. Or they have fled."

Pike was afraid of either answer. He ran around the perimeter of the clearing. "Lila! Weedaw!"

He reached the overlook leading down into Zevayne's overgrown interior. Just as he did, the rain and wind let up for a minute—and he could hear limbs cracking far below. Another wild animal, he thought—until he heard the whinny.

He cupped his hands together. "*Lila!*"

For several moments, he heard nothing.

"*Weedaw!*"

"He's gone," replied a voice from somewhere down in the dark. "And he's not coming back. Neither am I!"

Lila's words echoed everywhere. Pike couldn't tell where she was—and certainly could see no way to get down into that brush. "Lila, don't do this!"

"We're done, Christopher. Good-bye."

He looked down plaintively. Lila was the best wilderness rider he'd ever met. It was why he'd approached her for this mission, even knowing her feelings. If she didn't want to be found, he wasn't going to find her.

But maybe all was not hopeless. He turned to see Spock standing behind him. "You heard?"

"Yes, Captain."

Pike walked past him, heading for where they'd retied their horses. "If she's got Weedaw with her, she can't be going too fast. Maybe we can catch her."

"Or maybe Weedaw is dead."

Pike stopped and looked back. "What?"

Spock advanced past him to their horses. "These creatures were tied securely, Captain." He pulled against the restraints. "Warden Talley was here when the horses escaped. Her pursuit may have even provoked them."

Pike shook his head, water dripping from his hair. "You don't know her, Spock. You don't know what you're saying."

"I only know the facts."

Pike started to untie his horse. "There's got to be another explanation. Give me alternatives, Spock. That's your job."

Spock knelt and looked in the mud. "We could examine these boot prints.

We require no technology for that. Only light." He stood. "But I suspect you already know what we would find."

Pike looked down through the darkness at the water puddling in the imprints.

Damn it.

He resecured Shadow. "What happened, then?"

"I expect she heard our discussion of deactivating the Baffle, stole Weedaw's notes, and sought to prevent us from activating the system from here."

"That's what I was thinking. It just takes humans a little longer to get there." Pike turned back toward the overlook. "Do we search for them? Or for Weedaw's body?" The last sentence sickened him to say.

"Our only priority can be as you mentioned."

"Stop the Baffle, before it stops everything."

They hurried back into the temple. The torches were out this time. Pike found his pack and lit another. "Do you remember enough about Weedaw's translations to re-create your notes?"

"Not with specificity. The last panels were laden with coordinates and equations. The Strooh were evidently very learned."

"We have to transcribe everything. Then find someone who can understand the glyphs." Pike looked around. "Any stems and papyrus handy?"

Spock raised a finger into the air. "There may be an option."

He retreated into the shadows and came forth with a large pack. "This item was suggested to me by the Menders." He unfastened the clasps and opened it, bringing out an object Pike had seen only once before, in the impound room in Havenbrook.

"The optivator!"

"I had never heard the term before, but on examination it appears to be a self-developing camera. There is no motor to it, but the Menders did purloin film enough for twelve images."

"Twelve panels, twelve images." He looked back at the rondure, black as a new moon. "Lighting's a problem. Unless they also stole a flash bulb, we're stuck until morning."

He and Spock stared into the darkness for a moment—until they looked at each other and said the same thing at the same time. "The bag!"

Pike found the one he'd been carrying. He knelt, dumping out the contents carefully. "Can't use the rifle shells—black powder burns too slowly." But he had been given several other things by T'Var. "Yeah, here we go."

"The signal flares."

"You got it." *Thunderer* wasn't likely to remain at anchor for the whole time they were in-country, and there was no guarantee that Pike's company would emerge from the jungle in the same place it went in, if it escaped at all. The Vulcans had planned for just such a possibility.

Penknife in hand, Spock went to work, revealing a flare's contents. "Potassium nitrate and sulfur."

"Epheska doesn't have it all, but saltpeter and volcanoes it's got. And even Zheng He's era had signal bombs."

"Thankfully, T'Var's people have made some improvements. We should be able to repackage this for our needs."

"So long as we do it without blowing our hands off." Pike went to work alongside Spock. "When you joined Starfleet, I bet you never thought you'd be working with your captain on a pyrotechnic experiment."

"I have learned to keep an open mind."

CHAPTER 54

THE CONFRONTATION

"Hey, there's no running in the Care Circle!"

Celarius already knew he had stayed in Om Mataya too long, but now he'd seen everything. A group of people trying to run in floor-length robes, crossing straight through the no-shoes-allowed area of the great map on their way to the alcove and its lifter.

People had been running back and forth like mad since he got back from fishing. The fact the Matayan River ran right through the city had always been the area's only appeal for him. Standing in frigid water had taxed even his robust physique, but he'd been unwilling to investigate the first five times someone had dashed past.

He saw Zoryana on the great map, directing traffic as she stood atop the Helladan Desert. She seemed unusually flustered, and not because the fish he was carrying was dripping on her display. He got her attention. "What goes on here?"

"Your guests have left the chateau."

"No, they haven't. I saw them at lunch."

"While you were out amusing yourself, they infiltrated a sentinel training session. Your father saw them."

Celarius frowned. "What of it? They got bored. I would too."

"This isn't like the people you bring back here from your joyrides, and you know it. The general thinks they're intelligence operatives."

"He thinks *what*?" Celarius was flabbergasted. "He's delusional. What does that even mean?"

Zoryana put up her hands. "You and your father need to work out your own problems. These women are ours—and they are on the run." She stepped away and returned to her nervous breakdown.

Celarius dropped his rod and reel on the continent of Zevayne and let the fish drop onto an adjacent ocean, where he was sure it would confuse the hell out of some novice. As fun as that might have been to watch, he had other business.

He hurried into the alcove, only to find a crowd of pursuers waiting for the lift. Fortunately, while the general public didn't know he was heritor general, everyone here did, and he played the prince card to get to the front of the line.

"Full up," he declared, once he was inside. He kicked out the operator as well. "You too."

He figured he'd look first in the hangar. He was halfway there when his sharp senses detected something moving above. He pulled the cord to stop the car's motion.

"It's me," he called to the ceiling. "You can come down now."

Nothing for several moments. Then the utility panel atop opened up, and Una looked down. She gave a crooked smile. "Safety inspector."

"Come down. You're safe."

"I feel better up here." She looked around. "Hodgkin needs to write a paper on Parallel Elevator Development."

Celarius shrugged. "Everyone's looking for you. What's going on?"

"I went exploring."

"That I've heard. Is Uhura up there with you?"

She stared down at him. "You mean you don't have her yet?"

"I don't have anyone. I'm not looking for anyone."

"Right," Una said. "Not your problem, huh? I'd believe it if you weren't the heir apparent."

"I haven't got the slightest idea what's happening."

She studied him, apparently evaluating whether to trust him. Celarius sat down cross-legged on the floor of the car. "Those people downstairs can wait. We can pretend we're back in the forest, eating random plants."

She chuckled—and decided. "The *sah'ree* are powering your aircraft."

"Yes."

"You know this?"

"Yeah," he said. "The big envelopes are helium. The small sacs are propulsion."

"And the *sah'ree* are providing that."

He pointed his thumb upward. "They're part of the system running this lift too. Way up at the top. What of it?"

"They're life-forms," Una said. "You're harming them."

"Harming?" He'd never heard that before. He stood up. "Can you just come down here?"

Una shimmied down. He helped her alight on the floor. "Thanks."

"Easier on the neck," he replied. "Now, how do you know they're being harmed?"

"Uhura knows. She saw your people harvesting them from a caldera."

Celarius's eyes narrowed. "Una, I know what lives on this planet. The *sah'ree* have some kind of biological systems, I'll admit—autonomic responses that respond to the *zazics*. But it's no different than a flower turning toward the light."

"It's more than that. And she also says—"

A piece of metal jabbed through the edge of the door to the car. It was replaced seconds later by two sets of hairy fingers. The instant after that, the door snapped completely off with a noisome crack.

"Private conversation," Celarius said to the pair of beefy Zoldaari sentries beyond. "And you owe me a new door."

"It's *my* door," Drayko declared. He arrived from behind, flanked by more muscle. He pointed in at Una. "Hold her!"

The Zoldaari advanced—and both she and Celarius struggled. He didn't know what they thought they were doing, and he expressed his annoyance by punching one of the bruisers in the jaw. Una had beaten him to that with another one. But there was no evading the giants in such close quarters, and soon they were hauling Una through a hall and out onto one of the snowy terraces.

Celarius stormed after them. He'd made the mistake of stopping the car on the level with the guardhouse, he realized. It was a seldom-used facility, but it was getting a workout today.

If Drayko was upset with his son's treatment, he said nothing of it. His attention was on Una. The thugs stopped and turned her toward him. "Where is the other one?" he demanded.

Una nodded in the direction of the valley and gave a canny smile. "Outside—where you'll never find her. Uhura is Starfleet's top outdoors expert."

"She's a child!"

"She's got you fooled, then. She already crossed hundreds of kilometers on foot, living by her wits. And now you've sent her out with a warm meal. She's ready to go again."

"You are ready to go somewhere else." He pointed to the guardhouse, and the Zoldaari took her away.

Drayko was adjusting his sleeve when Celarius charged past. "I'm getting her out of there."

"You will not." He glared at his son. "What has she told you?"

"She says we're harming the *sah'ree*."

"Nonsense."

"What if she's right?"

"She isn't." Drayko walked onto the terrace, crossing his arms against the cold.

Celarius followed him. "We've been using them in our airships. If it causes them pain—"

Drayko gestured to the sky. "Do clouds feel pain? Does the ground scream when you use a shovel?" He laughed. "Or do you ask the *ollodons'* opinions when you—"

"I get it."

"We have plenty of experience with the *sah'ree*, my son. Saachi has been working with them since before you were born."

"But if Una's right—"

Drayko shook his head. "Your indifference to your role as heritor has cost you. There are things about our society, burdens that I have never shared with you."

Celarius glowered. "Do tell."

The general began to walk the terrace, which was recently swept of snow. "You know that centuries ago, we lost contact with the *Liberator*."

"The vessel charged with delivering settlers here."

"We knew then its crew no longer wished to support our project. We now know they took their last rescue, a human settlement, for slaves—only to lose control in a revolt."

"Serves them right, I'd say."

"We lost our one source of immigrants and supplies from the stars. For hundreds of years, we'd striven for self-sufficiency—but this was a blow. And once it became known in certain sectors on this planet, it bred unrest."

"I've never heard of that."

"That's by design. For it was just the hint that we were finally alone that drove Epheska's troublemakers—it's always the builders—to acts of defiance." He snorted. "Apparently you cannot rescue a human from a natural disaster without him spitting in your face, whatever planet you are on."

Drayko faced the sky. "Then as now, we had no army. When our words, our mission wasn't enough to still the unrest—we unleashed the *sah'ree*."

"You did *what*?"

"For the last several centuries, when a lookout has reported a citizen in violation of our rules on technology, sentinels have dispatched the elementals to destroy the offending machine."

"What?"

"It's no different than powering our airships. The creatures can be compelled to seek a target, through a proper suggestion from a controller."

"Proper!"

"No one is harmed—and people's fear is of the *sah'ree*, and not us. That is as it should be." He waved his hand. "It's a remarkable system. We have stockpiles of the creatures in the low stratosphere. We only need sentinels at the end with line of sight on the destinations."

Celarius couldn't believe it. He looked down at the ground. "All this time, we've been telling people the planet's been defending itself. But it's been us all along."

"You can't pretend you didn't suspect. Are you that oblivious?" He watched his son's expression. "No, no. You accepted it for the same reason we got every-one else to accept it. You liked the story."

"Who knows about this?"

"Zoryana. Saachi. The leaders of the various departments here. The cleans-ing detail is offered only to the most experienced sentinel crews."

"*Cleansing?*"

Drayko shivered. "I am going back in."

Celarius stormed after him.

Once in the guardhouse, Celarius saw Una again, under heavy guard. Drayko received a report that Uhura was still at large.

"It doesn't matter," he declared. "I was intending to use Una to flush out Captain Pike. I can do the same as far as her other crewmates are concerned." He addressed the Zoldaari. "Take her to the asylum."

"The asylum?" That, Celarius did know about. "She doesn't belong there."

"You're correct. She is not a member of our society, driven so mad with a desire to disrupt that she must be restrained."

Una smoldered. "Is that what you do to them?"

"In very rare cases. But you are not from here. All the same—you are cer-tainly disruptive."

The Zoldaari began to move her. Celarius moved forward to intervene—only to realize there was no getting her away from them. He looked to Una.

"It's okay," she told him. "I can take care of myself."

"I know you can. Still, I usually get what I ask for." He faced the guard he'd struck in his earlier scuffle. "Take me too."

The Zoldaari before him growled—but did nothing.

Drayko rolled his eyes. "That really is enough of this childishness."

"Yeah, I'm like that." He glanced at Una, who was looking at him with new respect. "If she's disruptive, so am I."

His father was about to argue further when Zoryana appeared, having scaled the exterior stairs. She leaned against a cornice, huffing and puffing. "*Someone . . . has broken . . . the lifter.*"

Drayko scowled at her. "Why didn't you send up a runner?"

Zoryana fought to catch her breath—and produced a folded paper from the shrouds of her cloak. Drayko snatched it from her.

Celarius saw his father's brow furrow as he read. "But this rondure hasn't been in operation since—"

He went silent. The blood drained from his face.

"I understand now." He crumpled up the paper. "You were right to come directly to me." He started walking.

Celarius whistled at him. "What about us?"

Drayko stopped to look back at them both. "I can't be bothered—not now."

Zoryana found her voice. "What is happening?"

"He is jailing his son," Una said.

Zoryana looked with surprise at her superior. Drayko waved dismissively. "A couple of weeks down there instead of out in some forsaken swamp makes no difference to me. It will be a safari of another kind for you."

"Some father," Una muttered.

"I am the conservator general—and I now have something more important to attend to." He headed for the stairs.

Celarius called after him. "Aren't you afraid I'll tell people there what I know? What you just told me?"

"If they're in the asylum, they may already know. And if they do," Drayko said, "they'll never get out."

CHAPTER 55

THE CATCH

At another time, the fact that he had lost his maps from *Enterprise* would have been a setback for Christopher Pike's venture. But Commander T'Var's people had the benefit—or curse—of an additional century to map their maritime environs.

T'Var leaned across the table in the great cabin on *Thunderer*'s quarterdeck as her subordinate spread out charts before her. "Thank you, Sivenda." The commander looked to Pike. "You bring grave news, Captain."

"That's why we hurried back." He and Spock had done it without a guide; the dire need to return was so great that the *Enterprise* officers had made straight for the coast, ignoring every threat and obstacle that came along.

"Is this thing so concerning?" Sivenda asked. "If this 'nodal rondure' makes other worlds into places like this, who is harmed?"

T'Var lifted her hand before her. "Young Sivenda is of the new generation, Captain. She is your age but has never known a working circuit. She does not know the extent of the damage that could be done."

Pike understood. He tried to explain the ramifications. "If it really controls the Baffle and if the Skagarans—or anyone else—were to misuse it, countless people could die. People aboard starships and starbases would asphyxiate, starve, or freeze. Colonies dependent on them would suffer. Flying vessels would plummet. Containment systems for antimatter reactors would fail." He stopped himself from going further.

"What is the probability that it really could have such range?" T'Var asked.

"Spock is still working with the pictures we took. Without Weedaw, there's no easy translation, but there was a Strooh section in the phrasebook he got from the people who rescued him. The problem is the glyphs are a more archaic form."

Sivenda volunteered that her crewmates were working to assist in the translations—and that they and some of the Menders were numbering the glyphs for transmission to *Enterprise*.

"Unfortunately, one of my top language experts is lost down here somewhere," Pike said. "But every little bit helps."

T'Var nodded. "I am told you informed *Enterprise* about the danger."

"First thing. I'm sorry I didn't come to you beforehand."

"Your duty is to your people. How did you instruct them?"

"They're remaining nearby for the moment, as Sivenda says—but I admit I'm torn. I'd love to tell them to keep helping us, because they increase our odds of thwarting this thing." Exhausted, Pike put his hands on the table. "At the same time, I want to tell them to run for civilization as quickly as possible and warn everyone before bringing back help."

T'Var's eyes narrowed. "I would be cautious of informing many, Captain. You might tell those who would misuse it."

Sivenda mocked the notion. "The commander is reliving her days in intelligence work."

"And my child is taking liberties."

Pike looked between T'Var and Sivenda, startled. "Your child?"

"On a world where people are few, nepotism makes sense," T'Var said. "But such license only goes so far." She came back to the matter. "The warden who fled, who destroyed the *zazics*. What was her motive?"

"Lila? I think she was trying to slow us down."

"And Weedaw?"

"We had reason to think he was on our side," Pike said. "But his horse was gone, so we assume he's with her." *I hope, anyway.*

"Seeking to delay a course you had not even set upon is a rash act," T'Var said. "Warden Talley had no idea I would even convey you to this place in the ice that you found."

"She knew you were castaways like us, and she knew you had brought us this far." He studied the aged Vulcan. "But that's right. I apologize, Commander—I hadn't even asked if you would be willing to take us there."

"We would only be able to take you partway, of course," T'Var said, gesturing to her map. "Much of the northern ocean is permanent icecap, and the abrupt changes to winter here make the extent of sea ice unpredictable." She pointed. "The most distant settlement we might achieve—short of the Zoldaari ones, which you must avoid—is Krykander, home of the Yuganan."

"Who are the Yuganan?"

"A quiet people," Sivenda said. "They take sustenance from the sea, until their fjord freezes. Then they make handcrafts."

"Sounds like Drayko's favorite kind of settlers," Pike replied. "I don't suppose they'd be that welcoming."

"We do some light commerce with others who trade with them."

"But you're renegades. I thought Drayko had rules about trade."

T'Var walked to the row of windows aft in the cabin. "We had little experience with sea cultures on Vulcan, Captain, but there seems to be something universal to them. Strangers from the land are feared. Those from the sea are often welcomed. I believe it is because they are more likely to visit and be on their way."

It's a good thing the Skagarans never kidnapped any Vikings, Pike thought. Then again, for all he knew, they did—and the descendants of those ancient seafarers were off in some distant corner he hadn't seen yet.

He remembered something else she'd said. "You mentioned the Zoldaari. My friend Carpenter is one. They're a problem?"

"They festoon the northern reaches," T'Var said, pointing sequentially at many spots on the map. "Hard people for hard lands. And fanatically devoted to the Skagarans' so-called project—we suspect they supply many personnel for the conservator general's actions. I do not know the leanings of the Yuganan, but the Zoldaari who lie beyond must be avoided at all costs."

"If they're such close neighbors, I'd worry the Yuganan wouldn't be much help either." Pike came to grips with the daunting route they were considering. "I know this is a big request—and it could put your fleet at risk."

"And I appreciate what is at stake. But while I am fleet commander, we are not a dictatorship, Captain. It is something that must be discussed."

Pike made his respects and withdrew, taking a second in the doorway to marvel at where he was. How many times, he wondered, had he visited a superior officer on another ship for a briefing—and how often had he thought about what it would have been like to do the same thing aboard a tall ship?

I wish I could enjoy this.

Feeling beaten, he went up to the deck. He had no idea how long it would take to reach a decision, but with personnel spread across her flotilla, he knew it wouldn't be settled quickly. He had something to decide, as well, as he felt responsible for the Menders and their families. As often as they'd assured him they were with him all the way, he didn't expect that included a last-ditch mission to the glacial highlands.

At least they were having fun, he thought as he looked across the harbor. While awaiting his return, several of the Menders had gone out in small boats to fish. They didn't know about Weedaw yet, and he didn't relish telling them—especially as nothing could be done to find him. He saw only glowing faces when a group of them came over the side.

"Some help here!" Joe shouted.

Pike assisted him. It wasn't his leg causing the difficulty—but the banana-bunch of fish that he'd caught.

"They're called yellowfins. Half of those are mine," Jennie said, ebullient.

The captain admired their catch. "Looks like everyone did well. What did you use?"

Jennie produced a handful of lures from her jacket. "The Vulcans gave us these little bobbers."

"They're a wonder, Captain," Joe said. "Enough to make you quit and change jobs."

Pike held the lures up before him. He'd fished, of course, though Mojave, California, wasn't exactly teeming with fishing holes. But that was a nice memory about Lila's place. Her father had tied the best lures. Hairy mixes of filaments of alternating colors, designed to entrance the canniest underwater denizen. These were fancier still, connected to brightly painted baubles sure to please the piscine eye.

Wait a second. He held the two flies in his hand up in the sunlight and evaluated them. "You got any more of these?"

Joe had one. Vicki produced three more. Pike stared at the lures. "Where did you get these?"

His question led to a Vulcan sailor, who opened a bin. "They come in trade, Captain. I agree that they are exceptional. They are tied by the Yuganans."

Pike rummaged through the container, examining one after another.

Yeah.

Spock arrived beside him, looking haggard. "Captain, if there is no more to do, I should like to retire."

"Retire later," Pike said. He shoved the bin into Spock's hands. "I need to see the commander again, right away!"

CHAPTER 56

THE DREAM

Enterprise's engineers had started a tradition. Upon leaving the ship's service, departing chiefs and many other engineers had scribbled notes inside the hatch of the Jefferies tube just outside main engineering. Graffiti being prone to less than serious advice, most of the statements were jocular in nature. Doctor Galadjian, whose shuttle had been no match for the Baffle, had nonetheless left Hemmer's favorite: *To convince a captain, take a bottle.*

Hemmer knew there was no hope of convincing La'an Noonien-Singh with alcohol. There was barely any chance of moving her with well-articulated arguments and evidence. The hours without the shuttle crew were now being measured in weeks, and all her options—approaching Epheska to try to help or exiting the nebula to call for it—had been stymied once Captain Pike got in contact with them.

It had forced her into the same position that chief engineers were in at every port of call: trying to find some way to be useful while the landing party did all the work. He knew she was spending hours each night alone in the conference room, sorting through stacks of padds and consulting *Enterprise*'s maps, looking for answers. Given the frenzy the latest news from below had caused, Hemmer didn't expect she had gone to bed at all.

And so, Avedis Galadjian's advice arrived at the door with a twist. "Coffee," Hemmer said.

"You're a wonder." La'an did not stand as she took the cup from his tray.

He regarded what she was studying. "What's this?"

"The databanks have been working overtime. At least six of the species Captain Pike has mentioned are familiar to us, and they are known to have been preindustrial at the time of the abductions."

Hemmer nodded. More phrasebooks to be sent down, if the sailing ships ever stopped moving long enough to pick them up. They'd just gone into motion, racing northeast.

"We've confirmed *Thunderer*'s wreck was never located. We've also found records of a tornado and wildfire that erased a town on the Purgatoire River in Colorado." Her tone lowered. "Purgatoire is French for a place between Heaven and Hell that nobody ever gets out of."

"You have described my last departmental staff meeting." Hemmer took the other mug and sat beside her.

She sounded weary. "This threat the captain's describing. The Baffle. Could it really do what he suggests?"

"All along, we've been discussing a force that interrupts the basic rules on which the universe functions. It should not occur within a space with a radius of a meter, much less a million kilometers. So any argument against it reaching a trillion kilometers is worthless."

"Do you think this relates to the Delphic Expanse? With what was going on with the Sphere-Builders?"

"The distortions here are much different. Indeed, I theorize that is why the Skagaran vessel crashed there. Whatever permitted it to operate around here was of no help there." Hemmer shivered. "The thought that there could be more than one kind of area where basic physical laws do not apply gives me a pain in a place I will not discuss."

He explained that he had examined *Enterprise* NX-01's records of the Skagaran wreck, and that they had provided little guidance. "The Skagarans pierced the Baffle with a tremendous transporter array that worked over a long distance. Nothing of the machinery survived. An amazing technological advance—and the only hint it ever existed is what lives on the planet below."

What they had already been able to decipher suggested that the nodal rondure, if struck by an energy beam or a torpedo, might well survive. Worse, it might trigger unpredictable effects, such as the calamity Spock feared it was capable of.

Hemmer sensed that the conference room's viewscreen was showing the current location of Pike's viridium patch. "They're making very good time."

La'an perked up. "They caught a gyre that will deliver them up a strait to Krykander—that fjord at upper right. T'Var knows her sailing."

"My respect. But she can only carry him so far. Has the captain yet explained why he thinks the people there will help him?"

"No."

"A gamble. Lovely." The Aenar engineer clasped his hands on the table and focused on them. The posture was an affectation, as he did not see them as others did—but it communicated information, and La'an noticed it.

"What's on your mind, Hemmer? Why are you here?"

Hemmer inhaled. "The fact is that apart from designing probes that cannot function within the Baffle—and repairing this vessel's EPS systems after every time we try to communicate by signal flashes—I have been reduced to helping to craft some very fine message containers."

"There is *Icarus*."

"There is." It was their last-ditch plan, already constructed. "*Icarus* has remained unused because we haven't got the resources aboard to duplicate it. There is only one shot. And so it, too, has been put on a very large shelf—along with me."

He rose and began to pace around the table.

"We have a situation below," he said, "where electricity is weak and where transtators do not work at all. Furthermore, many of the captain's allies below greatly fear the generation of motion by the use of fire. As such, to the disappointment of young Ensign Ghalka and those who like the kinds of stories she reads, there are no opportunities for steam-powered boats, engines, motorcars, or automated dogwalkers. I, too, am greatly disappointed, because the story about the giant metal kangaroo suggests quite the engineering challenge."

"Is there a point, Lieutenant?"

He stopped walking and faced her. "When I was young, the Andorians had many things that the Aenar did not. One of them captured my imagination. You could well say that obsessing over it helped get me into engineering. Wishful thinking plus envy."

"I don't see—"

"And I don't see as you do, as you well know. But that's another thing. How Aenar process images makes us extremely well suited for engineering. We understand where things are, and how things connect, both inside and out. You see a schematic. We think in schematics. We need not manipulate them to see all sides."

"You would like to suggest another gambit."

He tapped the side of his head. "There is something I have dreamt of since childhood that is locked right here. I know what it requires. I know how to construct it. I know so well, that with a dedicated staff and the right resources, I could put it together in days."

"Sadly, our resources here are limited."

"I only need a few things from *Enterprise*, and I know we have them. With your permission, I can appropriate them."

La'an moved to take a sip from her coffee. "You're the chief engineer. Why would you need permission?"

"Because without the supports under the mess hall, the deck might cave in."

La'an nearly spit out her drink. "Please say that again?"

Hemmer brought out a control mechanism from his pocket. "If you were Aenar, I could share with you exactly what I have visualized. Alas, we must do this your way." He directed her attention to the viewscreen. "I will need you to be patient—and to use your imagination."

"Very well."

"And just remember: if you say no, you will be crushing the dreams of a very old child."

CHAPTER 57

THE KINDRED

Of the journeys Christopher Pike had taken on Epheska, the voyage to Krykander was both the longest—and the fastest. T'Var had made all sail for the Pella Strait, catching fair winds and strong currents, heedless of the threat to her own vessels. She had even abandoned three of the slower ships after evacuating everyone. Spock said it illustrated the proper balancing of needs.

Before, they had been two people trying to get home. After the revelation at Agar, they stood for the needs of many more.

The time that elapsed had been put to good use. With the help of those belowdecks, Spock had gotten farther with his translations of the tablets. Much more remained to be examined, but in the main, Weedaw seemed to have spoken accurately.

Pike also spent more time with the Menders, who had learned of Weedaw's disappearance even as T'Var had set sail. All he had to give them was the hope that the blacksmith had gone with Lila, for whatever reason, and his judgment that she was a good person, if one with conflicting loyalties. If anyone could keep him alive in a wild place, he said, it was Lila—but what they had seen of Zevayne from the sea had not been encouraging.

Late in the journey, he knew that *something* was cooking on *Enterprise*, but clouds prevented him from learning many details. It didn't matter: all hopes, above and below, rested on the reception they'd receive at Krykander, home of the Yuganan.

Pike saw both from a distance as *Thunderer* entered the icy fjord. The city was a keep with a towering wooden sea gate, opening onto a ramp down into the water. He understood that it closed only during winter, and that further confirmed for him that T'Var had done right in hurrying. The tilting planet was already bringing on shorter and colder days, and the fjord was in danger of freezing at any moment. He owed it to the Vulcans to get his business done here quickly.

Engineering on Epheska was already frozen, and that made him think the Yuganan home planet must be impressive. The port had every hallmark of being constructed by people capable of building to colossal heights. When he saw the Yuganan who appeared outside to greet the great ship, he understood why: they were giants, nearly three meters tall.

He'd seen several large beings in the audience during the Jubilee. Unlike the Zoldaari, there was nothing coarse to the demeanor of the blue-skinned people who welcomed his small party as it arrived in *Thunderer's* jolly boat. The Yuganan seemed in all regards peaceful, dedicated to arts and crafts—and there were signs of their handiwork everywhere as he entered their domain.

Fine woodwork, beautiful tapestries: the titans' quadruple-jointed fingers made them excellently suited for detailed work, regardless of their immense stature. But their size also lent to immense furniture and soaring architecture: every room felt like a Viking mead hall. Rafters towered above, and there were birds flying inside the building and nesting on high. The Yuganan didn't seem to mind.

"Seeing a place like this is why I left the Zoldaari," Carpenter said, dazzled. "Amazing what you can do when you're not drunk all the time."

"My ears are burning," Joe said.

T'Var had invited Pike and Spock to bring along a few of the Menders on what was, in fact, her first visit to the city. A towering Yuganan female—they all appeared to be women—met them in a great workshop.

"I am Rivkin, warden of Krykander," she said, her voice a trilling purr. "The kindred of Yuganan welcome you." She bowed before T'Var, which brought her bald head to eye level for her guests.

T'Var returned the bow and identified herself—but not her guests.

"We have long known of your fleet," Rivkin said.

"I thought I hid our presence better," T'Var responded.

"You cannot hide your deeds. Many years ago, my aunt was lost at sea, along with her whole trawler. A mysterious vessel came to the rescue and conveyed her and her companions to shore. We know this was you."

"I could not have done otherwise."

"And I have heard of others you have helped." Rivkin tilted her oval-shaped head. "Successive conservator generals have inquired about your fleet for years. They call you the Orlights, after something in Skagaran culture. But we have always denied any knowledge of you or your activities. It is the least we could do."

"You have my gratitude." T'Var looked to the workshop behind Rivkin—long rows of tables where Yuganan labored at various crafts. "We have made much use of wares that originated in Krykander."

"If our goods have reached you, and you have appreciated them, I can only be happy." She looked to Pike and the Menders. "Who are your guests, Commander?"

Pike took a deep breath. He'd been in this position recently, where everything depended on his winning over not just one person, but a whole population. But on Kiley 279, he'd had a working starship above. Here, he'd have only his words—and what he carried in his pockets.

"I'm an admirer of your work," he said, producing a fishing fly for Rivkin to see. "What you've made here is really impressive. One of yours, right?"

Large spiny fingers took it. Rivkin smiled. "Ah, yes. A blue bobber. It's a favorite of the yellowfins."

"It won over my friends," he said, gesturing.

"Yes, it is a favorite design."

"Great," Pike said. "I'd like to see the machines."

"The what?"

"The machines in your factory."

"I'm afraid I don't follow you."

Pike emptied his pockets. He had ten more of the flies—hooks removed, for personal safety. The Menders produced even more. "Like I said, we're really big fans." He glanced at the tables. "You're telling me all of these were tied right there, at those tables?"

Rivkin drew up to her full height. "Of course."

"That's the thing," Pike said, pacing between the tall work desks. "Where I come from, fly-tying is really one of the last purely handmade crafts that's mass-produced. Even hundreds of years ago, when they had whole rooms full of people tying them for sale, each one was a little different. Sometimes just a millimeter here or there—they were tying according to the same models and had to try to keep the quality the same. But nobody needed absolute precision. The fish didn't care."

Rivkin just watched him.

Pike walked back to his companions. "We've untied your ties. We've measured. Every component is exactly the same size." He paced around her. "We've counted knots. We've even counted the hairs. How many, of each color, and of each length."

Spock withdrew calipers from his vest. "There is much time on a ship."

"We've looked at it all. The paint scheme on the bodies, the artificial eyes—they're all in the same place," Pike said. "Every detail that went into these is *exactly* the same. And that means you're either *really* careful—and some people are—or there's another answer."

Rivkin watched him. She looked to T'Var. "Commander, who is this person?"

"My name is Christopher Pike."

She did a double take.

"Yes. The one from the alerts you've been getting," Pike said. "I'm from outer space, but not like you. I got here less than a month ago. I know you've been warned about me already, over the rondure." He gestured to T'Var. "She's from space, as well—but she's been here a lot longer."

Rivkin's big eyes bulged at the news. "Really, I don't see why you would—"

"I'm telling you this to let you know that we understand technology," Pike said. "The need for it. The need to get back to it. And the need for people who have it now not to lose it." He gestured to the workers. "You have machines because they probably make your lives easier. But you're hiding them because you're afraid the Skagarans will take them away. Them, or some fire from the sky."

Rivkin looked back at the handcrafters–and then back at Pike. "What do you want? To see our machines?"

"I'm sure they'd be fascinating. The more important thing is you think like my friends here." He gestured to the Menders. "They're of like minds."

She peered at Carpenter. "You're Zoldaari. Even you?"

"We're not all alike," he replied.

"What I want is your help," Pike declared.

"Our help?" Rivkin asked.

He gestured to the Vulcans. "T'Var has taken me as far as she can go—and she needs to get out of here. I need to reach a location to the northeast. The only way is across the ice shelf that lies beyond here."

"The Kandrus? It is vast."

"That is what the map shows." Spock produced it and showed it to the Yuganan warden.

She gasped. "I have never seen such a map!"

"That should prove who we are," Pike said. "My starship made that image—sent it down just as we reached the fjord. Our ship is out beyond your moons, but it was able to see this."

Spock pointed to a location on the map. "This is our destination."

Rivkin took a close look at the map—and laughed. "You want to go to the Devil's Dish?"

Pike looked to Spock, and then T'Var. "Who named it that?"

"My ancestors did, after something in their language," Rivkin replied. "An explorer found it once, in a year of no sea ice. It is literally the end of the world."

"Well, it's definitely too far for horses," Pike said. "I'm also told there's a lot of Zoldaari that way—and they're not all as reasonable as my friend Carpenter there."

"*The Devil's Dish,*" Rivkin repeated, mesmerized. She let the map hang down. "Why would you go there?"

Pike spoke gravely. "We want to prevent a bad thing from happening. It may not hurt you, or the people here—but would destroy the machines of countless others in space. And those people would be hurt. Many would die."

T'Var quickly added that there was a cost. "If Captain Pike succeeds, advanced technology would function on this planet. Your world, your lives, could be changed."

Rivkin stood, taking it all in. "This does not seem a difficult choice to me. But I must speak to the rest of the Kindred." She took another look at Pike. "I might have *you* speak to them as well."

Her smile was encouraging.

Pike figured that of all the settlements on Epheska, Krykander had to be one of the most densely populated. Everything was within the ringed keep and courtyard—including the secret factory, which was everything Pike imagined, with ingenious water-powered machines galore. Nearby was the immense alpine-style hall where the Yuganan took communal meals together.

Pike had worked both Spock and the Menders into their presentation at dinner. "At a minimum, I'd like sanctuary for my friends and their families," he said. "Meanwhile, Spock and I would figure out some way across the Kandrus alone."

"At a maximum," Spock said, "you could provide us with a way across."

One of the Yuganan listeners spoke up. "We don't have anything like that."

"Maybe you could help us construct a way." Pike waved to the ceiling above. "You're builders. My friends are builders. We may be able to—"

Motion from the big doorway caught his attention. T'Var entered with a speed that belied her years.

"I must take leave of you, Captain. *Enterprise*'s forecast was correct. A vortex is forming. If we do not leave tonight, we will not be able to."

"Go," Pike said, offering a Vulcan salute. "With my thanks."

"I despise leaving, given what you are facing," T'Var said.

"Then remain," Spock said. "You have come this far."

She shook her head at him. "Spock, I am responsible for many."

"Many who are trapped. What is the better outcome for them?"

Pike didn't disagree, but he understood T'Var's split loyalties. "I appreciate what you're trying to do, Spock. But the commander has—"

Another interruption, through a different door. One of Rivkin's lookouts approached the warden. "There is a call from Om Mataya," the aide said. "A sentinel saw the sailing ships pushing toward the fjord."

"Then we are discovered," T'Var said.

Pike's heart sank. It was what they'd worried about. Racing to Krykander, T'Var had forgone her usual tactics designed to hide the size of her fleet. Whether or not they were trapped, they were certainly found out. Now they *really* had to go.

He watched as the elder Vulcan stood back and clasped her fingers. *I'm sorry*, he wanted to say. But she was looking down, lost in thought.

"Was that the entire message?" Rivkin asked her aide. "What do they want?"

"They warn us to be on alert. And say that if Captain Pike—or any other stranger—should arrive, it is General Drayko's order that those persons be brought before the rondure to speak with him."

"I'm guessing it's not just to say hello," Pike said. He looked to T'Var. "Don't wait. Weigh anchor."

Her forehead behind templed fingers, T'Var did not immediately respond. When she looked up, her question was to Rivkin. "What will *you* do?"

"I must obey," the warden said. "We have worked to ensure the Skagarans consider the Yuganan as loyal to the project. For the sake of my people, I would not sacrifice that unless we had some guarantee of a better outcome." She looked to Pike. "Can you give me one, Captain?"

Pike remembered his last broken communication with La'an—and decided. "There may be something. Let me make a call of my own."

CHAPTER 58

THE ASYLUM

Across the histories of several worlds, certain governments had interned dissidents in mental wards, attempting to "cure" them of their political views. Many had not been hospitals at all, but outright prisons.

The names of places in Om Mataya leaned hard on euphemisms, referring to the operations center as the Care Circle, security guards as "compliance aides," and bathrooms as "contemplation nooks." Una Chin-Riley was not surprised that the asylum Celarius had spoken of was known as the Warm Embrace—and she was even less startled to learn it was nothing more than a cold dungeon, where new prisoners, food, and water were dropped down a literal hole. Uneasy guards had offered to put down their ladder for the heritor general; Celarius had rejected that, diving in first and helping to break Chin-Riley's fall when they cast her down.

Drayko's regime didn't kill people, so far as she could tell, but it had no problem burying them alive, as long as they died out of sight.

The pair had been greeted the first day by a gray-haired Skagaran. Another prisoner, Kohsam was the self-appointed resident assistant, having survived in the catacombs for more than half his life. Pasty-skinned and emaciated, he directed the new arrivals to a chamber with unoccupied slabs that looked not unlike funeral biers—after which he served as their guide to the facility's extensive reaches.

"The rondure predated everything in Om Mataya," Kohsam said in a voice that connoted dignity, even amid intense deprivation. "Legend has it our first capital was reclaimed by the wild. The Skagarans were delighted to find a rondure sited in a protected place near a river."

Chin-Riley nodded. She'd already learned from him that the communications devices were *discovered*, and not invented, by the Skagarans. Celarius confirmed that as well. All the family secrets were coming to light.

"They laid down the first level of buildings on the shore alongside the temple," Kohsam said, "only to decide they deserved a larger, fancier home as more people were delivered to the planet. So they abandoned the early works and put down what you *think* is the bottom level on top of it."

The spindly elder gestured to the ceiling, where a little light filtered in through the gutter grates above. Water and cold air came in there as well.

"The people of Om Mataya walk right above us every day, some surely hearing our cries. Every few years, we close off another room as we store our dead. I expect in another century we'll run out of spaces, and the next level up will join the Warm Embrace."

As dark as the place was, Celarius had been in a darker one since arriving. The confident man of the forest looked bereft. "What you must think of my people," Celarius said, refusing to look to Chin-Riley. "I swear I didn't know it was this bad."

"Don't worry about what *I* think," she said. "Worry about Kohsam. He's one of your people too."

They walked through the icy puddles. Chin-Riley glanced from room to room, seeing abandoned people shivering. "It's awful," she said. "And surprising. I've been to places like this before. This is not what I expected."

"Did you think we were better?" Celarius asked. "Or is it the shock that we could be so uninspired about our punishments? You may have noticed all the imagination on this planet came from somewhere else."

"There's nothing wrong with that. The people I come from are very adaptive. It's just with all the energy your people put into staging every bit of your society and culture, they seem to have gone for the fastest nonlethal fix. My people send offenders to faraway places like Thionoga. The Skagarans couldn't even be bothered to put this place on the opposite bank of the river."

"Our prison lacks flair," Kohsam said, "but it serves its purpose—and its location reflects how quickly they must act when they perceive existential threats." He looked awkwardly at Celarius. "I find that for all the talk about the project's endurance, the leaders act as if it is as fragile as an egg."

Celarius agreed. "My father spent six years tending to a tree every day— only to rip it completely out when its roots threatened a bush he liked better. I suspect this is the sort of logic that ruined our homeworld."

Kohsam gave a wan smile. "I should probably not speak to you so—but then I consider where I already am."

The Warm Embrace held people from all across Epheska—and not just Skagarans. Inventors who would not abandon their interests would suddenly decide after an intervention session with their local warden that it was time to move away. An airship ride to the valley later, they were never seen again. As with the *sah'ree*, it was enough to instill superstition, but not actual fear of the state. Chin-Riley had already remarked that a goal of the Skagaran project was to pretend there was no state.

And then there were prisoners like Kohsam. The aged Skagaran, the commander had learned, had been a true believer. He was one of the novices who went through the same orientation that she had been jailed for infiltrating. He had learned how to control the fire creatures—and had done so for decades aboard sentinels.

But he had learned something. Something that Celarius told her he hadn't known until just before his imprisonment. It wasn't just that the creatures known as the *sah'ree* were alive, or that being manipulated against their will caused them pain. They were being directed against the settlers and had been for four hundred Standard years.

"I did it for a decade," Kohsam said, forlorn and ignorant of the drizzle dripping down on him from a grating above. "We said we were targeting evil *things*—flushing what the generals called the 'poisons of progress.' But I know for a fact that while the traveling flames did not intend to harm others, often they caused destruction that did."

"Not to mention the toll on the people," Chin-Riley added. She was trying to be understanding; Celarius still seemed shaken from learning about it, and he had been closer to the situation for his whole life. But there was no sugarcoating it. "The leaders here made the *sah'ree* into a weapon of terror."

Celarius slammed his fist against a stone wall. "I always knew there was *something*. But I was content to let the sentinels ferry me places, wild places where no one lived, where I wouldn't have to see it."

He had bloodied the back of his hand, she saw, but he turned his back and clenched his fist to his chest, refusing aid.

"Maybe that's why you're down here," she said. "You've seen every corner of this planet except the one right below your feet. This was overdue."

They went from chamber to chamber. Those sentenced for similar crimes gathered together; those of a similar species also did. Communal hopelessness, interrupted by food drops and punctuated by deaths.

But it was a single old woman alone in a chamber, staring into nothingness, who most grabbed her attention.

Kohsam looked in at the woman. "She is the saddest of all," he said. "Her people speak a language we could never interpret. Most of them have passed beyond."

"But why is she here?" Chin-Riley asked.

Celarius shifted awkwardly as he looked in at her. "I recall this. Her people's colony had failed, and my grandmother wanted to assign their rondure and settlement to someone else. The few of them were brought back to Om Mataya as guests. I wondered what had happened to them."

"She is still your family's guest," Kohsam said. "She is the last one."

Seeing that the woman was looking at him, he made a gesture of greeting. She responded to him in words the commander could not understand—but there was something about her joined eyebrow and sunken eyes that struck a chord in Chin-Riley's memory.

"She's Menk."

The old woman's eyes went wide. "Menk!"

"Yes. You are Menk." Chin-Riley entered the dark room and knelt. She placed her hand on her chest. "I am Una."

"Tooza. Menk Tooza."

"Your people are from Valakis."

The old woman reared back and bolted onto her feet. "Valakis!"

A stream of words unfamiliar to Una followed, and the woman clasped hands with her. "*Tooza zan Una kray. Tooza Valakis xeh.*"

Kohsam was mystified. "She has never spoken to anyone like this. Is Valakis her settlement?"

Chin-Riley shook her head. "It's her people's planet. Starfleet visited there a hundred years ago—but the Menk were a primitive people even then. I don't doubt that the Skagarans took them."

Tooza chattered more, mentioning her species and homeworld several more times. She didn't want to let go of Chin-Riley's hand—and Una didn't want her to.

But Kohsam's confusion continued. "Do you mean to say you are from space, Una?"

"Yes."

Celarius nodded. "It's why she's here."

The old man reached past him with surprising vigor and grabbed for the commander's wrist. He started pulling her away from Tooza.

"She doesn't want me to go," Chin-Riley said.

"Bring her along," Kohsam said. "This cannot wait."

She and Celarius looked at each other. *What can't wait in a place like this?*

Her arm around the still-talking Tooza, Chin-Riley guided the woman after Kohsam to a room at the farthest end of the chain of miseries. There, she saw people huddling under scraps of fabric against the cold. One man sat apart, wearing a jacket and vest that she recognized as being from the Old West.

His face she recognized as well. From a briefing document.

"Doctor Li?"

The bearded man looked up at the sound of her voice.

Una conveyed Tooza to Celarius's arm and went fully inside. "Doctor Li Chaoxiang?"

Cautiously, he replied. "Yes?"

"I'm fighting the urge to add 'I presume' to that. You're the captain of the *Braidwood*. I'm Lieutenant Commander Una Chin-Riley from *Starship Enterprise*."

As Tooza had, the middle-aged academic bolted upright. He clapped his hands, waking up his dozing companions. "She's from *Enterprise*!" he repeated, making sure everyone knew.

The moment Chin-Riley had with Tooza repeated several times over—with her surprise for them leading to a surprise for her. From the back corner of the chamber, an elderly Skagaran woman approached the gaggle. Her hair was white, but her eyes were wide and aware. "Did you say *Enterprise*?" she asked.

"I did. Do you know it?"

"Oh, I know it. But we probably know different captains." She extended her hand. "My name is Taliyah. Jonathan Archer changed my life."

CHAPTER 59

THE FACEOFF

Christopher Pike had made his signal to *Enterprise* but had no idea if there had been a response. Even with the longer nights, the weather system made sighting the starship impossible, and the Meteor Express deliveries had stopped back during the sea voyage. That left him nothing to do other than decide who should be in attendance when Rivkin called Drayko on Krykander's rondure.

He and Spock were obligatory attendees. The surprise was T'Var, who, heedless of the risk to her stationary fleet, remained for the call. "He knows we exist. It is illogical to pretend otherwise. I will not spend another century here avoiding the faces of tyrants."

Pike knew the night wind was unfavorable for getting the ships out of the fjord. But he appreciated her willingness to join them.

In the temple in the keep's courtyard, he and the others took *zazics* and settled in near the rondure. Rivkin triggered the device, and within moments, they were in the astral plane.

This time, there was no garden surrounding Drayko, only blackness and the whirling rondure. The Skagaran leader regarded Pike coolly but looked surprised to see the extra attendees.

"I have unexpected guests," Drayko declared, gravel voiced. "It feels like a dinner at Om Mataya."

"Om Mataya," Pike said. "Your home, as I recall."

"Indeed, you could have been having dinner here now, Captain, had you not taken flight." He laughed. "But what am I saying?" He clapped his hands together—

—and seconds later, a luxurious dining room came into view. Drayko took a seat at the head of the table—and gestured for the others to join him on either side.

A supersized chair had been provided for Rivkin away from the table. "Please stay and observe, Warden. I have a few words, and then some orders for you at the end."

"As you say, General." Rivkin's response sounded more dry-mouthed than Pike had heard from her before.

"Come, sit," Drayko said to the others. "The food is imaginary, but you might as well see what you're missing."

Guarded, Pike and his companions took their seats.

Drayko raised a chalice. "To our delayed reunion, Captain Pike. And to our new friends."

No one joined the toast.

Real or not, Drayko went through the motions of cutting meat. "I take it, Warden Rivkin, they arrived just after our alert."

"They are here," she said. She looked unnerved to be in this company. Pike didn't know how far out on a limb she'd go.

"And this pair," Drayko said, gesturing to the Vulcans with his fork, "must be our Orlights." He put the utensil down. "Three generations of my family have hunted you." He gestured to their ears. "You are no species the Skagarans brought here. Who are you?"

"I am T'Var, from the planet Vulcan. My people were trapped here many years ago." The commander stared directly at him. "We have not met—but we know all about you."

"And I know so little about you. But I expect that will change." Drayko looked to Spock. "Your junior? Your offspring?"

"I am Lieutenant Spock of *Enterprise*."

"Of—" Drayko leaned back and put his napkin on the plate. "The last of the lost is found!" He toasted the Vulcans. "This little alliance makes sense. Congratulations on finding one another."

Pike looked at the Skagaran, startled. "You said 'the last of the lost'?"

Drayko put down his cup and nodded. "Yes, it is time. I have someone here you might like to speak with." He looked from the table to the rondure. "Zoryana, she may join."

Pike saw a blurred figure—who suddenly snapped into view. *Number One!*

"Hello, Captain," she said. His first officer wasn't in uniform, but drab and dingy khaki clothing. She looked haggard. "I heard about you a lot."

"I haven't heard anything about you." Pike was horrified to think she might have been in Drayko's clutches all this time—but he was nonetheless glad to see her. "Is Uhura there?"

"She's alive." She glared at Drayko. "So far as I know."

"The young human is here," the general said. "She is not going anywhere." He nodded to Number One. "Can you behave well enough to sit at my table?"

"I'll stand."

"As you will." He looked to Pike. "Una has been our guest for some time. I can assure you she was well taken care of—until her curiosity clouded her judgment."

"Occupational hazard," Chin-Riley said. "They pulled me out of a perfectly good dungeon to take this call."

Pike frowned. "Don't harm my people, Drayko."

"And you weren't going to harm mine," he declared. "But everywhere you go, dissent and destruction follows."

"The only destruction is yours, General," Chin-Riley said. "Captain, the *sah'ree*—the fire beings—are controlled by the Skargarans. They make them power their airships and strike their enemies."

"Strike—?" The news startled Rivkin, who'd been watching, mesmerized, from her chair. "General, what is she saying?"

"Mad nonsense, Warden," Drayko declared. "These are the rantings that have put her in the Warm Embrace. But there are kind people there, seeing to her mental condition."

"No doctors," Chin-Riley said. "But there is a professor. And a lot of inventors. Dissidents. And, oh, yes—the crew from *Braidwood*. Captain Li sends his regards."

Pike's head spun. All the answers, at once.

Drayko gestured to T'Var. "It does not disturb me that you think I have this capability. Because your little fleet cannot be allowed to continue. My ancestors brought seagoing peoples to this planet—even some undersea ones. They never worked out. You will scuttle your vessels and live on the land—or we will burn your ships."

"He can't deploy the *sah'ree* without line of sight from the airships," Chin-Riley said.

"As I have always suspected," T'Var asserted, the old woman's resolve showing. "General, I will blow your aircraft out of the sky."

"Your ammunition will run out sometime," Drayko said, "and I know Warden Rivkin and the Yuganan will offer you no help. You may be frozen into the fjord there even now. When it happens, you will see my people arrive."

"What people?"

"Forces are mustering all across the Kandrus. They have been coming for days, summoned by us once we knew where you were headed." He faced Pike and gave a canny grin. "I know you are heading for—what is it your people call it, Warden, the 'Cold Dish'?"

"The Devil's Dish." Rivkin gulped audibly at hearing how much Drayko knew.

"It was a good gambit, Captain—and an incredible discovery that you've made. But you should know I would never allow you to reach it."

"You know what's there." Pike said it, more than asked it.

"Now I do. Thanks to you."

"How?"

Drayko looked over at Number One and chuckled. "It is amusing, really.

I had just decided to arrest your junior here—and to teach my son a valuable lesson—when a call arrived from Agar." He shook his head in wonderment. "No one had called us from that rondure in centuries since the founding of Om Mataya. When I learned who was calling, and what she had to offer, I dispatched sentinels to meet them on the coast right away." He glanced at T'Var. "That's right, Commander. It was so important, I risked the airships to cross your precious sea."

Drayko looked to the side, as if hearing something in his ear.

He rose from his chair. "Speaking of, I'm just informed we have even more special guests, calling in from a rondure significantly closer to you."

All eyes turned to the rondure, which glowed more brightly for several moments. When it returned to its normal hue, two figures flanked it.

Lila—and one other.

"Weedaw!" Pike said. "You're all right!"

The blacksmith glowered at him and Spock. "No thanks to you two." He faced Drayko. "*Pike was going to kill me!*"

CHAPTER 60

THE TRUTH

Pike had sprung from his chair on seeing Weedaw and Lila. On hearing the blacksmith's accusation, he plopped back down, as if struck by a blow.

He thinks I wanted to kill him?

Spock found his voice first. "I do not understand, Weedaw. We were working the translations when I stepped out to see the captain. What transpired next?"

"The warden came in." He pointed to Lila. "She warned me!"

Pike looked to Lila—silent, as she had been since arriving. "Warned you of what?"

"She told me the truth," the Strooh said. "She told me she was from space too."

Pike's brow furrowed. No, he hadn't shared her secret at that point. "She *is* from space."

"So it's true." Weedaw looked to Drayko, almost averting his eyes. "It's true, General!"

"I know it, my young friend." Drayko sat down again, seeming amused. "Tell him what else she told you."

Beads of sweat formed on Weedaw's forehead. "She told me we needed to hide from the Federation. That it's an evil organization—that your Starfleet runs around conquering planets!"

Pike's jaw dropped. "*She didn't.*"

"She did! She said you were spies. Advance scouts or something. You followed her here. All that stuff your ship rained down on the wagon train was to stop her from rescuing us from you. And the whole thing about turning off the Baffle—it's so you can come down here and take over!"

"I admit bafflement myself," Spock said to Pike.

Weedaw pointed at Spock. "She said you two were talking about killing me when my translations were done. That's when she set your horses loose—and she came in and saved me!"

Pike was flabbergasted. "Weedaw, I didn't—"

"I didn't want to join this call. But I wanted you to know: you lost. I gave her my notes. General Drayko said I'd be safe forever!" He stepped behind Lila's back—and made a fist over her shoulder at them. "We've saved the planet!"

Before Pike could object further, Lila spun and clapped a hand on the blacksmith's shoulder. "You've said your piece. You can go."

Weedaw glared at the Starfleet officers, bared his teeth—and disappeared.

Pike couldn't believe what he'd heard. "Those are lies," he said to the air. He faced Rivkin. "They're all lies!"

Lila adjusted her hat. "They were, and they weren't. You might not have been coming back to kill him. But you *are* going to destroy his world if you get your way."

Spock and T'Var joined in appealing to the Yuganan warden. "Rivkin, Vulcans do not lie," T'Var said. "We are incapable of it. This woman is not a Vulcan."

"No, I'm a warden," Lila said, walking over to face Rivkin. "I'm just like you. I'm protecting my settlement. And protecting the project!"

Drayko smiled. "A better example of devotion I have rarely seen, not even from those born here."

Pike looked around as if in a daze—and noted that Number One, who had been watching the spectacle the entire time, was now right beside Lila. His old friend and new friend fixed eyes on each other.

"What do *you* want?" Lila asked. "Who are you?"

"I'm Una Chin-Riley. You're the guide."

"What?"

"I spoke with Taliyah," the commander said. "The *Braidwood* crew told me that you betrayed them."

Lila's temper flared. "I did no such thing!"

Chin-Riley pivoted and faced Pike. "Do you remember hearing about Taliyah—the little Skagaran girl that Jonathan Archer met?"

"Hell, I've met her."

"Well, she's here, Captain."

Pike looked to Lila, stunned. "Taliyah's *here*?"

"That's right," Number One said. "An observer on *Braidwood*, not on our manifest. Taliyah told me she invited a human woman along as a pathfinder for the party. When *Braidwood* crashed, that scout left to find help. When the scout came back, it was on an airship." She paced around Lila. "She'd found the civilizations here and made contact with the Skagarans. So Drayko brought all the *Braidwood* survivors back to Om Mataya."

Lila glared at her. "What of it?"

"Drayko demanded that *Braidwood*'s crew all join the society here—give up any hope of leaving the planet. But they wouldn't all agree."

Drayko shook his head. "Extremely disappointing. Taliyah would have been a great asset. A Skagaran, who found her way back to us! She would have been a grand story at the Jubilee."

"They tried to escape," Number One said. "Only someone informed on them. Someone from their own crew." She stared Lila down. "The only one who's not imprisoned here now. *The guide.*"

Lila opened her mouth, but Chin-Riley spoke first. "If you're going to deny it, she said your name was Lila Talley."

"Bingo," Pike said acidly. He glared at Lila—and he got the sense that even in astral space, she could feel his eyes on her.

"It wasn't like that," Lila finally said.

Pike did not respond.

She approached the table. "They were going to ruin everything, Christopher!"

Number One circled behind her. "I take it you know this woman."

"I thought I did." Pike shook his head. "She betrayed me too." He stood from the table and faced her. "Back at Havenbrook, when I first got a package from *Enterprise*. You sent the lookouts to the farm after me. You told Drayko."

"For the protection of everyone here," Lila said. "Just as I was protecting Weedaw!"

Pike's first officer shook her head. "Permission to speak freely, Captain?"

He didn't look back. "Granted!"

"Your friend is a real piece of work."

Drayko pushed his chair back from the table. "And I've had quite enough of you." He pointed to Number One. "Zoryana, break her contact."

The commander started to say something—only to vanish.

"Where'd she go?" Pike asked.

"She will be taken back to where she was," Drayko said. "Don't worry. You'll see her again when you join her there."

"You seem awfully certain."

"I am."

Spock's gaze was fixed on Lila, Pike saw. "Why is she doing this, Captain?"

Pike was going to say he had no idea—but he thought for a moment. His eyes narrowed. "Wait a minute. You took Weedaw with you and stole his notes so we couldn't find out how to turn the Baffle off." He tilted his head. "Why is he still alive?"

Lila blanched. "I don't know what you mean."

"If what Weedaw saw on those tablets is an existential threat to Epheska and the project, then why didn't you kill him back in Agar?"

"I wouldn't do that. What kind of person do you think I am?"

"I'm not sure anymore," Pike said, circling her now as Number One had. "I'm not sure I ever knew."

Spock got Pike's point. "The reason Weedaw is alive is the same reason you took his notes, Warden Talley. You want the Skagarans to know what he knows. Not how to deactivate the Baffle. But how to modify its radius."

"To increase it," T'Var said. She shook her head. "She *is* mad."

"She's hurt," Pike said. He stepped toward Lila. She took a step back. "The families that lived in her community moved from Earth to Kelfour VI—and were annihilated by the Klingons." He studied her. "Is that it?"

She said nothing.

He read the answer in her eyes—and was staggered by it.

"*That's it,*" he said in a small voice. "You're going to do it." He spoke over his shoulder to Spock. "How far are we from the Klingon border?"

"Ten light-years. Qo'noS is eighty."

And Earth isn't much farther, Pike knew. But just the notion that the Baffle could disrupt technology in any part of Klingon space—

He let out a deep sigh. "Cold revenge."

"It's not revenge," Lila said.

"Are you going to tell me it's justice? Because a lot of people will die who aren't combatants."

"With the Klingons, there's no such thing. And we already know they don't care."

Drayko clasped his hands behind him. "You have it all wrong, Captain. It's not revenge or justice if I sponsor it. It's prevention."

"Prevention?" Pike asked.

"From what Warden Talley tells me, our location in your so-called Beta Quadrant suggests the Klingons would conquer Epheska in a heartbeat, if they knew it existed."

Pike couldn't disagree with that. "They don't know."

"*Braidwood* already found us. So did *Enterprise*. I know you're talking to them, by the way, with that ingenious device of yours—I'll need that. Should the Klingons hunt *Enterprise* down, they could easily find us."

"They won't. The war is over."

"If they are not at war with the Federation now, that only increases the odds they will visit, if the nebula seems a place you are interested in. Why shouldn't we cut that threat off?"

"Because you're going to kill a lot of people you've never met."

"And will never meet. A difference that makes no difference is no difference." Drayko paced from behind the table back to the rondure. He gestured across it—and the table was gone. They were all seemingly in space, as Pike had been during the Jubilee. "My people have visited dozens of worlds. We rescued just a fraction of the populations there. We couldn't take everyone. We wouldn't have wanted to take everyone."

"You've got yours."

"I have. And my people will continue to protect those in our care—whoever takes my office afterward." He pointed to various planets in the sky, all larger than they would naturally appear. Several had the lights of cities on their night sides. The lights of each of those worlds went dark, one by one. "Random visitations like yours will end—and war will come no longer in this region. The residents will thank us, eventually. Your people will too, Captain."

"Never," Pike declared.

"No matter." He waved his hand, and the dining room returned. He looked to Lila. "You're almost to Krykander?"

"We made it to Golaraad, the closest Zoldaari settlement. Weedaw's staying here until you're ready for him." She adjusted her sleeves. "Javu is here, with his force at the ready. He says the strait is freezing over. It'll be hard riding, but we can go as soon as it does."

"I know it is important to you to finish this," Drayko said. "Javu of the Zoldaari is the perfect enforcer, unescapable. Go, with my blessing."

Lila gave Pike a last look—and vanished.

With her disappearance, Pike felt as if the astral air had gone out of the room. A voice came from a forgotten corner.

"Excuse me," Rivkin asked. "What do you expect of *me*?"

General Drayko approached her and addressed her directly. "Hold the renegades. And then, dear Warden, I expect no more than your usual behavior. I know that the Yuganan abhor machinery as much as anyone on Epheska." He reached for her hands. "Help us deal with these wrongdoers, and your people can go back to what they always desired: an eternity of making crafts as they should be made. By your enormous, miraculous hands."

He smiled—and vanished. Pike saw only the ruby rondure, slowing to a stop. They were in the temple again.

He looked from Spock to T'Var. This was bad, and they all knew it.

Their only hope knelt nearby, clutching a *zazic* in her spiny hand. Rivkin, giant of the icy north, was shivering.

Pike stood and walked with her out of the temple into the night, followed by the Vulcans. He saw the silhouettes of row after row of Yuganan citizens, standing still as statues, waiting to hear what their warden had learned. From a low ceiling above, snow began to fall.

"Will you still help us, Warden?" Pike asked.

"I don't know," Rivkin said.

"An honest answer."

She stared up at the clouds. "I need something. A sign to say who is in the right." She looked wanly at him. "What you said earlier in the factory, Captain—I feel you understand us. We are like your Menders, ready for another life, ready to build. Drayko's people have protected us—but I do not think he really knows us."

Pike nodded in agreement. Then he saw something.

"What is it?" she asked as she noticed his gaze. "We do not see so well at night."

"I think it might be your sign, Warden." He grabbed her wrist. "And I think we need to run!"

CHAPTER 61

THE INITIATIVE

They landed one at a time, descending through the clouds precisely a minute apart. In the darkness, they at first looked like trees, falling from the sky. It was only after Pike and the Yuganan in the courtyard sought cover that it became apparent the tree canopies were, in fact, parachutes. And the trunks that landed in the snow outside the city walls were metal posts.

T'Var, who had been expecting aerial bombardment after the call with Drayko, had to be convinced not to make immediately for her ships. But the one girder that did enter the compound—clipping the outer wall as it drifted down—demonstrated to her and Pike both that it was not from Drayko at all.

"Duranium," Pike had said. *They're gutting* Enterprise—*and sending it to me!*

He didn't really believe that was the case, but no message had arrived either with that delivery, or on any of the various metal pieces, not all of them girders, that landed outside the keep. The rain of materials continued until just after sunrise, by which point the collective force of Yuganan, Menders, and Vulcan sailors had carted most of what had fallen into the courtyard.

Pike was about to query with his viridi-comm when one last parachute appeared—this one delivering something wide and squat. The payload spun wildly. It was targeted directly at the keep, and it clanged off the side of the temple before settling in the snow, covered in the next instant by its spent chute. The Yuganan attacked the ropes, trying to get to the latest prize.

"Slow down, folks," Pike said, approaching. "Some space, please."

It was an escape pod. Its parachutes were identical to all the others. Pike realized *Enterprise* must have scavenged all its other pods for chutes in the night's drops. Spare parachutes weren't just sitting around. Stenciled across the side of the pod was the name *Icarus*, which made some sense; down was the only direction this ship went. A line appeared around the main hatch, and the door opened.

A warmly dressed Hemmer took a step out—and collapsed immediately into the snow.

Pike rushed to him. "Are you okay, Lieutenant?"

"Cousin? Is that you?"

"Try 'Captain,' " Pike said. Hemmer was delirious. He tried to help him sit up. "You're dizzy."

Hemmer's head lolled about atop his neck. "It seems . . . electronic assistance . . . is helpful for attitude control."

"I don't know what you're doing here, but welcome to Epheska." Pike gestured toward the crowd gathered around. "These are the Yuganan. This is their home."

"Hello," Rivkin said, copying the Vulcan salute T'Var had given to her.

Pike didn't know whether the expression "seeing double" meant anything to an Aenar—but as Hemmer dared to stand, he was clearly startled by the size of the crowd. "I hope they're not all here because I landed on someone."

"Just the Wicked Witch of the East."

"What?"

"Never mind," Pike said. "Hemmer, I told La'an nobody was to come down. Four people stuck here is bad enough. What's the idea?"

The Aenar straightened—and brushed snow off his parka. "To be clear, Captain, you also ordered La'an to find ways to assist you that did not reveal modern technologies to the natives. You furthermore expressed an urgent need to get to the 'Dog's Dish'—"

"Devil's."

"—whatever. The lieutenant instructed me to seek ways to help, pursuant to the limitation that the bizarre conditions here prevent the use of anything electrical. And, oh, yes, we're to avoid fire because apparently on *this* planet fire comes alive, and your allies would be fearful of it." He took a frosty breath. "Have I overlooked anything?"

"No."

"These are significant constraints, with many potential conflicts that require a captain's judgment." Hemmer crunched through the snow toward one of the piles of girders. "Now, we could get our captain's opinions, were he not communicating via a piece of fabric and a box—which at least is better than our responses, which are limited to carrier projectile, when they're not requiring spectacular flashes that zero out all the clocks in main engineering."

Pike nodded. That was how it was.

Hemmer pulled a notepad out of his parka and counted girders as he talked. "Faced with these limits, I devised a method that I believe would assist you—but it soon became apparent that its complexities would require engineering personnel on-site. Knowing that—and knowing that I had already devised a single pod for a dead-stick surface landing—La'an decided to take *Enterprise* out of the loop. I had argued for one of my junior officers to make the trip instead, but apparently La'an has the 'greatest respect for my abilities.' I can't tell you how delighted I was to be so honored."

Pike couldn't help but grin. "So all this is your idea." He gestured. "What *is* it?"

"It is the Great Experiment, Captain. Or rather, it is my Great Experiment. It is inspired by another *Experiment*—with a capital letter, and in italics—and, oh, yes, a thing I have dreamt of building since I was a child on Andoria."

"You're not making sense."

Hemmer finished his count. "There are several units missing."

Pike shrugged. "They came down all over."

"I despise imprecision. Well, they can be obtained as we go." He turned his head about and breathed in the crisp air. "A taste of home here. I like it." He gestured to the crowd. "Now, do any of you bystanders have any interest in performing a massive feat of primitive engineering in an impossibly short window of time?"

The Menders' hands immediately went up. And as soon as the translations made it around, the rest of the hands followed.

Nyota Uhura knew a variety of phrases in different languages that had ceased to be meaningful years ago, yet their use had persisted. For an ostensible center of advancement, Starfleet in particular seemed stuck in its words, either owing to tradition or laziness. Officers still spoke of having "paperwork" to finish, had ordered her to "tune into" or "tap" a remote conversation, or had requested that she "wind back" a response. At least no one she could remember had ever asked her to "dial up" anyone.

Epheska was a fascinating study for a linguist, demonstrating not only alternative evolutions of known languages, but idioms that were still used to reflect their original meanings. Yet the anachronistic phrase she'd been thinking most often during her time in Om Mataya was "above her pay grade."

She suspected, for example, that somewhere in the codicils to the Prime Directive was a ban on setting fire to one's guest room on a foreign planet. Yet that was what she'd done, after she and Chin-Riley had become separated following the fiasco in the hangar. The first officer had attracted all the pursuers in her flight, allowing Uhura the chance to sneak back to the Garden House and reclaim the empatherm from the first officer's closet.

It had not been Uhura's intention to become trapped, nor had she wanted Empy to respond to her panic by setting the room alight. It had allowed her to escape, however, and while others were able to quickly contain the blaze, the moral and legal quandary lingered. Even so, she felt very much in Empy's place. Her commanding officer had told her to escape but hadn't had time to say how.

Her fiery friend knew she was in danger, but still didn't know the rules. Such matters were above *his* pay grade too.

The hours and days that followed had been an inversion of her long walk in the open. Every minute had been spent skulking from one sheltered hiding place to another, lit only by her friend within the precious lantern. Hundreds of years of expansions and renovations had left nooks and crannies everywhere. Unlike in the wild, food wasn't a problem this time; meal preparation at Om Mataya was a backstairs affair, meaning she just had to await her chance to grab something.

But while she had overheard that Chin-Riley had been captured, all of Uhura's nocturnal searching had been unable to reveal where she was being held.

After repeatedly thinking to herself that the wrong one of them had escaped, Uhura finally dared to visit one of the lower, more populated levels of the facility. She had long since abandoned her ungainly cloak, having purloined instead a laborer's uniform from the laundry—and while she knew precious little about the rondure she'd heard about, it *was* a communications device.

Any hope of reaching it—much less raising anyone friendly on it—vanished when she realized the temple sheltering the device was occupied every minute of the day and night. Runners went back and forth from it to the pavilion like they were running a relay race.

Lantern in hand, she retreated back to the crawl space she'd emerged from. It was one of many places she'd gone where the empatherm had made it more difficult to navigate—but she didn't want him floating freely. Reaching the end of the low tunnel, she placed the lantern outside it and prepared to emerge into the maintenance area alongside it.

She saw a large hand pick up the lantern and lift it. A tall Zoldaari glared down at her. "Who are you?" the giant asked in Skagaran.

Uhura looked about, grasping for a suitable response. "I'm working on the plumbing!"

He grabbed her shoulder with his other hand. "*I'm* working on the plumbing. I don't know why the mucky-mucks think they need inside pipes—or why they don't get someone smaller to repair them."

Uhura smiled awkwardly and gestured. "That's why they sent me!"

He put down the lantern but did not release Uhura. "Either you're taking my job or you're one of the people they're hunting. Both bad answers."

Uhura started to struggle, before pausing. "Did you say *people*?"

She got an answer when something struck the Zoldaari in the back of the head. He went down like a bag of hammers, forcing Uhura to dodge his fall.

Chin-Riley emerged from behind him, holding a metal crowbar. "I didn't catch all of that, Cadet. Was it important?"

"I was afraid I got my Skagaran plurals wrong." Uhura picked up her lantern and smiled. "Thanks, Commander. I thought they'd caught you."

"They did," Chin-Riley said, kneeling to check the Zoldaari worker. He was still breathing, Uhura saw. "A guy like this hauled me out of prison the other night to chat over the rondure with the captain and Spock."

"They're alive!" Uhura gushed.

"They're alive—but things are complicated. They got a little simpler when the guards tried to take me back to lockup." She looked awkwardly at the crowbar. "That time, it was a piece of lumber somebody had left sitting around. I'm afraid I broke both of their noses."

"Is there a regulation against that?"

Chin-Riley smirked. "I won't tell if you won't."

"I know there's a regulation against *that*."

"Never mind. How have *you* been? I don't guess they're still trying to send you back to your luxury suite."

It was Uhura's turn to feel embarrassed. "We kind of burned it down when trying to escape."

Chin-Riley laughed out loud. "And you're talking regs to me." She smiled at the lantern, which glowed blue in response. "Way to go, Empy. That's acting on your initiative."

"Don't be too congratulatory. A lot of your maps and books went up too."

Chin-Riley glanced around. "I think we have a good idea where we are by now."

"Extremely," Uhura said. "Are you ready to get out of here?"

"Not quite." Chin-Riley gestured to the storage shelves. "I'm here for the tools." She pointed to a wrench. "Grab that. Precious few metal tools here, but we need them."

"We're not leaving?"

"We're not leaving." Chin-Riley grabbed a coil of rope and turned up the hall. "I'll explain as we go. And keep your head and voice down."

Uhura looked back at the tunnel she'd crawled through. Keeping her head down was something she'd had a lot of practice at.

CHAPTER 62

THE CROSSROADS

As glad as Una Chin-Riley was to see Uhura, she had to admit the cadet's devotion to the empatherm surprised her. But confronted with a rusty grate that the two of them could neither pry nor pull off the ground, *Enterprise*'s first officer soon found herself admiring Uhura's foresight.

Uhura knelt over the metal grating, peering in at the occupants in the dank prison below. She'd already told them to stand well away from the opening overhead. She instructed her companion as well. "Don't think, Commander. *Feel* how upset you were to be trapped down there."

"I'm feeling." Kneeling beside the cadet, Chin-Riley thought of the others she'd met trapped down below. Taliyah and the *Braidwood* crew, who'd wandered into something they never expected. Kohsam, stuck down below longer than any, for the crime of caring. And poor Tooza, bereft and alone. She raised the lid of the lantern.

"This grating is causing us pain," Uhura said. "We don't like it."

The plasma being curled out of the lantern and spiraled toward the grating. Occupants below raised their voices in alarm as it laced in and out, prodding the bars almost in an act of curiosity. Uhura shushed them.

"Yes," Chin-Riley said. "We don't want the grate. The grate is harmful. We hate the grate!"

The empatherm thickened—and glowed brightly. The barrier glowed too—until it started dripping. Soon, a torrent of molten metal fell into the chamber below. The grating consumed, Empy grew cooler—and wafted his way back to the lantern.

Celarius stepped near the hot puddle and looked up at them. "I can't believe it. That isn't supposed to be possible without a *zazic!*"

"You never ask them," Uhura said. "You just order them."

Chin-Riley tied a rope to a nearby post. This building provided the winter housing for the recreational canoes and boats that the locals used to venture onto the Matayan River; she figured they were done for the year and that it would be a place where no one would wander in.

She grabbed onto the rope and let herself down. Celarius helped catch her—and held on to her a little longer than she expected him to. "You *are* amazing," he said.

"Told you I'd be back." She pulled away. "All hell is breaking loose. Captain Pike is in Krykander—"

"*Krykander?*"

"—and your father is sending the Zoldaari after him. I wasn't allowed to stay in the rondure call, but the captain and Spock have found some secret Drayko is after."

"My father and secrets."

Chin-Riley looked out into the hallway. Other prisoners were gathering. "We need to figure out what we're going to do," she said. "I'm here to get the *Braidwood* crew out—but we can't leave everyone else behind."

"I agree." Celarius cast his eyes below. "My father wanted me to learn a lesson. I have."

"What lesson?"

"He was expecting that all this—*this down here*—would continue in my name." He looked up in anger. "I won't have any part of it."

She nodded. "So?"

Her bland response startled him. "So?"

"So, what are you going to do? You won't endorse it—does that mean you're walking away from it?"

"I can't stop it. What else can I do?"

"I thought you were the heir apparent."

Above, Uhura called down. "Guys, we may want to hurry."

Celarius ignored her. "What are you saying, Una? That I should sit back and let these people down here suffer until my father gives up the job? He'll keep at it until his bones turn to dust."

"No, I think waiting is bad," Chin-Riley responded. "I asked what you were going to *do*."

Celarius looked back in the hallway—and again at her. He sputtered, flabbergasted. "You want me to lead a revolution?"

Above, Uhura muttered, "There are *definitely* regulations about that."

Chin-Riley rolled her eyes. "Withdraw, Cadet."

"Sorry."

She pointed to Celarius. "You don't have to overthrow anyone. But you have to take a stand."

"You would respect that? Is that what it would take?"

"I'm trying to get you to do something *you* would respect." She studied his eyes. "This hatred of Om Mataya you always talk about—it's hatred of yourself, for not looking more closely at what's being done on this planet. For not doing anything to change things. You'd rather manage the animal population than think about the sentient people here."

Celarius said nothing.

"There are people here who need a leader—and not just in this so-called asylum. You can remain a spectator, thinking your hands are clean until the day it becomes your problem. But the man I met in the forest wasn't willing to let everything go to hell. He had a plan for fixing things."

He scowled.

"We need to get people out of here," he finally said.

"Okay."

"Many of them are in no condition to do anything." Celarius scratched his beard. "I need safe places for them. I've got some apartments. And nobody but me comes to the *kuuko* stables."

Chin-Riley listened. "And?"

He nodded to the hole in the ceiling. "Out there we've got boats. The river won't have frozen yet. Downstream are limestone caves—and farther, one of the Chinese villages. The warden there is a friend. She'll protect anyone I send there."

"Better."

"*Braidwood*'s crew is in the best shape. We can get out on *Zersa*."

"I can see you've been thinking about this."

He shrugged. "There hasn't been a lot to do down here."

I bet you've been thinking about it a lot longer, she thought. "Let's get started."

The crack echoed across the fjord. On the wharf at Krykander, Spock saw one of the junks—a survivor that had outlasted dynasties and interstellar wars—shift in the ice, coming to rest at a perverse angle. T'Var's people had emptied and abandoned it hours before, but its fate was still a wretched sight. History was dying before anyone could get a look at it.

Some ships had already foundered in the cold snap in the day and a half since Hemmer's arrival. Others had been brought through the sea gate and up the ramp, out of the icy water entirely. *Thunderer*'s smaller craft had already been relocated, and Menders using horse teams were trying to bring as many of her cannons down and out of the ship as quickly as they could. But not all of them. T'Var had positioned the vessel so its port emplacements faced outward. Any approach by the Zoldaari on the ice would come from down the fjord. She would face it.

Spock found the aged commander on deck, her focus on her dwindling fleet. "You should go back to the others," she said, her back to him. "There is nothing to be done here. Your fate lies in the hands of an Andorian."

"Lieutenant Hemmer is an Aenar," Spock corrected. "The Andorians once abused them."

"They were all our enemies, when last I saw Vulcan." She turned to face the science officer. "I left my home to destroy his. And now, he comes to help you. I did not believe you when you told me the Vulcans and the Andorians have become allies—but seeing him, I admit its truth."

Spock studied her. She had seen Hemmer arrive but had not greeted him. "The Andorians have proved to be loyal allies. The lieutenant is a capable officer. I hope you harbor no ill will."

"What I thought long ago no longer matters." She waved her hand. "Assume we could return to space: What would be the logic in persisting in my past beliefs? So much time has passed. Drayko has already put into practice the greatest single attempt to freeze time without the aid of temporal physics—and I do not believe it was successful." She straightened. "We will not cling to old beliefs either."

"A reasonable conclusion."

"Epheska is nothing if not humbling, Spock. Staying here even a short while has that effect. Stay for a century, and you may find yourself open to many new ideas."

Spock was gratified by that—but there was an older idea that he was concerned about. "Sivenda tells me you intend to remain here, even when this vessel is destroyed, by fire or ice. This is illogical."

"My daughter speaks too much. The remaining guns here must be operated."

"And they can be. From shore emplacements." He knew what she really intended. "It is sensible to adopt some ancient maritime practices to run such a vessel. But not all traditions need be observed. We cannot cling to physical objects."

T'Var gestured up to the masts. "Do you know, Spock, it took us eleven years to sheet those yards properly? We had no idea whatsoever how to do it. We only knew these ships were conveyances. The rest came by trial and error." She shook her head. "Many of our number fell from the yards. The lucky ones drowned."

"An achievement, accomplished out of necessity." He gestured back to the keep. "There is a new need."

T'Var nodded reluctantly. "You are going to ask me for more of *Thunderer*. More than her guns and boats."

Spock nodded. "Lieutenant Hemmer's work is progressing, but he was not expecting that so many would need assistance. He believes much of this ship could be useful." He clasped his hands together. "It served you for decades. This would give it a worthwhile final task."

T'Var looked back down at the deck. "I had already decided, Spock."

"Is that so?"

"Yes." The uniformed Vulcan trod the boards of the deck. "If *Thunderer* founders here, it will despoil a perfectly good harbor. My people are already assisting yours. Your alliance in space exists here as well. You will have all that we have."

Spock was gratified. "And you will come with us."

"To space, even, if you can reach it. It will be good to go home."

CHAPTER 63

THE DOORSTEP

The great jailbreak took place over the course of a week, and as far as Una Chin-Riley knew, General Drayko was none the wiser.

Since the compliance aides—*what a name for guards!*—never actually entered the catacombs, they only saw those they dropped food and water down to. Chin-Riley and Celarius made sure that there was always someone there to receive those deliveries. Drayko's minions had noticed nothing amiss at all.

The boat storage area proved to be the ideal location, both for housing and for staging. The larger craft had places for the infirm to recline. Covers on the smaller boats provided hiding places for that time—always the same, every day—when a sole sentry went through. Casks of clean water were kept there, as were bags of hard biscuits; still better than what was served down below.

Uhura, meanwhile, had provided warmth to those who needed it with her magical lantern. Some of the former inmates had been terrorized by the *sah'ree*, and she did not expose them to Empy. But many of the Skagaran prisoners knew well what the beings were and could do.

Celarius had been as good as his word. He had led groups of boaters out in the dead of night, seeing that they survived the frigid waters to leave the valley. He then returned on foot. Una had seen him sneaking back into Om Mataya, always exhausted. He would collapse—and be ready to go again a couple of hours later.

Twice she had gone with him, to see the lay of the land. Each time, she'd been able to talk to him, feeling out his plans, understanding his level of commitment. He hadn't broken, not yet. Every day exposed to the condemned seemed to fuel him with more anger. He'd been told of the righteousness of the Epheska project. He still believed in it. But where he'd fully expected that a few compromises had been made to keep things running, the true number of them had stunned him.

And the fact that his agreement to it all was just assumed had incensed him. Not just for its insult to his character—but for the light it had cast everyone in his family into. "They were afraid I'd be the last of the line," he told her. "It might be just as well!"

With the more vulnerable escapees safely away, Celarius and Chin-Riley were down to two groups of people. The crew of *Braidwood*, she had already determined, needed to go wherever Pike was. That left the more able-bodied prisoners—and those who refused to flee, regardless of their condition or age. That included Kohsam, the Warm Embrace's longest tenant. There was a place for him in their plans.

What they hadn't expected was that the elderly dissident wouldn't want any part of it.

"I don't think you understand," Celarius said. "The only way we can get the *Braidwood* crew out is aboard *Zersa*. Nothing else can reach Captain Pike. Nothing else is big enough!"

"And how were you expecting to power that vessel?" Kohsam spat on the floor. "The only way you can. By continuing to exploit the *sah'ree*."

Sitting by the lantern with the gently glowing empatherm, Uhura nodded. "The *zazics* hurt them."

"It pains me to have it confirmed," Kohsam said. "I was a stoker for sentinels for years. If you were expecting me to do it again, Celarius, you are more like your father than I thought."

Celarius put his hands before him, palms up. "It's the only way, Kohsam. We're talking about crossing incredible distances. Una said Pike was in Krykander—and about to head even farther out."

Chin-Riley looked about the storehouse. "Isn't there something else we could use for propulsion? Don't the Skagarans confiscate inventions?"

"Contraband is held at the local level until there's enough to be dumped remotely," Kohsam said. "Then the *sah'ree* are dispatched to destroy it. *Those* missions, at least, harmed no one."

"I guess the last thing my father wants is a giant central warehouse of the forbidden." Celarius shook his head. "I'm sorry about the things you were forced to do, Kohsam."

The elder Skagaran calmed down. "I am glad of the things *you* have done, Celarius. They are helpful. But you have only just come to understand the *sah'ree*'s plight. It took me even longer."

Uhura looked confused. "I don't understand that."

"What?"

"I figured it out a lot faster than either of you—and you were around the empatherms for years. Why is that?"

Kohsam looked kindly on her and Empy. "I do not know, Uhura. But I admire the care you have taken with that creature. You have a rapport I have never seen."

"It's because we communicate—and because we've been together so long."

Kohsam took that in. "Perhaps *that* is why it took so long for me to realize what we were doing was wrong," he said. "I was never in the presence of a single specimen of the *sah'ree* for more than the time it took to make a single flight."

"It's like your *kuuko*, back in the forest," Chin-Riley said to Celarius. "You didn't mind sacrificing it to the *ollodon*. Why was that?"

Celarius shrugged. "I told you then—it was native to the forest. I found it and tamed it there."

Uhura raised a finger. "See, if it was something you'd known a long time— like a horse—you wouldn't have acted the same way."

Celarius nodded. "I guess there's a reason I never take any of my horses on those trips."

Kohsam continued to press the case. "If we all accept that the *sah'ree* are alive and sensible to pain, then the course is clear. You must find another way—or another stoker. I will not use those blasted *zazics* to propel another airship."

Uhura stared at Empy—and then spoke. "What if you don't use a *zazic*?"

Kohsam looked to her. "What?"

"What if you don't use one?"

"Then you cannot compel it to your will."

"I understand that. What if you don't *compel* it?" Uhura reminded him of how she'd gotten Empy to destroy the grating. "We asked it. We showed it how we felt about all of you suffering in prison."

Chin-Riley tilted her head. "These *zazic* things—they're tied to the ron-dures, right? Some kind of psychic amplifiers."

"Right," Celarius replied.

"So, what if the amplifier is just too loud?"

"It's hurting the fire's *ears*?"

Uhura shrugged. "Yelling, compelling—it's all the same." She patted the top of the lantern. "Maybe the reason nobody has a rapport like ours is because no one is exposed to a single empatherm for any length of time—and people have been trained from the start to just use *zazics*. You can't start a friendship if you're shouting."

Kohsam gazed at the lantern. "All those years down in that hole, I truly wished that just once, I could have engaged with these amazing creatures with-out hurting them—or anyone else."

Uhura opened the top of the lantern. "Here's your chance."

"Captain Pike!" Cyrus had his pencil and booklet in hand. "Got time for a few words for the *Post*?"

"The *Post*?" Standing in the courtyard in Krykander, Christopher Pike scratched his hairy chin. "You know, I haven't been getting my papers lately."

Cyrus grinned. "Our copy was so hot the presses melted—and our only employee has been away on assignment. But he's on a great story."

Pike was glad that Cyrus was feeling positive after leaving his life behind. The editor had been along for the whole journey, participating in the best way he could: keeping a record of the adventure. Pike thought it was important—but his own role, for the present, had come to an end. He'd run a horse team locating and recovering the rest of the pieces *Enterprise* had dropped down; now those were all in the Yuganan work area, as well as everything Hemmer needed from the fleet frozen in the fjord. It was all in the hands of the engineer and the small army of people he had working for him.

"You should see Carpenter," Cyrus said. "Hemmer's made him his deputy, and they're both running around directing the Yuganan. It's the first time Carpenter's ever met people who are taller than he is!"

"Sounds like a busy place," Pike said. "That's why I'm staying out of it. On *Enterprise*, I have my space and the engineers have theirs. No sense confusing the chain of command."

"What's going on back there is amazing. It's the biggest thing I've ever seen. The winches the Yuganan used to pull those boats up into the keep—they're immense. I don't think they ever imagined they'd use them for something like this."

"They hadn't met Hemmer before."

They walked through a gate to the wharf, where Pike beheld the carcass of *Thunderer* poking out of the ice. As a captain of another kind of ship, he felt it was worth a few words. "Laid down 1760 at Woolwich Dockyard, England. Scrapped, 2259, Epheska, Bullseye Nebula." He shook his head. "One year short of five hundred."

Cyrus expressed amazement at all the Vulcans had been willing to do for them. "A month ago, we didn't know they existed."

"Not all rescuers from the stars have ulterior motives. T'Var has done nothing but impress me."

"Don't leave yourself out of it," the editor said. "I won't, when I write the book on this."

"Maybe you should wait to see how it ends."

Pike hoped that Cyrus *would* be able to write a book, and that someone would be allowed to read it—but that prospect dimmed when he heard a distant horn.

The noise was soft, and he had to listen hard to hear it again. It was coming from the west. Down the neck of the fjord, to where the sea opened to the passage that led north to the Kandrus Ice Sheet.

"You hear that?" Cyrus asked.

"Yeah." Pike looked back and up to the ramparts atop the city walls. The platforms there had never been used for offensive purposes, Rivkin had told him; only to spot approaching vessels. But T'Var had put a watch up there, with their superior spyglasses, and shouts from above told him they'd seen something.

He hurried inside. Yuganan ladder rungs were no easy thing to master for the insufficiently tall, but he found that Sivenda and Spock were already there, looking west through their scopes. Rivkin arrived a few moments later.

Pike had heard airship horns during the wagon train chase and was not surprised to see sentinels on the horizon. The fjord was only about four kilometers across at that point, hemmed in by jagged upthrusts of land on either side; three dirigibles appeared about a kilometer apart, spanning the neck left to right.

"They are coming in low," Sivenda said. "They will be in cannon range if they continue much farther."

"I don't think they're what's coming for us," Pike said while using Spock's telescope. As the airships approached, a blur appeared flat on the gray line at the far end of the fjord. Slowly, dark objects came into view. They initially looked like tanks—until they grew nearer and larger. "Woolly mammoths?"

"*Ollodons*," Rivkin said. "The Zoldaari are the only beings who ride them."

Pike looked more closely. Like fur-covered triceratops, they had massive heads that provided both offense and defense to their riders. Nasty-looking horns sat amid shield-like facial plates.

"It's not just Zoldaari," Pike said. There were other species in the mix, both of the two- and four-legged kind; a marching barricade advancing east up the fjord.

"I have never heard of *ollodons* crossing ice," Rivkin said. Everything about what she was seeing seemed to unnerve her.

Pike saw wooden disks on the feet of the nearest animal. "They're on *hestestruger*," Pike said. "A kind of a snowshoe. They used them in Scandinavia and Newfoundland."

Spock stared. "I was not aware the Skagarans abducted people from those places."

"They didn't have to. Lila knows about them. I bet she's out there."

Another loud call from a horn. Pike saw this time it came not from an airship, but a massive rider at the center of the Zoldaari cavalry.

"It's Javu," Rivkin said. "He is the warden of Golaraad, on the west side of the straits."

"A bad customer?"

"It is good the Zoldaari dislike the sea, because we have never liked their company. The Skagarans are constantly issuing Harmony Notes, keeping them in line. They intimidate those of smaller stature." She glanced at Pike. "Your friend Carpenter is an exception. But even he yells a lot."

Sounds like he's on his way to being a chief engineer, Pike thought.

"The Zoldaari have rifles," Sivenda declared.

Rivkin was startled. "I've never heard of them carrying such devices." She had seen enough. She rang a large bell nearby, and the enormous sea gate began closing seconds later. "For Javu to appear, the strait must be completely frozen!"

Pike spoke in calming tones. "Don't forget, that means something to *us* too."

"It is still hard to watch such a thing from one's home."

He understood. "They're going slow. To protect the animals—but also because they can. They want you to have time to think about it, Warden."

"There is time for us, then," Sivenda declared. She looked down from the ramparts to the emplacements. "We must turn the cannons on them."

That wasn't what Pike wanted. "That could go very wrong—for them and for us." He faced Spock. "Tell Hemmer he's got to hurry. My horse is already sharpshod. I'll get us the time."

Spock stopped him at the ladder. "You will require an escort."

"No. Just me. Hemmer needs every hand he can get. Man the door and wait for my signal."

"What kind of signal?"

"I don't know yet." Pike glanced back at the horde on the ice. "Lila and I have played this scene before. It's time for another parley."

He had a feeling that one way or another, this one would be the last.

CHAPTER 64

THE RUPTURE

In a society that was monarchial by default, Young Drayko had been the model prince. He had done everything he was told, committed all his hours into learning his duties. Every hobby was, in some way, connected to the work he was supposed to one day perform. When asked once whether he would have become a gardener had he not been conservator general, he had responded with a blank look. A Drayko without the title was a Drayko who did not exist.

He had also followed the leads of many of his forebears by taking as a spouse someone who would neither embarrass him nor make demands upon his time, which belonged to the project and no one else. Issala had been so absent from his life that he had gone from her birthday dinner to her memorial service without seeing her in between. He knew she would understand, because he had purposefully selected someone who *would* understand. It was part of the criteria.

She had died the same way his mother had: of a malady that, back on Skagara, would have been immediately treatable by technology. They were better off dead, Drayko knew. Dead, they were examples that those who managed the project from Om Mataya were no different from all the others on the planet. Alive and cured? No one would understand that. Surviving would have shown a distinct lack of devotion on their parts.

There was no special treatment. The only perks that came with the Garden House were nice meals the conservator generals never had time to eat, and comfortable rooms they never had much time to sleep in. Nothing more.

Celarius was a child when his mother had died, and barely into adolescence when he learned that, had they lived offworld, she could have been saved. He had certainly not understood that, and the rift between father and son started that day. Drayko had learned there and then that he could only share difficult facts with his son a few at a time.

Celarius had discovered the facts of the project's weaponization of the *sah'ree* earlier than the general had intended, thanks to someone who was *nothing* like Issala. Innocent Una, the amiable house guest—and alien meddler. It was not too late for his son to forget about her, abandon his time-wasting pursuits, and find his duty. And Drayko had a new hope as well. The human warden, Lila

Talley, had been in every respect the exact kind of citizen the Skagarans wanted. Her intrepidity had brought him a chance to guarantee that Epheska would be protected forever—and she was at that moment running Pike and Spock to ground.

Maybe she *should be my heir,* Drayko thought.

That was nonsense, of course, but what she'd provided had changed the game—and, he hoped, would fix his problems with his son. Part of what had driven the general and his predecessors to work so hard was the fear not just that the planet could turn into another Skagara, poisoned by its own citizenry, but also that outsiders might somehow defeat the Baffle.

Now that he'd had a few days to cool off, he hoped Celarius would see the value of that, and accept his role. Una and Uhura, still at large, were likely long gone from Om Mataya if they had any sense. His son would forget them soon.

That hope of Drayko's lasted until he reached the guard station that housed the ingress to the Warm Embrace. A shamefaced compliance aide met him. "They're gone, sir."

"Who's gone?"

"Everyone."

Drayko thought the Zoldaari jailer might leap into the hole himself after that. "Where are they?" he demanded. "Where are the other guards posted here?"

"They're down in the Warm Embrace, General. Looking for them."

Drayko's blood boiled. The sentry topside had been spared his wrath only when a voice came from below. "They went up into the alley behind the boathouse!"

The general hied there, leading a parade of humiliated Zoldaari. More were waiting at the storage area. It was clear that people had sought refuge here, and that many boats were missing.

"Should we search downstream?" someone asked him.

"That's the kind of incisive thinking that's made this the premier posting on Epheska." It was best done from the air, he knew. He strode quickly out of the room, heading for the hangar. The Zoldaari followed.

He and several guards had arrived in the repaired lift when Saachi met him at the door. The flight trainer looked rattled. "General, I'm so glad you're here!"

"What's going on?"

"It's the heritor general. Celarius just came in to ready *Zersa* for flight. He's done that a hundred times—but he had those two interlopers with him."

"Una and Uhura."

"Yes. I thought they were being held in the Warm Embrace!"

Drayko had not publicized that Celarius was supposed to be there too—his little lesson might undermine his son's future authority. He charged down the hall. "I don't want them going anywhere."

"They won't be. All the *zazics* are locked up. They can't launch without them!"

He knew that was true—and he knew Celarius understood that to be true. So it didn't make any sense to Drayko when he saw Celarius and his cohorts in the hangar, preparing to unloose the giant airship and ready it for flight.

"That's quite enough!" the general shouted. He stalked onto the hangar floor, flanked by Zoldaari guards armed with truncheons.

Holding a rope, Celarius looked back at him. He threw the cable down in frustration. "Would five minutes more have been too much to ask?"

"The time for this is up." Drayko looked behind him to the passenger compartment in *Zersa*. "Who's that there?"

"My crewmates," the elderly Taliyah said, stepping out onto the floor. "Commander Una came for us."

"The traitor from the *Braidwood*." The general snorted. "*This* is your home. You're a Skagaran. You should act like one!"

"When I was a child, being a Skagaran—a *Skag*—meant I was descended from slavers. Lower than filth. Our neighbors learned to live in harmony with us, but I always wondered whether my people really were so bad." She shook her head. "You and this world have been a great disappointment."

"I don't care." He faced Una. "Pike and Spock are in hand. Warden Talley and the Zoldaari have them trapped at Krykander."

"Lila. Another disappointment," Taliyah said, looking down. "I don't understand what she's become."

"She's become an ideal Epheskan, which is more than I can say for my son." Drayko looked between Celarius and the Starfleet commander. "I've had enough of this woman's influence on you."

"He's making up his own mind," Una declared.

Drayko didn't think that was worth a response. He was ready to send the Zoldaari forward when he paused. He spied Uhura, who was kneeling beside a lantern whose top she had unfastened. The flame within had gone from blue to a nervous orange.

"Is that what you intended to drive the sentinel with?" the general asked. "That little thing?"

"You know the *sah'ree*'s appearance is unimportant," announced another voice. Drayko looked up to see an aged Skagaran stepping out of *Zersa*. "The flame can be fanned into a bonfire."

The general laughed out loud. "Kohsam? Is that you?" He had not seen Om Mataya's longest-serving political prisoner since a tour of the Warm Embrace many years ago. "You've forgotten how to run an airship. You don't even have a *zazic*!"

He turned and clapped his hands at Saachi. She used a key to unlock a cabinet and withdrew a tall *zazic*. Drayko asked for it.

"You know, Celarius, I used to travel, just as you do—touring our lands. I wanted to know everything." He lifted the staff in his hand. "Kohsam is right. At any size, a *sah'ree* can do great things."

He lunged forward with the *zazic*—and the flame creature in the lantern struggled. The container quaked back and forth, finally falling over and releasing the elemental.

"I admit I'm rusty." But Drayko waved the staff around, causing the *sah'ree* to respond.

"Empy, don't!" Uhura called out. The flame being, unable to resist the *zazic* and Drayko's will, spiraled around her.

"It serves us, as it should." The fiery serpent grew longer—and whorled around Una as well. The others stood back, fearful. "The *sah'ree* we direct against technology will not burn individuals," he said. "But in such close quarters, it will do as I command."

He mentally turned up the heat, and the *Enterprise* officers squirmed uncomfortably. It wasn't as easy as Drayko remembered; the being struggled against him. But he had the upper hand.

"Father, stop!" Celarius took steps toward Drayko. "Don't do this!"

"Stay back, son—or I *will* harm them. You aren't going anywhere—any of you." He looked up at the airship. "Where did you even think to go?"

"The Devil's Dish. Una told me of the rondure there, and what you intend to do to the Baffle. She says a lot of people will die!"

"People die every day."

"Including people who don't have to. Like my mother." Celarius stared at his father. "But I forgot. You don't care about that either."

"I don't care to continue this. Whether you are at my side or not—the project will be protected forever." Drayko glowered at Una and Uhura, entrapped by the circling *sah'ree*. "We're done with prisons. It's time for a different kind of Warm Embrace."

Una yelped with pain. But it was when Uhura shouted that something unexpected happened. The elemental circled the two faster, making a figure-eight between them, glowing a golden yellow. Then it lanced out from them, assaulting Drayko. The general felt blinding pain and staggered, dropping his *zazic*.

Armed Zoldaari lunged toward the prisoners. The fire creature found them, too, leaving Drayko and jumping from one truncheon to another, setting them aflame. The guards dropped what they were holding and ran. The creature then withdrew, creating a wall of fire separating the general from the escapees.

On his hands and knees, Drayko beat his clothing, trying to put out the fire the being had started. Saachi hurried to his side. His face was burnt.

The trainer was flabbergasted. "What is happening? This is impossible!" Saachi looked to the floor. "The general should not have been harmed. He had a *zazic*!"

Behind Uhura, Kohsam stepped forward. "It is as I always told you, Saachi— my old student. There is more to the empatherms than we ever knew."

"What . . . is an empatherm?"

"It's what's taking us out of here," Una said. She gestured for the others to reboard *Zersa*.

Pawing gingerly at his face, Drayko called out to them. "This isn't over."

Celarius looked down on him. "It is for me, Father. Farewell."

CHAPTER 65

THE EXPERIMENT

Days earlier in requesting her evacuation from Zevayne, Lila Talley had asked Drayko for two things. She wanted Weedaw's pony and Buckshot brought along, of course; she wasn't leaving them to the nonexistent mercies of the monsters of that jungle continent. She'd also asked for the honor of joining any mission to the nodal rondure.

The wise conservator general had obliged, directing her sentinel to the Zoldaari settlement of Golaraad, rather than Om Mataya. The Skagaran capital was hundreds of kilometers back, whereas Golaraad would be the logical jumping-off point for any expedition across the northern ice shelf. Sentinels could operate in that frigid region, but their performance was expected to be marginal at best. The journey would have to be made the hard way, and someone would have to ensure it went off properly.

So Lila wound up serving as wilderness guide yet again. Only this time, it was for the right people.

Having seen *ollodons* before in Epheska's temperate forests, she had been skeptical they could be broken at all. But Javu's people had been using the beasts for years in the northern reaches, and while traversing ice was new to them, her snowshoe idea seemed to be working out. She'd wanted to leave immediately for the nodal rondure, but the news that Pike was at neighboring Krykander changed all the plans. The Zoldaari needed to be evaluated on the ice anyway; this would make for a good test.

She cinched her jacket tighter and rode through the Zoldaari ranks. The Vulcan ships were gone, with only the skeletal remains of a large one stuck in the ice before the towering Yuganan keep at the end of the fjord. Several of the accursed cannon had been moved to emplacements on either side of the structure, giving them coverage looking down on the ice sheet before the great sea gates.

At the front of the Zoldaari line, mighty Javu stood tall in the saddle astride the largest *ollodon* of all. No rifle for him; no shirt, either, in this below-freezing weather. A silly display, just to frighten those ahead and impress the more oafish in the ranks behind him. But Javu was sharp, and at least he and his vanguard were more suited to this kind of work than the wardens and lookouts that Drayko had dragooned back at Leejo Point.

"So much for the dreaded fleet," Javu half said, half grunted. He pointed to each cannon in turn. "Still think the Yuganan aren't allied with Pike?"

"The offworlders are the problem," she said, declining to mention that she was one too. "We clear them out, and the Yuganan can get back to tying flies."

"Those guns don't even have to fire on us directly. They can blow the ice to pieces."

"They can use all the ammunition they want on it. Eventually they won't have any left to fire on the sentinels. And we can put people onto the land on either side, here, and work our way to the emplacements."

Javu snorted. "I never knew humans were so good at wars."

She decided that wasn't worth a response.

Lila didn't want to get into a long siege; the nodal rondure, and what it could do, was more important by far. She was gratified to see a single rider emerge from Krykander and head out onto the ice.

"Here comes a hostage," Javu said.

"Hush." *This might not take long after all.*

Bundled and bearded, Pike trotted toward her on Shadow. She had to give him credit: he'd kept the gelding with him all the way from Joe Magee's stable. They cared about much different things, but this was the one they had in common. She wanted to make this as easy as possible. She nodded to Javu. "Just you and me. Nobody else moves."

"Right."

The three riders met halfway across the ice. Pike pulled up and stopped. So did she. He touched his hat. "Lila."

"Christopher." She looked down at his horse's hooves. "Sharpshod?"

"Like you taught me. Not that we got a lot of ice in Mojave."

Javu, who had not stopped, rode his *ollodon* in a circle around the two humans, his mount growling rudely at Pike's horse. "Captain Enterprise. So *you're* the troublemaker."

Pike glanced at Lila. "Did you tell him we've done this scene before?"

"Settle down, Javu." Lila gave the Zoldaari warden a stern look.

"I'm just curious what gives him the nerve," Javu said, his animal tromping to a stop. "My ancestors were being hunted to extinction when the Skagarans saved us."

Lila couldn't imagine the Zoldaari having predators—but it was just like the Skagarans to rescue them.

"You seem to be doing better here," Pike said.

"You're damn right," Javu replied. "And we're not going to let you change everything, just so you can go back to space and tell everyone about us."

Pike shook his head. "It's not about that anymore." He looked to Lila. "Have you told him what's going on?"

"He knows enough," she asserted. "Javu knows if you get what you want, the Baffle will end—and everything will come apart. The *sah'ree* won't be able to stop it all. People will have steam engines in a month. Railroads. Gas vehicles." She gestured above and then below. "You won't be able to see the aurorae for all the filth in the air. This fjord won't even freeze in the dead of winter. And that's just what the humans will do!"

"It doesn't have to happen that way," Pike said.

"It did before. They may have left Earth, but they're the same people."

"We're not the same people."

Javu growled in disgust. "Are you here to surrender, or talk?"

"I don't know," Pike said. "That's a hard choice. I'll tell you what. Let's flip for it."

"Do what?"

"Flip a coin. That's the era-appropriate way, right?" Pike reached into his pocket and came up with nothing. "I forgot—I'm Starfleet. Got a coin, Lila?"

"No." Her eyes narrowed. *What is he on about?*

"How about you?" he asked Javu. "Got a coin we can borrow?"

He glowered at Lila. "What is this fool blathering about?"

"He's talking about money," she said. "Which he knows is something we don't use."

"Yeah, that's right." Pike scratched the side of his beard. "Took me a while to realize, actually. Coming from the Federation, it's not something we often think about. When Lem didn't charge me for a drink at the Dirty Duck, I thought he was just being nice. But it turns out *everyone here* is being nice."

"I told you," Lila replied. "People here help each other out."

"I've noticed. Oh, there's a kind of bartering, for sure, but it's more like horse-trading—literally, in some cases. But nobody keeps score." He pointed his thumb back toward the keep. "People have been supplying T'Var's fleet, even though she doesn't have anything to sell at all. All she has to offer is her good deeds, rescuing people who've been lost at sea. The trappers who fished Spock out of the ocean didn't set him out for T'Var's crew to pick up just because he was a Vulcan. They knew she took people home to where they belonged. Kind of what she's doing with me."

"Not anymore."

Pike ignored her. He turned and gestured broadly at Krykander. "You see, I've realized something. The people I've met—the Menders and some others I won't mention—aren't pursuing technology for wealth or aggrandizement.

They're doing it because they enjoy it, and because it gives them the one currency that really matters: time. Time to do other things."

"Like invading other planets and annihilating the populations?"

"You know what I mean. Recreational activities."

"A lot of so-called leisure activities are just as costly and destructive to the planet." Lila gave an exasperated sigh. "You know what my dad's people said about idle time."

"I know. Devil's workshop and all. But if you're going to tell me it's morally superior to ride a horse for work than for fun, we're going to have to disagree."

Javu gave Lila an angry look. "Are we done? He's stalling."

Pike apologized. "I did want to have this discussion." He looked to Lila. "I'm hoping you'll see reason about what we talked about over the rondure."

There it is. Lila put up her hand and scowled. "I'm not talking about that."

He studied her. "You're sure?"

"I'm sure."

"That's a pity."

Lila was surprised that he had let it go so easily—but maybe he was tired. She certainly was. "This can end very easily, and no one gets hurt. You just have to give the word."

Javu rode beside Pike and shoved his speaking trumpet into the captain's hand. "*The word,*" the goliath emphasized.

Pike turned his horse around and looked back to the keep. Spock emerged from a door beside the sea gate and faced the frozen fjord. He raised his hand—and then quickly brought it down.

She saw Pike nod. "By the way," he said. "I'm afraid I lied to you before. I *was* stalling."

Javu shouted. "*The word!*"

"Fine, fine. Here's two." Pike lifted the speaking trumpet to his lips and shouted toward the keep. "*Hit it!*"

A creak echoed across the harbor, announcing the opening of the sea gate. Once parted, the tall doors revealed the prow of something large, moving tentatively down the ice-covered ramp into the fjord. But while it did have masts, this was no boat being launched from the dry dock. The colossal structure sat on three razor-sharp blades, one forward on a pivot and two larger ones on either side.

As it nosed outside the keep, Lila saw Spock grab a rope and leap onto the conveyance. Seeing him do so helped her understand the sheer size of the thing. The blades sat beneath what looked like large pontoons, and between were some kind of wooden treads, driven by something she couldn't see. All that was encapsulated within a hull that rose higher and longer—and which appeared to her to be protected by armored plating of some kind, mounted forward and on the sides.

The massive thing teetered on the ramp for a moment—and then lurched forward, as the treads below it contacted the surface and went into motion. Thunder sounded across the fjord, driving the waves of *ollodons* behind her into a frenzy.

Even Buckshot reared. Lila sputtered. "What—what is this?"

"You were talking recreational activities earlier. This is one from Andoria," Pike said as the vehicle reached the frozen bay. "They race ice-cutters there—but the Aenar were never allowed to. My friend Hemmer always wanted to build the biggest ice-cutter ever." Pike smiled. "He finally did!"

"But how—?"

"The blades are forged from building blocks of *Enterprise*—as is that shielding mounted outside. The pontoons atop the blades are the hulls of the junks. The upper deck was repurposed from *Thunderer*. The Yuganan shipwrights had the equipment. Everyone's been working around the clock for days."

Fully on the ice now, the giant used its momentum from the ramp—and whipped around, making a long circle in the bay. Some Zoldaari bolted in its direction—but many others fled as they realized the wooden and metal monster was not just moving but speeding up.

Lila was flabbergasted. She looked to Pike. "How?"

"That would be all of our horses, driving those treads between the blades. It's actually an Earth idea. There was a horse-propelled ship, the *Experiment*, back in the 1800s. They used a screw propeller. Hemmer went the snowmobile route."

The ice-cutter whipped around a third time, and Buckshot backed up without Lila telling him to. She looked behind her. Some Zoldaari had found their courage and were firing—but the shots glanced off the armor. The barrage didn't last, as their mounts threw them the second the vehicle lurched in their direction.

Pike pointed. "In a few minutes, it'll hit top speed. Hemmer will disengage the equine engine, raise the treads, and let physics—the part that still works here—take its course. I need to get aboard first."

"Get aboard?"

He pointed. Heavy wooden panels several meters long descended on chains on either side of the vehicle. *Running boards.* A Vulcan was perched on either side, ready to help secure any late rider coming aboard.

"The landing bays are open," Pike said. "We've got two. We're leaving this planet, Lila. Come with me or don't."

She swore at him.

"Fine. Some of Rivkin's people are coming with us. Don't let Drayko hurt the ones that are left. They still have those cannons. And besides," he said, "I won't like it." He kicked his horse into motion with a loud "*Hyaah!*"

Lila followed—but Pike was already in alignment with the racing skiff and drove his horse up onto the platform. Seconds later, his horse was chained into place—and the mammoth vessel tore across the ice, responding to the sudden withdrawal of the treads. It raced pell-mell to the west and the fjord's exit, sending Zoldaari and *ollodons* running for the hills on either side.

Javu ran up to her. He'd lost his mount, and from the shirtless warden's condition, he appeared to have been dragged on the ice for some distance. He gasped for breath as he looked at the receding ice-cutter. "*What was that?*"

Buckshot was already moving. There was no time to explain. "Signal the airships," she yelled. "We've got to get to the Devil's Dish!"

Part Five
OLD FLAMES

KANDRUS ICE SHEET

CHILBIN

THE DEVIL'S DISH

NDRACINE MOUNTAINS

HELLADAN DESERT

FGC-7781 6
EXHIBIT 560-C
THE HIGH COUNTRY
SOURCE:
CAPITAL MAP LIBRARY
(STANDARD TRANSLATION)

NERATHOS

CHAPTER 66

THE RACE

"Red alert!" Christopher Pike called out from his position at the ice-cutter's forecastle as the frozen surface whizzed by. "Obstruction ten degrees off the starboard bow. Distance one kilometer."

Frigid wind blowing past him, he waited as the Vulcan sailors carried the word back to the quarterdeck. What they'd done here was admirable. Hemmer's design had retained the mainmast and mizzenmast from the original ship; they'd slung the sheets as soon as the ice-cutter exited the fjord, exposing it to the powerful gusts on the frozen sea. A runner came with a response moments later. "Fleet Commander requests recommendation, Captain."

Pike squinted through his scope. Staring at ice under the sun was always a challenge, but it was necessary. Several attempts by Drayko's forces to stymie the ice-cutter's progress had involved debris, dragged onto the open ice in narrower straits to create choke points. The roadblocks had been easy to avoid once spotted, and this one would be too.

"Recommended heading five degrees to—" Pike stopped, suddenly moved to take another look. "Belay that."

The course he was about to recommend had something on it he hadn't seen before: whitewashed stumps, randomly spaced. *They've driven posts in the ice.* A difficult undertaking—but well within the powers of the muscular Zoldaari. Striking the posts might not damage the ice-cutter's blades, but the impact might tear them from the rest of the vehicle.

"Correction," he declared. "Recommended heading fifteen degrees starboard. Skirt the side of the junk we can see."

The word went back, and it was so ordered. Pike felt the change in motion seconds later.

Spock, likewise bundled against the cold, arrived to relieve him as spotter. "Our opponents are growing more creative," he said.

"It's a race now. My money's on *Thunderer II*." Pike smiled. "Registry number NCC-1701 A.D."

"The first *Thunderer* was laid down well after 1701."

"That's the spirit, Lieutenant. Keep me honest." Pike handed his scope over and headed aft.

Jokes aside, Pike had determined the vessel's name apt. Much of the previous ship had gone into the ice-cutter, and while Hemmer had put every bit of his prodigious imagination into it, he hadn't come up with a name of his own. It also made some sense, as T'Var had agreed to command on deck. The sailors who had been part of *Xen'tal*'s crew from a century before had now served aboard three very different kinds of vessels. He admired their versatility—and her leadership. Pike had been more than satisfied to let her run the show.

The past two days had seen Drayko's forces take several actions to thwart the ice-cutter's progress. They had the advantage of long-distance communication, and Om Mataya had called ahead to Zoldaari settlements in the area to bring lookouts onto the ice. When a tactic failed, those at the next location learned of it—and adapted their approach. The result had been to make *Thunderer II* run a gauntlet, relying on its speed and armor to make its way.

Pike went down the hatch and headed to what they'd decided to call main engineering. The horses were idle, taking feed in stalls cannibalized from the equine ships—but the Menders were ready to bring them into position at a moment's notice should the wind and momentum fail, making the traction drive necessary.

Amid the noise was Hemmer, tirelessly moving back and forth. An officer who operated the most complex machines Starfleet had devised had put together a system combining turntables, hinges, and flywheels. Some of it was built from materials from T'Var's fleet; some of it the Yuganan had on hand. The rotors, gears, and several of the major structural supports had been ripped from *Enterprise* and reshaped before being launched to Epheska. In a real way, *Thunderer II* incorporated the efforts of everyone Pike had traveled with, both in his crew up above and those who were aboard with him.

Pike doubted whether his chief engineer had slept at all. "Isn't it time for a break, Lieutenant?"

"Are we stopping?"

"No, we can't. Far to go yet."

Hemmer laughed derisively. "Then I'm not resting." He showed the captain around. "Reengaging the treads when we slow may seem a simple matter. But the animals must be in motion, and their speed matched to the vehicle before they can be brought back online."

"You should be proud of yourself. You're learning a lot."

"I have learned to be careful about where I step." Hemmer's nose crinkled. "They aren't the most civilized of creatures."

A whinny came from the wings, as if in protest. Hemmer turned in that direction and made a gesture Aenar probably considered unkind.

Pike knew he couldn't pull him away. "Forget what I said earlier. I'm glad you came down. This is amazing."

"Building oversized models isn't the only reason I'm here." Hemmer stopped moving long enough to face Pike. "We took a lot of measurements of this so-called Baffle, both with the probes and otherwise. There may be an explanation for it—and how the rondures work—but I really need to discuss it with Spock."

"Who's here." Pike looked around. "And your every minute has been booked. Can you give me the synopsis?"

The Aenar's face was fraught. Pike rarely saw Hemmer express any fear of being wrong. This was different. It was a fear of being right.

"Spock and I really must speak. We may have stumbled on something even more dangerous than you have already imagined."

"Worse than sending everyone back to the preindustrial age?"

"Worse." Hemmer turned back to his work.

Drayko had forgiven his son a lot of things over the years. Many tumults, meaningless in the larger scheme. Celarius graduating to rebellion was far worse. It was obvious Chin-Riley had him under her spell, and even that need not be the end for him. A good gardener knew that wounds healed. Drayko was scarred and that would be hard to explain in the Jubilees. But he would come up with a story for it. He would proudly bear the imprint of surviving the storm, like any tree.

And yet Celarius had forced Drayko to do something he hadn't done in years, something he abhorred doing. He had been forced to leave Om Mataya.

He had not quit the capital, like some lowly dictator on the run; this was a mission of the highest importance. He had to go, taking *Zersa*'s sister ship, *Issala*. But while he had once made a point of visiting many of the distant settlements, in recent decades Drayko had preferred to manage from afar. So much could happen while he was in the air and out of contact.

And there was the small matter of terror. His own.

His face bandaged, Drayko sat in the middle of the airship's compartment, his cloth-wrapped wrists tucked underneath the armrests of a chair affixed to the deck. A black tarp had been thrown over the observation pane on the floor, so he could not see out. He had been flying in a sentinel as a young man when it had plummeted from the sky, the consequence of high winds and a poorly trained stoker. After that near disaster, his nervousness about flying grew—compounded by the fact that flight problems started plaguing even short jaunts.

Maybe there was something to the things Uhura had said after all. If the *sab'ree* really responded to raw emotions, that explained a lot. Including the very bumpy flight he was on now—despite the fact that no less than Saachi was aboard to operate.

"I'm sorry, General," she said through the aft door. "I've never known the *sah'ree* to be so agitated."

"Close the damn door!" He thought to dismiss her with a hand, but that would have meant releasing the chair.

It was all about holding on now.

Om Mataya had been in an unprecedented state of confusion when he left. Few people knew about the Warm Embrace, but those who managed it did, and there was no mistaking the uproar caused by all the searchers running about. They were still there, looking for escapees; Drayko was certain at least some of the dissidents had stayed in the city, preparing to cause unrest.

And while Celarius wasn't known outside the capital, many there did know him—and word about what had happened in the hangar had already gotten out in the ranks. So, too, had the story that the *sah'ree* had burned Drayko. That unthinkable news had resulted in several of Saachi's people balking at working with the fire beings.

Things had started to come apart, for certain, but the system was resilient. Nothing would resolve it like reaching the nodal rondure and ensuring the Baffle's permanence and spread. He trusted Warden Talley to do the right thing, but he hadn't heard from her, or Javu, in days—and since catching the easterly airstream, *Issala* had been too high for its pilots to read any of the signal flags down below. It wasn't something he could leave to anyone else. Zoryana knew the rondures as well as anyone alive; she would do what needed to be done.

If only she would leave him alone. "We've reached the Kandrus Ice Sheet," she said, returning to him from the forward window. "I think you should see this."

"I have seen ice."

"It is what is upon it." She gestured behind her to the forward port. "You will not believe me."

Drayko knew there would be no placating her unless he went. He released the chair and stood. He gave the covered window on the deck a wide berth and pawed his way across the bulkhead until he reached her side and looked out.

At first glance, he thought he was seeing a host of *harrownits* streaming across a white table. Then he realized that species of insect would be a lot more organized. The creatures below ran willy-nilly in all directions. Some parts of the ice sheet were missing, open to water; others, strewn with debris. As *Issala* descended, he finally realized what he was looking at.

"*Ollodons!*"

Curiosity overcoming his restraint, he turned back and whipped the tarp off the observation port on the deck. In a move that his injured body objected to, he threw himself to his hands and knees and looked down. "Zoldaari riders."

Zoryana knelt beside him. "That's the pennant of Javu's people. His flagger is there."

"Hold here!"

As *Issala* descended farther, Zoryana read the signal flags. What she said then made no sense to him. It prompted him to order the sentinel to land.

A minute later, they were on the ice—and Drayko was out the door, followed by a shivering Zoryana. They saw Javu lope up on an *ollodon*.

"Who's this guy?" Javu asked Zoryana.

"It's your general!" Drayko shouted through his facial bandages.

The sound of his voice startled the massive Zoldaari. "Sorry," Javu grunted.

"Get off that thing!"

Javu dismounted and regarded Drayko's condition. "What happened to you?"

"Never mind. What happened here? Where is Pike?"

"He's gone. Tore out of Krykander on a ship on skates."

"On *what*?"

"That's what I'd like to know. Just the sound of it scared the *ollodons* half to death." He pointed to the routed forces all around. "We've been calling ahead to towns up the sheet to stop the thing. But every group we've reached looks like this."

Drayko glanced about, flustered. "Get in the sentinel!"

The Zoldaari warden did as ordered—and soon the vessel was back in the air, with Javu narrating for Drayko a travelogue of frustrated efforts to stop the renegades.

"They've still got some of those cannons from the sailing ships," Javu said.

"Are they firing at you?"

"They fire at everything *but* us." Javu pointed to craters and open water on the trail as they headed east. "Sometimes they fire to keep us off the ice or just low enough to scatter the *ollodons*. We can't keep a barricade with them. Other times they'll catch us as we're trying to smash the ice ourselves. What they're traveling in is big, but it doesn't need a wide patch of ice to get through."

Drayko couldn't believe it. "You say it's some kind of sled? What's pulling it?"

"Nothing we can see. But whenever it starts to slow down, it takes off again."

"This is inexcusable," Drayko said. "Pure incompetence!"

Javu growled. "It's our first whatever-it-is!"

Drayko shook his head in disbelief. "What happened to Warden Talley?"

"She took off." Javu crossed his arms and leaned against the bulkhead. "Last we saw, she was headed east, toward the highlands." He sneered. "Guess she lost her nerve."

Zoryana and Drayko looked at each other. He remembered the map of Epheska he had memorized decades before. "The Andracine Mountains are like knives," Zoryana said. "They cannot be crossed."

"Scratch one warden." Javu shrugged. "I guess there are more humans out there, if you need a new one."

Drayko frowned. "It's *one* human that I'm worried about." His eyes narrowed. "Where would they be now?"

"Lots of islands in the ice where they're headed—zigs and zags, not many straightaways. They can't be past Chilbin."

Drayko knew they weren't out of reach yet. But neither was *Issala* likely to beat them to the rondure—not without leaving the sea and crossing the intervening mountains, which the aviators had said was impossible. If Pike could not be stopped, he had to be slowed.

Forgetting his pains and fears, the general charged around the sentinel issuing commands. "Get us to the nearest rondure site. Tell them to send every airship in the region to Chilbin—and get all the ground forces in the area there."

Listening in the aft doorway, Saachi looked at him with concern. "We can't push the sentinels hard in this climate. They won't last long."

"For what I have in mind, they won't need to."

CHAPTER 67

THE ASSAULT

The flights Una Chin-Riley had taken earlier on *Zersa* had been leisurely investigations of the scenery below. This time, she'd been in the clouds or above them for countless hours. Celarius had dropped out of the airstream only occasionally to look for a landmark, and to grab a little intelligence from a settlement's signal flags.

That was the problem with semaphore: without an accompanying code, it was an open communication for anyone to see—including a renegade sentinel. Several flybys had been enough to tell them that Pike was still on the loose, heading for the Devil's Dish, and that a commandeered airship was likely heading that way.

"They don't mention me," Celarius said. "My father must still think we can reconcile."

As dubious a proposition as that was, Chin-Riley was thankful for it. She knew firearms and ballistae existed on Epheska. And while *Zersa* had seldom been low enough for those to matter, just riding the raging gales had been dangerous enough without someone shooting at them.

The temple signals had also revealed something else: Drayko himself was on the way. *Zersa* had a significant head start, but the general would be able to ride the same winds they had. And while he might spare his son, she wasn't banking on any mercy for anyone else.

Uhura entered the cabin, chilled to the bone. Chin-Riley quickly went over to help warm her up. *Zersa* had stores of warm robes for its occupants, but the propulsion area was mostly exposed. The cadet coughed. "Kohsam won't leave his station. I don't know how he does it."

"He's been waiting a long time to do what he's doing," the commander said. "I respect his devotion, but we can't have him getting frostbite."

"There's a surprising amount of heat coming off the bag that Empy is in. It's something."

Chin-Riley still didn't understand how the empatherms lived or functioned, but Uhura had been right about what they could do. Knowing that Drayko's people had weaponized them against civilians was infuriating.

"We should be near Chilbin now," Celarius declared. The archipelago amid the ice of the Kandrus had been mentioned in several of the intercepts as a place where, for whatever reason, the Skagarans expected Pike would have to slow down.

Zersa dropped through the clouds. When Chin-Riley was able to see the surface, she realized Drayko's forces weren't done misusing the *sah'ree*.

"Look at all the sentinels!" Uhura declared. "Six . . . eight . . . *ten!*"

"And what are they chasing?" Celarius asked.

It looked to Chin-Riley like the top of an old British sailing ship married to some kind of armored undercarriage that rested on sleds. It was in motion—but it was also on fire.

She soon saw why. The cluster of sentinels carried red-cloaked *zazic*-wielders who were directing empatherms down from the sky, just in the manner that Uhura had described. It required the airships to come relatively close to the giant sled, and it was clear that some had paid for it. The ice nearby was littered with deflated sentinels that had made uncomfortable landings, and occupants aboard the great sled were firing rifles at the other airships.

But the giant conveyance had also suffered. The rearmost sails were afire, and sailors were on the yards trying to cut them away. And *sah'ree* continued to whirl near the mainmast. They hadn't contacted the speeding vessel thus far—but it was only a matter of time.

"You're sure that's Pike?" Celarius asked.

"Who else would it be?" Chin-Riley squinted. "Besides, they're flying Vulcan colors."

Celarius shook his head. "If warning shots aren't keeping them away, I don't think shooting them down is going to make any difference," he said. "Father knows how hard it is for sentinels to operate in this region. He must think this is his only chance."

She looked out the starboard window and saw ground forces advancing across the ice. Out the other side, she saw debris and open water. This was an attempt to bottle up their prey, and it had worked. She felt helpless. They'd crossed a measureless distance to find Captain Pike and Spock, only to discover them in time to see them captured.

Or worse. "They're not just trying to stop it," Celarius said, outrage in his voice. "They're going to burn it to the ground!"

And anyone inside. Drayko was done messing around. She could already imagine him crowing about—

Chin-Riley looked up. "The horn!"

"That?" Celarius gestured to a cone situated in the forward bulkhead. The commander had seen it used both as a speaking trumpet—and, most powerfully, as a flugelhorn.

She stepped over to it. "The stokers aboard the sentinels have to concentrate to control the empatherms, right?"

Celarius grinned. "Distract them!"

Uhura looked aft with concern. "Won't we distract Kohsam too?"

"Not if we warn him!" Chin-Riley declared. She showed Uhura the horn. "Hailing frequencies open!"

She looked fretful. "I'm too hoarse."

"Then you see to Kohsam. Go!"

As Uhura ran aft, Chin-Riley took station at the horn. She took a deep breath—and blew.

She'd never really looked at *Zersa*'s horn, but she'd heard it from afar outside the forest. It sounded far louder now. She could see how it spooked some of the animals Drayko's forces below were riding—and it definitely served to distract the focus of the stokers on the other sentinels. The flying flames threatening the fleeing vessel's mainmast somersaulted; after a second blast, they tumbled away from the ship.

It gave the sailors below time to cast off the burning sails—and then something below the vessel happened that shook the whole structure. It began moving uniformly, heedless of the wind, trying to escape the area. However they were doing it, Chin-Riley knew the horn trick wouldn't work for long.

Zersa was quickly closing on the other airships. It had approached unmolested by the Skagarans as no one else knew who was aboard it, but Chin-Riley figured they might be in danger of being shot at by Pike's people. It was time to stand and be known. She looked to Celarius and gestured to the horn. "You already decided, remember?"

He looked at it—and nodded. He took her place and removed the mouthpiece, changing it from a horn to a speaking trumpet. "They're expecting Skagaran."

Chin-Riley knew enough to understand him when he spoke. "Attention, sentinels! I am Heritor General Celarius! Stand down. I repeat, halt all operations!" He looked to her—and came to a final decision. "My father is no longer conservator general. You will obey me!"

Her eyes widened. "Will the forces below know who you are?"

"The sentinel pilots will. And when I make them land, they'll tell the others."

Indeed, the airships had stopped and were hovering in place, their occupants evidently trying to work things out. The ice vessel passed between two obstacles and resumed its escape.

Chin-Riley placed her hand on Celarius's shoulder. She didn't want to sound condescending to someone his age—but some words were appropriate. "Well done."

"It's only until they hear from someone who's got access to a rondure."

"I don't see one around here. For now, your word is law."

Christopher was still out there, still causing trouble. Lila Talley had seen the sentinels on the horizon far behind her on a couple of occasions where the view was unobscured by trees or clouds. The unnerving thing was that she and Buckshot were often higher than the airships.

She'd had time to study Pike's map, as well as the one Javu had of the Kandrus. She'd realized there was another way to the Devil's Dish. Drayko's airships would never be able to make it over the granite teeth of the Andracine Mountains; apart from the elevation, the winds and weather would have destroyed any sentinel trying to cross. She'd felt the violent downdrafts herself rounding several prongs, and a screaming williwaw atop a crest had lifted all four of Buckshot's hooves off the ground for several seconds.

Crossing the range was madness in any season, much less winter. There were no trails, no places of shelter. She'd brought nothing with her beyond some supplies she'd taken from the Zoldaari, including some feed and another blanket. It was for the stallion, not her. She'd stopped to walk him many times when the snow got too deep, or when she needed to clear the crystals building up on his fetlocks. When he'd lain down to rest, she'd tried to share a bit of warmth.

But she wasn't sleeping. As hostile as the Andracine was to sentient life, it still had its share of predators. She'd emptied her rifle already; now she was down to her Colt Navy. It was the only genuine one on the planet, having come with her as a family heirloom aboard *Braidwood*. She wondered how the manufacturers would have felt about their works being used on another world.

This wasn't trailblazing. Lila never expected any sensible being to follow her path, and she knew there was no chance she could retrace Buckshot's steps if she wanted to. It wasn't just the snow and the fog; parts of glaciers slid away just to spite her impudence in trying to cross. She was going too fast to care. Pike's contraption would have to round a lot of landforms to reach her destination. She would beat him there or die trying.

"Hang in there," she rasped to the Appaloosa as she swept the frost from his eyebrows. "Hang in there." For her life to ever have mattered at all, Lila knew she would have to do the same.

CHAPTER 68

THE PURGE

The fire was out and the flight was over—but Christopher Pike knew the real challenge had just begun.

Pike had seen the newly arrived sentinel earlier, and it hadn't taken him long to realize it was not like the others. He had never seen a happier sight than when he caught a glimpse through his spyglass of Uhura waving madly from the airship. After he assured T'Var's gunners that it was friendly, *Zersa* had then followed the ice-cutter through the frozen channel and into the final long passage leading to their destination.

During the day's travel, the airship had dropped a ladder allowing Una to descend, providing what may have been the strangest briefing a Starfleet captain had ever received. It certainly was a most unusual setting. And after more than three weeks since their last in-person meeting, he didn't know which one of them had more to say to the other.

The early winter night found both vessels at their final stop—though not at their ultimate destination. The Devil's Dish lay kilometers inland in what Rivkin had called the Andracine Range; the ice-cutter could go no farther and Number One's friend Celarius had expressed doubts that *Zersa* could voyage inland either. Pike had expressed his own doubts about Celarius on learning he was Drayko's son, but Chin-Riley and Uhura had vouched for him, and that was good enough. A further endorsement had come from Taliyah, whom Pike had not seen since he was a child when she visited the Bar T. No matter what, Number One had succeeded in their original mission in locating and delivering the *Braidwood* crew.

Pike called for a meeting in advance of the final leg. It couldn't involve everyone, of course: between the Menders, T'Var's people, several Yuganan, and those Una had arrived with, *Thunderer II*'s population had to rival the one he had in space. Instead, the four *Eratosthenes* passengers plus Hemmer sat with representatives of everyone who'd assisted them or been assisted by them. It was all on them: *Enterprise* was cut off from them due to the overcast sky.

Not only had T'Var's quarterdeck been preserved from *Thunderer*, but her table too—and it was strewn with maps as well as translations from the Strooh writings at Agar. And one very unusual lantern, which sat atop the table alongside Uhura, providing light as she translated.

Hemmer, finally freed from his duties running the ice-cutter's innards, looked ready to drop. But as the person who'd been most recently aboard *Enterprise*, he had research to report—and it turned out that he and Spock had independently reached similar conclusions.

"You start," Hemmer said.

Spock obliged. "At the end of the twentieth century on Earth, a pair of physicists postulated that gravity could leak into extra dimensions."

Pike remembered his academy coursework. "The Randall-Sundrum model?"

"Correct. Unconnected to that research, something like what they imagined seems to have come to pass here, only for electricity and magnetism. Fields larger than a certain size bleed into the extra dimensions, making electricity extremely weak."

"We're bleeding electricity?"

Sitting cross-legged on the floor by the bulkhead, Jennie sang, "*There's a hole in my bucket, dear Liza.*"

Hemmer scowled. "What bucket?"

Pike shot Jennie a grin. "Never mind. How big are these dimensions?"

"Not very," Hemmer said. "But there are apparently size thresholds involved, because basic chemistry still works."

Pike thought he understood. "We always assumed the rondures were distributed randomly—but maybe we're just using the wrong geometry. Do we think they're creating these extra dimensions? Or accessing them?"

Spock nodded. "I believe both. From what Weedaw and I were able to translate, the Strooh thought so as well. But perhaps Cadet Uhura has learned more."

The captain looked to Uhura, who was poring over all their notes from recent days. "There's some history here in the margins," she said, referring to one of the instant photos. "I think the Strooh were here even before the Skagarans!"

The statement caused some surprise at the table—but not nearly as much shock as Uhura's lantern, which briefly flared a bright blue color.

"Do that again," Pike said, staring at it.

Uhura didn't appear to know what he meant at first. Then she looked at the lantern. "Oh. Empy does that."

Number One had explained all about the empatherm to Pike—and that Uhura had established some kind of bond with this one. "I've been seeing that pulsating while you've been working there," he said. "Sometimes it changes colors."

"Or temperatures." She smiled. "It seems to literally be telling me when I'm hot or cold."

Pike looked to Celarius, who he expected knew the most about the so-called *sah'ree*. "Did your people know they did this?"

The mountain man prince shrugged. "We didn't even think they were intelligent."

Pike had seen many strange things in the cosmos, including the plasma beings in action. Still, questions remained. "How would it know anything about the Strooh?" He had another thought. "Cadet, you said these fire creatures are native to the planet?"

"As far as I know. I thought I saw Empy born from the volcanic seams—but who knows how old it is." She gestured to her work. "But yes, it seems like when I started looking at these glyphs, it got a lot more responsive."

Spock addressed Pike. "Both Weedaw and Jaddak believed their people were brought here by the Skagarans."

"Maybe that's just the story," Pike said.

Celarius nodded. "My family loves its stories."

The captain stared at the lantern. "Uhura, ask it if the Strooh built the rondures."

She did—and Pike noticed the flame turn to a very pedestrian orange.

"Not very animated."

Uhura thumbed through her notes. "I keep seeing glyphs calling the Strooh *helpers*. I'd assumed they were the helpers of the Skagarans, but maybe there's someone else involved. Someone earlier, that they don't refer to here." She looked up. "And Weedaw was definitely right. There is a way to regulate the size of the Baffle's effect."

Spock spoke up. "And this is why we know the system was created by an intelligence that was, if not benevolent, at least mindful of others."

That hit Pike like a brick. "How do you figure that?"

Hemmer explained. "I mentioned the electricity leaking into the other dimension." He raised a finger. "The effect is mostly limited to the planet's surface."

Number One frowned. "It didn't feel limited when we were on *Eratosthenes*."

"I said *mostly*. There appear to be random oscillations in which the impacted area increases in radius. These expansions last but a nanosecond—but it is enough to cause catastrophic faults in our transtators."

"And everything resets," Pike said. "No matter how hardened the equipment is. Because it's not an electromagnetic pulse at all. It's the opposite!"

Hemmer's expression suggested he would have described it differently—but he had other issues. "We come now to the very bad thing I have been worried about."

Pike looked to see the other listeners' expressions. *There's always a very bad thing.*

"If the affected area were *always* larger than the planet," Hemmer said, "Epheska would have no functional magnetosphere—and thus no protection from cosmic rays. Life here could not survive."

Chin-Riley's eyes narrowed. "So the extremely short expansions of the effect are enough to thwart our ships—but not long enough to harm life here."

Pike wondered if that had resulted in some of the unusual storms he'd seen.

But then he thought of something else. "Wait. You're saying if Drayko gets his way—if the radius is expanded—"

"That wipes out not only life on this planet," Hemmer said, "but on every planet within the radius."

Gasps emanated from around the table.

"It is a weapon," T'Var whispered. "A trap, left here to destroy us all."

"We do not know that," Spock said. "The fact it is currently set so as not to destroy this planet's life suggests some foreknowledge, if not friendly intent."

"Friendly!" The military woman profoundly disagreed. "It allows people to live—until someone sets it off. It is the most efficient method for purging life we can imagine." She faced Pike. "Did you ever eradicate those who created the Delphic Expanse?"

Pike didn't want to get into that, because he still wasn't sure the thing was a trap or weapon. But there was something he did need to be sure of. He looked to Uhura. "Spock said Weedaw thought the radius could be set to infinity. Was he right?"

Uhura's brow furrowed, and she searched for the relevant passage. She looked up, face fraught. "*He was right.*"

The empatherm pulsated in agreement. Then it burned so low Pike thought the flame would go out. He knew how it felt.

"Then we're all in. I'm ordering *Enterprise* to get away from here as quickly as possible. The Federation has to be warned—and everyone else." He stood. "The rest is up to us. The Devil's Dish at dawn."

CHAPTER 69

THE SUMMIT

It felt to Christopher Pike like the last ride, for better or worse. It certainly was the hardest.

Enterprise had created a lidar map of the Devil's Dish, sending it down with Hemmer. It was an absolute necessity. The Andracine Mountains were bathed in cloud, and while the great mesa was just a couple hours' ride from the icy coast, Pike's party might have ridden right past it without the map in hand.

He'd settled on a two-prong attack. *Enterprise*'s map had shown a potential route to the summit, but it was obvious the only riders besides himself and Celarius who were capable of it were the Menders, all of whom had grown up with horses. Getting the other personnel he needed to the summit meant *Zersa* would have to make an astonishingly hazardous ascent, with both Celarius and Chin-Riley at the controls. Pike's team would be responsible for carrying up iron stakes so as to tie the airship down before it blew right off the plateau.

Slowly he had scaled the circuitous route, maneuvering narrow spots where ice covered rock. Pike and Shadow set the pace for the others, with Jennie riding Cricket right behind him, followed by Vicki and Carpenter. It was just too strenuous for Joe—and while Pike had disliked the idea of having Jennie along, he'd come to understand the young woman was the best equestrian he'd seen outside of Lila.

When he dismounted at the shelf right beneath the lip of the bowl, the sun was setting: a fact he could now see. They were above an ocean of clouds. "Easy," he said. "One at a time now."

He scrambled up the final sharp incline, guiding Shadow up a slope the gelding never could have made with a rider on his back. The desperately relieved mustang ran free on the surface despite the pummeling winds as Pike turned to help Jennie and then the others with the final climb.

When everyone was at the surface, Pike and the others led their horses behind a boulder. Peering across it, he saw a temple near the center of the plateau. It didn't look any different from any of the others he'd seen—and he noted it didn't have the flags, which the other temple locations had.

"Unoccupied," Carpenter said.

It wasn't surprising, given how hard it was to get up here. Pike figured it was why Drayko couldn't simply call anyone here to trigger the nodal rondure. How the Strooh built the temple—if indeed they had done so—he had no idea. "You're on, Vicki."

As Vicki unrolled her bundle, Carpenter carted his payload of stakes toward the temple and Jennie deployed her own cargo to finish out a harness for her mustang. Vicki then headed with Pike to the northern rim of the dish. Minutes later, a variety of pyrotechnics were in the air, ranging from roman candles to a mortar round. Pike had assumed correctly the gunsmith had the least fear of fire, and T'Var's people had found her a lot of options for signaling.

As darkness began to fall, Pike worried that the signal had gone unseen. *Zersa's* transit over the Devil's Dish was likely to be a one-way, one-chance thing, Celarius had said; it couldn't go until the ground crew was definitely in place. But the airship soon appeared, emerging from the cloud bank to the north like a whale exiting the sea.

Pike and Vicki ran back to the center of the plateau, where Carpenter and Jennie waited with a sledgehammer and spikes. The wind turned one way and then another as they ran, and behind him, the captain could tell the airship was fighting. T'Var's sailors had spent the day attaching heavy ropes to the main envelope and gondola—a slew of umbilicals to keep the sentinel from rocketing off across the Andracine.

Zersa's nose dipped and the vehicle dove downward. Cables lashed past Pike and the others, causing them to dive away. When he got off his stomach, he turned to see a cable striking the temple like a whipcrack.

When a second one snagged momentarily on one of the outer pillars, he looked to Carpenter. "Change of plan" were words the Zoldaari had no chance of hearing in the gale, but he got the idea, throwing the hammer away and dashing for the temple. With mighty bare hands, he leapt for the line and grabbed on.

"Hurry!" Pike dashed forward and helped the Zoldaari haul the line downward. Jennie, who'd finished Cricket's rig with practiced speed, hurried to get the horse attached. When leverage combined with human, Zoldaari, and equine muscle to anchor the sentinel just over the roof of the temple, Pike waved to the sky.

Spock rappelled down first, using the temple dome to slow his descent. Hemmer followed, yelling something Pike could not hear. Both the lieutenants were on the ground and seeking lines to tie down when Uhura landed next. Pike saw she had the lantern with her. Nothing was inside it.

"Empy's still up in the envelope," she called out to Pike.

The elderly Kohsam, Pike knew, had not been up to the trip, forcing Uhura to coax cooperation from her empathermic friend in one of the propulsion sacs. Only Number One and Celarius remained aboard—but Pike couldn't see how they could escape, with the blimp whipping about like mad. A powerful gust caused *Zersa* to careen about the building, ripping loose every additional tether Spock and the others were trying to fasten to the ground.

A terrible rip sounded. Pike had thought it was the main envelope until Uhura's cry directed his attention aft. "Empy!"

The ruptured propulsion sac expelled the empatherm, which caught the wind and vanished. All control gone, *Zersa* followed a downdraft toward the temple again. Chin-Riley leapt from the cabin and slid off the stone structure, landing hard. When she looked up, the main line connecting the airship to the building and horse tore loose from the canvas above.

"Celarius!" she called out, scrambling to her feet. Pike ran alongside her as the balloon, powerless, was swept into the air and off the mesa, out of sight.

Panting at the edge of the rim, Pike squinted at the ever-darkening clouds below. "Can he survive?"

Chin-Riley looked in every direction. "The main envelope's helium. He could be in the Delta Quadrant." She turned to Pike. "He wouldn't leave the ship until I was down!"

It's his ship, Pike wanted to say. *He's the captain.* But it wasn't the right time.

Uhura arrived beside them. He'd heard her calling up to the air, repeatedly, for the empatherm. Pike couldn't see anything except the aurorae, which here above the clouds seemed to be more vibrant than anywhere else on the planet. If the rondures were indeed tied into the Baffle, it made some sense that the nodal rondure might be at the magnetic pole.

"There he is!" Uhura ran back from the edge, having spotted a will-o'-the-wisp straining against the wind. It looped its way downward to her, where she waited with her lantern. The creature reentered it, drawing a smile from Uhura.

At least someone's happy, Pike thought. He glanced over at his first officer, who remained at the edge. "Number One—"

"I know," she said, turning toward the temple. They had their own ship to look after—and perhaps countless more. It was time to go to work.

CHAPTER 70

THE TEMPLE

"I think, my friends, we are in mission control," Pike said on entering the chamber with Jennie.

"Or main engineering," Hemmer replied.

The outside of the temple was the same as the ones Pike had seen in Havenbrook and Agar, but the inside was different. It had the same chemical glowlights illuminating the place, but they lit a rondure that had three podiums facing it, each one with a *zazic* already inserted. A fourth station with a *zazic* stood outside the circle, taking the place of the many slots he had seen for Drayko's followers in the other temples.

Pike and Jennie stood near the wall as Chin-Riley walked the room quietly. Vicki and Carpenter were outside keeping watch, and would say if they saw any hint of Celarius's survival. The captain knew she'd been trying to get back to business after his disappearance. "Number One, was there ever any notation this place was important on Drayko's big map?"

"Not at all," she said. "I don't even know if they knew it was the magnetic pole. But it was marked as the rondure with the highest elevation."

"Fascinating," Spock said as he examined one of the inner podiums. "Perhaps this location is the upper limit of the Baffle's permanent effects. But it seems unusually coincidental that it would also be the pole."

"Maybe it's the pole *because* the nodal rondure is here," Pike said.

Hemmer regarded him drily. "Let's leave the theorizing to the theorists." He felt the glyphs on the fourth podium. "Cadet, what does this say?"

Uhura held her lantern near it to read—and chuckled. "Something like 'engineering station.'"

"Then I am appropriately placed." Hemmer stood beside it, careful not to touch the embedded *zazic*.

Pike watched as Spock ran his fingers across one of the three podiums in the center.

"I agree, Mister Spock," Hemmer said.

The science officer looked back at him. "I said nothing, Lieutenant."

Hemmer scowled. "You did not just say that you felt you were in something that equated to a ship's bridge?"

"I thought as much. But I was not touching the *zazic*."

"Nor was I."

Pike stared. "You know, I thought I heard him too."

Jennie nodded. "I think we all did."

Chin-Riley faced Spock. "Now you are thinking, 'Why would there need to be a telepathic communicator to speak across a room?'"

Pike looked around to all his officers. No one said anything until Hemmer clapped his hands. "Eureka!"

"What is it?"

"Is that not the right word?" Hemmer asked.

"It's what I want to hear. What is it?"

"Let's follow the bridge idea." The engineer pointed to the other two podiums. "Volunteers?"

Jennie started to bolt forward. Pike took Jennie's arm and stepped back. "Somebody needs to witness this."

"Aw!"

"I told your father you'd be safe."

Uhura passed the lantern with Empy to Jennie. "Can you keep him?"

She eyed the container with suspicion. "He's not going to burn down my house, is he?"

Uhura smiled. "Of course not."

The cadet joined Chin-Riley in approaching the rondure. The women stepped to the two other podiums alongside Spock.. Their mere presence caused the rondure to start rotating—and the *zazics* on all four podiums began to glow orange.

Pike had been reluctant to see anyone touch any of the crystal widgets, for fear that they might start an astral-plane call to Drayko, wherever he was. But this place looked so different, he was willing to let Hemmer experiment. "Now what?"

"If I understand the translation correctly," the engineer said, "now *this*." He grasped the horns of the *zazic* before him. His white eyes went black in that instant, and the rondure began to glow, going from dark red to orange.

Pike was concerned. "You okay, Hemmer?"

"*I am*," he replied, his voice sounding in Pike's mind. "*I am taking some time to understand how functions are organized.*"

"Take all you want." Pike knew there had been an incident many years earlier involving Aenar controlling drones by telepresence; something about their abilities of perception allowed them to interact with systems in ways that no outsiders really understood. La'an had made a spectacular decision in sending Hemmer to the surface.

He just hoped she'd left the system, in case something Hemmer did went wrong.

"*I can see them*," Hemmer continued. "*I have reached all the other rondures. They have activated.*"

"All of them?"

"*All three thousand one hundred twenty-six of them.*"

Spock looked back. "Five to the fifth power—plus one."

"Then we've come to the right place." Pike looked at the domed roof overhead, more visible now that the rondure was glowing. "What *is* this place?"

"*Our assumption was correct*," Hemmer responded. "*The system was constructed. The system was activated, thousands of years before. It has operated ever since, removing EM activity to another—*"

Pike saw him freeze. "Hemmer?"

"*I need the others to join.*"

"Others? In other temples?"

"*No. Here.*"

Pike looked to Number One, Uhura, and Spock. It seemed like permission to him. "Go ahead."

The three touched their *zazics*—and the rondure shot a meter up from its levitating cushion. This time, it picked up more than brightness and speed: the tiny sun was generating a low whine as it spun like a turbine in the middle of the room.

"*I have located the proper subsystem*," Pike heard Hemmer think. "*I believe I can cycle the Baffle's radius down to zero.*"

"Can you shut the system down permanently?" Pike asked.

"*I do not know. But Spock, Chin-Riley, and Uhura must under no circumstances leave their stations, or I cannot guarantee the results.*"

Pike felt Jennie reach for his hand, and he took hers. It was in the literal hands of his crew now, all clutching the crystal rams' horns.

"*I have opened the subsystem*," Hemmer declared. "*Now I—*"

Pike looked up. In the rear doorway, leading to the temple's back room, he saw a silhouetted figure—and a flash. A shot rang out, and a scream ripped through his mind even as he felt a searing pain in his side. Jennie apparently did, too, as she sagged against the wall—and he saw through a haze of pain that Chin-Riley, Spock, and Uhura were similarly affected.

He touched his side. There was no blood. Neither had any of his friends been shot—save one. Hemmer released the *zazic* and fell away from the podium, blue blood coursing from his side.

Realizing Hemmer had communicated his pain to the others via the telepathic link, Pike took a step toward him only to hear a familiar voice. "Stay back, Christopher!"

Lila stepped fully from the shadows. She looked like she'd been through hell. Her hair was ragged and her face was parched by wind. She'd lost her hat somewhere. But even ringed by dark circles, her eyes were wide—and focused on Hemmer. The revolver in her hand was pointed straight at Pike.

He didn't care. "Lila, let me help him!"

"I told you, stay back!"

She fired another shot. The bullet, fired over Pike's head, ricocheted off the stone wall. It was enough to drive Pike back to the side where Jennie was still doubled over with psychic pain.

Writhing in real agony on the floor, Hemmer gestured toward the trio at the center of the room. "Whatever you do," he shouted non-telepathically, "don't release the mechanisms!"

Lila strode toward the podium Hemmer had been at. "He got in. I've been listening. He got in."

"What are you doing here?" Pike asked.

"I got here eight hours ago." She gestured behind her. "Buckshot's in the back room, asleep."

Pike couldn't imagine how she'd beaten him here. "Eight hours?"

"I rode over the Andracine."

She said it matter-of-factly—but Pike knew it was no simple thing. It would have taken the skills of the best equestrian on the planet. Maybe any planet. "You beat me again."

She approached the now-vacant podium. "I've been trying to figure this out all day. I have Weedaw's notes, but they're not enough." She glanced down at Hemmer. "But he got in."

Pike put his hands before him. "Lila, you need to stay back from it. It doesn't do what we think it does."

"I heard him say what he thought it would do. It's not happening. You're not turning the Baffle off."

Hemmer rolled on his uninjured side and looked back at Pike from the floor. "Captain, the system balances as if on a pin. Push it too far one way and the dimensional portal will grow unchecked!"

Pike saw a glare out of the corner of his eye. In Jennie's hand, the lantern glowed. If it reacted to emotion, it certainly had a lot to respond to.

"Lila, leave it alone," he said. "It won't just eliminate technology. It'll eliminate the people too!"

She looked back at him, confused. "What are you talking about?"

"Cosmic rays. Right now the Baffle only impacts places on the surface—and thwarts starships and shuttles that come too close. You expand it and you'll wipe out all life in the zone—including here."

"So it wouldn't just crush the Klingon war machine—it'd kill them? Kill them all?"

"And us."

Her eyes fixed on the podium. "I can live with that."

CHAPTER 71

THE SPHERE

Pike was still bewildered by Lila's comment when Jennie, at his side, appealed to her. "Miz Talley, don't do this."

Gun in hand, the shepherd waved her away. "I told you back on the farm, Jennie. When predators get a taste for what's around, they never stop coming. Then we've got to act."

"But Captain Pike says you'll kill everyone!"

"I don't know that. Maybe I can avoid that."

Hemmer spoke from the floor. "You don't know how it works!"

"Well, you're not going anywhere, are you?" Lila gestured to the podium. "When I'm there, I can talk to you telepathically. You can talk me through it. Protect the people here."

"While you kill billions. I will not help you!"

Pike shook his head. "She doesn't care." He focused on her. "Your colony is gone, Lila. It won't—"

"Save it." She pointed her gun at him and Jennie. "You two get out of here."

Pike realized he was going to have to rush her—but he also knew he wanted Jennie out of the line of fire. He took the teenager's arm and urged her toward the entry hall.

"We can't let her do this!" Jennie pleaded.

"I know. Let me—"

Pike stopped. He heard gunshots through the entry hallway. Instinctively, he pulled Jennie back. "Get down!"

Four Zoldaari burst in from outside, struggling. Pike realized one of them was Carpenter, fighting against the other three. The captain ran toward the scrum. He was nearly there when Javu entered, a powerful hand on Vicki's shoulder and a sharp blade in his other hand.

"Stay where you are, Pike!" the Zoldaari warden shouted.

Vicki struggled against his hold. "Let go of me!"

"No." Javu glowered at the Zoldaari wrestling with Carpenter on the floor. "Can you manage that traitor, or do I need to handle that too?"

Vicki looked apologetically at Pike. "They leapt down from an airship. We shot at it—but we couldn't stop them!"

"On the contrary," said a voice from behind her. A figure with a bandaged face stepped in, holding a pistol. "Your shots were essential to our landing. Our sentinel deflated just before we went over the edge."

Javu glared at the newcomer. "Don't forget that you shot first. Fired into your own blimp. I'd have liked some warning."

"There wasn't time. Zoryana and Saachi are in worse shape than I am."

He spoke with a voice Pike recognized. "General Drayko."

"We meet at last." The Skagaran leader brushed his free hand against his bandages. "I'm afraid I'm not looking my best." Drayko faced the Zoldaari, who now had Vicki and Carpenter prisoner. Another had apprehended Jennie. "Have your people get these wretches out of here, Javu—and then come back inside. If they cause a problem, you have my permission to break them."

"The loving ruler," Pike muttered as his friends were escorted out.

"Nonsense." Drayko pointed the gun at him. "This entire trip is about saving my people. I will never allow you to turn off the Baffle."

"You don't understand—"

"*You don't*," the general barked. "We're able to give the people of this planet something amazing. A world that never changes. A life where what they learn in their childhood will still be useful when they reach old age—and a world where they're not forced to reinvent themselves over and over again to stay in step—or to stay fed."

"I'm trying to tell you—"

"There's nothing you can tell me." Pointing the gun, he prodded Pike back up the hallway. "I've read about life on Skagara before the collapse. People running around, constantly striving against one another, having to build higher and dig deeper. Every day harder than the one before, filled with some new shock. Warden Talley tells me that nearly destroyed Earth."

"I heard my name," Lila replied from inside the rotunda.

Drayko was surprised to see her. "How did you beat us here?"

"Cross-country." She gestured to the podium before her. "Near as I can understand it, the system is ready."

Drayko stared at her—and laughed. "You *are* impressive, Warden." He looked over to see Chin-Riley, Uhura, and Spock at the stands before the whirling rondure—and his voice grew cross. "What are they doing there?"

"They can't move," Hemmer declared. Pike saw that he was sitting up, holding his midsection. "The system is running. They're logged in, in a sense—components of the whole, acting in gestalt." He gestured to the podium before Talley. "Whoever is at that terminal must execute a procedure before they can release their *zazics*."

Drayko looked to Lila. "Do you understand what to do?"

"I think so."

He clenched his fist. "We can *save* the Earth, Captain. Stop the Klingons forever. Turn every world into one like Epheska. Yes, there will be some dark times at first. Some people will die. But you will only have to relearn once. Call it your penance for coming to the idea late. You should have listened to—what did Talley call them? The Luddites."

Pike had heard enough. "What you're really saying is you want *your* life to remain the same. With you and your people on top, Drayko. And Lila? You just want this so nothing else bad will happen to you."

"It didn't happen to me," she yelled back. "*It didn't happen to me!*"

"Tell him what we told you," Pike said. He faced Drayko. "We think the rondures are set as they are for a reason. If you expand the radius, you'll strip the magnetic field from Epheska, killing everyone."

The news left Drayko dumbstruck—but just for a moment. "What an effective lie. Much better than all the starships going dark. I applaud you. It must have taken a while to come up with."

"It's no lie. And if you expand it to impact other planets, too, it'll kill those people as well."

Lila looked to Drayko. "It *is* a lie, right?"

"Of course." The general looked to see Javu enter. "You are just in time."

Lila passed her gun to the Zoldaari. She clasped her hands on the *zazic* on the podium—and shook, as she stared out into a space only she could see. Pike knew there was no time. He had to rush them, do something.

Captain.

Pike looked up. It was another person's thought, but it didn't sound in his mind like Hemmer's or Spock's voices had.

It's Uhura. I think I've found a way to talk just to you.

Pike looked surreptitiously over to her, standing at her podium before the rondure. He was afraid to think anything, for fear that Lila would catch the message.

Captain, Empy helped us before. You need to release him.

Pike's eyes went to the lantern. Jennie had set it on the floor partway across the room earlier when Lila arrived. The flame inside flickered orange.

This machine—it feels familiar. I think Empy knows what it is, what's happening. But the vents aren't large enough for him to escape the lantern, and Drayko knows he's inside it. You can't let him see what you do.

Pike looked back to Uhura—and nodded.

Drayko was standing alongside Lila, now, watching intently whatever she was doing. In the middle of the room, the rondure rose another meter from the surface, spinning even faster and casting the whole room in orange light.

Pike took the chance. He stepped toward Javu and looked the bruiser in the eye. "Back," Javu said, waving Lila's gun.

"You really need that?" Pike asked, taking another step. He laughed. "Carpenter didn't think much of you people. No wonder."

Javu snorted. "You think that's going to work?"

"No," Pike said. "But this might." He hauled off with an uppercut—the only kind of punch he was able to make and connect with the giant's jaw.

Javu shook it off, glared down at him, and smiled. He tucked the gun in his belt and cracked his knuckles. "I'm going to enjoy this."

Behind them, Drayko called out from Lila's side. But it was too late. His bodyguard threw a mighty punch against Pike. The captain spun and hit the wall, rebounding just in time for Javu to strike him again.

When he recovered, Pike lurched forward, ready to grapple. Javu grabbed him and lifted him from the floor. The captain had gambled on exactly that—and when the Zoldaari warden threw him across the room, he tumbled toward the lantern. Shielding it from the shouting Drayko's gaze with his body, Pike snapped open the lantern's lid. "Go. Do whatever you do!"

The empatherm billowed out. Drayko, burned once, fired his pistol toward the flame being, a panicked and useless maneuver. But even as the general screamed, Empy did not touch him. Instead, it bypassed him, heading toward the *zazic* on Lila's podium.

Lila opened her eyes. "What's happening?" she called out.

Pike started toward her, wondering the same thing. The elemental swirled about her, only to stream toward one of the rams' horns on the *zazic* she was clutching. The crystal glowed—and Empy seemed to emerge from the other horn. This time, the creature shot, laser-like, directly toward the rondure.

The empatherm raced around it, a shuttle orbiting a globe, its glow vanishing into the radiance of the rondure. The sphere screeched as it rotated—

—and then a bubble of force materialized, centered on the orb and surrounding Chin-Riley's, Uhura's, and Spock's positions.

Incensed, Drayko took aim at Pike's first officer and fired. The bullet seemed to stop right at the edge of the sphere, only to spiral around it and sizzle back outward, sending Javu diving.

"Don't do that!" the Zoldaari yelled.

"I don't know what's going on!" Drayko looked to Lila, still clutching the *zazic* that Empy had transited through. "What's happening?"

Hemmer interjected. "She is connected to the system now as well. It is in the next phase. Removing her could be catastrophic!"

Lila shook her head. *"I've got this,"* she thought so all could hear.

Pike glanced at Hemmer, who spoke again. "The Skagarans discovered the rondures could be used to communicate—but the real communication was designed for this. So those *here*," he said, gesturing to where he was, "could talk with those *in there*." He pointed to the bubble, which was growing increasingly opaque with energy.

"*He's right, Captain*," Pike heard Uhura say.

Spock's voice came next. "*The* zazics *are not antennae. They are keys, for accessing the system. And for allowing the empatherms to interface with it.*"

Pike was stunned. "The empatherms?"

"*I'm still working through it,*" Chin-Riley declared. "*But when Empy entered, all the systems came alive.*"

Something more than that was happening. The rondure was lifting higher into the air—only this time, the force bubble surrounding it lifted, too, leaving a cavity in the center of the floor. Lila, at her podium outside the divot, called out. "*I'm inside the system. It's growing! The field is growing!*"

Pike's eyes locked on the bubble. The force sphere rose gently at first—and then rocketed upward, striking the skylight above and smashing through several of the stone structural supports. Large chunks of debris fell. One slab struck Javu hard, knocking him flat. Drayko stumbled away in the shower of stone and glass, only to be struck by something himself.

Lying on the floor, Hemmer pointed to Lila and yelled. "She must hold on, Captain!"

Dodging fragments, Pike made his way to her side and tried to steady her as more material rained down. "What the hell is going on, Hemmer?" He looked up through the smashed rotunda and saw the glowing circle heading up. "Are they all right?"

"*We are, Captain,*" Spock communicated. "*We seem protected.*"

"Is that some kind of—of ship?"

"*Negative,*" Number One replied. "*I think it's something else entirely!*"

CHAPTER 72

THE CHOICE

"I think we're in the Great Glass Elevator," Una Chin-Riley said.

Spock did not seem to find the reference helpful, but to her it surely felt like a scene from a storybook. The three of them had launched into the sky, with nothing beneath their feet but a transparent energy cocoon. Only this was a conveyance with handlebars, in the form of the *zazics*.

Hemmer had told them they couldn't release the devices. That wasn't a problem, because at least it gave them something to hold on to. Despite the fact they had felt no motion themselves—or even the impact of the temple dome— one could not look at what was happening around them without discomfort.

Uhura looked nauseated. "I don't know if I can take this," she said.

"Focus on the podium," Chin-Riley advised. *Her* eyes were everywhere else. During their rise through the atmosphere, she'd seen hundreds of shining stars rocketing from the surface. Rondures, she imagined, just like theirs.

"Captain," Spock said, intending to project his thoughts as well, "the rondures do indeed prescribe an outer limit for the interdimensional effects. Our pod appears to be the master unit, setting a level for all."

They all heard Pike's telepathic response. *"Is it activated yet?"*

"I don't believe so," Chin-Riley said. She hadn't seen any change to the aurorae as they'd ascended. "I think it's got to lock into position first."

Another mental voice was heard. *"And lock it will. The warden is seeing to it!"*

The women looked to each other. "Drayko."

Spock's eyes narrowed. "We are a component—but we are not in control."

"Lieutenant," Ortegas asked aboard *Enterprise*, "is there a kind of an alert I can issue when I don't know what I'm looking at?"

"Pretty much any of them will do." La'an walked behind Ortegas and sat in the captain's chair. She looked toward the main viewer. "What have we got?"

"Over a thousand contacts leaving the planet. And that's just on this side."

Enterprise had sat beyond Epheska's moons for days, keeping its vigil. After Pike provided his horrific news and ordered the ship to depart, La'an had made the possibly career-ending decision to send the shuttle *Copernicus* to depart the nebula with its warning. If the captain was right about the potential for an expanded Baffle to destroy all life within a wide radius, it didn't really matter who delivered the news. This way, *Enterprise* had been able to remain on station in case it was needed.

What *she* needed now was an explanation. According to observations from Mitchell, every single site identified as having a temple had just launched something.

"They're expanding outward uniformly," the navigator said.

"Find me the one that left from Pike's position—the Devil's Dish."

La'an waited until Mitchell pulled it up on the main viewer. "Enhance."

A glowing sphere appeared—with what appeared to be three figures barely visible in silhouette standing inside. Mouths dropped open all over the bridge.

Ortegas spoke first. "Is that three people in a turbolift—without the turbolift?"

"Or the ship," Mitchell added. Her lower lip curled. "I don't think we want to be inside that area."

"Agreed," La'an said. "Line us up with that object—but keep ahead of it. We'll try to match speed."

She sat back in the chair. What, indeed, *was* the proper alert for this?

Lila Talley was in another world. Pike felt her body shake under his hands. Her eyes were focused elsewhere. She was in the system, whispering to herself. He could hear her thoughts, a mishmash of directions and numbers. She was no engineer, but neither was this a machine in any traditional sense.

Or so he thought.

"*We're a battery,*" she said. "*We're sending electrical energy into another dimension.*"

"Just like Spock and Hemmer said." He watched her. "Why?"

She didn't answer. Instead, Pike looked over to see Drayko pointing a gun at him. Drayko was barely standing, propping himself up against a fallen pillar. One of his pants legs was shredded, with blood seeping from it. He was covered with dust, his clothes tattered from the sudden departure of the rondures. He seemed bewildered.

"Are you okay?" Pike clearly didn't think he was.

Drayko coughed repeatedly before looking up in a daze. "My rondures are gone."

"What's wrong? Not sure how you'll rule without them?"

"When she's done," he said, gesturing to Lila, "I won't have to care." He cocked the pistol. "I'm sorry *you* won't see how the story ends."

Strong hands took Drayko from behind and whirled him about. Celarius, his face streaked with blood and his own clothes dirtied and torn, grasped the gun in his father's hands. "We're done telling stories."

Drayko, dizzy, appeared to have trouble focusing on him. "Celarius?"

"I'm doing what you wanted. I'm taking over." He uncocked the pistol and took it from his father. Then he turned the old man about.

Pike marveled at the scene. "We thought you were gone."

"A backdraft sent me into the wall of the mesa," Celarius said. "The envelope ripped against it and caught on something. Good thing I wasted a few years rock climbing."

Pike saw Celarius supporting his father as he walked toward the exit. "Careful. There's Zoldaari out there."

"I made sure they knew—they work for me now." Celarius looked over his shoulder. "I saw the other rondures rising—and that one. Was that Una?"

"*It is,*" she replied. Pike heard her voice—as did Celarius.

Pike nodded. "We'll get her back."

Satisfied, Celarius led his father outside.

"*Captain,*" Spock said, "*we have exceeded the orbit of this system's fifth planet. And we appear to be accelerating.*"

Struggling to stand, Hemmer faced Pike. "The Baffle will expand at warp speed soon." He gestured to Lila. "When she stops it, it will activate in the new area."

"You can't take her place? Turn it off?"

"Not now."

Pike had no choice. It came down to Lila, and what had happened. He knew all about Kelfour VI, but not the victims. So many Luddites. So many members of her family's community. So many—

He walked around the podium and put his hands on hers. "Tell me about them."

She was lost in whatever it was. No response.

"Tell me about them. The people you lost."

"*I told you. The community moved. The Klingons killed them.*"

"*One billion kilometers,*" Spock called out.

Pike shook his head. "Not the community, Lila. Your family."

He saw her eyes clench. "*My parents died years ago.*"

"No, no. I know that." He grasped her hands harder. "Tell me about them."

"*Two billion kilometers.*"

"Lila, tell me about them."

Lila winced—and when she spoke, it was with her own voice. "I don't know what—"

Pike's hands moved to her wrists. "Tell me about your children."

Her face froze.

"What were their names?"

Tears began streaming from her eyes.

"There was someone," Pike said. "You told me. Eduardo. Eduardo Lopez."

"Four billion."

She shook her head, eyes still closed. "He . . . he went to Starfleet. I didn't want him to go."

"But he came back. Didn't he?" Pike moved his hands to her cheeks and wiped away a tear. "What were their names? Your children?"

"Isabel," she said in a small voice. She choked up. "Luisa." She bawled uncontrollably. "Jimmy."

"Like your dad."

"Eddie took them with him . . . to the new place. I was going to close up the ranch on Earth. I wasn't . . . wasn't with them." She opened her eyes—and tears flowed freely. "Christopher, I can't go on."

"You can. You're strong."

"I can't—"

"You're one of the strongest people I've ever known, Lila. You crossed those mountains, alone."

She shook her head. "I had Buckshot."

"You still do. And you've got me, and a lot of other people. You've got to save those people, Lila."

"I was trying to."

Spock spoke again. *"Eight billion!"*

"You've got to save them *now*. Save them all." Pike looked to Hemmer. *"Can she stop it? Dial it back?"*

"She can stop the growth," Hemmer replied. "Then it activates. She cannot return the Baffle to its previous size."

Lila looked up. "Can I repeat the process? Do it again, in reverse?"

Hemmer's face fell. "The rondures will not return to their previous positions. All the sites have likely been damaged, like this one. We may not be able to recall them at all."

"I concur," Spock added.

"We're approaching the inner nebular boundary," Number One declared. *"Once outside, we're into populated areas for sure."* A pause. *"Captain, we have to shut down the expansion—no matter the cost."*

Pike shook his head. All Epheska was at stake. There had to be another way—but better a star system than countless more. "If it's got to be, it's got to be." He put his hands back on Lila's. "Shut it down."

CHAPTER 73

THE DEPARTURE

Around Nyota Uhura, everything stopped.

The nodal rondure and its surrounding sphere, which had raced breakneck toward the nebular gases, stopped moving just shy of them.

Enterprise, which Uhura had seen enter and exit warp several times in an attempt to stay ahead of the bizarre bubble, had paused in normal space in her field of view. Rather than warp away as she had seen it do before, this time it just sat there.

And her companions weren't breathing. Chin-Riley and Spock sat frozen as statues, their hands on the *zazics*.

"Sirs?"

No answer.

She concentrated. "Captain? Hemmer?"

Still nothing.

She looked at the *zazic* with exhaustion. She'd been told not to release it, but if time was frozen, what did it matter? She pried her hands off it.

She turned about and looked through the bubble at space outside. There was the Epheskan star—and the planet she'd spent so long on, looking unbelievably small. Behind her, *Enterprise* was still doing nothing.

She took a deep breath and closed her eyes. She'd been alone so much lately. This was as bad as it got. Entombed in space, cut off from time.

Unimaginable.

She felt warmth—and opened her eyes. The *zazic* on her podium glowed—and in the next moment, a wisp of flame emerged from one end of the horn.

"Empy!" she said. But it was different. The plasma kept flowing, filling the space before the podium. By the time it was done, there was an Uhura-shaped figure of flame standing where she had been stationed.

She heard a whisper of a voice in her mind. *Hello.*

"You are Empy, right?"

We accept the name. You are our friend.

"And you are mine. I am Uhura."

You are our friend.

She looked about. "What's going on? What am I to make of this?"

We have not known what to make of this.

She took a deep breath. "I will listen."

Our home was in great danger. The energy that gave us vitality was dissipating. There was much suffering. To restore our health, we created what you call the rondures to open a portal to your space.

"To export the electrical energy."

Correct. When we arrived on the hidden planet, we realized there were beings there who would die if we did not carefully control our mechanism.

"The Strooh!"

And so we made sure our efforts left the planet's magnetosphere in place. In exchange, they assisted us in maintaining the rondures, protecting them from harm. We have no solid form in your realm.

"Did it work? Did you save your dimension?"

With our intake limited, the siphon required much time. And we had only begun the process when what you call the Skagarans arrived. They did not respect the Strooh—and did not understand what the rondures were.

"So they used them for communication. To build their settlements around."

We would not have objected to that. But they also discovered something we never expected. The zazics—the mechanisms that allowed our kind to interface with and control the rondures—could be used to control us.

It all made sense to Uhura. "But they didn't know they were harming you."

That, we could have endured. But they used them to compel us to harm others. We did not fully understand what we were doing. We thought, at most, we were destroying inanimate things. It was our time with you, Uhura, that taught us what was really happening.

Uhura looked about. Spock and Chin-Riley were still motionless, but somehow she had a sense that they were hearing this too—and perhaps Captain Pike and the others back in the temple on Epheska. She had one question to ask on behalf of them all. "What now?"

What you call the Baffle could serve our needs at this size. Faster, if it were to grow larger still. But just as we would not harm the Strooh, we will not harm you. We must act together, Uhura, to prevent our device from causing further injury.

"What do you mean?"

We believe you have the capacity to leave this sphere. I believe you also have the capacity to destroy it. We need you to do both, in that order.

"Destroy it?"

It will work.

"But what will happen to you?" She reached out to the flame being. A tendril of fire, cool and blue, touched her hand. "Won't you die?"

In our realm, as in yours, energy can neither be created nor destroyed.

Uhura shook her head. "I don't think I can do this."

You must. Make your call, without delay. We thank you—and will remember you.

At that, the being shrank and withdrew, re-entering the *zazic* and becoming one with the machine.

Uhura shook her head. "Make my call?" she said aloud.

It was then she saw a light on *Enterprise* blink. And then Chin-Riley and Spock blinked.

"Who's got a comm unit?" Uhura asked.

The first officer, confused, stared at her. "What?"

"Hemmer gave you a comm unit. Try it!"

"It won't—"

"Try it!"

She triggered the communicator. "Chin-Riley to *Enterprise*."

Uhura hoped to hear a response—yet La'an's voice startled her anyway. *"Is that you, Commander?"*

Without delay, Empy had said. Uhura shouted. "We need you to beam us out—and destroy this pod!"

Stunned silence. *"Repeat that?"*

Uhura looked to Chin-Riley. "You heard Empy, didn't you?"

The first officer was speechless for a moment. Then she committed. "Three to transport out—and destroy this pod!" She looked to Uhura. "Phasers or torpedoes?"

"Do it all. Just do it fast!"

Uhura watched as a torpedo launched from *Enterprise*'s aft. Chin-Riley looked at it—and then to her and Spock. "Boy, I sure hope *this* transport works."

Pike had just emerged from the ruined temple with Lila when the light show began. All the rondures on Epheska had traveled far into space, and while they were tiny objects, their explosions were immense enough to be seen millions of kilometers away.

The fireworks display didn't stop there, either, as a portion of the aurora above the Devil's Dish separated and lifted high into the sky, heading toward the starbursts.

"They're everywhere," Jennie called out, pointing from one direction to the other. Across Epheska, countless empatherms rose from their planetary bondage and left, heading back to their own domain.

Lila gazed up at it. They'd both heard the story Empy told Uhura. "They didn't save their home," she said. "They're just leaving."

"They made a choice," Pike said.

He looked over at the newly freed Menders and then at Celarius, Drayko, and their companions. All of them were watching the skies. Things would be a lot different here.

The first sign of it came in the form of a sound Pike had all but forgotten. He pulled his comm unit from his pocket. "Pike."

"*Captain!*"

"La'an. Where've you been?" He smirked. "Never mind. We need medical help down here. Hemmer—and, well, a bunch of other people."

"*Right away. La'an out.*"

He looked wanly at the communicator. "Guess I'm on the clock again."

Lila shook her head, exhausted. "I just want to see my dog."

"Let's get your horse first." They walked back inside.

CHAPTER 74

THE KING

Drayko sat in a garden, surrounded by someone else's plants. The flowers here were plentiful and colorful and part of someone's idea of a pleasant restful spot. To him, they were alien and absurd, and the room felt exactly like what it was: a cabinet attached to a machine.

The arboretum on *Enterprise* was a fraction of the size of the one he had left behind in Om Mataya. In place of the lovely aurorae and nebulae visible through the skylights was a large port showing what he'd been told were stars sailing by. Of course, the occupants of the starship had many panels that looked like windows but which were actually simulacra. He had chosen to think this one was a false image, too, as it was better for his stomach. Either way, they had reduced the beauty of the heavens to bright smears on a glass. Perfect, to go along with a garden in a closet.

The dolt watching over him—"security officer" was a laughable term for a member of a society in which no planet should feel secure—had tried repeatedly to show Drayko how the chair he was sitting in operated. It rode on the air, but not like the rondures did—and to operate it, he needed to master some kind of handheld agility puzzle attached to the armrest. He didn't bother on principle, though it meant he had to keep looking at the burping face of the dreadful pink flower staring at him.

He heard the door open and words being exchanged. His minder spoke to him. "You've got a visitor. I'm going to step out so you can talk."

Drayko did not respond.

A kindly-faced man entered. The general had seen him before. "The doctor."

"That is correct." M'Benga took a look at the abomination in pink, white, and green. "Ah, you have found the king protea."

Drayko looked at the flower and blanched. "This is the king of something?"

"An important flower of my continent on my planet."

"I recommend taking it back there and leaving it."

"The king will brook no insults." M'Benga cracked a gentle smile—and turned Drayko's chair in a different direction. He pulled up a seat of his own, across from the general. "I wanted to speak to you about your prognosis."

"I haven't the time," Drayko replied, idly looking instead at the alleged stars outside.

"In fact, you have more time than you would have had, if your injuries happened a month ago."

Drayko turned back to see M'Benga gesturing to the Skagaran's face.

"The treatment you received is continuing to repair the skin damage from the burns you suffered. As to your injuries from the collapse, your bones are repaired, but the tissues will need time to recover before I would recommend walking unassisted."

"My dear doctor, I have nowhere to go." He looked off to the corner.

When the physician did not immediately leave, Drayko glanced in his direction and spoke again. "Are you waiting for me to thank you? For me to admit I would have died, were it not for your technology here?"

M'Benga nodded deferentially. "We ask for no appreciation—but, yes, that would be accurate."

"Better I should have died with the project," Drayko replied. "You have ruined it all. Centuries of work."

"I have been told about this work—about your society." M'Benga clasped his hands together and rested his chin on them. "Your son tells me your wife and mother both died of Kasten's Syndrome, a cancer found in certain humanoids. They would not have died either, had it not been for the Baffle."

"Warden Talley told me of your world, Doctor. I know full well there are people here who avoid advanced medical practices on moral grounds—because of all else that comes with modernity. Would you have denied my family this same right?"

"It is one thing if they denied themselves," M'Benga said. "As I understand it, you made this decision for many others."

"Is this how it works here? Treatment, with complimentary judgment?"

"My judgment is not complimentary." M'Benga looked down at the deck and spoke quietly. "You nearly killed a member of *my* family. And would have killed countless more, had your plan worked."

Just another ploy. Drayko looked about. "This mystery family member is aboard ship? Or somewhere else?"

"Somewhere." M'Benga looked up. "Suffice it to say I do not remember delegating my rights—or *hers*—to you."

Drayko stared at the human doctor for several moments. It was clear M'Benga was in earnest. But the general wasn't about to express regret. *Enterprise* had no business anywhere near Epheska. Had it not arrived, he would never have learned of the nodal rondure's powers—or been provoked to use them.

He was blameless.

"Have they decided what is to happen to me?"

"I can answer that."

Drayko looked over to see Captain Pike's security chief, La'an, enter, holding a device. Drayko thought she was barely more than a child. M'Benga started to stand.

"Don't get up," she said.

"I wasn't planning on it," Drayko grumbled.

"I was talking to the doctor, not you," La'an replied. "To you, I can say that you've kept several departments within the Federation and Starfleet very busy."

Drayko looked to the overhead. "What *will* I do with such an honor?"

She ignored him. "We have found individuals on this planet from at least twenty different civilizations. Some of those are Federation members. Some aren't. Some of their original societies are completely gone." She walked around Drayko's chair. "Some are places that would welcome the return of their citizens. In other cases, the people are safer right where they are."

"Do tell."

"There are further reintegration issues, as we found with the culture that Jonathan Archer discovered."

"The *Liberator* survivors."

"Not what I would have named the ship. But yes, this is requiring the consultation of a host of experts on culture, mental health, and physical health. Some people have hundreds of years of immunizations to get caught up on before they go anywhere."

"So you are taking them all away." Drayko crossed his arms. "I expected no better."

"No, it's not like that." She stopped behind M'Benga's chair and looked down on Drayko. "When the rondures left, all the settlements were severed from the only support system they'd ever known. The word has spread slowly, and we're working to soften the shock. In a sense, it's like twenty different first-contact scenarios. It's inevitable they'll find out, because with Om Mataya gone—"

"Gone!" Drayko bolted upright—and felt pain in the process. M'Benga was right there with a ready hypospray, but the general waved it off. "Om Mataya is gone? What have you fools *done* to it?"

"Nothing," she responded. "The rondure is gone, so your command center had nothing to work with. The empatherms left, so that ended the airships. We're fortunate—none of the vessels fell from the sky. Without drive systems, they just meandered until they put down on their own." La'an added, "It turns out that a secluded capital completely dependent on resources from the outside does indeed get abandoned when there is no more outside."

Drayko steamed.

"At any rate, we have made contact successfully with several races on Epheska, Skagarans included, about their future disposition. And the one thing they agree on is this: they do not want you back."

He winced at the statement—and then couldn't help but laugh. "Sweet child, my people love me."

"They'd love you to be somewhere else."

A lurch, which even Drayko felt in his chair on air. The lines outside the port vanished and were replaced by oily mud.

"And here we are," La'an said.

Drayko's eyes narrowed as he tried to figure out what he was looking at. A wretched soup, greasy and vile. It took him a moment—and motion from *Enterprise*—to understand what he was looking at was not a larvae-filled pool, but rather a planet.

It turned his stomach. "What is that disgusting place?"

"I'm told you've talked enough about it," La'an said. "I'm surprised you don't know."

Drayko looked at her—and then back at the world. His eyes bulged. "*Skagara?*"

La'an moved in front of the port. "Our first officer, Commander Chin-Riley—"

"Who?"

"Una."

"Oh, yes. You people have too many names."

"As I was saying, she was able to retrieve your library and recover records relating to your people's arrival on Epheska. They spelled out the location of your true homeworld." She gestured to the surrounding space beyond, blotchy with orange. "Another nebula. Lots of planets out there we haven't explored."

"It looks worse than I ever imagined. How long did the Skagarans survive?"

"Excuse me?"

"Before dying out."

She finally caught his meaning. "It's not like that. We established relations with them last week."

He couldn't believe it. "They live?"

"Not happily, but they are there, and they answered our hails. No Prime Directive issues there at all."

Drayko shuddered. He had long known that many did not support the Epheska project and had remained on Skagara to die. He couldn't contemplate what their lives must have been like.

He could, however, predict what the sadists of Starfleet intended for him.

"Is this place supposed to be my fate? The hole where you will bury me?" He fiddled with the chair control, trying to get it to turn so that he wouldn't see the place anymore, even by accident. "I will not go."

La'an stifled a chuckle. "Believe me, you haven't been asked!"

M'Benga nodded. "You are a king without a country."

Drayko grimaced. "Then why bring me here? Cross the stars for spite?"

"It is not all about you," M'Benga said. He rose. "This has been enough excitement. I will call for someone to bring you back to sickbay."

"That's today." Drayko looked from one human to the other. "What is my place after that? I demand to know!"

"We will find somewhere for you," La'an said. "It's taking some time. Some think you should be advising historians at Memory Alpha. Some think you should be locked away in a place like Thionoga."

Drayko crossed his arms. "Wherever it is, I am to be confined."

"Likely." La'an exited the room.

The general wouldn't have it. He clutched the armrests. "You're taking me away—and confining me, on a planet not of my birth!"

M'Benga paused just outside the doorway. When he looked back, he wore a sad expression. "General, what you are describing is a fate many have suffered. But in your case, at least, it will have been earned."

He walked away, and the doors closed behind him.

CHAPTER 75

THE FORSAKEN

Una Chin-Riley had just turned onto the street when the building at the end of it collapsed. Floor by agonizing floor, the structure pancaked onto the surface, sending clouds of debris billowing toward her. She pivoted and dashed back around the corner, finding an alcove to crouch in while the shower of particles passed.

She tightened her face mask when she emerged—and saw her Skagaran guide, Pellana, standing nearby, dressed head to toe in her dusty clothes and face covering. The woman didn't seem to share Chin-Riley's agitation.

"Was that a bomb?" the commander asked.

"No, it's just autumn."

"Excuse me?" The universal translator was working now, she thought. "Did you say it's autumn?"

"In autumn, the buildings fall." Pellana took her by the arm and turned her about. "We'd better take another street."

Pellana, the commander had learned, was a survivor of a people whose towers had soared to the sky—and whose technology had once been so powerful that it had enabled those with the Epheska project to pluck villages and sailing fleets from other planets for relocation. But the same ecological catastrophe that had made that project necessary had set the Skagaran homeworld back a long way.

Much of what Chin-Riley had been through in recent weeks seemed familiar. She had been unable to leave a planet run by Skagarans. This was a planet Skagarans could not leave—because they no longer had the vessels to depart or the communications tools to reach farther than the immediate area. When Starfleet dispatched a scout vessel to check out the reported location of their homeworld, the Skagarans answered. And while they had not entertained guests in centuries, they still took a certain pride in the place.

"I wanted to meet you here in Turgan, for it best recalls what we were," Pellana said, voice scratchy. "Its elevation protected it against the tidal waves, which meant the surrounding oil fires could burn unabated. The smoke pillars seem to have contributed to a heat dome over the city, redirecting most of the heavier particulates away. But ashfall season still takes down a few buildings every hour."

"That's horrible."

"That's Skagara. And nobody lives in them. It's all right."

It was not all right, and Chin-Riley could tell Pellana didn't really think it was. For centuries, her people had existed in shadow, migrating from place to place as conditions worsened.

And yet, some trace of what they had remained. Pellana—whose age was undetectable to Chin-Riley given her garb—worked with the university. When asked which one, Pellana had replied that there was only one, and that it had no geographic connection. "The university is wherever people who work for it—or learn from it—happen to be. We are all the university."

Their little splinter was all that remained of any of Skagara's institutions, and it was the only body that had been capable of responding to Starfleet's hail. As the first communications revealed, Pellana and her colleagues were well aware of Epheska and the Skagarans who had relocated there. And while they had no interest in seeing anyone still devoted to that cause, they welcomed a chance to speak with any who had abandoned it.

Down a side street, Chin-Riley saw two other masked members of her party—people for whom the visit had already been emotionally devastating. Yet they had wanted to join the trip to see the place they came from. Taliyah, whose *Braidwood* companions had finally achieved their goal of unraveling the North Star mystery, walked arm in shaky arm with Kohsam, her equal in age. The pair gazed about from place to place, understanding what had led their ancestors to abandon the world.

A third Skagaran darted into view from an alley: Celarius. He was back in his ranger garb, having been given the chance to stop in at Om Mataya before *Enterprise* left—and he appeared frantic when Chin-Riley saw him. "Were you near that?"

"The building? No."

He expressed relief. "I just can't believe this place. It's worse than the tales we were all told."

"Let's get to the plaza," Pellana said. "It's better there."

Chin-Riley walked behind as Pellana spoke to her cousins, centuries removed. Her people had initially been of two minds toward the Epheska project, she said.

"Some wanted to keep working here to fix the planet, not to abandon it. They looked on the idea of leaving as disloyal, as desertion in our hour of need." She shook her bundled head. "By the time things got so bad they wanted to escape, the Epheska project had already turned to kidnapping. And no one would countenance being a part of that."

"This is why you didn't want Drayko to come here."

"It was an outlaw movement—and the conservators general the chief outlaws." Pellana looked over to Celarius. "You truly have no further regard for the project or your father?"

"The project ended when the rondures vanished," he said. "And my family ended when my mother died."

Chin-Riley watched as he let out a deep breath and resumed his silence.

The plaza was just a place where everything that could collapse already had. She saw Captain Pike there, alongside his party: members of the *Braidwood* crew, as well as several of the Menders. It was not enough, he'd decided, that the Skagarans aboard *Enterprise* who wanted to see their homeworld have the opportunity to do so; the descendants of those the project had abducted deserved to see why it had all happened.

"It don't make it better," Joe Magee declared, looking about. "Just makes it sadder."

Chin-Riley thought that said it all.

Pike greeted Pellana. "There's a lot our Federation can do for you."

"There is a lot *to* do."

"And we will. But it's going to take some time. You'll see other captains and other ships, but given our recent experiences, we wanted to see what we could do to kick things off." He looked around at the ruins. "History is a complicated thing, and it can take a long time to untangle. Definitely my planet learned that. But there's always somewhere to start."

"Your visit is one step." Pellana gestured to the visiting Skagarans. "I understand the world you came from had troubles. But it does sound like it could be a refuge for some here who may not make it much longer."

Joe chortled. "I left a pretty nice farmhouse back on Epheska. Maybe some of y'all can move in."

Chin-Riley looked at Pike. There'd been some discussions about assisting Skagarans in migrating to this planet, if they so desired, but nobody had ever considered reverse migration. "There are a *lot* of settlement sites that were prepared on Epheska but never used."

Celarius nodded vigorously. "I know where they are."

Over his protective mask, Pike looked quizzically at his first officer. "Can we really solve this by moving *even more* people around?"

She considered. "Yeah. People are adaptable—if *they're* the ones to choose. But we'd have to be careful, just as we are with those who are leaving Epheska."

"Keep a watch for environmental impact," Celarius said. "Really think through existing populations, and the effect on them. And *only* those people who want to go." He looked at Pellana. "The way my family should have done in the beginning."

Pellana peered at him. "You would not be trying to restart your own regime there, with more Skagarans?"

Celarius shook his head. "No, I'll be here."

Chin-Riley gawked. "Here?"

"Yeah." He strode the plaza. "I've lived all my life in paradise. Enjoyed years of being catered to. Not knowing what it was costing." He gestured. "Here, I can try to do what I could for the place." He looked to Pellana. "Are there any animals?"

"A very few."

"We'll bring them back. But no transplants. No animal species from anywhere else. What this planet was is still here somewhere. We'll find it." He faced Chin-Riley. "And when anyone who needs to be evacuated to Epheska or anywhere else comes back, maybe they'll find it a place worth coming back to."

She marveled. *Okay, the prince has grown up. Guess it's never too late.*

Kohsam spoke. "I am too old to meet these challenges, I fear. But I never saw enough of Epheska when I was there. If some would move, I would help." Beside him, Taliyah expressed her interest too.

Pellana hung her head. "It has been so long since there has been any hope," she said, exhaustion evident. "All this, in so short a time. It is overwhelming."

Pike stepped forward to shake her hand. "This is just the start. And now I've got to finish what *I* started." He used his communicator and ordered *Enterprise* to beam up the Menders. As they transported, he said, "I'm still not sure how this ends for them. It's complicated."

Taliyah approached him. "Captain, I may have an alternative for you—if you don't mind adding another stop to your journey."

"If it removes the need for more stops later on, I'm all ears." He nodded to his first officer. "See you later, Number One. And Celarius—thanks. Good luck. *Enterprise*, two to beam up."

Chin-Riley and Celarius lingered on the plaza. They walked amid the debris—the place so different, in every way, from the planet he'd lived on. "I honestly thought you'd jump at the idea of resettling people back there," she said.

"My family has moved enough people around. I trust the Federation to know what to do and when to do it."

"You could do both. Work here and also there."

"That'd be cheating. Just like Om Mataya. Pampered when I'm not out in the wild."

She glanced about. "This won't be a week in the woods, that's for sure."

He looked sideways at her. "I don't see you coming here on vacation."

"We call it shore leave."

"No kitchen open all night. Not even any tasty wildflowers."

She thought back on the *llaoths*—and laughed. "They were *not* tasty."

He smirked. "No, they were not."

"Glad you admit it."

"I admit I liked the company." He looked at her—and then down at her uniform. Their eyes met again. "We're just never going to fit, are we?"

The mask muffled her laugh. "You are something else."

"What?"

"You're the person who gets everything he wants. And instead of in the big palace, or in the clouds, you ask *now*!"

"In the middle of the apocalypse."

"In the middle of the apocalypse." She brought him in for a hug. "We're both still going places, Celarius. Things to do. But there's time."

"We'll see." He looked down at her in his arms. "You're wrong about me, anyway. I don't get everything I want."

"Oh, yeah?"

"I'd like to kiss you. And you have that mask on."

"So do you. But trust the space woman on this. They're not permanent features."

CHAPTER 76

THE ROUNDUP

The Menders of Havenbrook were not the only Menders that Christopher Pike had gone cross-country with, and they were not the only people who'd asked to go to space. However, he did feel a responsibility to them. They'd helped him, and if he'd never crashed, nothing would have happened to their businesses.

Pike had been concerned about promising anything. Certainly, since boarding *Enterprise*, Jennie Magee had spoken of nothing except Starfleet, and she was no doubt hoping her father would permit her to throw her cowboy hat in the ring. But the specialists had urged caution—the *Braidwood* personnel had studied in great detail how Jonathan Archer's visit to the town of North Star reshaped the lives of those who resided there.

Yet nobody could beat the experiences of Taliyah. Having grown up adjacent to one time-lost community, she knew what it took to prepare people for a leap to modernity. Her suggestion to Pike had included something he hadn't heard of before, and on further research, he determined it was worth bringing his *Enterprise* to visit the original "cowboy planet."

There was no need to hide, as Starfleet's existence had been well known since the first of Miss Bethany's students had won approval to leave the world years earlier. As Spock and Pike guided *Galileo* down, Taliyah explained the process to the few Menders aboard.

"Captain Archer had been afraid of culture shock at the time," the white-haired Skagaran said, "and encouraged us to hit the books and learn about Earth things before we thought about leaving."

"Books we understand," Cyrus said.

"We understand everything," Jennie said, fidgeting in her seat. "I thought the tests were to get into the Academy, not to get to see it!"

Joe patted her arm. "Calm just a mite." The farmer had been humbled a little by seeing Skagara—and his mood had improved after receiving something else. "We don't know everything. You see what Doc M'Benga got me." He gestured to his new prosthetic leg. "He's saying they might be able to do a lot more than this, even."

Taliyah nodded. "That's exactly it. There's a lot of good things that have come out of the years you didn't get to see—but people learned a lot of hard lessons too. Advances come with costs *and* responsibilities. You need to know what you're getting into—and it takes more than a couple of hops on a starship to get you ready for that."

Spock called back to them from the pilot's chair. "We have arrived over the first location."

"Everyone up front," Pike said. He surrendered his chair to Taliyah. "Lean on the chairs if you need to."

After the others had gone forward—and Carpenter had banged his head on the overhead for the fifth time since boarding—Spock pitched *Galileo's* nose lower so that the passengers behind him could see fully out the forward port.

"Cheat!" Joe shouted, suddenly not as amenable. "It's a cheat!"

Jennie looked forward to see a dusty Western village, complete with horses and taverns. She then stared at Pike in shock. "You took us back to Epheska?"

"That's not Epheska," Taliyah said. "That's North Star. I grew up near there."

As Spock brought the shuttle lower, Vicki looked forward and squinted. "This is the place the other people were brought to?"

Pike nodded. "This is the planet where *Liberator* crashed. As you can see, the place here is a lot like yours."

Carpenter shook his head. "Not *just* alike. I don't see any people like me."

"There wouldn't be," Taliyah said. "This was just humans and Skagarans. And the societies aren't *exactly* alike—but it's interesting that the technology never changed much. We now know it was because the Skagarans who brought them here inveighed against advancements while they were still in control. There was no Baffle here, but their pronouncements seemed to have worked."

Scribbling notes furiously, Cyrus shook his head. "Doesn't seem as busy as our towns. Did they all leave like you did, Taliyah?"

"Not quite."

Pike waved. "Back to your seats, folks. One more stop."

He nodded to Spock, who lifted the shuttle's nose. *Galileo* accelerated, crossing hundreds of kilometers quickly.

Once the shuttle set down, Pike rose and headed to open the hatchway. "Watch your step, please."

Joe gave him a wary look. "If it's like Havenbrook, I know what I'll step in."

Pike smiled. "Come on. You'll see."

What Joe and his companions stepped on was not dirt, but asphalt—and what they saw, they did not immediately understand. Vicki pointed at the maroon-colored wheeled conveyance rolling past. "What in heaven's name is that?"

"That," Pike said, "is a sedan."

"A Tucker 48, actually," Taliyah said. "We have it on loan from a collector in California."

The Menders wandered out into a village not much larger than the one they'd seen. But if North Star looked like a Western movie set, this was Main Street from a later era.

"Your people were abducted from the 1850s," Taliyah said. "Our experiences with Miss Bethany taught us that it would be handy to see what life was like in the 1950s." She pointed to the post office, which was home to a forty-eight–star American flag—and white letters announcing the location: *Advance, Beta Quadrant.*

"The town of Advance is a pilot project that the *Braidwood* team began here," she explained. "We keep it separate from the other areas—another time zone, you might say."

Pike looked at the blank faces. "You see, you didn't get that joke. But you will."

A truck trundled toward them. It honked its horn, and several of the Menders stared at it in shock. Pike and Spock helped them get to the sidewalk.

"That's kind of the idea here," he said as the vehicle went past. "It's a training area, just like an astronaut would prepare for spaceflight."

"A what?" Scribbling furiously, Cyrus was running out of pages fast.

"People who rode the first spaceships. They came along in this time too. You'll see—and you'll see why adjusting to things in stages is useful."

Spock looked about approvingly. "Historical decompression. A sensible approach." He looked to Taliyah. "Are there other such sites?"

She smiled. "Jonathan Archer visited us in the 2150s, so Archerville is off to the west."

Joe did some mental arithmetic. "There's one missing. What's wrong with the 2050s?"

Pike, Spock, and Taliyah exchanged glances. "You'll see when you get the history lessons."

Jennie looked at the traffic signal and telephone poles—and then back to Pike. "Do we really have to start here?"

Taliyah put her arm around the girl's shoulder. "The quick studies don't stay long at all. We're talking weeks, not years."

Pike leaned against the flagpole. "And keep in mind, nobody's *making* you do anything—or making you move anywhere. There's been enough of that. It's your choice. Earth right away, here, Epheska—"

"*No!*" came the collective response.

"It's better than learning this at a starbase," the captain said. "I think it could be an idea that others from Epheska might use. North Star, Advance, Archerville—they're kind of stepping-stones."

Vicki looked down. "Poor Weedaw should be here for this."

"I found him before we left Epheska," Pike said. "He was still frightened—but when he realized the Baffle was gone, he knew he'd been lied to. He's back with the Strooh on Epheska. They have a lot of history to catch up on—turns out they were home all along."

"It's not my home," Carpenter grumbled. "I'll be happy to stay here with you little people."

"At least someone will be able to reach the stuff on the tall shelves," Joe said.

"And build them!"

Pike strolled toward the mailbox. "The good news is that wherever you choose to be, we promise you can all still stay in touch. Whatever planets you're on."

"Is that possible?"

He opened the door of the mailbox with a creak—and slammed it shut. "I *could* explain it all—"

"Don't tell us." Jennie put her hands up—and looked around to her elders. "We'll figure it all out ourselves. You'll see us in no time."

Pike finally set foot in North Star just as the sun was setting, soaking up a bit of the ambiance before saying his good-byes to the Havenbrook Menders, who'd decided to make their start here.

"This is as close as I'll get to Earth for a little while," he said, glancing around. "I want to thank you all for looking after me."

Joe choked up. "Cap'n, you just can't know what it means."

"I think I do." Pike gripped his hand. "You take care of Jennie. And watch the engine work."

Jennie, already in tears, hugged him tightly.

"I know," the captain said. "Good things—but a lot of changes."

She sniffled—and heard a whinny from around the corner. She pulled away from Pike. "Cricket! I forgot about Cricket!"

"We transported your horses to the livery in Havenbrook," Pike said.

Spock nodded. "Chief Kyle found the episode most diverting."

"They're being looked after. We can bring them here eventually—if you want them."

"You think of everything," Jennie said. "Thank you."

"Peace and long life," Spock said, hand in the air.

The Menders' response was almost right, Pike thought. *They'll get there.*

He and Spock turned and strolled a street that Archer had ridden a century earlier. Both were eager to return to *Enterprise*'s main mission—but Pike knew there were things left undone.

"There is still the matter of our other passengers," Spock said.

"I know. I feel like we're playing musical civilizations here."

Pike raised his hand preemptively, but Spock spoke anyway. "I understood the reference. This episode has shown us that individuals can be misplaced—but they can also be shown a path back. I believe that I, too, may have a workable solution to offer."

"Glad to hear it. Tell Number One. Wherever we need to go, let's do it." Pike took a last look at the town—and noticed a North Star resident lighting lamps in the street. *You know*, he thought, *there's someone else I've been meaning to see* . . .

CHAPTER 77

THE CANDLE

Like any cadet, Nyota Uhura had the usual bad dreams—including the worst one, sleeping through the start of her shift. She had therefore awakened into a living nightmare soon after returning to *Enterprise* when she realized she had slept through an entire twenty-four-hour day.

It was authorized, and she certainly deserved it. She did not deserve her roommates Carter and Probasco driving her into a panic the second she opened her sleep pod, but then cadets never deserved anything they had to endure from one another. She might be able to walk across half of creation and to get fire to talk, but she'd never change that.

Many days had passed since her return, but now she was sure Probasco was pranking her again. "Captain's coming to see you!"

Seated at the edge of her sleep pod folding her clothes, she gave her roommate a withering look. "Captain Pike. Coming down to the cadets' quarters." She shook her head and sighed. "You never learn."

Probasco was going to say something in response when she heard Pike's voice from outside. "Straighten up there, Cadet!"

Her fellow cadet snapped to attention—and she stood as well, barely noting she was still in her clothes from the gym. Pike poked his head into the room and saw her. "Oh, that was for him, not you." He thumbed down the hallway. "Take five, Probasco."

"Yes, Captain!" Probasco stepped into the corridor, only to turn. "Er— Captain, is that five minutes, or five laps around the ship? Because Commander Chin-Riley usually means—"

Pike gave a placid smile and said, "Cadet's choice."

Probasco vanished.

Uhura relaxed as the captain entered. "I always heard in the Academy that you should never give a cadet a choice."

"He's going to pick the longer one, just to impress me." Pike shrugged. "Shouldn't discourage that kind of initiative—or bold ambition. That's our next admiral, running in circles."

Pike found one of the other open sleep pods and put the pouch he had slung over his shoulder onto it. He looked back to her. "Go ahead. Sit. We've all needed laundry done."

Uhura did as instructed. "I was in the same clothes for two weeks."

"I guess I can't complain about having been in someone else's clothes the whole time." He tugged at his collar. "What they used for cotton back there was itchy as sin."

Uhura smiled—and then her face fell as she recalled the abandoned farm she'd visited, and its would-be cotton gin.

Pike read her emotions. "It's hard coming back, isn't it?"

His reaction put her at ease. "There was just so much I didn't have. And then Om Mataya was this haven, but then it wasn't, and then I was hiding in walls."

"You've had an experience. It's going to take a while. But you'll manage."

Uhura appreciated hearing that. She next heard the low hum that in these quarters indicated the ship was preparing to go to warp. "Where are we headed, Captain?"

"One last stop to make, getting people where they belong." He remembered the pouch. "Speaking of, I brought you something. This was one of my saddlebags."

He reached in—and handed her a small stubby candle.

"Er—thanks!"

"And can't forget this part." He withdrew the old lantern from the bag. "Science team's analyzed it. No trace of anything unusual at all."

She took it from him and held it by the handle. "I'm sort of sorry to hear that," she said. "But I know they went somewhere they needed to go."

"Well, we used all our instant film before we got to you, but there's a way you can remember when you want to." Pike's eyes went to the overhead. "Computer—engage birthday fire-safety protocol."

"*Working*," the computer responded.

Uhura watched him. "It's not my birthday."

"Nor mine," Pike said, opening the top of the lantern. "I'm surprised none of us had one during the time we were down there. The protocol basically tells the ship to decrease oxygen levels and allow a small, localized fire for five minutes. Spock has something like that for his cultural needs."

He watched her holding the lantern and candle—and then realized he'd forgotten something.

"Oh." He pulled out a wooden match from his pocket. "This is another place the Menders were kind of holding out on the Skagarans: 'strike-anywhere' matches." He struck it against the heel of his shoe and then applied the flame to the candle in her hand. She placed it in the lantern and closed it.

"You said five minutes?" she asked.

Pike eyeballed the candle. "Seems about right."

He started to rise, only to snap his fingers. "Forgot something else. Computer—grant birthday fire-safety protocol status to Cadet Nyota Uhura. Authorization, Captain Christopher Pike."

"*Working. Status granted.*"

He rose and left the pouch on the pod's mattress. "A few more candles and matches. That, I didn't forget." Upon reaching the entrance, he paused and looked back. "I need you to work on a special assignment."

"You need more information on Epheska?"

"No, it's not for me. There may be another opportunity." He looked in the hallway. "And here he is now."

Uhura was startled to see Hemmer in the doorway. Captains rarely came to the cadets' quarters; the current chief engineer never had. He didn't look thrilled to be there.

"I was afraid you'd gotten lost," Pike said.

"For some reason, projectile removal makes one move more slowly," Hemmer said. "Have you told her?"

"I was leaving that for you."

Hemmer passed Uhura a padd. "I realize that constructing an enormous vessel out of sticks and bolts may be difficult to top, but I have a feat in mind that may improve upon it."

Uhura read the first lines—and knew she didn't understand a word. "I'm not a particle physicist."

"Nor do we need another. But I believe there is a way to create a reactor that will replicate the dimensional transfer of electromagnetism in a safe manner—and in quantities that will satisfy your empathermic friends."

Uhura's eyes widened. "We can help them?"

"I cannot speak for what has transpired in their realm in the interim, or even how time passes there. But I have no desire to open a rift and start shoveling—without seeking some way of hailing those within it first."

She smiled. "Hailing."

"Right up your alley," Pike said. "And you already know people." He looked to Hemmer. "I think she's in."

"Wonderful. I warn you it could take some time. We will not unravel this mystery tomorrow. But my staff is fully briefed on the project. A positive legacy of our experience."

"I'll be here," Uhura said. "And ready."

Pike put his hand on the engineer's shoulder as he turned to depart. "Great work, Hemmer. On all of it."

"Of course it was."

"He knew I was going to say that." Pike smiled in at her. "See you later, Cadet."

She let out a deep breath as the door closed behind them.

She knew Hemmer was probably right. They wouldn't find a solution tomorrow. But they would try. It was hope, for creatures that had given her hope. She would do her best to ensure they wouldn't have to wait long.

She placed the lantern beside her and asked for the computer to bring down the lights. And when she started to sing, she thought she saw the flame dance.

CHAPTER 78

THE JUDGMENT

Sarek had been too busy to see him. Spock tried not to be disturbed by this, but he had just been missing for a month and had nearly died. He had also come with *Enterprise* all the way from Skagara to Vulcan, to deliver some truly surprising passengers.

And yet, his father was not one of those present at the meeting of the Vulcan High Council on the matter of the crew of *Xen'tal*, gone for so long. T'Var had stood before them in the ancient building, wearing a subcommander's uniform of a style that had not existed when she last left the planet. She had testified about her experiences, as had several of her oldest crewmembers. Sivenda spoke for the next generation, filling in details of the exploits of the phantom fleet.

Then Spock testified, describing his time with T'Var and presenting as further evidence the just-published stories of an actual native of Epheska: the journalist Cyrus Hodge. Being able to speak before a figure as revered as T'Pau was an honor for Spock, and he had wanted to provide as complete a record as possible.

"I thank thee for the corroborating report," T'Pau said from her chair. "It is a remarkable account."

Spock's part was over. Now judgment would fall.

"Is there anything more from the accused?" T'Pau asked.

T'Var, still years younger, stepped back into the light in the chamber and clasped her hands behind her back. "I say only this. The changes are fascinating. You, T'Pau, had only just gained responsibility when my force left to provoke war with the Andorians." She looked down—and then around at the elders. "From what I have seen of Vulcan—and from the actions of Lieutenant Spock, Captain Pike, and the other members of Starfleet—my judgment then was in error." She gestured to her comrades in the wings. "We have lost our time—and our place. I ask that you visit any judgment solely upon me."

T'Pau raised her hand from its position of repose. "This is not a logical request."

T'Var took a deep breath. She was about to say something else when the Vulcan elder spoke again.

"I would not have thee lose thy position, when thee are uniquely suited for another purpose." T'Pau gestured to Spock. "This we have discussed before."

T'Var looked to Spock, startled. "You spoke earlier?"

"We did." Seeing he had permission, Spock stepped forward again. "The Skagaran named Taliyah hailed from a world that lived in the past and left to join one that lived in the present. She made it her mission to find out if there were others. You, T'Var, have a similar case."

She did not see the analogy. "We left our present and became trapped in someone else's past, Spock. Are you suggesting there are more planets with a situation like Epheska had?"

"Certainly not. But there are Epheskans who have told us they might consider emigrating, but they fear making the transition. They do not have your advantage of ever having lived in the wider galaxy."

"I understood the Federation was providing resources to assist such people."

"It is, but we speak of a large population. And in the wake of our recent war with the Klingon Empire, the demands upon those personnel are extreme. It would be a great service to the Federation if you would assist."

"How?"

"Help them as you helped me. And the other castaways you found. Provide passage—and knowledge."

T'Var stared at him. Sivenda spoke for her. "We do not have a ship," she said. "Of any kind."

T'Pau nodded to the Vulcan to her left. He read from a padd. "You departed from Vulcan in 2154 in a military transport named *Xen'tal*." He looked up. "The vessel was never read out of the service."

Spock saw T'Var almost react with emotion. "That is true," she said, "but I certainly cannot restore it to you now!"

"That was not our aim." T'Pau's aide consulted his notes again. "Subcommander, it appears that you were not released from the service either."

Her eyes narrowed. "No. What is—"

T'Pau intervened. "It is unforgivable that one with thy seniority would be denied a posting. It has been agreed that thee shall be provided a new transport."

Her aide added more. "Your current crewmembers who are interested are, of course, welcome—and we will stock the vessel with noncommissioned officers who understand current technology." He put down the padd. "But we have no doubt that you will adapt quickly."

T'Var stared, seemingly trying to work it out. "You realize we are deserters? My entire crew was away without leave, after the effort to mount a sneak attack on the Andorians failed."

"We told them that was all a misunderstanding," came a voice from behind.

Spock and the others turned to see Pike approaching in his Starfleet uniform. T'Var greeted him. "Captain, I am the one who does not understand."

"Sorry I'm late." Pike bowed to T'Pau before facing T'Var. "Spock and I filled in all the blanks. It isn't the service record before that matters. It's the one from the last century—and, in particular, this last month that weighs the most."

T'Pau clasped her hands. "Indeed. Thee aided castaways before. Thy home-world expects you to do so again."

Sivenda grasped her speechless mother's arm. "I think the subcommander does not know what to say."

"Which reminds me," T'Pau's aide said. "That is an inappropriate rank for a leader of such a vessel." He stepped over and passed T'Var the decoration. "Congratulations, Commander."

T'Var swallowed—and took the insignia.

"What do you think of that?" Pike asked.

T'Var cleared her throat—and straightened. "I think I was a fleet com-mander. But under the circumstances, this is sufficient." She turned to Pike and Spock and bowed. "I thank you."

"*We* thank *you*," Spock said. An exchange of Vulcan salutes, and the officials led T'Var and her companions to where their new ship awaited.

Spock thought it was over—but T'Pau called out to him as he and Pike were making their respects. "Excellent work," she said to him. "We will be watching thee."

Pike and Spock walked from the chamber. "Did you see your mother?" Pike asked.

"Yes—but not my father. He was too busy."

"Uh-huh." Pike shrugged. "Well, you know, these things have a way of working out, in any family. You have that to look forward to."

"I look forward to returning to the ship."

"I've got one more stop first."

Spock stopped walking and looked at Pike. "Are you going to see her?"

"Who, your mother?"

"No, I mean—"

"I know who you mean." Pike reached for his communicator. "And, yes, I am. But I'm going to change first."

CHAPTER 79

THE RESCUE

"Come on. Where'd you go?" Lila Talley glanced over her shoulder. "You're getting lost back there."

It was hard to actually lose anyone in a place where the beige sky blended in with the desert floor below, but the nights were hot enough without something protecting you from the wind. The sun was setting, and the young ones needed to get back to their shelter.

They just weren't the kind of young ones she was used to minding.

"Come on," she said, looking at the Vulcan child on the pony at the back of the group. "Let's go, Sava."

"Sorry, Miz Talley." The girl urged her horse ahead.

Lila had wanted to go home, but she had understood that likely wasn't going to happen. She only got as close as sixteen light-years away. But there were days when Vulcan felt like Mojave, when the grounds of the rehabilitation center felt like the Bar T.

The attendants who had been working with her were obviously not the oversized personalities of the Old West—or even the domesticated variety she'd found on Epheska. But they were kind, and they had made honest attempts to try to bring her peace.

Proof of that had been the job they'd given her. No, not given—*created* for her. No one taught horse riding on Vulcan because there were no horses. But the center was interested in activities for the young who resided there and accommodations had been made.

She'd only been at it a short while and didn't feel she'd made much headway yet. Half of her students couldn't tell one end of a saddle from the other, and there wasn't a child here who had successfully tied a knot. But they were trying, and it was the effort that counted.

"Stay in the tents after dinner," she called out as the kids moved their animals to the stable. "I don't want to hear about any hijinks."

Sava looked back to her. "What are hijinks?"

"You're a hijink. Go."

She saw them on their way and then turned her horse back out onto the desert. She hadn't gotten fifty meters when she heard a horse behind her. *Kids and sheep: not good at listening.* She turned—

—and saw Christopher Pike. Wearing civilian clothes, he rode from the stable toward her on his horse from Epheska.

She observed his approach and spoke drily. "That's Joe Magee's horse. You'd better get him home."

"He is home." Pike nodded to her stallion. "I see Buckshot made it."

"He did. I hear you had something to do with that."

"I doubt he'd let anyone else ride him."

"And they sent me Rufus too."

Pike shrugged. "Gotta have a dog."

"What are you doing here, Christopher? Don't you have stars to chase?"

"Not today. I sent off some of the Menders—and then we just got T'Var's people taken care of."

"I'm glad," she said. "I guess those wooden ships were their homes."

"Well, a ship's just a way to get you from one place to another. It's—"

"If you're going to tell me it's not a home, I'm calling you on it. I know you don't believe that."

Pike changed the subject. "I saw some of the place here on the way in. It's nice—and new."

"There are a lot of orphans from the Klingon War. Colonists' kids. Mostly Vulcan here, but some not. They were looking for an activity to give them, and the idea of a ranch came up."

She dismounted, and he did as well. As they walked together, flanked by the horses, she spoke of the project the Vulcans had set up, pointing out all the features on the makeshift ranch.

"Looks like a good place," Pike said, "and a good idea. It doesn't seem out of place at all, strangely."

"I'm just ashamed anyone's gone to all this trouble. It's kind of a make-work thing for me."

"Not a chance. They're helping you. You're helping the kids."

Lila took that in. Her shoulders relaxed. "Tell Spock to thank the Vulcans."

"They're good people."

She looked out. There were no fences within sight, but she wasn't kidding herself. "It *is* a prison. But not too bad of one."

"Lots of kinds of prisons." He chuckled. "It's funny. Everything down on Epheska—the ships, the horses, the ice—it was kind of like going to camp. I should feel like I've just come off a big shore leave. But it was work—and it's created a lot more work."

"I can tell."

He spoke of what had been done on Epheska, and she listened. She was glad to hear some of the residents were staying, and the other things he described sounded good too.

"It's important work," he said, "but it's been taxing."

"You'd like to fly away—but flying away is your job. Poor pitiful Pike."

He laughed. "Next you're going to say, 'Your eyes are telling me your soul needs a vacation.'"

"Dream on." She rolled her eyes. "That kind of airy-fairy stuff was the sort of thing you heard from what's her name back home—Freida?"

"Freena."

"The free spirit." Lila laughed. "You were never an item, I hope."

"No. Just a friend."

"Like *we* were." Lila stopped walking and looked down. "Christopher, I am so sorry—"

"Don't." He stopped beside her. "Don't do that to yourself. You don't have to."

"Yes, I do." She wiped a tear from her eye. "What I was going to do—*what I would have done*—it's unconscionable. Unforgivable, if anything ever was."

Pike took a deep breath. "Look, I'm not going to say it wasn't. But there's a way that you and your family were right about technology."

"There is?"

"Your dad said the reason there were so many bandits in the old Westerns is that it took less effort to pull a trigger than to plant a crop. It wasn't too long after that it became possible to level a city by pushing a button—or bombard a whole planet by saying a word."

He looked up to the sky, where Vulcan's aurora was becoming visible.

"So we find the empatherms, who had the ability to turn physics off for *everybody*, just like that. We still have no idea what drove their technology. Maybe it's a good thing it's all gone, because I don't think we're any better at comprehending the scales involved—or the stakes. It's more power than anyone could be expected to have."

"You sound like you've had some experience with this."

Pike looked off to the sky. "Yeah, a little," he said. "When your thoughts can reshape reality, you can have a brain that's twice the size and it'll *still* be hard to know what the right thing to do is." He put his hand on her arm. "You just try to think of others and try to do your best."

"Like you tried to do for me." She leaned in, and they embraced.

It lasted for several seconds—until his communicator beeped. "Technology," she said.

"Yeah, speak of the devil."

He answered it—and Lila listened as Uhura told him of events that required his attention. She could tell from the tone of his response that the starship captain was back.

He closed the communicator. "There's always an emergency somewhere. Guess I have to hit the trail."

"Riding to the rescue." She took his horse's lead. "I can take him from here."

"Thanks."

She watched as he stepped away, preparing to transport up. "You think you'll ever be satisfied to stay in one place?"

He stopped and looked back, a peculiar look on his face.

"I don't mean *here*," she said, quickly recovering. "I mean—"

"I understood you. No, I know it all ends someday, one way or another. I just want to do what I can, while I can."

She nodded. "Can't expect you to have time to visit an inmate."

"No. But I will always see a friend." He smiled as he triggered the comm. "Energize."

ACKNOWLEDGMENTS

In 2021, when I wrote this section for my last novel, *Star Trek: Picard—Rogue Elements*, I said I crafted the story for a pandemic-ridden planet in need of a break, and that I hoped the coming year would find the world in a happier place.

Well, shoot. Let's try this again.

When I was asked by *Strange New Worlds* co–executive producer Kirsten Beyer and my Gallery Books editor Margaret Clark to write the first novel for the TV series, I was delighted to return to writing about Christopher Pike, whose adventures during the Klingon War I had chronicled in *Star Trek: Discovery—The Enterprise War*. As that novel's action was almost entirely shipboard and my following *Discovery* novel, *Die Standing*, had spotlighted several completely alien civilizations, I gave a lot of thought to where I'd want to spend the next year.

The idea of "one planet, many worlds" intrigued me: a massive quest for the characters to undertake, without the aid of technology. *Rogue Elements'* exploration of the Chicago mobster Iotians also got me thinking about many other *Trek* stories about transplanted communities from human history. How much more was there to those people's stories?

I also wanted to take a look at a utopian society many centuries after its founding—and one which, as Kirsten suggested to me, still might work for some of its citizens, even as it was compromised in many ways. Any situation that sets up tensions between what Starfleet officers can do, want to do, should do, and must do is very much suited for *Star Trek*.

There began *The High Country*, a novel which was partially written during a time in which—and I am not kidding—my 1853 farmhouse had to be lifted off the ground for a week for an emergency foundation repair. I suppose I should be glad it wasn't whisked off to the Beta Quadrant. It's hard to get good cat food there!

Obviously, much inspiration came from the *Star Trek: Enterprise* episode "North Star," written by David A. Goodman. Further ideas came from the *Star Trek: Discovery* episode "New Eden," teleplay by Vaun Wilmott & Sean Cochran, story by Akiva Goldsman & Sean Cochran.

I am further indebted to the *Strange New Worlds* team for inspiration, including the series actors Anson Mount, Ethan Peck, Rebecca Romijn, Celia Rose Gooding, and Bruce Horak among others. Their portrayals served as my guiding lights. And of course, much inspiration came from the work of Nichelle Nichols, whom we sadly lost while this book was in production. She will be a part of everything we do in *Star Trek*, always.

My thanks go to Margaret Clark, Ed Schlesinger, and the team at Simon & Schuster/Gallery Books, as well as to Kirsten Beyer, John Van Citters, and the crew at Paramount. Thanks as always to Dayton Ward, and to Scott Pearson, who again provided peerless copyediting.

I am grateful to Don Lincoln, senior scientist at the Fermi National Accelerator Laboratory, who listened to my ideas for how the Baffle behaved and suggested some explanations that would be workable for the *Star Trek* universe—even if, as he cautioned, they'd be unlikely to survive the scrutiny of another particle physicist. (Don't try to build your own Baffle, in other words!) The model referenced herein developed by Lisa Randall and Raman Sundrum is real; there's more about their work in Randall's *Warped Passages: Unraveling the Mysteries of the Universe's Hidden Dimensions*.

My deep appreciation goes to equestrian expert and longtime friend Beth Kinnane, who has now advised me on matters equine in two different universes. Thanks also go to astronomer Michael L. Wong of the Carnegie Institute for Science, off whom I bounced many planetary ideas. My son, John Miller III, also contributed ideas relating to time-period-appropriate technology.

Given the role of maps in this story, I'm delighted we were able to include my original ones, which I designed using Inkarnate Pro with the assistance of James Mishler. Interstellar locations are based on *Star Trek: Star Charts* and *Star Trek: Stellar Cartography*.

My thanks go again to my two proofreaders: Brent Frankenhoff, who knows his *Trek*, and Meredith Miller, number one on my bridge.

And my best to you, dear reader. Here's hoping the year that follows *this* book is more peaceful—and that your own house stays rooted firmly to the ground!